KT-418-120

80 003

Discarded

ng
d

FOOLISH LESSONS
IN LIFE AND LOVE

Penny Rudge

ABACUS

First published in Great Britain in 2010 by Abacus
This paperback edition published in 2011 by Abacus

Copyright © Penny Rudge 2010

The moral right of the author has been asserted.

*All characters and events in this publication, other than those
clearly in the public domain, are fictitious and any resemblance
to real persons, living or dead, is purely coincidental.*

All rights reserved.
No part of this publication may be reproduced, stored in a
retrieval system, or transmitted, in any form or by any means, without
the prior permission in writing of the publisher, nor be otherwise circulated
in any form of binding or cover other than that in which it is published
and without a similar condition including this condition being
imposed on the subsequent purchaser.

A CIP catalogue record for this book
is available from the British Library.

ISBN 978-0-349-12247-2

Typeset in Bembo by M Rules
Printed and bound in Great Britain by
Clays Ltd, St Ives plc

Abacus
An imprint of
Little, Brown Book Group
100 Victoria Embankment
London EC4Y 0DY

NORTHAMPTONSHIRE LIBS & INFO SER	
80 003 235 742	
ASKEWS & HOLT	25-Jan-2012
AF	£7.99

For my brother, Pete,
who was the first to listen to my stories

CHAPTER ONE

Taras jerked awake with a thud of the heart that cancelled the dream, like a TV set going to black. He needed to lie still and let the panic evaporate, wallow in the dregs of sleep, but his mother had already wrested away the furry blanket and was tugging at the sheet corner.

'Taraşhu! Wake up, little piglet. Time to wake up.' Three firm pats to his cheek. 'Up, up, up!'

An aromatic, tannic scent in his nostrils said it was morning, though the click of the bedside light disagreed.

'Pourchi, are you awake? Your tea is here, look. Extra sugar, for energy.'

He let out a groan and unscrewed one eyelid. The Blessed Virgin loomed into focus: etched into a giant teardrop of red-tinted glass, she was ignoring the infant on her lap in order to enfold Taras with a sweet, drooping gaze. Her expression was one of infinite sorrow, seeming to encompass all the wickedness of the world.

This icon had been fixed to his wall ten years ago, on Taras's thirteenth birthday; a gift from his mother who had been alarmed by his explosion into puberty. Shamed, he'd understood her intention, but still lacked self-restraint. The besetting sin of his childhood had been greed, unstoppable despite the ballooning misery of puppy-fat. Adolescence stirred new demands somewhere beneath those lolloping

1

folds of flesh. His mother, baptized Maria like every first-born daughter in her homeland, called on a more powerful Mary for support. But not even the Mother of God could stop the sin; it relocated to the bathroom, where the bolt on the door proved an added blessing. Probably neither mother was deceived but since they couldn't intrude, Taras felt less guilty.

'*Mamaliga* going on stove now. Do you hear me, pourchi?'

He nodded, still incapable of conversation. Both mothers looked reproachful. The Holy One remained perfectly still: his own rattled open the curtains and advanced on the bed.

'I'm getting up, Mami,' he croaked.

An approving kiss smacked his forehead. '*Mamaliga* available for eating in fifteen minutes.' She whisked out of the door.

Taras turned away from the Virgin and snuggled back into his lumpy pillow. Warmth infused his veins; he was disassociating from his body, slipping blissfully back into the dream. Then an apparition burst forth: a thick, grey ponytail, coarse and stiff, twitching like the back-end of a horse, it lashed to and fro, twisting to reveal a pair of baggy, contemptuous eyes.

With a squeak of protest, Taras jolted upright and clutched at the mug of black tea. His hand shook, stirring up the gritty leaves which then stuck to his teeth. He dislodged some with a finger and wiped the debris on the lip of the mug, then glanced towards the digital clock. Sprouting from a clutter of coins, receipts and splayed keys, it blinked back at him. 05:50.

Exhausted, he slumped back. His bed was jammed into the room, enclosed on three sides by inward-sloping walls, hemmed in at the fourth by a square desk. As a child, he'd found this comforting, but now it was claustrophobic. He was trapped in a giant cot, able to push simultaneously against all four corners without straightening a single limb. His mother's room was even smaller, not a room at all, just a space behind a temporary partition. They'd swapped when he started big school, to give him a place for his homework. After university graduation he'd offered to switch back, with predictable results: 'Why I need big room? What I do with desk? You think I am mother to trample on Son? Never!' Thumping her chest for emphasis. 'Never, Never, Never!'

A sugar-laden sip of tea provided enough strength for his feet to edge down to the worn carpet, and he wriggled his toes into his slippers before standing up. Now he was faced with Russell Crowe in a leather-fringed skirt brandishing a sword over the threshold. The poster was frayed and one corner had curled up where the Blu-tack had dried and dropped away. Taras raised his arm in a gladiatorial salute and pulled open the door.

His room was the lowest in the flat, and guarded their bolted and chained entrance. Shuffling up a half-flight of stairs took him past the kitchen, which in turn opened on to the narrow parlour. His mother was out of sight. That meant she was in her room, the screened-off, coffin-sized space behind the sofa. Another short set of stairs brought him to the bathroom, tucked into the roof space. The white-tiled walls were scrupulously clean but cold, like the inside of a refrigerator.

Taras creaked the electric dial round to maximum, and let the shower run full-steam while he used the toilet. That not only took the edge off the chill, it provided cover for any noises. He'd often wished his mother's prudishness extended to bowel functions, but the smallest encouragement transformed her into a Grand Inquisitor of Frequency, Consistency and Strain.

Washing his hands brought him eye-to-bloodshot-eye with the small mirror above the sink. His skin was grey and there was a sticky mess in his hair. It must have been a good night. He prodded the ridge of flesh where his stomach overhung his briefs. It wasn't that bad. It had been worse. Far worse. Still, this was going to be the year of the new Taras. On New Year's Day, he'd done ten press-ups. The day after, he'd run around the block. His head was throbbing; today was going to be a blot on the new regime. Was it making a difference yet? By balancing on the bathtub and contorting, he could inspect his body in specimen-like sections, as if it were smeared on a laboratory slide. Ugh. No obvious improvement there. Hmm, maybe . . . but steam was clouding the mirror. Twisting, he tried to catch a glimpse of his buttocks before they disappeared.

Footsteps came pounding up the stairs. 'Taraşhu!' The door rattled.

'Aargh!' He slipped and tumbled into the bath, cracking his head on the ceramic tiles.

Another battery of knocking. 'What is matter? Open door!'

'Nothing, Mami.' He cradled his head. 'I'm fine. Go away.'

'We are late!'

'I'll be down in a minute!'

With relief, he heard her retreat, and curled up like a wood-louse under the shower-spray. The dream was re-forming in his mind, slowly; different images muddling together. There had been a girl. Not just any girl: Katya.

She'd spent their last date sobbing, the glow of the London Eye highlighting her puffy skin. The tickets were stiff in his back pocket but she was gulping and sniffing too much to be crammed into a crowded pod, so they'd leaned over the railings, backs to the elbowing stream of tourists. He'd squeezed her shoulders, staring at the blue and orange glitter on the water. Above them, the giant wheel slowly turned. In

4

another reality they were up at the highest point, gliding over the city lights, not rooted in this street-level misery.

Had she come to last night's party? He'd invited her – casually; it was good to be mature about these things – by sending her a text. Pain was splintering through his skull, making everything hard to remember. He just wanted to lie still, but if he didn't get a move on his mother would bang on the door again. Partially uncurling, he reached for the yellow coal-tar soap and shivered. This paltry spray left half his body out in the cold. They ought to get a proper power shower. He'd offered to pay for it, but his mother refused to contemplate such rash expenditure. 'Foolishness and waste, pourchi. What need for this?'

He dragged himself to his knees, lathered and rinsed. A horrifying picture broke loose: Katya's small form nestling into a grizzled embrace; a grey horse-switch of hair triumphantly swivelling. Taras gulped hard. What kind of nightmare had this been? Snapping off the shower spray, he left a trail of drips as he scurried down the stairs. His towel slipped to the floor as he snatched up his mobile phone, wet fingers scrabbling at the keypad.

Nothing. He scrolled up and down, not believing it. Her number wasn't there. This didn't make sense. His head felt heavier than a bowling ball, its balance on the frail, straw-like support of his neck too precarious for thinking. Action was effort enough: he'd puzzle this out later, when he felt stronger. Concentrating on each movement, he strapped himself into his darkest suit, discarding the tie he'd worn yesterday in favour of one not blighted by a mysterious amoeba stain. Automatically, he reached for the little white lens case, and then stopped. Scraping contacts across his shrunken corneas was out of the question; this would have to be a steel-rimmed day.

*

Upstairs, the *mamaliga* was hardening. His stomach curdled. 'I'm not hungry, Mami.'

'Who knows what customs these people are having? Maybe they will not feed us.' A ladle-shaped mound of polenta thudded into his bowl. Tutting from the back of her throat, she stirred in two dollops of sour cream and a generous sprinkle of feta cheese. 'You look very bad, Taraşhu. Are you having constipation?'

'No, Mami,' he said hurriedly, before she reached for the prunes.

'Then it is not enough sleep. Very thoughtless friends keeping you out late. I am worrying about you. Twelve o'clock, one o'clock, still no Taraşhu.'

'You should have gone to sleep, Mami.'

'Sleep! I have dress to finish. Hem, sleeves, buttons all to do. And who can sleep when noisy boy crashing in at quarter two in morning, stamping and rattling and knocking over tables?'

'I'm sorry, Mami. I just had a drink with a few friends, for my birthday.'

'Birthday! You think you need to tell me about birthday? Ha! I am the one with scars to remind about birthday. You celebrate with your friends, but it is not they who are having blood and screaming to give you birthdays. Come! No time! Eat!'

Taras pushed the bowl away.

'What is matter?' His mother put a hand on his forehead. 'Very bad luck to have early celebrating of birthdays. I am telling you not to be doing this.'

To silence her, he sliced off a flaccid spoonful and swallowed it whole. As soon as she was out of the room, he buried the rest under curls of potato peel in the bin and craned his head into the parlour. Scraping, swishing sounds behind the paisley screen indicated she was getting changed. A moment or two later, she emerged, giving her dress a satisfied tug. It was a deep, rich black, so dark that it had given her a headache to sew: he'd seen her frowning over the stitches. From start to finish, it had taken her three days non-stop: she'd left all the regular orders draped over the machine and concentrated on this; hand-sewing the high, embroidered collar, precisely tapering the sleeves so that the cuffs hugged her wrists, inserting more and more darts until the skirt swung out like a church bell.

'What is wrong, Taraşhu? You don't like?'

'No, Mami, you look . . . well . . . you look . . .'

The intense dark shine threw into contrast the dewy paleness of unlined skin preserved by a lifetime spent indoors. With her hair twisted into a mahogany pleat, she looked younger, closer to her real age, which was just forty-seven, and less like his own Mami clucking about in her apron and triangular headscarf, domestic as a dishcloth.

"You look . . . well . . . different.' It was the best he could manage.

'Silly boy. Come, sit.' It was a custom she always insisted on. They had to sit quietly for a minute or two before embarking on any journey.

Taras had no patience for it. 'I'm ready, Mami. We can go.'

A commanding flap of her hand quelled him. He sat. She bent her head, and he watched her wide mouth silently working, as if repeating a prayer. His stomach was pulsating: hangovers always made him queasy.

'Come, pourchi!' His mother was on her feet.

'Why go at all, Mami?' Reluctantly, Taras helped her into her belted coat. 'I never even met her. She was just our landlady.'

'Respect, pourchi. Mrs Bartlett good woman. Strong woman.' Chains jangled and bolts slammed as she wrestled with the door. 'Quick, quick. Very bad manners to be late at time of funeral.'

CHAPTER TWO

An oil-slick of light was pooling below the street lamp as they emerged. Dawn was still an hour away. All along, Taras had known there was no danger of being late; his mother was chronically early for everything. Countless hours of his childhood had been spent killing time: soaking up germs in the doctor's waiting room; shivering outside St Dunstan's long before the doors opened for Holy Liturgy. When he was six, they'd gone to visit Bunica Elena's grave in Harwich, an expedition that began with three stagnant hours at Liverpool Street Station, where they were able to watch the departure of the train before the train before theirs.

'Let's get a taxi, Mami. It's freezing. I'll pay.'

'Taxi?' She sounded as if he'd suggested conjuring up a magic carpet. Her gloved hand urged him to the kerb side of the pavement, the rightful place for a man. 'Come now, pourchi. Quick quick.'

Above them reared the high wall along the train tracks running into London Bridge Station, shot through with eerie, luminous tunnels. Ahead, a stray traffic cone lay askew. Tutting, his mother stepped around it, out into the side road, her heels clicking against the tarmac, just as a mud-stained van lurched round the corner. Trapped in the headlights, eyes startle-wide, with the buttermilk silk scarf (all she had to remember Bunica Elena by) shielding her hair and neck, she might have blown in straight from the Carpathian foothills.

The van driver beeped his horn and swerved, then stamped on the brakes. Sticking his cropped head out of the window, he yelled, 'Look where you're going, you stupid cow!'

Taras would have defended his mother's honour, but preserving her life was the first priority. He grabbed her arm and tried to hustle her back onto the pavement.

'Go on, get out of it!' The driver was impatient.

'What does that person say?'

'I don't know, Mami, it doesn't matter. Mind the kerb.'

'Bloody foreigners!'

Drawing up in outrage, his mother tugged loose and marched over to the van. Taras trotted after her, beginning to sweat. Tyres rasped as a black Audi pulled up behind the van and parped its horn. 'You are rude, ignorant person,' his mother informed the van driver, wagging a gloved finger for emphasis. A furrow creased the driver's flat forehead, but now a third vehicle had joined the queue and the Audi was tooting again, so he ignored her and honked back, jabbing an upthrust digit of his own at the side-view mirror.

'Come on, Mami,' Taras pleaded, plucking at her sleeve.

Instead, she rapped on the door. The van driver's big head swung round and his red-veined face bulged with astonishment.

'I am not permitting rudeness in street.' She slapped her chest for emphasis. 'Son and I are having British passports, meaning equalness for all and no need for shouting.'

'Bloody hell.' He turned to Taras. 'Where'd she escape from?'

'Er . . . Bukovina.' Taras said, with a placatory grimace that felt like a betrayal. Escape was the right word. How his mother had managed the perilous journey to England, he had no idea, and yet she had: aged just twenty-two and accompanied only by Bunica Elena, who collapsed with a

9

massive coronary as the grey cliffs of Essex loomed into view. 'Sorry for getting in your way.'

'You want to take better care of her, mate.' The van driver's big bull-head bobbed towards Taras's mother. 'It's all a bit different here, see, love. No bloody manners.' The Audi's horn blared. 'See what I mean?' He leaned out of the window and bellowed, 'Shut up, wanker!' before courteously waving Taras and his mother back to the pavement.

'There, pourchi.' Taras's mother's voice was ripe with complacency as the honking cavalcade sped off. 'This is how to be teaching proper respect. This is showing ignorants that we are not persons of no account.'

Taras's faith in God was shaky at best, but today felt like His idea of punishment. Dawn was only just approaching: a grey wash of sky lurched into view as they emerged from the maze of backstreets. Like a runway to oblivion, Tower Bridge Road veered upwards, breaking off in mid-air. The north-bound traffic was backed up as far as the eye could see, and the south-bound direction, where they wanted to go, was completely empty, with all the buses trapped on the other side of the river.

'Look, Taraşhu! Now what to do?'

A pulse began to throb at the base of Taras's neck. 'I don't know, Mami. Wait for the bridge to come down, I suppose.'

'How long is that, pourchi? Very bad.'

Closing his eyes, Taras found his strength failing him. Please God, he thought, just drop the bridge. Please. Let's just get this next hour over with, so I can go back to bed. Do it now, and I'll send fifty pounds to the monks, okay?

'Moving!' His mother clutched at his arm, giving him a fright. The blue railings were dropping back towards the horizontal. A swoosh of cyclists, a roar of motorbikes and his mother gave his cheek a delighted pinch as the cars grunted forwards. 'Clever pourchi!'

Taras had never had a prayer answered before. What a waste. For fifty pounds he should at least have got his hangover erased too.

'Quick, quick, Taraşhu. Bus is coming!'

They scuttled over the road. An auburn-haired girl was lounging against the bus stop, one hand tucked into the waistband of her tight jeans. She was looking right at Taras. He sucked in his stomach. Let her smile at me, God. Or speak, and I'll make it a hundred quid for the monks. Deal?

A square-nosed bus pulled in, and the girl bent her long legs to pick up her suitcase. Taras felt his mother prod him from behind. 'Be helpful, Taraşhu. Not gentleman-like only to stare.'

Reddening, he reached for her bag, but the girl was already lifting it, and they collided. She glared at him and muttered a few words which Taras considered cancelled his debt to the monks, and made his mother hiss and fold her arms. 'Not nice girl. Bad mouth and too-tight trousers. No more helping, Taraşhu.'

The bus was already crowded and they had to stand in the aisle. The embroidery of his mother's silk scarf was rubbing Taras's nose, but he didn't want to turn and risk catching the auburn-haired girl's eye again. He preferred dark hair to red anyway. Like Katya's. Was she there last night? A memory was blossoming . . . ugh! Someone in here smelled of cheese. Nausea surged up his throat. He concentrated on the window, staring at mile upon mile of stifled south London streets and trying to breathe slowly. When they'd finally jostled their way off the bus, he'd had to consult the *A–Z*, turning away from a row of workers' caffs and discount stores to face down a long residential street.

'How is this right?' His mother jabbed a finger in the air. 'This is council estate. Mrs Bartlett not have burying in such!'

But the church was there: a low brick building sheltering behind a large billboard. 'SALVATION ARMY. Everyone Welcome.' The sign was contradicted by a large padlock on the door. The lights were off. As usual, they were too early. His mother wanted to wait outside: letting a destination out of sight made her anxious. But Taras, eyeing the shattered windscreen on a nearby Honda, persuaded her to retreat to the main road.

They went into the least dirty of the caffs. Taras ordered a milky coffee and three tea-cakes to make up for the fact that his mother refused to have anything.

'You can't just sit here without ordering, Mami.'

'Belly not in need of filling,' she said, tutting with disapproval as he opened his wallet.

Not for the first time, Taras wondered how his mother had managed to spend a quarter of a century in this country without absorbing the slightest understanding of its customs. It must be Balkan stubbornness, since Katya wasn't that way. Five months after leaving Moscow, she was more at home here than Mami would ever be. A gulp of coffee revved up his body but didn't help his head. Last night's dream was making him more and more uneasy. That twitching grey ponytail . . . Something itched, like a scab on the dull pulse of his headache. He had to get help. Now.

'Mami, I'll go and check if the church is open yet. You stay here, in the warm.'

'Good, kind pourchi!' Her delighted beam gave him a stab of guilt, but this was an emergency. Skilfully evading a kiss, he hurried outside and round the corner. His phone was already flipped open. One keystroke and the green call button was all that was required. Speed-dial, two.

It rang, once, twice, three times.

'This is the Orange answerphone . . .'

Taras hung up, tried again. Pick up, Roy, come on.

Straight to voicemail again. He flicked through the dial

list, found Roy's home number and hesitated. The display on his phone gleamed 07:30. Too early. Averting his eyes, he let his finger slip on to the call button. One ring, two—

'Hello?' A female voice, sleepy, irritated.

'Oh . . . Astrid.' He should have known. Couldn't Roy even answer his own phone any more? Let a woman move in and she took over. 'Sorry, it's Taras.'

'Taras, is something wrong?'

'No, no.' He wanted Roy, but it seemed rude to say so. 'Did you have a good time last night?'

'You're not still out drinking are you? I told Roy we should have taken you home. You weren't in any state—'

'No, I'm fine.' Taras hesitated. 'I had a bit of a funny dream, that's all. Is Roy—?'

Her voice muffled: she'd put her hand over the receiver, then she came back. 'Taras, was Katya in this dream?'

'Yes!' How did she know that? He wondered whether to mention the grey ponytail too.

Her voice softened. 'Well, it's bound to be a bit disturbing, isn't it? I mean, even though you're fine about it all, it is quite soon, so—'

'What?' Taras panicked. 'Fine about what? What're you talking about?'

'Katya, of course.' Astrid sounded perplexed.

'She was there? Last night? What happened? Did something happen? Why isn't her number in my phone any more? What—'

'Taras, calm down. Stop and listen . . . No, listen . . . No . . . OK, I'm passing you to Roy. Hold on.'

Her voice muffled again, then at last Roy was there. 'Chill, Kroheman. Don't you remember Katya turning up around midnight with her new bloke? Older guy, a bit arty-looking.'

Nausea flooded Taras's throat again. He hunched down against the brick wall. 'Does he have a grey ponytail?'

'That's the one. Distinguished, Astrid reckons, but what does she know? You're OK about it though, right? You said you didn't give a shit. You even drank a toast to them.'

Taras's hand was on his mouth, twisting his lips. 'Yeah,' he said, through clenched fingers. 'Yeah, I'm fine.'

'Bollocks,' Roy said cheerfully. 'I knew you'd freak once the alcohol wore off. That's why I deleted her number from your phone.'

CHAPTER THREE

Things had begun so well on their last night together. Taras had cornered a squashy leather sofa at Wine Wharf and ordered a bottle of Veuve Clicquot, a big excited smile spilling over his face. 'It's our anniversary,' he told the bartender, who passed him a complimentary bowl of cashew nuts.

Katya's little pixie head with its acorn-brown cap of hair had bobbed over the champagne glass, wrinkling her nose at the bubbles. Taras wanted them to drink from each other's cups, arms in a snaky entwine, but the choreography didn't work. Katya licked a splash from her hand and made a face. She didn't usually drink alcohol, but Taras had insisted. 'It's our anniversary. We have to celebrate. It's exactly three months since we met.'

'That is not anniversary.' She forced down a gulp, trying not to grimace. 'Anniversary means year, silly. It is from Latin.'

This was one of the things he loved about her: she knew so much. English wasn't even her first language and she could still correct him. It made him proud. All the other people in the bar must see how lucky he was; he felt the glow of their approval.

When they emerged into a frosty wind an hour later, Katya was teetering on her spiked ankle boots. She didn't want to walk a mile down the cobbled river path, but he'd already bought tickets for the Eye. They compromised on a cab. Taras had to tap Katya for cash: he'd emptied his wallet giving the barman a tip.

'You want me to pay?' She stared.

'No! Well, just temporarily. We'll stop at a cashpoint. I'll pay you back!'

She didn't look pleased, but inside the cab she forgot her annoyance and snuggled into his shoulder. Then his phone purred.

'Ring, ring again! Can you never turn it off even for romantic evening?' Her accent was stronger when she was upset; the heavy roll of her 'r's sounded uncomfortably like his mother's.

'It's been on silent, I'm not making any calls, I promise. Could I check my messages, just quickly, that's all?'

'What is so important that you need to check now?'

'I don't know.' That was the point. He hated being out of touch. It gave him the uneasy sensation that something exciting might be going on, and he was missing out. That wouldn't please Katya though, so he searched for a more acceptable answer. 'What if something happened to my mother and she couldn't get hold of me?'

'What can happen to your mother? She is at home. She is always at home. What is going to happen to her there?'

'Accidents happen at home. Or there could be a break-in.' Scenarios took shape in Taras's mind, igniting a genuine flare of anxiety.

'OK.' Katya skidded away from him. 'So check your messages.'

There were three, all within the last hour. He turned the volume down as far as it would go, one eye on Katya's small, dissatisfied face.

'Hey, Casanova, how's it going?' That was Roy. 'Tonight's the night, eh?'

16

Hastily, Taras pressed the skip button.

'Woo-hoo, man, you in the mile high club yet?' Jamal from work, pub sounds in the background. 'Colin says the Eye is 0.01 miles high, so we reckon if you do it one hundred times—'

Skip.

'Mr Krohe, you are a lucky winner in our luxury cruise prize draw. To claim your free holiday, just dial—'

Delete.

He stuffed his phone back into his pocket. Katya was staring at her own reflection in the window, her back rigid. A white beret was pulled down over her hair and a matching scarf swaddled her neck. There wasn't much bare skin to aim at, but he had a go anyway.

'No, do not! Get away!' She pushed him off and scooted further into her corner. 'So, was there an important message saying your mother is dying, you must come running now?'

Silence.

'There, now I sound evil and horrible. It is your fault. Why must you do this?' Katya hiccoughed, burst into tears and fell against him as they pulled over behind County Hall.

Taras dealt with the situation manfully. He cajoled her out of the cab, then took a ten-pound note from her purse, and told the driver to keep the change. The driver, a hefty bald man, nodded laconically and said, 'All right, mate.' That made Taras feel better, as though he'd found a rock to cling to in this sea of feminine emotion.

'I can't do this,' Katya sniffed.

'We don't have to go on the Eye right away, we could get a coffee first.'

'Not the stupid Eye. Us, Taras. You. Me. I cannot go on in this way.'

'Oh.' They leaned against the railings, buffeted by the passing crowd. 'What's the matter?'

'What is the matter? You ask me what is the matter?' She counted off a small, white-gloved finger. 'For example, you make me drink alcohol which I do not like, and now you want me to go up a big wheel which makes me scared.' Next finger. 'For example, you promise that you will switch off phone and then you want to take messages.' On to the third finger. 'For example—'

'All right.' Taras wasn't sure how many examples there were going to be. 'I get the point. Basically I can't do anything right.'

'This is not fair!' She stamped her foot, which made him want to laugh, even though he was getting angry. 'You are always . . .'

The words rushed at him, stinging like hailstones.

'Careful, Katya.' Overriding her squeaky voice with his deepest, calmest tone made him feel strong, like the cabbie; the kind of hero who would be unmoved by a woman's flailing fists. 'I won't take this. One more word, and I'm done, we're finished.'

'One word? I will say many words! As many as I please.'

He couldn't back down now. 'Fine. Then it's over.'

'Good! This is what I want! I am glad!'

18

CHAPTER FOUR

Taras wanted to dash his head against the caff's brick wall. Why had he pushed her so far? And then he'd let her walk away. Drunk, wobbling in her heels, crying. What sort of idiot was he? Discoloured patches of moss protruded from the cracks in the wall, like parasitic, clawing fingers. Like geriatric liver-spotted hands crawling over Katya's smooth flesh, squeezing, prodding, exploring. His breath was coming too slowly, as if someone had dropped one of these bricks in the cistern of his lungs; he couldn't force enough oxygen through. His little Katya.

'Taraşhu?' His mother was at the doorway, adjusting her hat. 'Taraşhu, is church opening now?'

'Yes. No. I'm not sure, Mami,' Church? She couldn't expect him to deal with something so trivial when his heart was breaking. But telling her so was out of the question, so back they plodded to the low brick hall.

'This is very strange,' his mother said. 'Mrs Bartlett rich woman. Owner of many properties, not only little flat for us. Why have funeral here? Why not in grand cathedral?'

'Maybe it's the wrong place,' Taras said hopefully. 'Let's go home, Mami.'

'Mrs Krohe!' A stentorian voice rang out from the other side of the street.

Taras turned and groaned. The Bartletts' stout solicitor was puffing towards them, hampered by a boxy overcoat.

'Oh, Mrs Krohe!' For several moments, he was unable to say any more and had to content himself with pressing his chest; working his lungs like bellows and emitting little clouds of frosty breath.

'Yes, good morning, Mr Banerjee.' Taras's mother tilted her head and waited while he recovered.

'Mrs Krohe, whatever are you doing here?'

'Son and I are here for funeral, of course. This is correct place?'

Mr Banerjee wiped his brow and upper lip with a folded tissue, missing the symmetrical drops of condensation that clung to the tips of his moustache. 'It is a private service, Mrs Krohe, for invited guests only. Mrs Bartlett did not wish you to have contact with her family.'

Taras's mother lowered her eyes, which had a softening effect on the tips of Mr Banerjee's moustache. He began to nod in a paternal way, loosening the globules of condensation until they began to slide.

His quarterly visits to collect rent and arrange repairs should have taught him better, Taras reflected. Mami wasn't giving in so easily. 'Sitting at back only. No contact-making. Mrs Bartlett good woman. Deserving respect.'

'Mrs Krohe—' Mr Banerjee began, but a young, urbane voice broke in. 'Is there a problem, guys?'

Condensation plopped on to Mr Banerjee's collar. 'Nothing, Gideon. I will deal with this. Go on inside.'

'Gideon?' Taras's jaw slackened as he stared at the tall lean body in a charcoal suit and open-necked white shirt. Purple-tinted sunglasses held back long, dark-blond hair. Taras's mobile phone all but twitched in his pocket. It took enormous will-power not to call Roy immediately.

Gideon stared back. 'My God, it's Flounder.'

It was seven years since their last encounter, at London Bridge Station, just before Christmas in Taras's GCSE year.

A Salvation Army brass band had been belting out carols as Taras and Roy crossed the concourse. 'Hey!' Roy had dropped his school bag and prodded Taras in the ribs. 'It's the Mad Monk!' There was their ex-classmate, half strangled by his peaked cap and gold braid; the tallest, lankiest member of the ensemble, protruding from the back row, neck writhing like a stringy tortoise as he tooted on his shiny cornet.

He looked very different now. Taras sucked in his stomach and wished he'd put in his contacts.

'What are you doing here?' Gideon sounded bemused.

'Ah. Mrs Krohe wanted . . . ah . . .' Mr Banerjee lost his bearings and broke into a cough, so Mami finished. 'Son and I here for paying of respects.'

'Oh.' Gideon glanced at Taras with a slight frown and looked back at Mrs Krohe. 'I don't mean to be rude, but did you know my mother?'

'She was our landlady,' Taras said, surprised. Didn't Gideon know that?

Apparently not. Gideon blinked and raised his eyebrows at Mr Banerjee, whose moustache was drooping. 'Oh? It seems Ma was full of surprises.' With a shrug of his charcoal-suited shoulders, he dropped the purple-tinted sunglasses over his eyes and stepped aside. 'Come on in. The more the merrier.'

Taras couldn't resist any longer. As they entered the brick church, he grabbed his mobile and tapped out a message to Roy.

Rmembr Mad Monk? Nt mad anymre!

'Taraşhu!' His mother didn't approve of texting.

'Something important, Mami,' he said, knowing she'd think he meant work.

'Darling!' A cry from outside made Taras's head whip round. Actually, it sounded more like *Dawlin'*, in a throaty American accent. It had come from a blonde, leaning through the window of a black cab. Pushing open the door as it drew to a halt, she leapt out, skittered across the pavement and wrapped herself around Gideon. She was tall, almost as tall as he was. Her hair skimmed his shoulders, glistening in the wintry light as she pressed her mouth to his.

Taras pulled his phone out again, and typed another message to Roy.

Bllcks. Nt monk either.

CHAPTER FIVE

For most of Taras's childhood, the name 'Gideon Bartlett' had been held up as a model of accomplishment. Mami would prise information out of Mr Banerjee at each rent-day visit, and feed it back to Taras in motivational chunks. Gideon Bartlett entered a national competition for spelling and won third place. Gideon Bartlett had a commendation from his church for youth leadership. Gideon Bartlett studied for three hours every night and got top marks in all his tests. Looking back, Taras recognised the questionable pattern in these achievements, but at the age of ten he hadn't doubted their value, and he'd been awed at the prospect of finally meeting this paragon.

On his first day at St Bartholomew's School for Boys, tightly packed into a stiff maroon blazer, feet wincing in new shoes, he'd nodded eagerly as his mother reminded him. 'Must be taking care for being polite to Gideon Bartlett.'

'Gideon is class prefect, Mrs Krohe,' said Mr Banerjee, looking over his moustache at Taras. 'And junior captain of music. He will not have time to notice a new boy.'

It wasn't a rent-day visit: Mr Banerjee had made a special call, and his presence made everything more formal. Taras's mother pretended not to be nervous, but she kept touching Taras: straightening his tie, adjusting buttons, brushing away non-existent fluff. Each time, more agitation transmitted itself, until his stomach was a tight, heaving churn.

'This is best possible opportunity,' she told Mr Banerjee, still fiddling with Taras's fringe. 'His whole future, all starting here. He will work hard, pass all exams with floating colours. Look at him, so smart!'

Mr Banerjee looked and saw a fat little barrel of a boy, a cotton-brained stomach-on-legs destined to disappoint his mother. He didn't say so, but his moustache drooped, and Taras could tell. Sandwiched between the downward pressure of this disdain and the upward thrust of his mother's expectations, Taras felt breathless. Each seemed to squeeze harder; his gut squirted hot pulp and he had to scuttle for the bathroom.

Ensconced on the cold lavatory seat, he relaxed, feeling safe. Fragments of the conversation downstairs drifted in. Mr Banerjee's indistinct murmur, then his mother interrupting vehemently. 'Best for Son, yes, this is absolutely what I am wanting!' More murmuring, then, 'Best school, same as for Gideon Bartlett. Why my son not deserve this best?' It seemed as if Mr Banerjee was nettled; his voice briefly became audible, '. . . is getting the same, Mrs Krohe. But he will struggle. Is that really for the best?'

The volume sank down again, and although Taras strained his ears, there was no more to be heard, until an urgent call of 'Taraşhu! Taraşhu!' came.

'Taraşhu, you are being late! What is matter? Where are you?'

He reached for a scrunch of toilet paper. 'Coming, Mami!'

When he emerged, the bathroom pipes still creaking from the effort of the flush, Mr Banerjee and his mother had moved on to a new discussion.

'Runny tummy,' Mami was saying. 'He is getting often, I am worried about not enough nutrients.'

'A boy his size is not missing any nutrients,' said Mr Banerjee, unaware that Taras was in the doorway.

24

Burning inside, Taras wanted to rap the dome of Mr Banerjee's freckled head and watch it crack and glaze. It made him brave. 'Why will I struggle, Mr Banerjee?'

Mr Banerjee looked as if he regretted saying that. He stroked his moustache. 'Taras, this is a rather different school than you have been used to. Mrs Bartlett is a governor, and some special exceptions have been made for you. You will have to work hard to keep up.'

Taras took these words to heart. Trailing at Mr Banerjee's heels through the school's high black gates, he flinched as a group of boys his own age came sprinting past them. 'Me! Me! Murdoch! Throw it to me!' came the cries. The fastest, evidently Murdoch, turned and threw a navy cap up in the air, and the others jumped and twisted to catch it. With an impatient 'Hmmph!' Mr Banerjee strode across the quad-rangle in the boys' wake, and Taras trotted breathlessly behind, inwardly quailing. Already he was having trouble keeping up.

Half an hour later, waddling down an unwelcoming aisle of faces, Taras saw Murdoch again, leaning back in his desk with boredom. He turned and whispered something to his neighbour as Taras approached, and the other boy snorted. Taras wanted to turn away, but the only empty space was in the next pair of desks. The position was alphabetical (Krohe, Lewin, Murdoch), but as soon as his seatmate turned around, Taras felt victimised. The boy had spectacles with jam–jar lenses and frames that seemed to have been scrawled on to his pallid skin with a crayon. On either side of his head, a long ear protruded from a frizzy black cloud of hair.

He looked as underwhelmed by the meeting as Taras felt. As a ripple of sniggers spread outwards from Murdoch and neighbour, he muttered. 'Great. Put the two ugliest freaks together. Just so everyone knows who to pick on.'

25

No one had called Taras ugly before. He was acutely conscious of being fat, but he was still his mother's handsome boy. Crestfallen to the point of tears, he stared down at his hands, hardly hearing the barked announcements from the teacher.

Half the class were new; the rest had been at the school a year already. The lining of Taras's stomach was almost eaten away with anxiety: he had absorbed his mother's acid determination that he do well. He tried to concentrate on the teacher, whose stiff gingery hair stood up like the bristles of a hairbrush, jutting back from a prominent forehead. A short, slight man, with a self-important air, he was striding about at the front of the room.

'Manners maketh man. When a master enters, you stand up and greet him. You address him as "sir". I will not have rudeness. Lateness is unforgivably rude. By wasting another man's time, you are showing you do not respect him. I will not have this in my class. Punctuality is the first rule.'

Taras quivered. He was being singled out. It wasn't his fault he'd been the last to enter the class. Mr Banerjee had taken forever over the forms in the secretary's office. He kept staring at his hands, but the heat of an invisible spotlight was getting closer.

'Krohe! What is the first rule?'

The teacher, no, master, was leaning over the front of his desk, arms braced on the wooden lid. Willing him away wasn't working. There was a snort from one side, and he lowered his head further under the heat of Murdoch's scornful, freckled gaze.

'Punctuality, sir!'

'I didn't ask you, Lewin. I asked Krohe. With your name, Krohe, I expect you to be an early bird in future.'

A prickle of laughter ran round the class. Taras felt shamed. This was an unfamiliar, hostile world, with none of the happy rush and jostle of his primary school.

Minutes later, a folded piece of paper slid across the desk. Taras hesitated, but his scribble-haired desk-mate was nodding, black spectacles jouncing on his nose. Warily, Taras opened it up and found a doodled cartoon. There was a ponderous crow snatching up a terrified, wriggling worm topped with a red brush of hair. Underneath, a title declared 'THE EARLY BIRD GETS HIS REVENGE'.

Taras read the cramped signature: '*Roy Lewin*', then grinned at his new friend. Though the style was for boys to call each other by their surnames, Roy and Taras never did. It might just have been Roy's insistence on subverting authority, but to Taras it symbolised the special depth of their bond. This wasn't a tactical alliance of two misfits, it was a brotherhood forged in the fire of adversity – Taras had seen enough war films to know how that worked.

Roy had been there a year already and so he took charge. At break-time, they perched on the back wall of the top quad, under the domed shadow of the cathedral. A list of names rapid-fired from Roy's thin, elastic lips: boys to fear; boys to despise; boys to avoid. Below them, Murdoch was hurling a tennis ball to bounce into someone's groin. Shuffling his large bottom along the parapet, Taras shrank into himself.

'Hey,' Roy had said suddenly, nudging him. 'Over there, see? That one, with the prefect's badge. He's in our class, but he wasn't in registration. That's Bartlett.'

An unfashionable ear-skimming bowl of blond hair bobbed above a starched white collar. The knot of the tie, over-large, protruded from a tight grey pullover. Lanky legs, a gawky pre-pubescent frame, and a pile of sheet music clamped under his elbow.

'Gideon Bartlett?' Taras asked.

'He'll probably try to convert you. He's a Jesus freak. He tried to give me one of his stupid godbothering leaflets once. My dad rang the Head and complained. I call Bartlett the

27

Mad Monk.' Roy squinted at Taras. 'How did you know his name? You know him?'

'No,' Taras said hurriedly, feeling like St Peter denying Christ.

CHAPTER SIX

What a friend we have in Jesus,
all our sins and griefs to bear!
What a privilege to carry
everything to God in prayer!

The words scrolled up the projection screen: purple font dissolving into a green background. The singing was patchy in the parts of the room where smart hats interleaved with shiny pink pates, but where the clothes were poorer and unrestrained children ducked in and out of the aisle, voices rang out lustily. Taras decided these were the Salvationists, and the others must be Mrs Bartlett's friends or her husband's business acquaintances. From the front row, like a beacon, shone the silky blonde head of the girl who'd leapt out of the taxi. That was well-fed American hair, Taras thought: plush, satiny, expensive hair. No wonder Gideon's immaculate grey shoulders were drawn back: who wouldn't stand tall, with a girl like that? On his other side rose an even loftier figure, but these shoulders were hunched and topped by a head of silvery hair. His father, Taras thought, as Gideon's hand came up and briefly pressed the older man's back.

Can we find a friend so faithful
who will all our sorrows share?

A wistful feeling enveloped Taras; he wished he'd known his own father, or even knew a bit more about him. If he asked questions, his mother clammed up. Until he was eight and the daughter of the Ukrainian family living in the basement flat had disdainfully pointed it out, he wasn't even aware that his surname was German. Seeing fathers and sons together always made him feel lonely. He glanced at his mother, whose lips were firmly pressed together. Taras wondered if she was perplexed by the exuberance of the singing. Eucharist at St Dunstan's was a more solemn affair. Even though he no longer accompanied her, Taras remembered the acres of silence pressing down on him from a high, arching roof, with God himself acting through his mother's fingers to administer a sharp pinch for any rustles or wriggling.

Mami had an appealing contralto voice, but she didn't waste it on English songs. Her lullabies used to coax Taras to sleep until, aged five, he'd stomped home from school demanding a proper English nursery rhyme. She'd temporarily stopped up his pout with a sugar cube, but that night his fat little legs, straining in their fleecy pyjamas, had drummed at the mattress each time she began crooning '*Nani Nani Puiul Mami*'. 'NO, NO, NO!' he'd roared, thrusting his fingers into his ears. 'NOT THE LITTLE CHICKEN! I WANT BAA, BAA, BLACK SHEEP!' Now she only sang while she was sewing, and then only if Taras was out of the room.

> *Are we weak and heavy laden,*
> *cumbered with a load of care?*

Taras definitely felt cumbered with a shedload of care. The blonde was holding Gideon's hand. She turned and whispered something in his ear. A burst of longing for Katya twisted in Taras's chest. At their first meeting, in the Roadhouse, the thumping rock music meant he couldn't make out anything she said, but her white shoulders, flickering under the strobe lights, leaned closer until he was swimming in the liquescent shine of her eyes. Ever since then, he'd loved the way those small, bright pupils fixed on him, as though he was a mystery that she was trying to disentangle. Not even his mother attended to him with such intensity. He'd found it both flattering and disturbing, in more or less equal measure.

Do thy friends despise, forsake thee?

Oh, Katya, Taras thought.

Take it to the Lord in prayer!

God, give me Katya back, Taras prayed silently. I'll start going to Holy Liturgy again, if you do. He opened his eyes as the hymn's last notes drowned amid a sputter of coughs and the scraping of plastic chairs. Spread-eagled under the windowless electric light, the room was grey and drab, and the Nativity figures huddled together under the sparse fronds of the Christmas tree, as if apologising for still being here in January. The silence elongated into a low, scattered murmur that was quickly hushed as Gideon rose to face them.

'Thank you all for coming today.' There was no tentativeness in his voice, no throat-clearing or abrupt changes in volume. He was comfortable in front of a microphone. 'I doubt if this hall has ever held so many people at one time, but this is an exceptional occasion. My mother was an exceptional woman. I'd like to say a few words in her memory.'

Was Mrs Bartlett truly exceptional, or was that just the sort of thing people said at funerals? Taras didn't know; this was his first. He imagined himself in Gideon's place, dignified under the burden of grief, attracting the admiration and

31

sympathy of the multitude. Not that there would be a multitude. Just him and Mami. And she wouldn't hear his speech. She'd be dead. He gulped back an alarming swell of distress, sliding his fingers over hers for reassurance. She misunderstood, and slipped him a throat lozenge.

'My mother was a woman of strong faith. She believed in the power of prayer. My arrival – when both my parents were well into their forties – might be proof of that . . .' An appreciative ripple ran through the crowd. What a performer. He had them in the palm of his hand, Taras thought resentfully. '. . . My mother's family have been stalwart Salvationists pretty much since William Booth's time – although she broke with tradition when she married my father . . .' More chuckling. That wasn't even a joke. '. . . She instilled her own strict precepts in her only child – me. It was perhaps the bitterest moment of her life when I turned my back on her faith . . .' He lowered his well-shaped blond head. There were murmurs of sympathy. '. . . and started a new life in New Orleans as a jazz musician. But I know she always hoped I'd see the error of my ways and return home.'

New Orleans! Taras nearly burst with envy. Jazz musician! How cool was that?

'. . . I admired my mother's practical approach to life, and I learned a great deal from her strength . . .' Admired. Strength. Nothing about love. To Taras, it seemed a stark omission. Perhaps his face showed it, because Gideon's gaze, scanning the audience, snagged on Taras's for a moment. '. . . My mother believed privilege is also a responsibility. Her good works and devotion to charitable causes speak for themselves . . .' Taras felt Mami stiffen and glanced sideways. Colour was rolling over her cheekbones. The unplucked eyebrows that swept, vivid and black, across her face, had squeezed together to force a deep vertical crease. Her nostrils had taken on an ominous flare. The prayers and Bible reading that followed didn't cool her displeasure. When the service came to an end, she shot over to buttonhole Gideon by the exit.

'Why you are looking to us when you speak? We are not charity-takers!'

'Mami!' Taras scurried after her, elbowing mourners aside, and prised her fingers off Gideon's suit.

Gideon straightened his sleeve and raked a hand through his blond hair. He looked perplexed. 'Mrs Krohe—'

'Place to be living and bring up Son only what is right. Mrs Bartlett understanding this. You are not to be insulting.'

'Mrs Krohe!' Mr Banerjee pressed through the crush. 'This is not the time. Please, come away now.'

Then a tall, stooped figure was looming from the crowd – all bones and joints topped by a cloud of silvery hair. It was the tall man from the front of the church: Gideon's father. His face was set in an expressionless cast, but the deep grooves of its angular features and his heavy, puckered eyelids gave him a weary look.

'Oh dear,' muttered Mr Banerjee. 'Mr Bartlett, I don't think—'

The tall man spoke over him. His voice was detached, almost cynical. 'Hello Maria. Outspoken as ever, I see.' The thickened eyelids swivelled to Taras, flickering up and down with lizard-like swiftness. 'And this, I suppose, must be your son. Sigi's boy.'

CHAPTER SEVEN

Sigi's boy. Taras had a brief but embarrassing instant of incomprehension. Although he knew his father's name was Sigismund, he'd never heard it abbreviated before. 'Sigi' sounded affectionate, even playful; not at all the mood evoked by Taras's mother on the rare occasions she alluded to him. 'Passed-away husband,' she would say frigidly, when confronted with official questions, or 'Father of Son', never according him a name of his own.

Since she made very few new acquaintances, she didn't have to mention him often. This was just as well: she'd been outraged the time a clipboard-wielding market researcher hovering at the supermarket checkout had asked if she was a Miss or Mrs. Small, duffel-coated Taras, clutching uncertainly at his mother's skirt, had immediately been bundled out of the automatic doors into a cold wind.

'Rude know-nothing,' hissed his mother, pulling up his hood, so it came over his eyes and he stumbled. Detecting traces of the jammy dodger he'd already sneaked into his mouth, she pulled out her handkerchief to scrub at his chubby face. 'Must be clean and standing up straight,' she said, giving the duffel coat an admonitory shake. 'So rude persons are not mistaking you for no-good illegitimate.'

'And where is Mr Krohe?'

The over-friendly father of the Cypriot family who'd

briefly inhabited the basement flat had asked that, a year or two later. The man didn't have a clipboard, but he was a rude person all the same. Head level with the overhang of his belly, Taras had inhaled the dark, fermented smell of *latakia* tobacco. It leaked from the man's pores, curling around the black hairs that pressed against his undershirt. Tears sprang as its spicy harshness hit the back of his throat. The Cypriot man had two sons: the youngest was seven, the same age as Taras, but stringy like a runner-bean whereas Taras was plump as a pea. Sometimes Taras imagined that the Cypriot man was really his own father, not theirs. He harboured a secret fear that one day the wobble of his bulging little tummy would give it away. The runner-bean boy would dash upstairs to live with Mami, and Taras would be banished to stew with the fat man in the basement's oily fumes.

Mami shifted her small bag of groceries into the other hand in order to unlock the door, and little Taras clutched her skirt, apprehensive that at any moment he'd be claimed by the hairy-bellied stranger.

'Nine weeks we have been here,' the Cypriot said, drawing a little closer. 'No sign of Mr Krohe. He must be a very busy man.' His red-veined eyes wound around the firmness of Taras's mother, from chest to waist to hips and back again.

'Yes, husband is being busy,' she said flatly, stepping inside and dragging Taras after her. 'No time for talk.'

The bruise-like flush on his mother's cheeks warned Taras she was angry, though he wasn't sure why. She went up to the bathroom and came down with reddened eyes. At first he'd thought she'd been crying, but she'd just scrubbed off the eye-shadow she'd been wearing. Later, he saw the little grey pot in the pedal bin. Trying to straighten out the conversation in his head, he came up to the sewing machine and asked what his father was so busy doing.

'Oh, pourchi,' she said, sounding tired. 'You know he is being dead.'

For a long time after this, Taras imagined that it took a great deal of effort to be dead, and pictured his father one day jerking awake and coming home. The thought kept him quiet for a few months, until the Cypriots were replaced by the Ukrainians. Then, after being humiliated by their skinny-legged, haughty daughter, he'd come snivelling up the stairs.

'Mami, Aleksandra says we're German. She says Krohe is a German name.'

'And what is this mattering?'

'She said Krohe is German, and crows are ugly and black. She says I'm an ugly black German crow. I said that my father isn't German, he's dead, but she won't believe me. Come and tell her, Mami, come.'

His mother pushed aside her bundle of sewing and rubbed her finger along the rim of her headscarf. The black sweep of her lashes stood out against her oyster skin. 'Taraşhu, your father is being dead *and* German, both at the same time.'

Her sewing hunched broodingly in the corner: a jumble of suit trousers for hemming, skirts to be taken in or let out and jackets with missing buttons. She used to advertise in the newsagent's window, till Mr Banerjee suggested that dry-cleaners might be a better route. He'd even negotiated with the two nearest on her behalf, and now she fetched a bundle from each on Monday evenings and had them ready for return Thursday mornings. Taras hated them: cast-off shells of strangers that might suddenly come to life.

'Why don't I know anything about him?' he wailed, feeling hot and betrayed.

'Nothing more to be knowing.'

'I don't want to be a German crow.' He kicked at a trouser leg that had edged out from the sewing bundle.

'Taraşhu . . .' Her headscarf was a good indicator of her mood. When she was calm, it was smooth, neatly outlining her scalp. If disaster was looming, then the ends untucked themselves, fanning out into a crazy starfish. Today it was somewhere in between.

'I DON'T WANT TO BE A GERMAN CROW!' He ran at her, head-butting her lap.

She put her arms around him. He rocked and bucked and then gave in, collapsing into her warmth and letting her heave him up into her lap.

That evening, she gave him something he'd never seen before: a picture of his father. Taras slept with it under his pillow. He held it up to the bathroom mirror, comparing his own thick brown sweep of hair and wide forehead with his father's lighter, fine-boned looks. Since the picture was a grainy black and white, the deep-set eyes appeared grey, but they could just as well be brown, like Taras's, or even blue. Despite its limitations, the picture became a talisman that he kept to himself for the next three years.

Then, in his second term at St Bartholomew's, he'd shown it to Roy.

'Bit good-looking, isn't he?' Roy was holding it right up against the black-rimmed spectacles. It was obvious that a new prescription was overdue, but Taras knew Roy was delaying for fear the fish-eye lenses would get even thicker.

'Yes, he is,' Taras said proudly.

'Doesn't look anything like you.'

'I know.' Taras had long concluded that his father's genes had been completely overpowered. He had his mother's thick, straight hair that shone like well-polished leather, and her burnt-toast eyes. Unfortunately, these blessings were submerged in a squidgy adipose layer that was all his own.

'It's not a proper photo, though.'

'What d'you mean?'

'The paper – it's print, not photo. There's a caption under it and everything. And it's ripped out of somewhere, there's a great chunk missing. Are you sure it's your dad, and not just some bloke your mum saw in the newspaper and fancied?'

'Of course it's my father.' Taras snatched the picture back. 'Look at the name, bat-eyes. See what it says? Sigismund Krohe. Krohe! Like me.'

Even the name was a kind of amulet. Taras repeated it to himself at night sometimes; it had a comforting certainty that helped him fall asleep. Another of their transitory neighbours, the lady from Bratislava who wept a lot, had got tired of hearing him tramping past, chanting a syllable with each stair – Sssig-iss-mund. Whipping open her door, she'd hissed at him, 'Not Sssig-iss-mund. Zig-iz-munt!' before dissolving into sobs once more.

In his second year at St Bartholomew's, crammed into the art department's multimedia cubby-hole to watch a pirate video of *Romper Stomper*, Taras saw the name Russell Crowe roll up the screen, heading the credits. 'Did you see that?' He nudged Roy. 'Crowe. Like me.'

Roy was unmoved. He hadn't liked the film. 'Neo-nazi shit.'

'Sssh.' Taras didn't want Murdoch to hear that: he'd smuggled the video in, and Taras was hoping to impress him. 'We're probably related.' It felt like the kind of thing that could be true.

A few boys picked up on it, taking the piss out of him, but something stuck. When they were taking GCSEs and *L. A. Confidential* came out, someone said, 'Isn't he some sort of cousin of yours, Krohe?' and Taras had ignored Roy's snort and said, 'Yeah, kind of.' When *Gladiator* hit the screens during their A-levels, Roy said nothing, and Taras swelled with family pride. He'd been thinking about changing his name to Terry, among his school-mates, to fit in better, but now he didn't need any anglicisation; he was proud of his name, all of it.

He stuck the poster of Russell Crowe as Maximus up in his room. His mother hovered suspiciously. 'What is this man in skirt?'

'It's a film, Mami.'

She inspected the shining breastplate and fringed leather skirt. 'What kind of film? Is it having ladies too?'

Did she suspect it of being a dodgy film? There had been an incident recently where his mother almost found a *Penthouse* at the bottom of his wardrobe. She'd been cleaning it out, and he'd grabbed the magazine just in time. It made him burn just to think of it. After that, Taras kept anything illicit under the mattress.

'The actor's got the same name as us, Mami,' he said quickly. 'Crowe. Like my father. Something to be proud of.'

'Oh Taraşhu.' She sat down on his bed and crossed herself. 'Can be proud of Bunicu Bogdan instead. Fine man. Fighter for Romania and Orthodox Faith.'

Taras was still cringing over the time he'd boasted about his grandfather to Dr Lewin. 'Mami, the Iron Guard were fascists.'

It was an old argument. 'Bunicu Bogdan good man. Brave man. Your father . . .' She waved her hand. 'Enough. No need for bad rememberings.'

Since that moment with his mother, he'd kept quiet about his father. He stuffed the picture in the back of his wallet, and didn't look at it so often. At university, if anyone asked, he said, 'My father's dead,' and left it at that. So hearing the name 'Sigi' now wasn't only unexpected, it was shocking; as though a secret was being exposed to the world. His father was private and now a stooped, silver-topped stranger was letting 'Sigi' roll off his tongue. It made Taras feel like an outsider; a pretender trying to sneak his way into a long-established circle.

'You knew my father?' he asked.

'Yes.' Those half-lidded, amphibian eyes slid over him. 'You don't resemble him in the least.'

'I know.' Taras felt excluded again as the gaze swept across to his mother. She was standing very erect, shoulders stiff. The flush in her face had died down, and now she was radiating absolute determination.

The silver-haired man seemed to recognise this. 'I don't know why you're here, Maria, but I suppose you'll get what you want. You usually do.'

Turning, he sagged. Gideon immediately moved to his side and the press of mourners stepped respectfully back, letting father and son reach the waiting car.

CHAPTER EIGHT

Taras's hangover had reached the hollow-stomached, trembling stage by the time he'd dropped his mother back at their front door. As she tilted her head to kiss him goodbye, winter light flooded her face, exposing the faint creases around her eyes, and he wished he could smooth them away. He didn't like seeing her begin to look careworn, but before he could think of something comforting to say, two road-workers in orange vests strolled by unwrapping greaseproof paper. The hot steaming smell of burger hit Taras's nostrils and his stomach let out an angry growl.

'Must be eating, pourchi.' His mother rummaged in her bag for emergency supplies.

'Don't fuss, Mami.' But she pressed a Walnut Whip into his palm, and he crunched on it while walking down the road, stifling a touch of nausea as warm chocolate ran down the back of his throat.

The open gullet of London Bridge Station sucked him in and hawked him up the steel escalator, spitting him out on to the main concourse. He weaved through the crowd, and out on to the forecourt where a bendy 521 bus was filling up. No chance of a seat, but he rested his forehead against the cold window as they trundled on to the bridge. Upriver, the spoked hoop of the London Eye bit into the skyline. In some other universe, he and Katya were slowly spinning round in a pod, laughing and kissing. But that didn't happen and now she was with a grey ponytailed geriatric. What a mess. Being alone with his thoughts was depressing, so he rang Roy. No reply, but five minutes later, he got a text.

At hsptl, cant talk. Wots this abt Mad Monk? Drink 2nite?

The suggestion of inflicting alcohol on his hangover made Taras feel ill.

no he texted back.

B a man. Jst the 1. Camel at 8

Taras was about to resend *no* but the giant dome of St Paul's was frowning through the window, as severe now as when he and Roy had perched under its shadow on the wall of the school quad.

OK he texted as the bus rumbled over the viaduct, *Cu l8r*

Off the bus, across the street, through the revolving doors. Taras didn't rush. If he was lucky, the morning meeting would be over. He nodded to the fragile red-headed receptionist, who ignored him as always, and sauntered into the lift just before the doors clamped shut. A laminated plate listed the building's occupants. Taras jabbed the button next to Floor 4 – International Business Scalability. Not that they were international yet, unless you counted a client in Cardiff. As a new graduate two and a half years ago, he'd been grateful to get this job, but the feeling was wearing off. Perhaps the Chief had hoped the name would imbue his fledgling firm with the size and authority of IBM. Unfortunately, most people who saw the IBS logo thought of Irritable Bowel Syndrome. On cue, Taras's gut rumbled again.

Annoyingly, the meeting was still in progress. The rest of his team were corralled in a small, windowless cell. Taras peered through the zoo-like glass porthole in the door, and saw that feeding time was over. The remnants of a Krispy Kreme box were splayed across the table, and Francis was brushing sugar from his jowls. He was an oddly proportioned man: his chest and stomach were soft and succulent, padded with forty-five years of indulgent living, but from them sprung a pair of undersized chicken-legs. Sitting down disguised these defects, but not the shiny crown or the large, winged eyebrows, which were currently drawn together in a preoccupied frown. All Francis's expressions were coded: this one signified 'executive with weighty matters on mind'. Taras interpreted it differently. To him, it shouted 'befuddled, squinting fool'. Pressing closer to the glass, he widened his field of vision until he found the focus of the frown. It didn't take long. Across the table, their senior programmer's lips were contorted and his head was jerking like a demented puppet. Bracing himself, Taras pushed open the door.

'Ah, our tardy pwoject lead.' Francis's eyebrows peaked, then flattened forgivingly. 'Sit down, Taras.' As usual, his inability to say the letter 'r' meant he pronounced it Tao-ahs. 'Colin's just giving us an update on these . . . ah . . . sub-woutine pwoblems.'

'I keep telling you.' A weak-wristed slap on the table rattled the pens clipped to Colin's shirt. 'The subroutine isn't the fundamental problem . . .'

Taras felt indescribably weary. He slid into the seat next to Jamal, who had fallen into his usual chin-to-chest meeting slump. Even half-asleep, he didn't show any traces of hangover: as ever, the crisp collar of his lilac shirt was impeccable, and the dark grain of his skin kept its secrets. Taras felt envious: but cheered up when Jamal lifted his head, revealing eyes that were laced with pink spider-veins.

'About time, mate.' Cobwebbed eyes gave Taras the once-over. 'Been sleeping off the tequila?'

'No!' Taras exclaimed as Francis's eyebrows vaulted upwards.

Fortunately, Lisa came to his rescue. 'Jamal! He's been to a funeral, haven't you, Taras, love?'

Like Francis, Lisa was older than most of the other IBS employees. The Chief favoured youth: he mistakenly equated it with energy. But whereas Francis was a clueless, irritating twat, Lisa made herself useful. She was competent at system testing, which Taras and Jamal both found boring, and she fussed over them all like an auntie.

'Here, I saved you a glazed chocolate custard.' Lisa's head, helmeted in a tight perm, nodded encouragingly at Taras.

Cramming it in his mouth, he used a napkin for cover and flexed his wrist in a wanker sign at Jamal, who just grinned and pushed a cardboard packet across the table. 'The new business cards got distributed. I picked up yours.'

'Oh, thanks.' Taras was about to have a look, but Francis was glaring, so he shoved them hastily in his pocket.

'All wight! Let's recap for Tao-ahs's benefit.' Francis closed his eyes and pressed his middle finger against the ridge between his beetle-brows. This was his 'don't test my patience' expression. 'Who's been taking minutes?'

Rifling through her A4 pad, Lisa started reading in a loud monotone. '*Item one*. Merger status. Talks with the Americans continuing. Discussions sensitive so details not available. Francis to channel further updates from the Chief as and when. *Item two*. Meeting minutes. Last week's minutes were not distributed because Jamal's notebook went missing. In future, minutes to be distributed by close of business same day. Also, everyone to keep an eye out for Jamal's notebook which is red and has his name on the inside cover. *Item three*. Testing progress. Two weeks behind, due to subroutine errors making the region crash—'

A strangulated wail interrupted her. A spit-bubble was convulsing in the corner of Colin's mouth. 'Why doesn't anyone listen? It's not my subroutine! The tables are out of sync because the region refresh wasn't done properly . . .'

'Well that must be wesolved.' Francis's eyebrows bulked together. 'This is a high-visibility pwoject and the Amewicans are taking a close intewest in its pwogwess. The

Chief says it's mission-cwitical that we meet our milestone date for UTA testing.'

'UAT, you mean,' said Lisa. 'User Acceptance Testing.'

Francis waved her aside. 'Who's going to pick up this one? Jamal?'

Jamal snapped out of his torpor. 'Pick up what?'

'Slot Jamal's name against the action.'

'Can't do, sorry.' Jamal waited for Francis's forehead to bulge, then added, 'Off on holiday . . .' Thrusting out his arms and miming a skier slaloming down the slopes. 'Won't be around to see it through.'

Brows knotting, Francis looked round the table. Taras strategically filled his mouth with chocolate doughnut and studied his hands. What was it like being a jazz musician in New Orleans? Gideon probably got up at sunset and drank bourbon on the rocks. No wonder he could pull a stunning blonde. Would Katya have liked Taras better if he could blow a trumpet? Perhaps he should have demonstrated his ability to thump out the intro to 'House of the Rising Sun' on a keyboard.

'Tao-ahs!' Francis's eyebrows were bristling.

'Umpf?' Taras coughed on his doughnut.

'Jamal has just pointed out that as the new pwoject lead, it should be your wesponsibility to sort out the testing pwoblem.'

Taras swallowed, coughed again, and shot an outraged glare at Jamal, who leaned back with a sliver of a grin. 'It's difficult . . .'

'Why?'

Taras cast about for a valid objection but had to settle for, 'It's my birthday.'

Francis gave this the respect it deserved. 'Put Tao-ahs down to wesolve the . . . ah . . . TUA issues by liaising with . . . ah . . . all welevant parties. Now. Next item, ah yes, missing documentation. Also your action, I think, Tao-ahs?'

Taras froze. 'What?'

Francis rested his forehead in the 'V' of his thumb and forefinger, speaking with exaggerated slowness, 'The Version 3 Business Architecture document. Still outstanding. You were going to look into it.'

'Oh yes. I've done that.'

'Good.' Francis brightened. 'The Chief wants a copy for the Amewicans, so forward it to me asap.'

'I can't.' Taras caught Jamal's eye. There was a glint of sympathy in it, but not enough to expect any support. 'It doesn't exist.'

'Nonsense! We've got eight clients wunning on Version 3.'

'The system, yes.' Taras wriggled in his seat. 'But the document didn't get written.'

'No document?' Francis sounded upset. 'Who's wesponsible for that?'

Silence. Jamal flipped the end of his silk tie thoughtfully and gazed at the ceiling, while Lisa concentrated on twisting the tab off a can of diet Dr Pepper.

'Well, that's you, isn't it, Francis?' Colin said, insensitive as usual to the subtleties of office politics. 'The Chief put you in charge of standards and documentation.'

'Who was wesponsible for witing it, I mean.' Francis said brusquely, but his eyebrows were sagging.

There was a rap on the porthole. Through the glass, the Chief's buxom secretary mouthed 'conference call' and pointed at her watch.

'All wight. We'll have to stop here.' Francis's low-slung legs were already propelling his weighty torso towards the door. It didn't do to keep the Americans waiting.

'We never used to bother with documentation and all that. Back-of-the-envelope requirements. Coding by the seat of our pants.' Colin stroked his wispy scalp wistfully. 'Glory days.'

'You think it's bad now, see what happens if the Chief

manages to flog IBS to the Yanks.' Jamal was first through the door. 'Gory days. He'll make a mint, we'll be out on our ear.'

'Really?' Colin followed them to the analysts area: a tight square of three desks. Jamal's was a polished shine: since it held nothing but a keyboard and mouse, the cleaners lavished it with attention. Lisa's supported a display panel of family photos and a mass of stationery, while Taras's desk was a muddle of poly-styrene cups and ripped-out sheets from an A4 pad.

'They wouldn't do that, would they? Sack us?' Colin's thin face went grey.

Lisa arrived, tucking the meeting minutes into a transpar-ent folder and adding them to the colour-coded pile in her out-tray. She glanced at Colin's drawn face and clucked loudly. 'Oh, you boys. You never learn.'

'Never learn what?' Francis materialised. He had an irri-tating ability to move almost soundlessly; Jamal said it was because his feet were so small, like a goblin's.

'The boys are a bit the worse for wear,' Lisa said comfort-ably. 'After their night out.'

'Oh?' The eyebrows furrowed. Francis was never invited to anything social.

Colin didn't pick up on the subtext and said informatively, 'For Taras's birthday.'

'Indeed.' Francis sounded resentful. 'The Amewicans are on the line, and they're wery keen to see this architecture document. I've told them we've got it in hand. Just a few fin-ishing touches.'

An instant message popped up on Taras's screen. 'TOO SLOW!' And then, Jamal was saying brightly. 'I'd do it, but I'm off to Meribel. Bet Cow-arse could put it together in no time though.'

'Good, good.' Francis stroked down the hairs in his left eyebrow. 'Ah, Tao-ahs. Just one thing. The Amewicans need it by lunch-time.'

'What?!' Taras stared. 'It's twelve already!'

'Oh, don't worry. West Coast time, not London.' Francis was already turning away. Over his shoulder he added, 'So you've got . . . ah . . . another eight hours in hand.'

CHAPTER NINE

Blackness poured through the plastic slats of the blinds, lapping at the corners of Taras's desk, while overhead a stark white beam flooded his terminal. At night the lights were triggered by a movement sensor: even the one directly above him flicked off every fifteen minutes, and he had to rock back in his chair, hands flailing above his head like a man drowning, to make it switch back on. This was no way to spend his birthday. Last night's pre-celebration seemed a million years ago.

With bleary frustration, he stared at the boxes and arrows on his screen. Re-reading the last line nearly pushed him into a coma.

The release profile will also be informed by the need for flexible access to ensure a stable platform for deployment.

Hmm. He reduced it to 4-point font and dropped it inside a hexagon. Better. The lights clicked off again, plunging him into the dark, and he didn't have the energy to move. The electronic glow of his monitor was sucking him into its eerie world. Time dissolved away.

'Brrring!' The shrill of his desk phone sent him leaping up in shock, and the halogen beam overhead snapped on.

'Pourchi, you are very late.'

'I'm still working, Mami.'

'Not good for eyes, *pui-pui*. Must be blinking and taking breaks.'

Two years ago, he'd made the mistake of bringing home an HR booklet called 'Your VDU and You'. His mother had picked it out of the rubbish and pored over it, lips parted, head nodding as though studying her catechism. 'I'm going to be late, Mami. Don't make dinner.'

'Already making, pourchi. *Sarmale* with carrot added. Very good for eyes.'

He sighed and looked at his watch. After seven already. He was due to meet Roy at eight. 'All right. I'll be home when I can.'

'Man telephoning for you, pourchi.'

Taras's hand was already on his mouse again, highlighting a section of text on the screen. It took him a moment to follow what she'd said. 'What? Someone called me at home?'

'He ask for you. I tell nothing.'

This was no surprise. His mother didn't trust strangers.

'Who was it?'

'Not leaving name. But I have number.' She sounded triumphant. 'Caller display show, and I write down. You want, pourchi?'

Taras let her read him the number. Mildly curious, he punched it into his mobile, and pressed dial. No name showed up, which meant it wasn't anyone already in his address book. He killed the call quickly before someone picked up.

His mother was still talking. '*Sarmale* cooking now, pourchi. Big shame to spoil.'

He was almost done, anyway. But his concentration had been broken. He hung up and stared at the screen. It stared back. Stalemate.

'Pile of crap,' he muttered, and jumped up, stretching out his cramped limbs. Lights flicked on overhead, tracking him like a stage spot. He executed a little spin and threw out his arms, like a cheesy ballad crooner. Suddenly a pair of button-bright brown eyes was in his mind. No. He wasn't going to think about Katya. He wasn't a performer any more, he was a criminal on the run. Dodging behind the photocopier, he darted from desk to desk, trying to outrun the search lights. Faster! They were on his trail. Aaargh! He crashed into the glass front of the snacks dispenser. It rocked on its pedestal, and a Caramac bar thudded down.

'Result!' A sticky mouthful of something sweet would give him the energy to finish up and get out. He strolled back to his desk the long way round, setting every light blazing. At Francis's office, he paused and pushed the door ajar, just enough to insert his backside into the gap and let out a trumpeting fart. Ha! That'd teach him.

An answering vibration from his desk made Taras whirl round, feeling guilty. His mobile was jumping about. Scurrying back, he snatched it up.

'Mmmphm.' Caramel was clogging up his mouth. 'Taramph.'

'What? Who is this? I just missed a call from this number.' The hard voice was unmistakeable.

'Mmph-n.' Taras dislodged the caramel with a finger and tried again. 'Gideon? Gideon. It's Taras.'

'Oh.' The voice was short. 'Hold on.'

Taras could hear traffic and voices. It sounded like Gideon was getting into a car. A door slammed, and suddenly it was quieter. 'Hello?' He was afraid he'd been cut off. 'Hello? Are you still there?'

'Yeah. You and I need to talk.'

'Oh. Well, I'm a bit busy. I'm at work.'

'I didn't mean now.' Gideon paused. 'Though . . . why not? You weren't too busy to gatecrash my mother's funeral this morning, were you? Where's your office?'

'Um, Holborn.'

'Well, that's easy. Hop in a cab and meet me at Gordon's on Villiers Street. I've got half an hour to spare.'

CHAPTER TEN

Taras should have refused such a peremptory command. But what did Gideon want to talk about? The detached, patrician voice of Gideon's father was still ringing through his head. '*This must be Sigi's boy.*' Either curiosity or the Caramac had overpowered his hangover: he felt surprisingly perky. No point in wasting time trying to finish the document. He just slapped a giant 'DRAFT' across the title, and fired it off to the Americans, then ran out to get a cab.

Villiers Street was a tiny pedestrianised stub along the side of Charing Cross Station, but Taras had to walk up and down it twice before he saw the dingy sign that read 'Gordon's'. It was like a secret lair: a long flight of dusty steps led him downwards, and at the bottom, brick walls papered with press cuttings funnelled into a dimly lit cellar, which was crowded with bodies, all hunched over upturned wine-casks, their voices rising above the guttering candles. Cautiously, Taras pushed his way through, fighting a sense of claustrophobia. The low, crumbling roof was holding in a packed sardine-can of noise and flesh.

At the bar, he found they didn't serve beer, only wine. Not wanting to look a fool, he pointed to the nearest bottle, which happened to be Chianti. He could really have done with a burger, but the only food on offer was bread and cheese, so he made an equally hasty choice, thinking he'd cram it down before Gideon arrived.

Naturally, things didn't turn out that way. He'd only had one bite, when a red-faced party of lawyers jostled their way out, revealing Gideon seated in the far corner, fingering a bottle of mineral water.

Taras stuffed a wine glass in each of his jacket pockets and edged through the crowd, crouching to avoid the sharp incline of the cellar roof.

Placing the bottle and plate of cheese on the table with a flourish, he said, 'Glass of Chianti?', feeling rather sophisticated.

'I'm driving.' Gideon looked at the pungent mess on Taras's plate. 'Isn't Italian wine completely overwhelmed by a Stilton?'

'No.' To prove it, Taras washed down a wedge of cheese with a robust mouthful of wine. The harsh blue tang mingled with the soft grape and formed a hideous acidic mulch.

'You'd be better with Pecorino or even a Brie.' Gideon continued.

How did Gideon know stuff like that? 'You're so . . . different,' Taras couldn't help blurting. 'What happened?'

'Since school? A lot, Flounder.' Gideon sounded impatient. 'So, you and your mother live in a flat Ma owned. How long has that been going on?'

'Well, always. You really didn't know?' Taras was shocked. 'But I thought . . . at school. I thought that's why you – you know – sort of looked down on me.'

'Actually, I looked down on anyone who wasn't saved,' Gideon said dismissively. 'So, what's the big secret? Old Banerjee's being very close-mouthed. Says it was a private arrangement between your mother and mine. Dad won't talk either. Is something funny going on?'

'Like what?'

'Something's up. I want to know what it is.' The candle flame cast distorted shadows over Gideon's face as he leaned across the barrel table. Around them, noise and laughter bubbled up. Hollowed by the flickering shadows, his grey-green eyes looked like his father's.

Taras thought of Elliott Bartlett's thin lips mouthing '*Sigi's boy,*' and shivered. How had Mami got mixed up with this family? 'What does your father do?' he asked.

'Do?' Gideon frowned. 'He ran a firm that made shoes. The sturdy, hard-wearing sort. Popular with traffic wardens and social workers. Old family firm. Dad sold it a while back.'

For a moment, that seemed disappointingly prosaic, but if Mr Bartlett had been the owner, it meant boardrooms, tailored suits, share options. No wonder those heavy-lidded eyes had been full of arrogance. But what did someone like that have to do with him and Mami? He needed to know more. 'How—' he began, but Gideon interrupted.

'Why did Ma pay your school fees?'

'What?'

'Don't try and weasel out of it, Flounder. I found her papers. Five thousand pounds a term, paid in advance, for eight years.'

Taras had known St Bartholomew's was expensive, but hearing the figure was a shock. 'I had a scholarship.' Under Gideon's narrowed eye, it sounded weak even to Taras's ears. He'd never actually questioned where the money came from, let alone the likelihood that he'd been selected for any kind of competitive prize.

'One hundred and twenty thousand pounds on your fucking education . . .' The Monk didn't swear in the old days but he looked mad now. Taras had never seen him as bad as this before. Gideon narrowed his eyes. 'Dad's not well. He's taken a sedative and gone to bed. Why did seeing you and your mother upset him?'

'I – I don't know.' Taras's throat felt as dry as crêpe-paper, and the throb of his hangover had started up again.

'Fine.' Gideon leaned back, hands spread on the wine-cask

between them. 'Then you'd better get ready to move. In the circumstances, we don't feel comfortable letting the two of you carry on living there.'

Before Taras could take this in, Gideon's gaze jerked up, over Taras's shoulder and towards the doorway. 'Damn.' He rose, stooping because of the incline in the roughly plastered ceiling, which gave him a look of his father again. 'She's early, for once.'

He raised his hand, and Taras turned to see the sleek blonde from the funeral unbelting a white velvet coat. With a dissatisfied pinch of the lips, she squeezed through to their table. 'You like to hang out in this old hole?'

'It's got character, Desirée.' Gideon leaned across to kiss her cheek. 'Full of history.'

'And dirt.' She took the candle from the table and held it up to the wall. 'I'll bet there's spiders in here.'

'I thought it'd be convenient for your hotel.' Gideon accepted the coat she thrust towards him.

'Yeah. And a long way from your pop's house. Where I'm not invited to stay.'

Gideon ran his hand through his hair. 'You know Dad's not well, and—'

'After coming all this way and everything.'

'I didn't actually ask you to . . .' He broke off, looking at Taras, who belatedly climbed to his feet too. 'I think you and I are done here. Banerjee will take care of the legal stuff. A month's notice, paperwork, whatever. OK?'

'Fine.' Taras didn't want to make a fool of himself under the searchlight of Desirée's cold gaze. Striving for urbanity, he extracted a business card from the new pack in his pocket and flipped it across the table. 'In case you need to contact me.'

'I doubt it.' But Gideon scissored the card between two fingers.

Taras waved Desirée towards his vacated seat with, he

55

hoped, a suitably wry smile. 'Bye, Desirée. It was good to almost meet you.' He tried not to think about the £15 bottle of Chianti sitting, barely touched, on the table.

'Yeah. Likewise,' she said, without a trace of humour, but blinking her wide anemone eyes in a way that seemed flirtatious. It gave him a pleasing sense of control; he straightened his back as far as the sloping roof would allow.

'Interesting choice of career, Flounder.' Gideon was still holding the business card, one eyebrow cocked.

Taras accepted this with a curt nod and turned away, feeling professional and rather superior until, in the corner of his eye, he caught Desirée mouthing, 'Flounder?' as if it was the silliest name she'd ever heard. That brought back all his childhood clumsiness and he blundered away, knocking against people and tables as if his hips were sheathed with an extra doughnut of flesh.

The name was born during a swimming lesson. The PE master stood at the pool side, arm raised, whistle in mouth. Heading the queue of ten-year-old boys at the diving board, Murdoch was bouncing impatiently on sturdy, freckled legs. The whistle sounded; he cut through the water with a strong, neat splash, and held the rubber brick triumphantly aloft. Next, Roy's pale Twiglet body looked barely capable of supporting the chaotic frizz sprouting from his scalp, but moments later, he spluttered to the surface, brick clutched to his narrow chest.

The blue briefs cut ridges into Taras's skin: they weren't made for someone who carried his own subcutaneous lifebelt. Hitching them up hopefully, he curled his toes over the edge and belly-flopped in. His arms scooped, his legs kicked, but it was no good, his excess flesh bobbed to the surface. He was unsinkable. The whistle shrilled. 'Stop floundering about, Krohe, and get out!' the master yelled.

'Flounder!' Murdoch started the jeering chant, as Taras heaved himself on to the tiled edge. 'Flounder! Flounder!'

And then Gideon Bartlett was standing astride Taras's dripping body, arms folded, facing Murdoch. 'God defends the cause of the weak. Leave him alone.'

'He likes it,' Murdoch prodded Taras's shoulder with a wet toe. 'Don't you, Flounder?'

Who was Gideon calling weak? 'I don't mind,' said Taras, though he did, and from then on, his own name, like the brick, proved irretrievable.

CHAPTER ELEVEN

'Where are you, Taraşhu? *Sarmale* getting cold.'

She always snatched up the phone like that, voice rising in panicked anticipation. Unless Taras was home; then she'd hold the receiver a suspicious half-inch from her ear, and demand, 'Yes?'

'Still at work, Mami.' Taras was at Charing Cross Station. He jumped into the last carriage and let his voice droop with exhaustion as the doors beeped and the train pushed out.

'Very noisy, pourchi.'

'The printer's going. It's chaos here.'

'Do you leave now, pourchi?'

'No.' He was terse, business-like. How was he going to tell her what had happened? It made him feel sick. 'There's a lot to do. I'm going to be late.'

'Remember to be blinking, pourchi. Are knees at right angles?'

He was sprawled across a seat, but this made him pull his legs in. 'I've got to go. My manager needs to talk to me.'

'Important keeping Boss happy. *Sarmale* can wait.' She sounded almost humble: the professional world was an anxious mystery. Taras basked in the artificial feeling of importance until he realised another call was coming through, which flustered him and he cut her off abruptly.

The second call was Roy. 'Where the hell are you?'

'I'm right there,' Taras gabbled. 'Seconds away. You're still at the Camel, yeah? I'm on the case, mate.'

'You're on a train, you plonker.'

'It's just pulling into London Bridge. I'll be with you in two minutes. Five, tops.'

'I can hear the announcement. You're at Waterloo East. And you're an hour late. You'd better have a good excuse for once.'

'Yep.' Taras was almost pleased to realise he did. 'I've just been evicted by the Mad Monk.'

Twenty-five minutes later, wiping cold foam from his lips, he told Roy all about it.

'Bastard,' Roy said. 'Still, might be a good thing. You need your own place. You can't live with your mother for ever.'

'But Mami couldn't manage without me.'

'You'd be the one struggling. Do you even know how to switch on a washing machine? Or make a cup of tea? You've got it too easy.'

Taras emitted a fizzy burp. 'Doesn't Astrid do all that for you?'

'Some chance. She's barely been home since she moved in. This new job of hers is a nightmare. Bloody charity. It doesn't even pay well. We'll never get a house deposit together at this rate.'

'You're thinking about buying? Really?' Taras was startled. That sounded a bit permanent. They'd be getting married next. It was a chilling thought.

'I'll have to go into plastics and start creaming off private patients.'

'Astrid wouldn't approve of that. Nor would your dad.' Taras had sat round the scrubbed kitchen table in Hendon enough times in his teenage years to know Dr Lewin's stringently liberal views. Keen for approval, Taras had even found himself voicing an ambition to join Médecins Sans Frontières and save lives in deprived African nations. Luckily he hadn't got the grades for medical school, or he might have felt too awkward to back out.

Resting his elbows on the pine bar, he imagined a stethoscope round the neck of his reflection in the window on to the dark street, and creased his eyebrows in a stern, intense expression, like Alan Alda in *M*A*S*H*. A couple next to them noticed him looking, and he quickly changed his expression to one of scrutiny, as if he was weighing up the Camel's merits. Hmm. Large windows, new wooden floor, chalked specials board and cheerful Aussie staff. Taras had always liked it here, but now he was wondering if it was a bit lacking in history or character or something. 'Have you ever been to Gordon's?' he asked Roy. 'A sort of wine cellar by Charing Cross Station.'

'No. Sounds crap.' Roy was already signalling to the barman. 'Same again?'

Taras checked his watch. He ought to get home, tell Mami the bad news. She'd be devastated. 'All right. Just the one.' He waited while Roy handed over the cash. 'It's a bit weird that Mrs Bartlett paid my fees for St Bart's. Why would she do that?'

Roy took a gulp of Guinness. 'Didn't you have some sort of bursary? Maybe she administered that. She was a governor, wasn't she?'

That made sense. But Taras wasn't sure. 'It sounded like she paid it personally. Why else would Gideon be so angry?'

'The Monk's a rule to himself. Who knows why he does anything?' Roy picked up his phone. 'Astrid ought to be done by now.'

'You didn't see him. He's not the Monk any more.' Taras said. 'He's changed. He . . .'

But Roy's head was bent over his phone: he was busy texting. Taras would have thought that after two years, there wasn't much left for him and Astrid to say to each other.

On the face of it, no pairing could have been less likely, but Roy had been hooked from the day he'd seen a limber figure wriggling through the wooden slats of the mathematical bridge, wearing a red t-shirt emblazoned with the slogan 'THE PERSONAL IS POLITICAL'. Taras had heard the whole story. The girl was stringing a large banner from end to end: 'PAGE 3 DEMEANS WOMEN EVERYWHERE. BAN THE SUN NOW.'

'Want to sign a petition to ban the *Sun* from the JCR?' Hands on cargo-pant hips, a supple stretch of skin revealing the stud in her belly-button, the girl was watching his reaction.

'No,' Roy said truthfully.

'Why not?'

'Er . . . good sports coverage.'

'So you're happy to support a system that degrades half the human race, in exchange for a few pages of crap about football?'

Roy had a choice here. There was still time to pick the right-on approach, (*When you put it like that . . .*). Or he could play the bluff new-lad, (*Yeah. So?*). The first seemed craven, and he didn't have the bruising rugby-player looks to pull off the second. So, he went for a typically Roy response: the unexpected.

'I'll tell you later.'

'What?' She leaned over the bridge. 'You'll what?'

But with a casual wave of the hand, he was already walking away.

Asking around, Roy discovered her name was Astrid, she was in the second year, like him, and was standing for Student Women's Officer at Queens. He barricaded himself behind a pile of books in the library and set to work. An hour later, he'd dropped a hand-drawn cartoon in her pigeon-hole. The first frame showed a gangling, bespectacled frizz-head settling down to read the sports page. In the second, he was surreptitiously gawping at a pair of outsize page-three breasts. By the third, he was flat on his back, hands ineffectively warding off the spiky-haired, cargo-panted avenger aiming a steel-capped toe at his crotch. A speech-bubble screamed 'I'll sign! I'll sign!' It was a gamble, but it paid off. The next time she saw him, she smiled. By the end of the year, they were friends.

That hadn't been such an easy idea for Taras to grasp. Back in London, enrolled on a Business Information Management degree at South Bank University, he was finding girls nearly as far out of reach as they had been at school. Though he'd managed a few incompetent snogs, the concept of female friends just didn't compute. It was a relief when, just before graduation, Roy admitted that he and Astrid had become an item. Relinquished to the status of girlfriend, she was made safe. Taras's role as best mate was no longer under threat.

CHAPTER TWELVE

Roy was still tapping out his text, so Taras was first to notice the boyish figure in jeans and an army surplus jacket, with spiky blonde hair, pushing through the door. He nudged Roy.

'Astrid!' Roy banged down his phone. 'I said I'd come and meet you.'

'Well, this was quicker.' She ruffled his hair.

'It's not a safe area. What the fuck do you think I'm doing, trailing all the way down here? The whole point is that I come and pick you up.'

'Oh, really?' She raised an eyebrow. 'I thought it was so you could drink with your little friend. Hi Taras.'

She gave him a kiss. Taras responded the way he always did with other people's girlfriends, turning his face exaggeratedly to the side to make sure any contact was clearly cheek to cheek.

'Yeah, right.' Roy was still grumpy. 'He's only just turned up. I've been sat here on my tod.'

'Well, now you can have a drink with us both. Lucky you.' She pulled one of his curls and let it bounce back.

Though still a mess, Roy's hair had lost the startled frizziness of schooldays: Taras suspected Astrid had something to do with that. Her influence was generally a shaping, controlling one. Taking a swig from Roy's Guinness, she demanded, 'Do you know how big a problem sex-trafficking is?'

'Jesus, Astrid,' Roy groaned. 'You've just done a fourteen-hour day. Let it go.'

'It has a global turnover of twelve billion dollars. Twelve. Billion. Dollars. Only drugs makes more.'

Roy made a 'don't care' face and she took a swipe at him. He ducked, and she caught Taras instead, splashing his lager over his trousers.

'Whoops. Oh, no, Taras, I'm so sorry,' Astrid said, putting a nail-bitten hand to her mouth. 'I'll get you another one.'

'It's all right. I've got to go, anyway.' Taras dabbed at the spreading wet patch below his groin and extracted the cardboard pack of business cards. The top few were slightly damp, but below that they were fine. The new font looked good. He wondered if it would look knobby to give Astrid one.

'Well, there's something I should tell you first. Katya's invited us out for dinner next week.'

For a moment, Taras thought that 'us' meant all three of them, but it didn't.

'With that ponytailed geriatric git?' Roy said. 'Christ, I hope you told her no.'

'I said yes, of course.' Astrid ignored the roll of his eyes. 'Taras, we can all be adults about this, can't we?'

He tried to say yes, but the beer-dribbling mumble stuck in his throat.

'It would be stupid for us to drop the friendship with her just because you two broke up, don't you think?' Astrid said briskly.

It didn't seem stupid to Taras at all. His insides were curdling. 'Wh . . . where are you going?'

'A Korean place, I don't know it. Somewhere behind Oxford Street, I think. The new boyfriend's a vegetarian.'

'I hate all that pickled cabbage,' Roy said sourly. 'And we can't afford a meal out. We're supposed to be saving.'

Taras would have preferred Roy's objections to be on the

grounds of loyalty, rather than cost or cabbage, but it was better than nothing.

'She said it's cheap,' Astrid said. 'And she offered us a lift home. The boyfriend lives somewhere in our direction, and he's driving. So . . .'

The barman came over, and she turned to order a drink. Taras grimaced at Roy, who raised his hands. 'Nothing I can do about it. You shouldn't have pushed the two of them together, you were desperate for them to be friends.'

'Not any more,' Taras said plaintively but Roy just shrugged.

Astrid turned, crooking her fingers in the shape of a drink and raised her pale eyebrows at Taras, but he shook his head. 'Got to go.' Draining the rest of his pint, he clunked the glass on the bar and said, 'See you.'

'See you,' Roy said. Astrid would have leaned over for a goodbye peck, but Taras was already backing away. She nuzzled against Roy instead: white-blonde spikes merging into black curls, and neither of them watched his exit.

Would he have had more chance of holding on to Katya if he'd been living in a place of his own, he wondered, turning off Tooley Street and under the neon-lit railway tunnel. Grey ponytail had an unfair advantage: he was geriatric enough to have bought decades ago, when houses were cheaper than chips; no wonder he could afford to run a car too. How was Taras expected to compete? Why couldn't the old git stick to female wrinklies, instead of coming after an eighteen-year-old? Jamal had called Taras a cradle-snatcher, and that was only a four-year difference. Well, five, as of today.

That channelled his resentment in a different direction. Emerging from the tunnel, he waited for a solitary motorbike headlight to pass, engine reverberating as it entered the orange glow, and turned into the silence of Crucifix Lane. No one had so much as said happy birthday to him. Had they all forgotten that last night's celebration was a day early, to take advantage of two-for-one Mondays? He wasn't expecting anything major, but an acknowledgement would have been nice. Trudging up Weston Street, he plunged into a fog of depression before his key was in the door.

The bulb in the shared hallway had gone, and a pile of unwanted mail skidded under his feet. Perhaps moving would be a good thing; they could go somewhere smarter; somewhere with their own front door. He thumped up the stairs, and unlocked their internal door. The corridor was shrouded in darkness; so was the narrow parlour. Through the shadows, he made out his mother lolling back in her chair, head to one side. She'd changed out of the funeral dress and her hair was hidden under a neatly tied scarf. A stuffed pincushion was on the table beside her; a pile of mending at her feet. She'd been waiting up.

Next door, in the kitchen, a spotlight burned on a plate of cold, sad-looking cabbage rolls. He wasn't hungry, but they'd taken hours to make. Stuffing one into his mouth, he swallowed it down without chewing, and flicked off the light.

'Pourchi, is that you?' His mother appeared in the doorway, rubbing her eyes. 'Taraşhu?' She flipped the main light on, and he saw the cards spread out over the table. Twenty-two of them, one from each birthday he'd had to date. There was the 'Now You're One' card with a teddy bear waving a balloon, and the 'Five Today!' card with a big red car, and the 'Eleven Years Old' card with the footballer in Newcastle United kit for some reason, right up to last year's which just said 'Birthday Boy!' and had a rude innuendo inside, which Mami hadn't understood. The first few were inscribed in Romanian, with big looping letters, but after that she'd switched to English, and a more careful, cramped writing style. The final message was always the same: '*La Multi Ani* Taras very dearest Son from loving Mami.'

This year's card was still in its envelope, on top of a long, flat parcel wrapped in a lurid interlock of plastic. Gift wrap was an unnecessary expense: she saved carrier bags, cut them into strips and wove them together to make little present sacks. Astrid had seen one, and said that Mami should sell them; they'd fly out of her hands at Camden Market. Taras hadn't reported that back: he didn't like to think of Mami standing behind a stall.

'I'm sorry for being late, Mami.' He felt terrible. Why hadn't he come home earlier? 'I didn't realise . . . I thought . . .' She'd been so cross when he said he was going out last night, and then this morning they'd had to rush off to that stupid funeral without so much as a happy birthday.

His mother bent down to ease the cake out of the fridge: a tower of sponge layers in different colours: strawberry, vanilla, chocolate, oozing jam and bedecked with cream: she must have been baking all week. 'What, pourchi? You are thinking that Mami forgets birthday?' She laughed merrily and nodded at the flurry of plastic. 'Come, open, open.'

He knew what it was: she always made him shirts from fabric she bought cheaply at a Caribbean shop in Elephant and Castle. This one was striped: tangerine and sunshine-yellow.

'Does it fitting, pourchi?'

Reluctantly, he peeled off his jacket and work shirt. Of course it would fit, she knew his measurements to the millimetre.

'Oh, pourchi!' She was looking at the damp stain over his flies.

'It's nothing, Mami. Just a spill.'

'Always accidents.' She shook her head. 'Give, give.'

He found himself climbing out of his trousers and handing them over. Tsking between her teeth, she fetched a cloth and started rubbing it over the wet patch. Taras stood, shivering in his stiff new shirt, underpants and socks.

'Mami, I've got some bad news.' He plucked at the shirt's tangerine cuffs. 'We have to leave this flat.'

'What silliness is this?'

'Gideon Bartlett called me.' He avoided saying they'd met up, since he'd told his mother he was working late. 'He's giving us notice. Don't worry, Mami. I'll take care of everything.'

He had a vision of himself striding into estate agencies: rejecting, selecting; escorting his mother through the door of her new home. Perhaps they could have two flats, next door to each other. With a connecting door, even. Then he could have girls stay over: he'd just have to lock the connecting door. Would that work? An image formed of his mother hammering on the door while he chivvied some unimpressed female into her clothes. The imaginary woman was slight and brunette, like Katya; he deliberately transformed her into a full-figured blonde.

'Nonsense-talk, pourchi.' His mother examined the soiled patch again and, apparently satisfied, hung the trousers to dry over the kitchen table. 'We are living here for always. Arrangement with Mrs Bartlett.'

'She's dead, Mami. And Gideon said—'

'Foolish boy.' It wasn't clear whether she meant Taras or Gideon. 'I am speaking with Mr Banerjee. All is same – staying, no moving.'

The image of the bachelor's flat with the connecting door evaporated. Taras plumped down on the hard kitchen chair and jabbed another cabbage roll. 'Mami, who paid my school fees?'

'Why?' She scrutinised his face. 'What is Mr Gideon Bartlett saying?'

Taras's mouth was crammed with cabbage, he couldn't reply.

'Leave me to be dealing, pourchi.' She kissed the top of his head. 'No need you talking with Bartletts. Come, eat, eat.'

She carved him a tricolour wedge of cake and slapped a pan on the stove, to sizzle the *sarmale* till they were piping hot again.

He opened his mouth to protest, but she was so busy and pleased that he didn't have the heart. 'I think this is the best cake yet, Mami,' he told her instead, and champed down on another slice with gusto, ignoring the chill of the unheated kitchen and the cramp in his bare legs as they pressed against the formica table-top. Engrossed at the stove, she said nothing, but he saw her smooth down the headscarf, so it lay sleek and satisfied over her forehead, and it gave him a glow of warmth inside.

CHAPTER THIRTEEN

On the day of Katya's double-date with Roy and Astrid, Taras spent the morning searching through Google for Korean restaurants and texting Roy, whose phone was off. By midday, he was slumped in front of his terminal and doodling on Post-it notes. It took a good thirty seconds before he registered the impatient harrumphs from behind and realised that Francis was craning over his shoulder. Fortunately even Solitaire was too demanding for Taras's current state of misery, so his screen happened to be displaying a complicated Gantt chart.

'Ah Tao-ahs. Sowwy to tear you away,' Francis sounded tetchy. 'Would you step into my office for a moment?' He stalked off without waiting for a reply.

'Uh-oh,' Jamal put on his new Oakley ski goggles and propped his arms behind his head. 'Wotcha done now, Cow-arse?'

If Jamal put as much time and creativity into his job as he spent inventing nicknames, he'd have supplanted the Chief by now. Cow-arse was a spin-off from the fussy lisping way Francis said 'Tao-ahs', thereby managing to mock both Taras and Francis simultaneously.

'Tao-ahs!' Francis was gesticulating from his office door.

This was London. Capital city, international marketplace, global financial centre. Beyond these plastic blinds, power-wielding movers and shakers were whizzing up sky-scrapers to cut mega-deals. Taras wanted to be one of them. Like Elliott Bartlett, running his own company and selling it off for a probable fortune. Instead, he felt little better than a schoolboy being summoned to the housemaster's office. Gopher-like, heads popped up at the scent of trouble. Lisa's protuberant eyes had brightened, and even Colin's sparsely tufted scalp was swivelling.

Taras trudged into the so-called office, which was really just a cubicle with a lid. Francis was hunched in front of his screen, so Taras caved into the spare chair and fixed his gaze on a stained carpet tile, readying himself for the worst. Perhaps Francis knew he'd farted in this office last week. Could CCTV cameras pick up a fart? He imagined an infra-red heat-sensing device charting waves of hot air emanating from his trousers.

It turned out he wasn't in trouble. The Americans simply wanted to review the document he'd sent them.

'I thought it would be good experience for you to be involved,' Francis said, but Taras knew better. There was no way Francis had digested a thirty-page document: his eyes glazed over if he had to press Page Down in an email. He wanted Taras there to take any flak.

'I'll just pwint this off.' Francis fidgeted with his mouse and peered at the screen. His legs were crossed at the knee, calves parallel like a girl. Taras tried it himself and found it wasn't possible with normal-sized thighs. Only Francis, with his skinny little knobble-kneed shanks, could do it.

The printer outside started to whirr. 'Shall I get that?' Taras offered, regretting it when Francis, not listening, sighed heavily and said, 'Just hold on, Tao-ahs, I'll be with you pwesently.'

Taras got up anyway, and went out to the printer. The glass front of the cubicle-office was tinted, allowing Francis to peer out without being seen. Now it was reflecting a sepia-coloured version of Taras. It gave him a nostalgic feeling, and he began thinking about the night he and Katya went to the open-air theatre in Regent's Park. It was a magical evening, just a few months ago; a stifling September night when the darkness had slid down without the hint of a breeze. They'd sat in the wooden bar area; close enough to feel the damp heat from one another's skin, drinking wine under the glow of white lights strung through the trees. It was perfect: like the cover shot for a Caribbean brochure. He'd knotted her hands between his and as he leaned forward to kiss her nose, a middle-aged couple had smiled and raised their glasses in a silent toast.

His reverie was interrupted by Colin dancing about in front of the printer like a demented elf. The paper-tray had jammed again.

'Is this yours?' Colin brandished a page in condemnation, skeletal arms jerking. 'You're not supposed to send big documents to this machine.'

Taras felt weary. Jabbing a thumb towards Francis's office by way of explanation, he grabbed the rest of the mangled print-out and retreated.

'That diagram's not right, anyway,' Colin called.

Taras shrugged. He didn't care any more.

Inside the office, Francis was stabbing numbers into the desk phone with a panicked frown, as if he'd never done this before. 'Come on Tao-ahs, sit down. We're late . . . ah . . . oh.' He held up a finger to command silence, and then said in a loud, over-enunciated, particularly pompous voice, 'Ah . . . Fwancis Erskine. London.'

He flapped his hand at Taras, who slumped into a chair. 'Yes, Leo. Yes. I've got the document in fwont of me . . .' His voice tailed off and he looked around with some panic, until Taras pushed the crumpled pages forward. 'And young Tao-ahs is on hand, in case we need to get into any, ah, technical issues.' Francis had a finicky way of saying the word 'technical', as though it was rather sordid but unavoidable, like a festival

Portaloo. He sat with the phone clamped to his ear, eyebrows working, saying 'Yes, Leo . . . no, Leo . . .' in a fussy way.

A swell of frustration rose in Taras's chest. That was Leo Harding, Sales & Marketing Director of the American firm whose voracious takeover appetite was on the point of gobbling up IBS. In the Chief's absence, Francis was the only conduit of news on this topic, and he hugged all contact with the Americans close to his plump chest.

'Ah, page twenty-four, yes,' Francis said, riffling through loose paper with a perplexed furrow. 'Let me see . . .'

A small twang went in Taras's ribcage, like an elastic band snapping. He flicked the telephone console to speaker mode. 'Can I help? I wrote this, after all.'

There was a pause. Francis stared at Taras in surprise, his soft hand still clasped round the receiver.

'Wey-ell, Tear-ass.' A confident voice, with long, drawn-out Southern vowels boomed out between them, filling the cubicle.

'Yes, sir.'

'Y'all call Francis sir too?'

'No, sir.'

A loud laugh. 'So, Francis. You reviewed this?'

'Ah. Yes. Well. Quick glance thwough, of course, but no time for an in-depth weview, as such, not yet, no.'

'No time, huh? So Tear-ass there is the content guy?'

'Under my genewal diwection, of course, but, ah, yes.'

'Got it. OK, here's what we're gonna do. Since Francis isn't up with the detail, let's go head-to-head on this one, Tear-ass. What's your direct line?'

Taras gave it and rushed back to his desk, unperturbed by Francis's indignant face.

'Got the sack did you?' Jamal said. 'That'd cheer me up, too.'

Taras waved him away. 'Watch my phone for a minute, would you? I'm expecting a call.'

He dashed over to the programmers' pit and found Colin. 'What's wrong with that diagram?'

Colin stared at him.

'Quick. Leo Harding's about to call me. What's wrong with it?'

Nothing pleased Colin more than being asked for advice, but he was incapable of getting into gear quickly. One bony hand came up to scratch at his scalp, and his mouth flapped a couple of times in preparation for sound-production.

'No time. My phone's ringing. Send me an email? Thanks.' Taras scooted back to his desk just in time to hear Jamal declare 'Cow-arse Krohe's phone,' then blink for a moment before his back jerked straight. 'Yes. No. Yes. Sorry, I'll get him for you right away. Handing the receiver to Taras, he mouthed '*leo harding!*'

As nonchalantly as his feeling of glee would allow, Taras nodded and sat down. 'Hi, Leo.' He savoured Jamal's look of amazement.

Unfortunately, the rest of the call wasn't quite so satisfactory, and Taras would rather have taken it in private. Leo was tough, and left Taras stammering in his wake as they trawled through each page of the document. Leo detailed countless changes and additions, impressed upon Taras the need for a complete restructuring, demanded a new set of appendices, and finished up by making it clear that spelling with an 'ess' instead of a 'zee' was outlandish, if not plain deviant. 'It's a tough market out there, Tear-ass. You gotta give the customers what they want.'

'But "esses" are what our customers want,' said Taras. 'They're all British.'

A loud laugh reverberated in his ear. 'All British, huh? Wey-ell, Tear-ass, you're talking to the guy that's gonna change that.'

Taras didn't get a chance to respond. Something distracted Leo, and Taras was put on hold with Whitney

Houston belting down the line. Doodling again, he wondered what kind of impression he'd made. The document didn't appear very inspiring, but Leo's tone had stayed friendly throughout. That must be a good sign. Perhaps Leo would keep him on when the Americans bought IBS.

'You stitched me up,' Jamal said.

'Sssh. I'm on hold.'

'Did he know who I was?'

'I don't think he gives a toss. He and I are having a head-to-head. Shush.'

'Should have been me. I know more about Version 3 than you do.'

'You should've written the document then,' Taras pointed out, choking down the last word as Leo came back on the line. 'Yes, sir . . . OK, that sounds good . . . Yes, of course . . . Right . . . Thanks Leo . . . Bye.'

As he hung up, an email pinged into his inbox. It was from Colin. Six pages of impenetrable explanation about why that diagram was wrong. Too late, but Taras sent it to the printer anyway. It might help with the revisions. Then he sat back, waiting for a barrage of questions from Jamal and Lisa.

None came. Jamal had his head down, apparently concentrating. Lisa was staring vacantly at her screen. Taras noted the way she sat: tilted forwards with her legs crossed at the knee. Unlike Francis, she didn't have her calves parallel: there was a forty-five degree angle between them. Fat thighs, Taras thought to himself. Not like Katya. An image of her in her favourite stone-washed jeans materialised. They were very tight, with pale streaks down the front that accentuated the inward hollow of her legs. When she stood straight, her knees didn't touch. Bow legs, she said critically, but Taras found them unbearably attractive.

Shaking the thought away, he announced 'Leo says he's coming over in a couple of months for a look-see.'

'Oooh,' said Lisa obligingly, but more because she'd just noticed the time. Three-thirty every day was a fixed routine: it was even scheduled into Outlook as a recurring appointment. Reaching into her desk drawer, she extracted two clingfilmed chocolate digestives, and settled down to munch.

Taras turned to Jamal and waited expectantly.

'Look-see.' Jamal snorted. 'Dumb Yank.'

'He's not dumb.' Taras was still smarting from Leo's stringent observations. 'It's our chance to make a good impression.'

'Mmmm.' Jamal wasn't jumping at anything. 'You've perked up. Not mooning over the Kit-Kat any more?'

Instantly, Taras's mood plummeted. Kit-Kat was Jamal's name for Katya, because on the night they all met, she'd been wearing a red top and crinkled earrings that looked like silver foil. Jamal had been the first to speak to her, and was always bemoaning the fact he'd passed her on to Taras. It wasn't a sentiment Taras appreciated, but that was Jamal's sense of humour. Like his quip a few weeks ago, when Taras told him they'd split up. Returning to his desk after lunch, Taras had found a Kit Kat wrapper on his terminal, slogan uppermost. '*Have a break,*' it said, with a big DON'T', inserted in marker pen above the *Have a Kit Kat.*

Then, Taras had been bullish about the split. Now he didn't feel that way at all, but Jamal was hardly his choice of confidant.

'Oh, that,' he said. 'Haven't really thought about it.'

'Ri-i-ght.' Jamal stretched out his hand for the pile of Post-its on which Taras had been doodling all day. The top one, elaborately decorated and coloured in, said in large block letters: 'KATYA.' Further down the pile, on separate leaves, came different versions of her name: 'Ekaterina. Katya. Ekaterina Romanchuk. Katya Romanchuk.' 'Kit Kat' was there a few times, also 'Sweetie' and 'Squirrel'.

The last one was a private joke. Squirrel was his special

name for her: on their first date he'd watched her take twenty minutes to eat a muesli bar he would have devoured in two bites. Her bright eyes and small nose; the way she held the bar up to her mouth with both hands for each nibble; it all reminded him of the squirrels that collected round Roy's parents' bird-feeder. 'Vermin,' Mrs Lewin had called them once, but Dr Lewin had said, 'They have to eat too,' and Taras agreed.

'A bit of grovelling and you'll get her back,' Jamal said.

Taras was offended by the image. 'Who says I want to?'

'Ri-i-ght.' Jamal said again, in that irritating drawn out way. He drew a Post-it out from the bottom of the pile, and loudly read out. 'Katya Krohe.'

Taras reddened. He'd just been thinking, what if Roy and Astrid did get married? He wouldn't want to be left behind.

'Katya Krohe?' Lisa rejoined the conversation. 'That's pretty. Sounds like an actress.'

'Yeah,' Jamal gave Taras a meaningful look. 'I wouldn't mind seeing her in something. *Confessions of Katya Krohe.*'

Taras snatched the pad back. He knew Jamal had an eye for Katya. He'd just screwed it up by playing it too cool in the club that night, and Taras had got lucky. Taras felt sure that all men, everywhere, lusted after his sweetheart. Even Roy, who was practically married. A week after they'd first met, Taras had taken Katya round to meet Roy and Astrid.

Katya had chosen not to sit next to Taras, and was framed against the darkened window instead. Her slight figure, wrapped in a stretch of dark green, wriggled like a mermaid as she offered round a tube of sweets: old-fashioned Love Hearts.

'Look,' she said. 'They have a little message.'

Roy reached over and took one. 'Pet me,' he read out.

'What does it mean?' Katya wanted to know.

Roy told her. She giggled. The beads on her slash-fronted

top shivered, drawing attention to the small, creamy curves below her collar-bone. She always hugged herself when she laughed. 'Not a pet animal? That is the right word, yes? A tame animal that will follow you?'

'Yes,' Roy said, adding softly, 'like Taras.'

Katya giggled again. Although Taras was pleased that they were getting on so well, he also wanted to punch Roy. Luckily, Astrid intervened and told Roy to shut up.

'Taras is not my pet,' Katya said, her mischievous brown eyes glinting. She gave his name the same stress on the last syllable that his mother did, but ending with a sibilant 's': Tuh-rass; her tongue running over it quickly, lightly, in a way that made him wish she would linger.

'Maybe I am his.' She gave him a quick glance, a private smile. Later he realised she'd been referring to the way he called her his Squirrel, but at the time he was just dazzled by the feeling that swept through him. Switching seats, he nuzzled down beside her, wrapping his arms around her small-boned frame.

'Ugh,' said Roy, exchanging a look of puritanical disgust with Astrid.

Taras was too happy to care.

His mobile rang. Finally it was Roy, sounding rushed. It wasn't always easy to call from the hospital, and the background noise suggested he was in the car park.

'What's up, Kroheman?'

'Do you think I should call Katya? Just to say I know she's meeting up with you guys tonight and it's cool.'

'No, I don't. And I'm not giving you her number. This is exactly why I deleted it from your phone in the first place. Just chill out, all right?'

'OK,' Taras said, deflated. There must be another way of getting Katya's number back. He didn't have numbers for any of her friends, and he'd have felt like a loser going via them, anyway. Last night he'd considered calling the student administration office and saying it was an emergency, but it wasn't really an emergency. Not yet.

'And before you ask, I'm not giving her your business card either.'

That had just been an offhand suggestion. Taras had given Roy a fistful of cards, in case. It might remind her that he was an up-and-coming professional, with as least as much potential for the future as her old geriatric. 'You don't think . . .'

'No, I don't. And, by the way, you should take another look at those cards before you hand them out to anyone else. So, what are you going to do tonight?'

'Oh, I've got a few options.'

'Like what?'

'Well . . .' Taras considered. 'There's a party in Chigwell.'

'Sounds crap.'

Taras thought so too. And the invitation had been a round-robin email from a guy he hadn't seen since university, which smacked of desperation. 'Or we could meet up. What time are you finishing dinner?'

'Yeah, sure, Astrid'll be cool with that. I'll just duck out, and leave her some cash for the bill and a cab home.'

'Great!' Taras started, before he realised Roy was being sarcastic. 'I don't mean leave dinner early or anything. Just, you know, after it's all done and over with. Hook up for a few drinks, that's all.' He really, strongly, wanted Roy to say yes. Somehow it would all feel better that way, if the dinner were just a blip in the evening, to be got over and swept away. 'Astrid too. Have a nightcap.'

'Maybe, I don't know.' There was a clatter of voices in the background. 'I've got to go, Kroheman. Lives to save, y'know.'

Taras put down the phone, wondering what Roy had meant about his business card. He pulled one out from his wallet. It looked good, a big improvement on the old ones. The font was more stylish, plus the IBS logo was swirlier and embossed which partially made up for its unfortunate connotations. His name was spelled right, no problem there. Oh, no. He couldn't believe he hadn't seen it before. It wasn't his name that was the problem, but his job title. Underneath the 'IBS' logo, the card announced him as 'Taras Krohe. Analist.' *Analist?*

'You bastard!' He brandished the card under Jamal's nose. 'You doctored my order form, didn't you?'

Jamal's eyes widened innocently. Taras ripped the card up and let the pieces flutter down on to Jamal's pristine desk, but it was hardly satisfying. Bloody Francis would never authorise a reprint. All Taras could do was wait and hope for a promotion to Senior Analyst, with an accompanying new set of business cards. He'd have to destroy these. So that's what Gideon meant the other night. Interesting choice of career, indeed. Bastards, all of them.

Head sunk in his hands, he failed to see Francis approaching.

'Ah, Tao-ahs. A moment, if you please.'

Taras didn't, but he supposed it was unavoidable.

'A little task for you. I've just been having a chat with Leo Harding.' That was supposed to sound impressive. Taras refused to be impressed. 'He's going to pay us a visit at the end of the month.'

'I know,' Taras said. 'He told me.'

Now Francis looked displeased. 'Ah. Leo and I thought it would be a good idea if you were to put together a little pwesentation.'

Taras's head jerked. He saw that Jamal was paying attention too. No one was fooled by that 'and I' crap. This was straight from the stallion's mouth. Leo talking.

'Nothing fancy,' Francis said. 'Just a summawy of the London technical situation. Where we're ... ah ... at, what we've got.' He was clearly parroting Leo's words. 'That sort of thing. Of course, I'll be supporting you on this. We'll work on it together.'

Taras's head was still reeling as Francis disappeared. Jamal let out a low whistle. 'Sounds like you're well in with the Yanks.'

'Leo and I understand each other,' Taras said coldly, still smarting over the business cards.

Instead of meeting this with a put-down, Jamal twiddled thoughtfully with a grinning gnome pen-holder from Lisa's desk, and invited Taras along on a stag night that evening. 'If you fancy it. Sounded like you were at a loose end. Should be a laugh.'

Taras didn't bother to answer. He'd had enough for one day. 'I'm going home.'

'Now?' Jamal glanced at the clock. 'What'll Francis say?'

Taras glanced over at the tinted office. Bravado swelled within him. 'Who cares?'

CHAPTER FOURTEEN

Hands stuffed in his pockets, Taras trudged round the bend of Chancery Lane. He paused at Ede & Ravenscroft to examine the cufflinks in the window. Would Katya have liked him better if he'd dressed more smartly? Taras only had one shirt which took links and he hardly ever wore it. Perhaps he would look sophisticated with little silver golfers at his wrists. Or dollar signs. Or was that tacky? It was hard to tell.

That first night at Roy and Astrid's flat, he'd walked Katya to the tube station, feeling very coupled-up, his arm around her shoulders. They kissed on the escalator, and an overweight teenage boy going the opposite way glanced at them enviously which gave Taras a massive boost: he used to be that boy.

'We'll wait for a Bank train,' he'd said as they reached the platform. 'Angel for you, London Bridge for me, that way neither of us has to change.'

He said this in complete innocence and failed at first to understand Katya's reaction. She was horrified that he was not intending to see her home.

'But this is almost the last tube,' he protested. 'If I walk you to your door, I'll have to get a taxi back.'

No use. She was adamant. Taras felt ill-used, but he obeyed. When he told Roy about it the next day, Roy roared with laughter. This was typical. Sometimes Taras felt that he was the butt of a giant joke; a walking punchline put on earth by God to lighten things up for everyone else. Only Katya took him seriously. It could be disconcerting: she didn't make allowances for him, the way other people did. She got annoyed when he turned up late, forgot important events, or made some major faux pas, whereas everyone else accepted it as part of his general entertainment value. Katya expected more. She didn't want an overgrown boy; she wanted a man.

And now she'd got one, but it wasn't Taras.

Tears welled abruptly, and he brushed them away as he cut through the hush of Inner Temple to the river. Embankment hummed with activity: raised voices, joggers weaving through gaps in the crowd, children stamping and jumping. It made him feel lost, the only one with no purpose. He was a loner, encased in a bubble of hopelessness. A spaniel trotting by at the end of a leash smelt the desperation and strained forward, barking.

He needed to get home; climb into bed, pull the pillow over his face and escape from everything, but first he would have to negotiate Mami. She was on the doorstep as he came down the street, headscarf and second-best coat on, off on a foray to the shops. When she saw him, her hand flew to her cheek in surprise and she rushed to his side.

'What is matter, Taraşhu? Why you are home?' She felt his forehead. 'You are sick?'

He fought her hand away. 'No, Mami, I'm fine.'

'Not lost job? Trouble with Boss?'

'No! I'm just tired, that's all. I'm going to go to bed and rest.'

She peered at him, and he turned his face away to avoid scrutiny. 'I am fetching you treat. Something sweet for tempting appetite.'

He didn't want anything, but it was easier to let her go. When she returned he was lying in bed, staring at the ceiling. He heard her go into the kitchen, and the hiss and rattle of the stove.

'Mami,' he called. 'Don't bother. I'm not hungry.'

The sounds continued. With a deep sigh, he got out of bed and trailed up the two steps to the kitchen.

'Tart-pops!' she said triumphantly. She'd bought Pop-Tarts and, lacking a toaster, was frying them in butter and sugar. The kitchen was so small that Taras could feel the blast of heat as caramelising sugar tickled at his nostrils.

'I'm not hungry.' He sank down at the table.

Mami was very worried. 'What is matter, Taraşhu? Not strong, healthy Son any more. Shrivelling up skeleton of boy.'

They were in their usual positions: Taras seated, his mother standing over the stove, but without the exchange of food, everything was disrupted.

'I can't stop thinking about Katya, Mami. You don't understand.'

'I understand this is very wicked girl, to treat you such way. Not good heart. You must be forgetting this bad girl.'

Her headscarf was up on end, letting the dark, shining coil of hair slip down her neck. She was pushing the Pop-Tarts around the pan with vicious thrusts of her spoon, as if they were bad Son-hurting girls.

'No, Mami, don't say that. She's an angel.' He'd never spoken so openly about Katya to her before. Screwing up his courage, he admitted, 'I really like her, Mami.'

'Not good liking. Must stop.' She gave another prod to the tarts, releasing a thick black ooze of jam that looked like a clot of blood.

'I can't, Mami.'

'Nonsense-making of very foolish kind.' She bandaged a Pop-Tart in kitchen-roll and tried to force it into his hand. 'Eat, eat!'

The smell was tempting but Taras shook his head, almost enjoying the sensation of power this gave. Her forehead creased with frustration: if he was smaller, she might have prised open his jaw and crammed the sugary mess down his throat. They stared at each other, and then she snapped off the hob and plumped herself down opposite him, wedging her elbows on the formica and taking his hand between both of hers.

'You think I am stupid know-nothing fool? Taraşhu, I am absolutely understanding, this is why I am telling you to be full of forgetting.'

The directness of her gaze was like a spotlight, it made him want to wriggle his hand away. They never sat face-to-face like this, at meal-times she was always on the move, jumping up to stir, to fetch, to clear away, only adding to her plate when she could pile no more on to his.

'Your hair's coming loose, Mami.'

Instead of setting it to rights, she tugged the scarf free, not letting go of his hand. Her thick rope of hair slithered over one shoulder, and Taras averted his eyes as if something intimate had been exposed.

'I am having this bad kind of feeling also.' She gripped his fingers. 'Long time past, with results of much painfulness and hurting.'

Overly conscious of the heat of her palm against his, Taras fixed his eyes on the grouting behind the sink, faded from years of scrubbing.

'No happiness in loving if love not coming back same way.' Finally she released his hand, and the table received a resounding slap. 'Time to stop!'

'Yes, Mami,' he murmured.

'Good, better. This is being a man.'

As if the skin had been pricked on an over-ripe tomato, Taras's emotions burst out in a pulpy mess. Everything was crumpling: his face, his bones; he was a gelatinous puddle.

'Mami, I can't. I want to be with her so much and now she doesn't care about me at all.' Fat tears dripped down his cheeks.

'Oh, Taraşhu.' His mother moved round the table and took him in her arms as if he was seven years old again.

'I wasn't good enough to her. I didn't treat her properly. It'd be different now. I just want another chance.'

He burrowed his head into her lap and she rubbed his back, making inconsequential soothing noises. He relaxed into her, feeling secure and comfortable again for the first time in days. He imagined her buying the Pop-Tarts in the tiny newsagent's, looking perplexed. She might have asked the white-haired Bangladeshi owner for assistance, but probably not. Stomach-tempting treat for boy was a private matter; she'd have studied the shelves until something jumped out. A new wave of emotion built up in his chest, not for his own misery now, but the pain she was feeling on his behalf.

She was warm and soft and the outside world was far away. Her hand moved to stroke his hair and in a low, gentle voice, she began crooning the little chicken song from his youngest years. '*Nani, nani, puiul mami . . .*' He didn't understand all the words, but their sound was so familiar that a heavy, peaceful sensation settled over him.

The sound of the doorbell was a jangling intrusion. Taras lifted his head and Mami stood up, straightening her skirt. Someone from one of the other flats must have opened the main door because footsteps sounded on the stairs.

'Who's that?' He went to the door and looked through the peep-hole. 'It's Mr Banerjee. What's he doing just turning up?'

'Open door, pourchi, quick, quick.'

His mother was bustling around the kitchen, clearing away the remains of the Pop-Tarts. Catching sight of her discarded headscarf, she bundled up her hair and slipped it on, checking her reflection in the window.

Taras felt mutinous, and made a business of unfastening the bolts and chains. Pulling open the door, he stepped immediately back out of the light, afraid that his face might still be blotchy.

Mr Banerjee was looking spruce in a checked jacket over a shirt and tie, and beige trousers with a sharp crease ironed in. He carried a leather briefcase with a shiny clasp and his bearing was business-like. Always punctilious, he waited to be invited into the narrow living room, and maintained his usual polite fiction of appearing unaware of activities in any other room, even though the thin walls made this patently absurd. Taras's mother was thus able to finish tidying the kitchen before she swooped in.

'I hope there is not problem, Mr Banerjee,' she said. 'I am not expecting visit.'

He had stood up to greet her, and made a business of hitching up his trousers and sitting down again, 'There is something rather important, Mrs Krohe. Something we must discuss.'

There was a momentary pause. Taras could feel both his mother and Mr Banerjee looking at him, and knew they wanted him to leave. His mother was cautious about financial dealings. She didn't trust ATMs, and she had closed her post office account because 'it is not the business of poke-nose lady clerk to know what money I am having.' She always excluded Taras from her quarterly meetings with Mr Banerjee.

'All right,' he said grumpily. 'I'm going out anyway.' This display of petulance had done him no favours with Mr Banerjee, he could tell, and, stung, he added, 'Don't make dinner, Mami. I won't be home till late.'

CHAPTER FIFTEEN

Hunched forwards against the wind, Taras crossed London Bridge, then turned west, veering away from the river. It was some time before he admitted to himself where he was headed, and even then, he kept pretending he was about to turn back. Only when he dipped under the arched roof of Smithfield meat-market did he allow himself to notice his surroundings, even managing to conjure up a little plume of surprise.

This wasn't a tourist area: even to a Londoner like Taras it was unwelcoming. During the week, like today, it was clogged with traffic, whereas on weekends he was able to zig-zag across the silent residential streets without once needing to pause for a car. Once, he'd ventured to ask Katya why she wanted to live in this bleak City hinterland.

'It is cheap,' she'd said, shrugging. 'And I can walk to my classes.'

She shared a flat with two other students: a tall, flat-footed Korean girl and a boy from Uruguay with long eyelashes and soft, accented English. There was no living room (it had been converted into the Uruguayan boy's bedroom) and Taras had been dubious about the enforced intimacy until a few more visits had shown that the boy studied sixteen hours a day and had no time for seducing his flatmates.

None of them had a car, obviously, and the space opposite their front door was usually occupied by an ancient Triumph belonging to the teacher couple who lived upstairs. Today, however, there was a different vehicle in place. It was a sea-green Bentley, a vintage 1950s model; polished and restored with care. Sparkling chrome bumpers and gleaming wheel spokes caught the light, and the soft leather interior, a perfect match to the unusual bodywork, was set off by deep, burnished wooden trimmings. Not wanting to be caught with his nose pressed against the glass, Taras recovered himself, and ducked into the tiny health-food café over the road, his heart nearly stopping as he ran into a woman at the counter. But it wasn't Katya. Nothing like her: mousy-haired and at least thirty.

The woman was engrossed in conversation with the heavy-set, grizzly bear of a man behind the till, and from experience, Taras knew it would take a while. Even if he dressed like a vegan, Grizzly was red-blooded enough to have an eye for his female customers. Pretending to interest himself in the contents of the drinks fridge (heavily soy-based, with a total absence of essential food groups like carbonation and sugar), Taras covertly glanced at his phone, and then out over the road. It was almost six. Katya was meeting Roy and Astrid at six-thirty, so she should be coming out any minute now.

'Waiting for your young lady?' Grizzly had spotted him. 'Haven't seen you two for a while, thought you'd gone off somewhere.'

Although he didn't want any attention, Taras was grateful to learn that he had not been completely replaced. Ponytail geriatric obviously didn't follow the same routine of coming here with Katya on Saturday afternoons. But the Bentley was worrying: a pale, sleek beast guarding the lair.

The last time he and Katya had sat here, they'd had an argument. A builder had paused in the street outside the café to answer his mobile. The small boy perched on his shoulders was framed in the window, and Taras had let out a deep sigh.

'What is the matter?' Katya had eyed him impatiently.

Taras jerked his head at the boy, who had begun bashing his father around the face, Still talking, the man turned his head one way, then the other, enduring the blows with stoicism. Taras felt that familiar pang of envy. If Sigi had lived, would he have carried little Taras like that?

Katya looked. 'Horrid little brat.'

'You can't say that about a child!'

'That is not a child, it is a bug-eyed monster.' The boy screwed up his features into a protuberant grimace and thumped both fists into his father's nose. 'Ugh. I would drown him like a kitten.'

Taras was shocked. 'I thought all women loved babies. I want lots.'

'Well, you will not have them with me,' Katya blew vicious bubbles through her straw. 'I have one big kid as boyfriend. I do not need more.'

A stifled chuckle from the counter had made Taras hunch over angrily. Grizzly wasn't even pretending not to listen. In a heated whisper, he said, 'I can't imagine being with someone who doesn't want children.'

A mulish look gripped Katya's small face: she didn't bother to lower her voice. 'No problem then. There is easy solution.'

For a foolish moment, he thought she'd given in, but the angry tilt of her head as she marched off to the toilet forced him to reconsider.

'That told you, didn't it?' Grizzly leaned over the counter. 'Never mind. Too many people in the world already. Make a donation to UNICEF instead. Ha ha!'

Taras didn't want to be dumped in front of a heckler. When Katya re-emerged with a defiant slash of lipstick applied, he salvaged the situation as best he could, which involved a humiliatingly profuse apology. Unfairly, it had proved more of a patch-up than a long-term fix – ten days later, he'd been propelled into the disastrous night at the London Eye.

Today, he was assuming a lofty indifference, but it didn't last long. When the mousy-haired woman finally tore herself away, Grizzly stroked his chin thoughtfully, his gaze running past Taras towards the open door. 'How about a glass of sarsaparilla, young fellow? Just the thing for emotional upsets.'

Taras spun round to see Katya on the steps outside her flat. She was rocking skittishly in kitten heels, sparkly purse dangling from one shoulder, head tilted towards the slim figure in a suede jacket who stood on the pavement. His grey ponytail jutted out at Taras, waggling impudently as its owner leaned in to place a possessive kiss on Katya's nose.

Taras's buttocks clenched in anguish. Ponytail was taking Katya's hand, leading her over to the Bentley's passenger door with a stiff-legged gait. He handed her in, then paused to flick his silk scarf over one shoulder. Taras hated him, with a deep, boundless loathing that he'd never previously experienced. He wanted to stuff the silk scarf in that thin, superior mouth and watch him choke. Jumping up, he hurried to the door, not knowing exactly what he intended to do, but ponytail had already crossed to the driver's side and was easing himself in, unaware of the emotional fury raging only yards away. Katya, though, had seen him. Silver hoops bounced below her ears as her eyes widened into little round 'O's. Her mouth opened, but the glass between them made it soundless. The engine purred into life, and the Bentley pulled away.

CHAPTER SIXTEEN

Twelve hours later, Taras woke up spread-eagled on bare tiles, feeling as if a small but pungent buffalo was sitting on his head. Levering himself to his knees, he put a hand to the crick in his neck and found an unfamiliar cluster of bristling hair, which startled him so much that he let his palm drop without investigating further. He seemed to be in a bathroom: larger and dirtier than home, with water-splashes on the floor and screwed-up towels everywhere.

Instinct prompted him to pull the lever on the sludge-coloured lavatory, producing a noisy cascade that made him wince, but lessened the acrid stench. Then, bracing both hands on the bowl, he pulled himself upright and confronted the mirror. It was worse than he'd thought. His shirt had disappeared, replaced by a splatter of dried vomit, and the unfamiliar hair belonged to a pair of artificial blond plaits tied in a knot under his chin. These protruded from a Viking helmet crested with horns and rammed low over his brow, with a purpling line around its rim that suggested his blood-flow was being dangerously restricted. He managed to tug the helmet loose, but unpicking the tightly knotted plaits was too difficult, so he let the whole thing dangle around his neck like a bellicose bonnet.

Something was pressing against the bathroom door, and it took all of Taras's depleted strength to shove his way out.

The obstacle turned out to be a comatose male body, similarly horned and shirtless, collapsed in the hallway. From the door opposite a rattling snore issued, dissuading Taras from taking a look inside. Instead, he fumbled his way down the darkened corridor to a living room that in other circumstances would have been bland and suburban, but today made a gruesome sight. A weaker stomach than Taras's, or one less recently voided, might have been turned.

Twisted carcasses were strewn across floor and furniture; helmets and shields lay scattered; torn blond plaits hinted at mutilation. A hot, sour stench hung over the gloom. It could have been the violent aftermath of a Norse raid: if the room had been silent, then it would have had an eerie feel of death and destruction. It wasn't silent though; there was a vigorous hum of breathing, interspersed with snorts, farts and belches.

Stepping between slumped bodies without inhaling, Taras reached the window and threw it open. A shaft of light from a street lamp cut through the thickened atmosphere and struck a slumbering Viking across the bridge of his flat nose. He blinked, opened his eyes, and regarded Taras with momentary bemusement before recognition glimmered. 'Top night, eh?' he remarked, and draped a plait over his eyes.

'Have you seen Jamal?' Taras asked.

'Think . . . urggh,' The flat-nosed Viking had to clear his throat of phlegm, '. . . think he went off with a girl.'

That sounded entirely plausible. Wasn't his flight to Meribel sometime today? With any luck, he'd miss it. Enlivened by that bright spot of hope, Taras went in search of the kitchen and a glass of water. It seemed that this was the only room not draped with corpses, perhaps because the galley shape wasn't very accommodating. A tepid draught of tap-water made his stomach gurgle, but he wasn't hungry, especially when he saw that the timer on the oven said it was only 5 a.m.

A glance at his mobile showed he had received a stream of texts from Roy last night. He didn't recollect any of them. Still bare-chested, he wiped himself down with a dishcloth to remove the worst of the vomit, then slid to a sitting position on the floor. The helmet dug into his back when he tried to rest against the fridge, so he wriggled his shoulders and was nearly garrotted as the knotted plaits buried themselves in his throat.

Spluttering, he managed to stand up, and braced himself against the counter. His phone wasn't set to save sent messages but he'd obviously been pressing Roy for information.

19:35 *korean ok, if u like pickled veg*

19:42 *old git ok 2. making an effort anyway*

19.51 *said ok thats all. not much in common*

19:58 *with me i mean arse-brain. k happy enough. think they r holding hands under table*

20:07 *well u asked. no more txt for while, astrid gtng annoyd*

22:30 *yes still here. having poricha*

22:42 *no, korean barley tea worse luck*

22:49 *well girls not drinking n old guy teetotal. how stag?*

22:55 *cant. got 2 take Astrid home*

22:58 *shut it*

23:04 *said shut it.*

23:11 *shut up or im turning off phone*

23:32 *cant call u now. old guy gvng us lift home*

23:38 *he lives hampstead app. so on way sort of. nice car*

23:42 *yes k here 2*

23.44 *no fuck off*

23:48 *stop calling i wont answer. u cant speak 2 her*

23:54 *arse. turning off phone.*

Taras could see that he had subsequently made four screenfuls of calls to Roy between 23:45 and 00:52, none of which had been answered. Sometime after that, he'd received a call from a withheld number. Maybe Roy had relented and called from home? Tentatively, he gave his mobile a try now, but it was switched off. A cold draught was seeping in from the living room. Spotting an old plastic anorak scrunched on the side, Taras dragged it over his head, feeling it pull uncomfortably tight over the horns on his back.

Next he checked the pockets of his jeans and found his wallet and keys, which was a relief, but the rest of his clothes could be anywhere. He needed to go home. Flipping open his phone again, he dialled Zingo, and waited while the recorded woman's voice kept repeating 'we are finding you a licensed cab,' in a deliberately classless Estuary accent.

'Right, where are you, mate?' A man's voice, impatient: he'd been switched through to the driver.

'Umm, I thought you could tell where I am from my mobile?' Taras realised he himself didn't have the slightest idea.

'Are you taking the piss?'

His eye fell on a pile of bills, and he grabbed the top one, unfolding it. 'No, got it. Here you go.' He read out the address.

'Right.' The driver sounded wary. 'I'm round the corner, be there in five.'

Outside, Taras felt himself to be an unprepossessing sight. The anorak was making him sweat, without providing any protection from the wind, and underneath it, the helmet was bulging out like a giant hunchback. His belt had also disappeared, so his jeans were slipping and he had to keep hitching them up. He was cold, clammy, and unwashed. He wouldn't have blamed the driver for taking off, but the man let him in. Twenty minutes later, he must have regretted that kindness.

'Sorry,' Taras rifled through his wallet. 'I don't seem to have any cash.' He tried an apologetic smile, but it didn't work. 'Er. Could I pay by card? Oh . . . don't seem to have any cards either. Shit! What happened to my credit cards?'

The driver looked over his shoulder. 'Think you're funny?'

'No.' Taras didn't feel the slightest bit amusing. 'Uh, I could get some cash from inside. My mother . . .'

'Yeah, I've heard that one before. You're not doing a runner from me, mate.'

A lively discussion followed, during which the driver refused to accept any of Taras's offers of surety, turning his nose up at a watch, and becoming almost violent at the suggestion of the anorak. In the end, they agreed that he would accompany Taras into the flat.

Not wanting to frighten his mother with this unwanted intruder, Taras rang the doorbell. It was 6 a.m. There was a long wait. The driver's breathing was getting increasingly uneven. Taras rang again. And again, holding the bell down, until finally the door rattled and his mother appeared, belted into a long dressing-gown, with her hair down her back.

'Taraşhu! What is matter?' She pulled on his hunch, sending the knotted plaits shooting up into his neck again so that he choked and spluttered. 'Oh, pourchi! Come in, quick, quick!'

The driver moved, and she turned to him. 'He is very good boy, sir. Never in trouble with police before. Thank you for bringing home.' She made to shut the door.

'Oi, no you don't! I'm not going anywhere till he pays up.'

'Corruption and dirty-deals, this is not being accepted! Laws against this, you should be ashamed. We shall not pay! No! Never!'

She tried to force the door shut again and the driver, with equal determination, wedged it open. Everyone was raising their voices, even Taras, who was feeling queasy again.

'Mami, you don't understand!' he begged.

'Always it is me who is not understand.' Dramatically, she let the door swing wide so the driver toppled in, collapsing to his knees on the battered lino. 'Very well. Come! Take all. Television, wedding ring, mug for golden jubilee, these are only valuables we are having. May Blessed Virgin forgive you!'

Picking himself off the floor, the driver looked stunned, then disgusted as Taras leaned over and vomited, narrowly missing the man's boots.

'Oh, pourchi!' Taras's mother elbowed aside the driver, as if this was his fault, and patted Taras's giant hunch. 'What is wrong?'

Busy wiping acidic bile from his mouth, Taras heard the inner door to their flat swing open, but didn't look up until a voice said, 'What is this commotion, Maria?'

From the top of the stairs, a squat, heavy-set figure was frowning down. It was Mr Banerjee. In the same khaki trousers and blue blazer that he had been wearing yesterday evening. As smartly turned out as ever, but with one glaring fault. A glimpse of crumpled white shirt-tail protruded from his flies.

This was a situation Taras had never even remotely envisaged, and was entirely unprepared for. Gulping down his horror, he tried to face it with dignity, but was hampered by the Viking bristles which had worked their way out of the anorak and tipped him into a sneezing fit.

'What is all this noise? Taras, who is this fellow?' Mr Banerjee came down the stairs, ponderously. 'Stop this, immediately.'

The driver, recognising the tone of authority, stated his case for payment. With an expression of severe disapproval, Mr Banerjee took out his wallet and silently counted out seventeen pounds, then asked for a receipt.

The driver left, and Taras was now in the awkward position of being indebted to the man who'd obviously just spent the night with his mother. There was probably a sophisticated way of dealing with this. Taras sneezed again.

'Pourchi, what is wrong with back?' His mother's nimble fingers located the bristly knot, and worked it loose.

'Mami . . .' He was being swept along by the force of her habitual authority. Then, over her shoulder, he saw Mr Banerjee become aware of the protruding shirt-tail. Hastily dropping his eyes, he tucked it away.

It broke a spell. 'Mami . . .' Taras said again, more sharply. The plaits flopped loose. She stood back.

'Mami. I . . . How . . . ?'

The two of them looked back at him. It was all too horrible; Taras couldn't bear to face them any more. He turned and ran. Halfway down the street, he was so out of breath he had to slow to a jog. He could feel the loosened helmet working its way down under the anorak, but he didn't want to stop. As he reached the corner, it slid out over his bottom and bounced, one, two, three, into the gutter.

CHAPTER SEVENTEEN

Taras had just enough money on his Oyster card to get the tube to Highgate. Astrid's eyebrows arched in surprise when she opened the door, but she was on her way to work, even though it was a Saturday, and couldn't stop. She banged the battered aluminium coffee pot on the stove, yelled for Roy, and rushed out of the door.

Blinking, Roy emerged in striped pyjama bottoms. 'Look at the state of you. No! Stop!'

An offensive odour was escaping as Taras unzipped the plastic anorak.

'Jesus Christ, you stink.' Roy folded his arms across his lanky chest. 'Keep that thing on.'

'Couldn't you lend me a t-shirt?'

'Not unless I want to cremate it afterwards.' Roy grabbed the pot as the spout began to hiss. Waving it in front of him like a priest releasing incense, he didn't stop until the rich scent of coffee had overcome Taras's reek. 'Have a shower or something.'

But Taras was too upset. With the coffee pot on the table between them, Roy was persuaded to sit down and listen as he told his story.

'Jesus Christ.' Roy was shocked. 'Motherfucker!'

Taras leapt up, and Roy hastily apologised. 'It's just an expression. Really, Kroheman, sit down. I wouldn't joke

99

about this. Christ. How long do you think that's been going on?'

'I don't know,' Taras said miserably.

Roy said nothing but poured them some coffee, and sipped his with raised eyebrows.

'Oh my God,' Taras said suddenly. 'What if he's still there when I go back? What if he moves in and expects me to call him Dad?'

The death of Sigismund Krohe had left Taras with a giant father-shaped hole in his psyche. Five years ago, he'd embarrassed himself in the Leicester Square Odeon by shouting 'Bastard!' during *Gladiator*, when Commodus taunted Maximus in the gladiatorial arena. Gloating over his son's murder was bad enough, but claiming the boy had sobbed like a girl had made Taras burn with feverish hate. The poster in his bedroom was an act of homage to the final act of paternal vengeance. A stepfather of Maximus's stature might have filled the hole. But the prospect of Mr Banerjee was simply horrible. He wasn't the right shape. It would be like trying to stuff an aubergine into Excalibur's scabbard.

'Can I stay here?' Taras begged. 'Just for a while. I don't want to go home and see him.'

'He probably won't be there,' Roy said. 'You might be blowing this out of proportion.'

Taras turned on a puppy-like look of desperation.

'Oh, all right. If Astrid says it's OK. Just for a few days. And you have to wash first.'

'Oh my God,' Taras said suddenly. 'What if they've been having an affair for years? What if . . . what if Mr Banerjee is my actual father?'

Hurrying into the bathroom, he stared at himself in the mirror. The lines of his face seemed different; merging, melding under his horrified gaze. His skin darkened a shade, his features blurred into that stern frown, and suddenly it was a younger Mr Banerjee staring back at him.

Roy appeared behind him in the mirror. 'Don't be stupid, Kroheman.'

'You don't think . . .'

'No, I don't.' Roy picked up a towel and threw it at him. 'But while you're in there, do me a favour, and get in the shower, OK? You really do stink.'

By the time Astrid came home, Taras was clean and wearing a hooded sweatshirt and old tracksuit trousers: the only items of Roy's skinny wardrobe which he could squeeze into. They were stretched uncomfortably tight but felt cosy: it was like being a baby in a sleepsuit. He and Roy were sprawled in front of the TV, playing on the Xbox, and when Astrid slammed the door, Taras jumped up guiltily.

'Do you want a beer, Astrid?' he said, seeing her glance at the empty cans. 'I'll get you one.'

She said she wasn't in the mood. Taras had been instructed not to mention that he needed a place to crash until she was good and relaxed, so he hovered around her chair, trying to think of things she'd like. It didn't seem to be helping.

'How about a biscuit?'

'For God's sake Taras, sit down. I've had a shit day.'

'What were you doing?'

She sighed. 'We're working on a campaign to raise awareness of sexual exploitation. A lot of people just don't want to hear about it.'

Taras thought he might be one of them. 'What's the problem?'

'Each year over a million women are trafficked for prostitution round the world.'

Taras tried to emulate one of his mother's tuts, but it sounded like loose phlegm rattling in his throat. 'Er. Sorry.'

'People just don't realise.' Astrid kicked off her sheepskin boots and stretched her legs, wriggling her toes in red socks.

'They think it's some sort of conservative myth put about by uptight farts who disapprove of sex for money.'

'You disapprove of sex for money,' Roy pointed out, putting down the Xbox controller.

'That's not the point.'

'Some people would say it is.' Roy got to his feet. 'Some people would say you're trying to impose your personal morals on a world that doesn't need them.'

Taras shot a look at Roy. They were supposed to be softening Astrid up, not provoking her. 'What about dinner? Shall I order a takeaway?'

'Nope.' Roy loped towards the door. 'I'm going to make chilli. You can help.'

Taras would rather have paid for the takeaway, but belatedly he realised he had no cash.

'Don't let Roy make it too hot,' Astrid called as he left the room.

Taras wondered if this was a good moment to ask if he could stay, but when he put his head back round the door, she'd already closed her eyes and pulled the woollen throw over her lap.

'She looks tired,' he told Roy.

'Yeah. She needs a break. We're going to take a couple of weeks off at Easter, go somewhere relaxing.'

If Taras and Katya were still together, they could have gone as a foursome. It would have been great. A couples' holiday. They could have been planning it now.

'My life's a mess.'

Roy passed him an onion to chop. 'You ought to ring your mum. Tell her you're staying here.'

'Why hasn't she called me? Doesn't she care where I am?' Taras made some ineffectual stabs, until Roy took the onion back and chopped it himself.

'Check your phone. Maybe you missed a call.'

'I'd have heard it.' But he went through to the spare room

anyway. 'Shit! It's not there!' He dug inside the pockets of his beer-encrusted jeans again. 'I must have dropped it in the cab!'

Now he had a vision of his mother in a state of panic, calling the police, hospitals. Did she know how to call the police and hospitals? He wasn't sure. She'd be rocking back and forward in her sewing chair, starting up at every creak of the plumbing or footstep in the communal hall. 'I'd better call. Can I use your phone?'

He hurried through to the living room and dialled. Astrid was asleep on the chair. Her face looked softer: normally he was a little in awe of her. She seemed to care so much about everything, not personal things – Taras could have related to that – but abstract things like third-world bank loans, and the exploitation of women she didn't know. Big things. Issues. He'd find it exhausting living with someone who was so intense. But now, with her cheeks slackened and her lips slightly apart, unconscious of his gaze, she was a different, more gentle person. It gave him a sense of how she and Roy might be together in their private moments. Suddenly conscious that it was rather intimate to stare at his best friend's girlfriend while she slept, Taras turned away, pressing the receiver into his ear.

'Taraşhu?' His mother's voice was sharp. 'Taraş, is this you?'

'Yes, Mami. I lost my phone. I'm sorry if you were worried . . .'

'I am not worrying, Taraş. I am having embarrassment.'

His stomach constricted at the thought of her apologising to him. He couldn't bear to hear it. 'It's all right, Mami. You don't have to say anything. I just wanted to tell you I'm OK. I'm at Roy's.' He badly wanted to know if Mr Banerjee was with her, but getting the words out would make him gag. He needed space to deal with this. 'I can't talk now, Mami.' Panic was gripping his chest. 'I'll call you tomorrow, OK? Bye.'

Though he'd been desperate to get away, now he found it difficult to put the receiver down. It fitted solidly in his fist, compensating for an ache, like emptiness, somewhere in his chest. He wanted to be at home, with steam rising in the kitchen and dishes clattering in the sink. Mami would be clearing away dinner, though without Taras there, she wouldn't have cooked. She didn't bother making meals if he was out, just picked at bits of bread, or leftovers from the fridge. Or was Mr Banerjee there, wiping sour cream from his moustache? Taras shuddered. He couldn't go home and see him there, squarely planted on Taras's chair in the kitchen, thick wool coat jostling up against Mami's lighter one in the hall. He just couldn't.

CHAPTER EIGHTEEN

Slouched over his desk on Monday morning, Taras sniffed an unfamiliar waft of lavender from his shirt. Astrid bought a different washing powder from Mami. Nothing wrong with it, but it just didn't smell right. On impulse, he picked up his office phone handset, holding down the button to silence the dialling tone, and rehearsed what to say if Mr Banerjee picked up.

'I'd like to speak to Mami, please.'

No, no. Too feeble.

Or, 'I'll have a word with my mother. In private, if you don't mind.'

Ugh, no. Pompous. He sounded like Francis.

'Bog off, frecklehead.'

Perfect. But he knew he wouldn't dare.

Lisa dumped herself down in her seat, and Taras put down the phone. He didn't want an audience. Between her and Jamal, there wasn't a minute in the day when he got an opportunity to call. How did people manage before mobile phones? There must have been no such thing as a private life. He'd buy a new phone on the way home: Roy was covering him with cash till his cards were replaced. Oh. Not home. Roy and Astrid's. To relieve his feelings, he borrowed Lisa's hole-punch and experimented with how many Post-its he could stab through in one go.

*

While the new phone was charging that evening, he called his mother from Roy's home phone.

'Taraşhu?' Her voice was just the same. No one else said his name the way she did: lilting from the rolled 'r' to a long, soft 'shhh'.

'Mami, is Mr Banerjee . . .' He couldn't bring himself to finish the sentence. 'Is he . . .'

'There is need for apology, Taraş. I . . .'

'No, Mami,' he said quickly. He'd forgive her and they'd never mention it again, everything could continue as before.

'Yes, there is need,' his mother said robustly. 'Son running away like mad person? Am I no-account baba to be treated like such? Is Mr Banerjee to be thinking this is how I teach for behave? This is very bad, Taraş.'

Taras's mouth flapped open. He slumped down into the beanbag.

'I am very ashamed, Taraş. You must be apologising to Mr Banerjee.'

In his mind, Taras saw a beige-cuffed hand close over his mother's narrow one, its square knuckles interlacing her fingers. He would not apologise. The idea was repellent.

'Mr Banerjee very shocked that you not coming home at night. No call, nothing. We are sitting, waiting. No Taraşhu.'

'He's there now?' Taras pictured him frowning over Mami's shoulder. 'What's he waiting for?'

'Now, no. On Friday. What is wrong with you, Taraşhu? He gives notice from Gideon Bartlett. To say we must be leaving. Ha!' Her voice was rich with scorn. 'I say, no, we will not to leave. Not mattering what Master Gideon Bartlett is saying. Forget son, go straight to father. Tell Mr Elliott Bartlett that we are to stay.'

'Just like that?' Taras didn't think his mother had a full grasp of tenant–landlord rights. 'I'm not sure—'

'Mr Banerjee make protest also. He say he must wait and speak with you if I do not understand. I say he can wait but make no difference. We will not to leave.'

A ray of light illuminated Taras's head. 'Mami, is that why . . . did Mr Banerjee wait all night on Friday just to talk to me?'

'He is very cross when you are not coming home. This is not correct way for Son to treat mother, he says. Indian son never stay out and not tell Mami where is.'

Taras doubted this, but Mr Banerjee had no children of his own, so was hardly an expert. It didn't matter. A possibility of hope was gathering. 'Mami . . .'

'When late, he telling me to be going to bed. He is waiting up for speaking to you. Then he is very cross to find that I am sleeping in parlour. He says Son should be on floor, giving mother bedroom, but I tell him this is our business.'

'So he waited in my room?' Taras was almost gabbling with excitement.

'I think he is falling to sleep. I knock on door to offer bedtime tea but I hear nothing. So I push door open, little bit only, and he is lying down, no shoes, trousers loose, everything, so I tippytoe creep away . . .'

Lying down? On my bed? Taras screwed up his face, but a wave of relief was already crashing over him, sweeping away this minor objection. Flopping back in the beanbag, he closed his eyes.

'. . . Then I also am to sleep. I worry for you, pourchi, but still I sleep. Having man in house is great burden off neck.'

'Shoulders,' Taras said automatically, sitting up again. What was this about burdens? His mother already had a man in the house. Him. He was about to say so, but a door slammed in the next room. Heavy footsteps: Roy coming home. 'I've got to go, Mami.'

Dropping the phone, he rushed through to the kitchen, where Roy was carving a doorstop of bread off the end of a loaf. 'It's all right! There's nothing going on between them. I got the wrong end of the stick!'

107

'Wishful thinking, Kroheman.' Roy smudged butter on top, then dolloped half a jar of blueberry jam over it. Taras only had to look at that to put on weight, but Roy's metabolism was on permanent overdrive. 'Astrid and I went out for dinner with them, remember. It's definitely a relationship.'

'You went out for dinner with Mami and Mr Banerjee?'

'What?' With a mouthful of bread and jam, Roy couldn't talk, but his eyes popped.

'I just spoke to Mami. I got the wrong end of the stick about her and Mr Banerjee. There's nothing going on there.'

'Oh.' Roy waved a hand, understanding now. 'Good. Has Astrid spoken to you?'

'She's not home yet. Why?'

Stuffing in another fistful of bread, Roy mumbled, 'Katya wants to see you.'

Taras thought he'd misheard. 'What?!' He had to wait an age for Roy to swallow down his mouthful of bread.

'She called Astrid today. Said you weren't answering your mobile. Wants to see you tomorrow, before work.'

'Shit!' Taras froze. 'What do you think she wants to talk about?'

Roy gave an expressive shrug.

'Do you think she wants me back? Oh shit! What if the geriatric proposed to her? She wouldn't accept, would she? Maybe she's giving up her course and going back to Moscow. I'd never see her again. It'd be better if she did marry the old git. Oh, God, no it wouldn't. I can't bear the thought of him touching her. Ugh. I saw them kiss. It was disgusting.'

'Yeah, you told me. Look, Kroheman . . .'

Taras grabbed a handful of Roy's bread and jam. This was no moment to worry about dieting. 'Does she want me to go over to her place?'

'She wants to talk to you alone,' Roy said reluctantly. 'Apparently there's a spot on Parliament Hill where you went once.'

108

They'd kissed for the first time there. Taras slapped Roy's back. 'Ye-esss!'

'Don't go overboard,' Roy warned. 'You don't know what she wants yet.'

But Taras was already doing a victory jig around the living room.

CHAPTER NINETEEN

Despite his best efforts, Taras was late, and had to break into a jog as he reached the edge of Hampstead Heath. It was a cold morning, but in the city below, the mist was clearing and the tip of the Post Office Tower had broken through.

Katya was at the top of the hill, walking back and forth to keep warm. She was wearing Taras's favourite tight, stone-washed jeans and a roll-neck jumper under a denim jacket not thick enough for the weather. Her hands were tucked under her armpits. Taras wanted to chafe them between his till the blood came back, but he didn't have the right any more.

'Hey,' he called, from a few yards away, slowing down to a walk, and she turned. He wasn't sure whether a peck on the cheek was appropriate, but she settled it for him by plumping herself down on a bench before he got close enough. Her bag was there, an impractical little clutch-purse which didn't have space for anything but lipstick, and also a supermarket carrier bulging with everything else. She never used the handles on the carrier, just scrunched the top of it in her hand, so it looked like an afterthought, nothing to do with an otherwise co-ordinated outfit. Whenever Taras pointed out how silly it was not to have an ordinary handbag large enough for what she needed, she'd shrug and say, 'It is the Russian way.'

Now he didn't know why he'd wasted time criticising

such trivia. Despite his anxiety about what she was going to say, it felt wonderful to be next to her. The sharp air in his lungs made him feel alive, and the fearful pitter-patter of his heart became a full, strong beat.

'Katya,' he began, but she interrupted.

'Taras, I want you to know that nothing happened between me and Jamal.'

He stared. Her little nose had pinched up against the cold and an orange bobble hat was hiding her hair. She didn't look at him.

'Jamal?'

'I do not trust him. I had thought he was a good person, but he is not.'

'What are you talking about?'

'Oh.' She looked up. 'He has not said anything?'

He shook his head.

'When I came to find you, he took me home—'

'Katya . . .' he protested, 'I don't know what you mean. Find me? What are you talking about?'

The story that unfolded appalled him. He had no memory whatsoever of Katya ringing him during the stag night.

'I was worried,' she said. 'You kept calling Roy. I don't know, I mean, I just had a feeling that something was wrong. So I called, and you were very happy to hear from me.'

Apparently, he had been too drunk to manage anything more than slurring 'I want you,' over and over again. Jamal had taken the phone from him and spoken to Katya. He'd painted Taras's condition so black that Katya had become even more worried, and she'd insisted that ponytail drive her to the club where the boys were drinking. He had been reluctant, and on the way they'd had a fiery quarrel which ended with her jumping out of the car and refusing ever to speak to him again.

That bit of the story Taras liked. However, he was less

keen on the part where Katya found Jamal in the club and was told that Taras had gone next door to the strip show.

'How could he say that?' Taras was outraged.

Katya looked at him. 'It is not true?'

'Well . . .' This was more difficult. 'It was a stag party, Katya. I was just swept along with the crowd.'

'Anyway.' She moved on. It seemed that Jamal, learning about the ponytail's tempestuous dismissal, had insisted on seeing Katya home himself, and on the way his behaviour had deteriorated to match his Viking dress.

Taras was boiling with rage. 'I can't believe it. I can't believe he did that.'

'You do not believe me?'

'No, no.' He snapped back into the present. 'I mean yes. It's terrible.' It was against every rule Taras had been taught. You didn't mess with your friends' exes. Never. Not unless you asked first, and even then it was frowned upon. Bloody Jamal. If there was any justice, he'd break his neck in Meribel. Or Taras would break it for him when he came back.

'It was not nice. I was very upset.'

'Yes, of course.' Taras realised he was appearing distracted. 'You're all right, aren't you? I mean . . . nothing happened. He didn't . . . ?'

But he had just made a drunken, rather crude pass. She'd ordered him out of the cab, and there had been an exchange of insults. And that was that.

Except, Taras realised belatedly, that all this had happened because Katya had been worried about *him*. *She* had called *him*. *She* had insisted ponytail drive her in search of *him*, Taras. Sunlight glowed through the frost-covered grass, shimmering like a halo over the distant City skyscrapers. Everything was wonderful.

He reached for Katya's hand. She let him take it.

'I'm sorry I messed things up between you and your new boyfriend,' he said untruthfully.

Katya shrugged. 'There were many problems. He is too old.'

Taras bit down on the inside of his cheek, just to assure himself that this was real, not a dream he'd scripted himself. 'You always said I was too immature.'

'Oh yes. That was not good. He is sensible, and he has very nice manners, and he treats me properly.'

Taras regretted starting her off down this particular track. He wanted to say he would treat her properly, if only he could have another chance.

'But . . .' She chewed her lip, thinking. 'He is cold. I mean, inside. Always rational, like he is measuring out feelings in little doses. Not warm, like you.'

Taras squeezed her hand tighter, trying to be as warm as he could.

'You are very stupid. And you annoy me all the time. But you have a big heart. I find I cannot stop remembering you.'

Taras's heart somersaulted painfully in his chest. He clutched her hand and planted kisses all over it. 'Katya, I'll do anything. Anything at all, if you'll just give me another chance.'

'Taras, it is not so easy. We will just have the same problems as before, and this will make us both miserable.'

'What problems? I'll change them.'

'Your mother does not like me.'

'She hasn't even met you.'

'Exactly.' She pulled her hand back, leaving him bereft. 'You are afraid for her to meet me.'

'I'm not,' he lied. 'It's just—'

'You cannot change people, Taras. I am me and you are you.'

They sat in silence.

'I'll change,' Taras blurted. 'I'll do anything. You can make me anything you want.' He put his hand on her denim knee, holding it tightly, not daring to edge any

113

closer. 'Just remember, Katya. Remember how happy we were together. How right it was. Remember that night in Regent's Park? When we went to the theatre?'

'I remember,' Katya said. 'I do not know if you do.'

'Of course I remember! It was magical.'

'What play did we see?'

Taken aback, Taras faltered. There was a pause. 'Shakespeare,' he said, feeling he'd made a good recovery. 'Anyway, that wasn't the magical bit. I meant me and you.'

'I remember you did not like the play. You complained that it was long and boring. When the interval came, you tried to stay in the bar instead of going back. You said you were too hot to pay attention and this was true, you were very hot and sweaty. Also drunk. It was not very nice.'

This was a shock to Taras. He had thought the evening incredibly romantic. Not knowing what else to do, he laid his head in her lap, and clasped her around the waist. 'Katya, I'm yours. Completely. Just come back to me, please.'

She held stiff for a moment, and then he felt her soften. She put her arms round his back and hugged him. 'Oh, Taras.'

'Yes? Does that mean yes?'

'I don't know. This is not why I asked you to come here. I am in trouble.'

He jerked up. 'What do you mean? Not . . .'

She stared at the hand gesticulating at her midriff. 'No! You know I have never even . . .'

Thank God for that. For months Taras had been manoeu-vring towards that particular goal, and he didn't want to find the old git had sauntered up and taken a free kick. 'What then?'

'I might lose my scholarship. It is a condition that I do not work, and they found out that I am giving Russian lessons. Perhaps they will take it away.'

'Is that all?' Taras was just thankful it had nothing to do with ponytail.

'All? It is disaster! Scholarship pays tuition and also money for living expenses. Not enough money, already I cannot afford but without I will have nothing!'

'It's all right, it's all right.' Now it was Taras's turn to comfort her. He hugged her tight. 'I'll sort it out. Everything's all right now.' He wasn't sure if he was talking to her or to himself. 'I'll make you so happy. You'll see.'

CHAPTER TWENTY

'Taraşhu! Is that you?'

'Yes, Mami.'

'Why you not say you are coming?' She appeared in the hallway: herring-boned wool skirt, slippersocks, grey headscarf. The short time apart evaporated in an instant. He stepped over the threshold, kicking off his shoes, and she bent down to push his slippers on to his feet. 'No food, pourchi, there is nothing. I don't know you are coming. I can make *papanashi* only.'

'I'm not hungry,' Taras said, untruthfully.

'Nonsense-talking, pourchi. Who is feeding you? Royck? Ha!'

She liked Roy, although she suspected his parents of neglect as he was so thin. Taras had not told her about Astrid moving in.

'Come, come now.'

He followed her into the kitchen, but didn't sit down. The radio was on, something by Beethoven, and she turned it up. Radio 3 was a political tool in her hands: volume went up for Liszt and Brahms, whom she considered to have Romanian influences; down for any Russian composer; off completely for Prokofiev or Stravinsky.

'Tomorrow, shop shop, fetching food for proper welcome home,' his mother said, hooking her apron over her neck. When he didn't reply, she looked up. 'What is matter, pourchi?'

'It's about Katya.'

Two sharp tugs fastened the apron strings. 'I am telling you, this is bad girl. Time to be forgetting.'

This was the reaction he'd been afraid of. 'No, Mami.' An object caught his eye: large, black, hooked over the back of his chair. 'What's this?'

'Umbrella, Taraşhu.'

He could see that. 'What's it doing on my chair?' It was big, masculine, intrusive; like a brooding vulture. It was Mr Banerjee's. He didn't need to be told.

'Mr Banerjee has been coming today.' His mother bent down to get the eggs out of the fridge. 'Bartletts are making difficulties.'

Taras rubbed his hand over his forehead. 'Mami, let's just move. Then we don't need to deal with the Bartletts or Mr Banerjee any more. We could even get somewhere bigger.'

'Waste money on big flat?'

The image of two flats with that connecting door, rose up in his mind again. Maybe not a connecting door even. Just next door to each other. 'I'm earning a salary now. We could—'

A vehement shake of the head. His mother smacked the chipped pyrex bowl down on the counter. 'No moving. This is home. I am living here twenty-four years. Who are these Bartletts to say we must move?'

'Well, they do own it, Mami. And it might not be such a bad thing.'

She cracked an egg with a smash against the bowl. 'Taraşhu, I am dealing with. All making smooth. These Bartletts,' another smash, 'will be sense-seeing.'

'Mami, I . . .'

'This is home!' Her voice rose sharply. Yellow egg yolk dripped from her fingers.

Taras didn't know the details of his mother's early life. He knew she'd still been a child when Bunicu Bogdan died, leaving the family without income, but he didn't know what hardships they'd endured, or the struggle it had been for Bunica Elena to embark on the emigration that killed her and left Mami alone, aged twenty-two, in a strange country with only a few words of English and no skills beyond the domestic. But something of this was in her black eyes as she wheeled round to face him, and in the clutch of her hands crossed at her waist.

'All right, Mami.' He pushed the image of his bachelor pad away again. 'You're right. This is home.'

She studied his face for a few moments then, apparently satisfied, said, 'Good, pourchi. Now, sit, sit.' Taking the plastic whisk off the hook by the stove, she set about the eggs with gusto.

He obeyed then leapt to his feet again. 'Mami, I want you to meet Katya.'

Although she was turned away from him, he could judge her reaction by the way her shoulder blades scissored together. 'It is not enough that Russians take our land, kill Bunica Elena mother and father? Make big hunger and sending Bukovina people to die far away? Now you wish to bring into home?'

'You'll like her, Mami, I promise.'

'This is foolishness, Taraşhu.' She was gesticulating with the whisk, abandoning the eggs to whip herself into a frenzy. 'Russians not for trusting. Only bad distorting lie-making talk. This is people that is causing much trouble for us.' Her head-scarf was standing on end, blood had rushed into her cheeks, and the whisk cut swathes through the air, boxing Taras in behind the rubbish bin.

'Mami!' he exclaimed, arching backwards until his head banged against the rack of ceramic pots. 'Ouch! Mami, stop it!'

She dropped the whisk and collapsed into a chair, breathing hard.

Taras edged round her, till he reached his own chair, and sat down. He took her hand in his. 'Mami!'

'No Russian girl.' Her black eyes were firm.

He let his mouth droop, pleading, and then sighed. 'OK, Mami.'

In a moment, she was back at the stove, satisfied and sizzling *papanashi* as if nothing had happened. Taras tipped his chair back, balancing it on two legs. He couldn't stay for dinner now, but he didn't know how to tell her. 'Mami,'

There was a knock. Soft, tentative, at the internal door of the flat. The flap of the letter-box creaked, and a voice called gently, 'Taras?'

His mother turned, slowly this time. 'Russian girl is here?'

Taras dropped his eyes. This wasn't going as planned.

She pushed the pan away. 'No.'

'Taras?' Katya called through the letter-box, louder this time.

'Mami . . .'

'No.' She folded her arms, bare to the elbows.

Did she have any idea what she was doing to him? He'd just given up the idea of a bachelor pad so that she could feel secure in their home. That meant there'd still be nowhere for him and Katya to be alone together. They'd never spent the night together: obviously he couldn't bring her back here, and she didn't feel comfortable enough with her flatmates to let him stay there. Taras had thought about it and decided that was the fundamental flaw in the relationship. No sex. Once that was sorted, everything would be OK. He'd been incredibly lucky to get this second chance with her; there wouldn't be a third. Happiness was within his grasp. How could Mami deny him this?

'Mami, you have to meet her. I told her you would.'

'No Russian person is setting feet in my home.'

It was his home too, Taras wanted to say. The letter-box flapped shut and Katya rapped on the door instead.

'Tell her to be going away, Taraşhu. Come, *papanashi* ready.' His mother turned back to the stove.

She was treating him like a child. It was humiliating. She wanted a son moulded to her needs, but he was a man with his own life to build. Taras jerked back his chair and stood up, knocking Mr Banerjee's umbrella to the floor. 'I won't do it, Mami.'

His mother switched off the radio. The only sound was fat spitting in the frying pan. They looked at each other. 'What you are saying, Taraşhu?'

'Katya is my girlfriend. I brought her here to meet you. I'm not going to leave her standing outside the door.'

'You speak like this to Mami?' She shook her head. 'Mr Banerjee is correct in his estimation.'

'What's he got to do with it?'

'Many times, he warn me I am letting Son to spoil, but I refuse to listen. He is good boy, I say. Sometimes he make mistake, but he loves Mami, he is right-thinking boy at heart, always.' She rubbed the back of her hand over her eyes, shielding her face. 'Now, all is plain. Too much love not best way.'

He could see she was holding back tears, and part of him wanted to throw himself at her knees and capitulate, but somehow the pattern had to break. 'I'm not a boy any more, Mami. I'm twenty-three. I'm the man of the house.'

'Man now?' His mother's hand dropped and she cast her eyes up to the ceiling. Her lips moved for a moment, without sound. He suspected she was calling on the Blessed Virgin. Then she looked back at him. 'You behave with rudeness to Mr Banerjee, who is here for helping us. You stay with Royck three nights, four. I am not knowing when you come home. This is boy, not man. And now you bring Russian girl.' She threw out her arm. 'Too much, Taraşhu.'

'I'm asking for one thing, Mami, the only thing that matters to me.' On his feet now, Taras kicked the umbrella under the table. 'And if you won't accept Katya here, then I can't stay either.' He marched down to his room and scooped his suit out of the wardrobe, then stuffed freshly ironed shirts and underwear into a rucksack. From the back of the door, Russell Crowe watched impassively, a tower of gladiatorial strength. 'This is your last chance,' he called up the stairs.

'I am not slave-person to be given orderings.' She was on the top stair, her nostrils a whitened flare.

'All right then, I'm going.' He undid the bolt and lifted the chain. 'I'm going.' Silence. He wouldn't look back. This was it. He hesitated, then stepped out. 'I've gone!'

CHAPTER TWENTY-ONE

He found Katya halfway up the road, and held up the bag. 'I've left. For you.'

She pushed back her woollen hat to look at him better. A small hand wriggled into his. He squeezed it, and they walked on together to the bus stop in blissful silence.

When the bus came, Taras handed Katya into a seat in his most gentlemanly manner. She smiled at him, but a moment later she rubbed her nose and frowned. 'Your poor mama. She will be upset.'

'It's all right,' he told her, as much for his own benefit as hers. 'She's got to learn that I'm not a child any more. It feels hard at the moment, but it's for the best. She'll come round.'

'You think so?' Katya gazed out of the darkened window, and her ghostly reflection stared back at Taras.

'It's about negotiation skills.' He filled the words with conviction and slung an arm around her shoulders. 'You just have to know when to make a stand.'

'Perhaps you could negotiate with Carlos for me.' Her small face peeped at him from under the nodding orange pom-pom of her hat.

Who was Carlos? Oh yes, the Uruguayan flatmate. 'What about?'

'I owe him money.' Her cheek felt cold against his arm. 'He wants it back.'

'What money? How much?'

'Two months' rent, a bit more. I was waiting for the next scholarship payment. If it does not come, maybe I will have to move. But without money, that is also difficult.' She shifted away from him to lean against the window. 'London is an expensive city.'

Thoughts spun round Taras's head in a fruit-machine whirl, and then with beautiful simplicity everything clicked into place.

'I've got a better idea. Move in with me,' he said. 'I'm getting my own place. Roy's right, it's about time.'

She didn't believe him at first. It took the whole journey to convince her he was serious. At her stop, he followed her off the bus and eagerly caught her arm under the street-lamp, his breath misting in the cold.

'I mean it, Katya. Why not? We'd be great together. We could get somewhere with a spare room, like Roy and Astrid have got, so there'd be space for you to study.'

A smile lit her face. Bobbing closer, she kissed his cheek. 'Taras, this is very nice offer.' She tapped his chest. 'This is why I like you. Your heart is very warm.'

He caught her hand before she could take it away. 'You see, Katya? This is how things are meant to be.' Lowering his head, he trapped her mouth into a long kiss: the first since their break-up. Her small lips, slightly chapped by the cold, gave way under his and excitement exploded within him. He pressed closer as she broke away for air. 'Shall I come in with you, just for a bit?'

She shook her head. 'House rule. No visitors at night.'

He sighed. 'All right.' The sooner they moved in together, the better. He watched her run up the steps and let herself in the front door, then waited until he saw the light click on in her room. A week ago, the Bentley had been parked here, right by this lamp post. He glared over at the wholefood café, shut up for the night, and wished the grizzly owner was there to see him reclaiming his territory.

All the way back to Roy and Astrid's, he made plans, and in the narrow spare bed they circled through his mind. He netted £1,200 a month after tax. £500 went to his mother, and of course that would continue, even if he moved out. What if the Bartletts insisted on her moving out? Anywhere new would cost more. Say £600. That left £600, of which £250 was needed for his credit-card repayments. Was £350 enough for a flat? And bills? Not to mention day-to-day living costs. By 3 a.m. he'd decided the Bartletts would definitely let his mother stay in the flat. That would release another £100. And Katya could contribute something from her Russian tutoring. At 4 a.m. he remembered that IBS pay reviews came up in June. Perhaps he'd get a promotion, or at least a hefty rise. Then there'd be no problem. At 4:05 a.m. he reassured himself that he deserved a rise. By 4:08 a.m. he was sure he could count on it, and at 4:09 a.m. he coasted to sleep on a swoop of relief.

CHAPTER TWENTY-TWO

Taras was on a high. Even the reminder on his Outlook calendar that Jamal was due back today didn't dampen his spirits. He'd give the treacherous bastard a welcome he wouldn't forget. Katya didn't want any fuss but Taras wasn't sure he could hold himself back.

'What more is there to do?' she'd said. 'He pushed his hand into my shirt, I pushed him out of the taxi. We are even.'

'That's not the point. It's the disrespect.'

Katya had brushed this off. 'I have more important problem right now.'

Taras had actually meant the disrespect to himself, not her, and there was no way he was letting it rest.

'Have you heard about Jamal?' Lisa dumped herself down with a cup of tea. 'He broke his ankle. He'll be off at least another week.'

What?! To relieve his feelings, he annexed a corner of Jamal's desk for his in-tray, and pushed a couple of old Styrofoam cups over the boundary for good measure.

Colin was a metre away, hopping from one foot to another. 'Did you hear about Jamal?'

'Yes.' Taras didn't want to talk. He plugged in his iPod, but Colin was still fidgeting about so, with a sigh, he took the earpiece out again.

'I can't do the table upload until Jamal tells me which region he wants.'

'Well he's not here, is he?'

'No.' Colin was persistent. 'But do you know when he'll be back?'

'Never, I hope,' Taras said, but Lisa butted in.

'He can't walk, poor love. He'll struggle in when he's up to it, but his leg's very sore.'

'Good.' Taras had intended to keep this strictly between himself and Jamal, man to man, but Lisa's sympathy was too much. 'I hope it drops off.'

'That's not very nice,' Lisa said reprovingly.

'Nor is trying to steal my girlfriend.' He couldn't hold it in any more. Pushing back his chair, he gave them the cold, hard facts, then waited for their righteous anger.

'Oh, you boys,' said Lisa. 'It's always something.'

Had she not understood? 'He tried to pull my girlfriend!'

'But you'd split up,' said Colin with programmatic exactitude.

'That's not the point! You don't go after a mate's ex. Everyone knows that. It's a rule.'

'Jamal didn't pork her though, did he?' Colin was still pondering the niceties of the situation.

'Colin!' Lisa said.

'It's the principle,' Taras had to breathe out through his nose to calm himself. Gladiator Maximus would have ripped these fools apart. 'Never mind. Go away. I don't give a toss about your table upload. I'm busy.'

Plugging in his earphones again, he opened an internet screen and got down to some serious research. Google Images was his first call. Humming along with Franz Ferdinand, he typed in 'broken ankle' and assuaged his anger with pictures of painfully shattered bones.

His reverie was interrupted by his desk phone. He took out one earpiece to answer it.

'Taraşhu?'

'Mami.' He was startled. 'Is everything all right?'

'Nothing is right. Taraşhu, Bartletts say we must be leaving flat. Mr Banerjee carries my message, but no attention is being paid. I do not understand.'

The stand-off between them seemed to be temporarily lifted. Perhaps this was his opportunity to set things on a more adult footing. 'Don't worry, I'll take care of things. I'll find another place for you, a nicer one.'

'I am not wanting other place. I am wanting this place.'

'Mami.' Why did the Bartletts have to make things so difficult, right now? They were wealthy; the flat couldn't matter to them. Taras entered 'Elliott Bartlett' into Google. Nine pages of results appeared.

'In this sink here, I make bath for baby Taraşhu. In this chair here, I feed and rock to sleep. All memories, everything, they are here. This is home.'

'I know, Mami.' A Reverend Elliott Bartlett had performed a Methodist funeral in Indiana thirty years ago. An Australian eighth-grade student called Elliott Bartlett was ranked ninth for mathematics across the Queensland region in 2003.

'I cook, clean, keep nice. All to make good home.'

He restricted the search to UK sites only. A Professor Phillips, Elliott had co-authored a paper on Quantum Mechanics with a Bartlett, G. He was momentarily distracted by a Mr Bertram Elliott Bartlett who had apparently recited 'in a vivacious manner with accompanying gestures 'The Charge of the Light Brigade' at the Bridlington Town Hall in 1897.

'Home is where you also are belonging, Taraşhu. Forget trouble-making Russian girl, and come home to Mami now.'

The appeal caught him unawares. 'Mami—' He broke off. He was seeing Katya tonight. And Roy had finally given in and agreed to let her stay over. His skin tingled at the thought of it. The silence stretched on. He dug his biro into the side of the desk, wincing with the effort it took not to give in. The nib snapped and he gave up. 'OK, Mami, I—'

A paper dart bounced off his eyebrow. He glanced up in annoyance and saw Colin waving a hand. Signalling that he was on the phone, Taras held it closer to his non-iPod ear. Strengthened by the interruption, he said, 'Mami, I'm at work, I can't talk now. Maybe Mr Banerjee didn't do a very good job of explaining things. I'll call Mr Bartlett myself and ask him to reconsider.'

'Call? What is this call? I am telling you to be coming home, not to make call.'

'Do you have the Bartletts' number? On a rent statement or something?'

'Taraşhu, do you not listening? I forbid you to be meddling and call-making. No number. No.' She hung up the phone.

He looked at the receiver and frowned, then stuffed the other iPod earpiece in, to block out the office noise, which was worse than usual. Determined not to be fobbed off like this, he googled 'Bartlett' and 'St Bartholomew's School for Boys'. Bingo! There: Ursula Bartlett, on the board of governors from 1988 to 1993. There was a link to the text of a speech she'd made about the new library. Taras downloaded the PDF and scanned through. Near the end, she made a passing reference to her home in Blackheath. Switching to BT.com, Taras typed in 'Bartlett', 'E', 'Blackheath', and pressed enter. Ha! Telephone number, and an address on Shooter's Hill. Brilliant. He should have been a detective, not an IT analyst. Another paper dart pinged off his neck as he sent the page to the printer.

Colin was back, bouncing on his toes like a child needing the toilet.

Taras pulled his earpiece out. 'How am I supposed to get anything done round here? Don't you have anything better to do?'

'We might none of us have soon,' Colin said, eyes bulging. 'Have you seen Francis's email?'

An envelope was blinking in the corner of Taras's monitor. He clicked through and the screen filled with text. It was about the prospective takeover by the Americans; a few phrases jumped out as he skimmed down the page:

'Roadmap for the combined business going forward . . . Consolidate product lines and service nodes . . . Gaining efficiencies . . . Opportunities for restructuring . . .' His eye whipped back and read that last one again. 'Opportunities for restructuring?'

'Yup.' Colin sounded American already. 'They're just buying us for Version 3. They want the product, not us. We'll all be unemployed by Easter.'

'Who says that?'

'Everyone.' Colin gestured round the room. It was a hive of activity. People were clustered around desks: a huddle of heads blocked the door to the Ladies. There was a muffled thump as someone kicked the chocolate machine.

'Francis isn't here. He must have sent it from home.' Colin gestured a bony hand towards the crowd. 'He's too scared to face us.'

Taras saw Lisa's frizzy head bob past. He was annoyed she hadn't alerted him to the email. He must have looked a right knob working away, oblivious to all this.

'Someone called the Chief's mobile, but there's no answer. Now they're trying any number they can find,' Colin reported. 'He's selling us all down the river.'

This was no time for Taras to lose his job. If he let Katya down on this, then he'd never win her trust again. He wished Jamal was here: even if he was a slimy girlfriend-pinching low-life, there was no one like him for sniffing out information. He'd have all the facts by now and be tipping back in his chair with that infuriatingly smug smile, waiting for Taras to humble himself and prise it out. But it'd be worth it. Taras could feel his heart rate accelerating to the kind of rush that normally took three cans of Red Bull.

He needed to stay calm. What would Jamal do? Right, Taras told himself. Identify the most likely source of information and separate them from the pack. Targeted precision hunting. But his legs were already propelling him upwards, he could feel his head whipping from side to side as he stumbled out into the room, panic blurring his senses.

'Isn't that your phone?' Colin trotted after him.

Taras wheeled round, not knowing what to do, and leaned across his chair to snatch it up. 'Mami, I can't talk now.'

'You whut? Tear-ass?'

Taras's back straightened. The wheels on his chair shot off at an angle, wrapping him in the phone cord and dragging the telephone halfway across his desk.

'Tear-ass? You thay-re?'

'Yes, sir!' Taras didn't dare disentangle himself in case it cut him off, so he stayed bent.

'What's going on? Some fricking idiot's calling from the UK. I've got four messages and I don't 'preciate being called into the office at five-fricking-a.m. I can't get a hold of Francis.'

'He's not here,' Taras said. 'But everyone's a bit upset about the email he sent.'

'Whut email?'

Craning round so that he was even more thoroughly tangled in the phone cord, Taras managed to reach his screen. He read the email out. There was a brief silence.

'Wey-ell. So you guys're pretty upset, huh?'

'Er, yes.' Taras said, managing at the last moment to stop himself from saying, 'Sure thing.'

Suddenly Whitney Houston was belting down the line, and he realised he'd been put on hold. Resting the receiver on the desk, he began unwinding himself. Halfway through, he heard his name and grabbed it again.

'Yes, Leo, sorry.'

A couple of heads turned. In moments the news of who

he was talking to had rippled through the office, and a crowd gathered.

'Sounds like Francis went off half-cocked down there, Tear-ass. He in the habit of that kinda thing?'

'Sure is,' Taras said, then bit down hard on his tongue. 'Yes, sir.'

'Wey-ell, this is the thing. Now, this is just between you and me, OK?'

Taras shut his eyes on the circle of faces pressing in. 'Yes, sir.'

'Some pretty heavy plans're coming together right now, Tear-ass. And I'm coming over to take a look at the set-up you guys got going. But thay-re's still a way to go and hollering won't help any. You with me?'

Taras wasn't sure, but he barked out another 'Yes, sir.'

'Yes, sir. Ha. Thay-att's good. Now, I got a real important task for you, Tear-ass. Think you're up to it?'

Almost certainly not, Taras thought, but he assented heartily.

'OK. Now it sounds to me like you've got a bad case of the discombobulations going on over thay-re.'

Did they? Taras had no idea. Was it some sort of infectious disease? 'Yes, sir.'

'We gotta get the team pulling together again. I'll bring forward my trip. Week of the first. We'll have a big night out. Whole office. All on me. You make the arrangements.'

'Er . . . what sort of arrangements?'

'What sort of arrangements? Hey, you're the content guy, right?'

'Er, right.' Taras said.

'So then. Whatever you guys like doing. Whatever sizzles your bacon. I'll get out thay-re and you guys can show me how you do it in London. We got a deal?'

'Yes, sir.'

'Yes, sir. Uh-huh. Oh, and Tear-ass? When Mister Francis shows up, you tell him to give me a call.'

131

The line went dead. Everyone waited while Taras unwound himself from the phone cord, then a frenzy of questions erupted. With an intoxicating sense of power, Taras held up his hands and shook his head. 'Sorry, I can't divulge anything.'

This was true. Mainly because he wasn't entirely sure what he'd been told. But Leo clearly had him pegged as his main man, and that could only be a good thing.

'There's Francis,' someone said. Taras turned. Still in his overcoat, which had military epaulettes and only made his shape more unbalanced than ever, with enormous shoulders and tiny little pointy feet peeping out beneath, Francis strode through the door, seemingly unaware of the commotion he had caused. Pausing by the printer outside his office, he glanced through the output tray, frowned, and picked out a sheet of paper.

Holding it aloft between two fingers, he came over, 'Tao-ahs. Is this yours?'

Taras would have denied it, but his user-ID was printed at the top of the page. There was Elliott Bartlett's address, phone number, and a map showing his street.

'We have a wule about personal pwinting, Tao-ahs. Like personal phone calls, personal emails, personal faxes, etcetewa. Not to be done in IBS time or using IBS equipment. I think you've been here long enough to know that.'

What an arse. No one obeyed those sorts of rules. 'It's not personal, actually, Francis. Leo Harding asked me to carry out some research for him.'

Francis's saggy cheeks bagged out with surprise.

Taras didn't give him a chance to question further. 'And he wants you to call him. He's not happy about the email you sent. If I were you, I'd get on to it straight away.'

It felt so good. He plucked the page from Francis's hand and swaggered off.

CHAPTER TWENTY-THREE

That evening he floated back to Roy and Astrid's flat still on a high, and coasted into the living room ready to regale Roy with the news of his day, but was promptly brought down by the sight of Astrid reading a book called *Sex Traffic: Prostitution, Crime and Exploitation*. That hardly made for a relaxing evening. He dropped into a beanbag and wondered if she'd mind if he put the TV on.

'I'm making Swedish meatballs for dinner.' Astrid put the book down. 'Do you want some?'

That was better. 'Can I invite Katya?'

'I suppose so.' Astrid tapped him with her foot. 'I'm pleased for you, Taras. But be careful, won't you? You don't have to rush into things.'

Taras didn't want to be careful, he wanted to be happy, but this morning he'd heard Astrid ask Roy how long he was planning to stay. To head off any discussion, he said, 'You're absolutely right.'

Astrid's white-blonde eyebrows lifted.

'Thanks for the advice.' Pleased with the success of his charm offensive, Taras bounced off to call Katya. Dinner here would save him money, and set up the situation perfectly for him to broach the idea of her staying the night.

She arrived late, wearing a patchworked jersey dress that was a bit too artistic for Taras's taste, but still made him want to stroke her. A green sparkly flower clipped her hair away from her face, making her look like a child going to a party. She'd brought a box of dome-shaped Russian chocolates for Astrid, who gave her a kiss and said how pleased they were that she and Taras were friends again.

Katya's eyes widened slightly. Taras grimaced. He hadn't meant to understate things, he'd just wanted to avoid a lecture. 'Well, a bit more than that,' he said hastily. 'But, you know, taking things gradually.' He hoped Katya wouldn't mention moving in together yet: he didn't want to look a complete fool.

Roy appeared in the hallway, wearing the 'Kitchen Bitch' apron that Taras had given him when Astrid moved in. 'Just give us warning to be out of the country next time you dump him.'

'Oh . . .' Katya looked uncertain. Taras knew she couldn't tell whether Roy was joking or not. Following him back into the kitchen, Taras said, 'Be nice to Katya, will you? She's nervous.'

'I'm pouring her a glass of wine. That's pretty nice.'

'You know what I mean. Don't be sarcastic, she doesn't get it.'

'She's not the only one.' Roy put the corkscrew down. 'Look, it's just a bit weird, that's all. She's going out with you, then she's going out with the geriatric, now it's you again.' He picked up the bottle and started pouring. 'Be careful, all right?'

Why did everyone keep saying that? 'Whoa!' Taras raised the hand holding a glass, and purply-red liquid sloshed on the floor.

Roy sighed. 'Get a cloth before Astrid sees that.'

When they headed through, Taras wished they'd been a bit quicker. The girls were on the sofa and Katya was looking at the book Astrid had been reading.

'. . . lad mags to strip clubs to brothels,' Astrid was saying. 'It all reinforces the entrenchment of patriarchal attitudes.'

Taras hoped Katya wasn't going to ask him to explain that.

'You do not like strip clubs?' Katya said, casting him a mischievous look.

Oh God, he thought. Don't let her mention that to Astrid. Shit. Shut up, shut up, shut up.

'They're completely exploitative,' Astrid said, marking the last word with a chopping motion.

Taras didn't think he'd exploited anyone on the stag night. If anything, he was the one who'd been exploited. He'd spent a lot of money and couldn't even remember if he'd had any fun.

'Wine?' he said loudly, thrusting the glasses forward.

'I do not think it is so bad,' Katya said, oblivious to the meaningful look Taras was sending her. 'It is just what men do.'

'Hand over cash to make a girl who's poorer than them get naked?' Astrid said.

'Why not? If the girl is happy to do it, then what is the harm?'

Roy, leaning over the back of the couch, started laughing. 'The law of supply and demand,' he told Astrid. 'She's studying economics, don't forget.'

'Perhaps soon I will not be studying anything.' Katya's small white teeth bit her lower lip. 'The scholarship committee have scheduled a special meeting to discuss my case.'

'I'm sure it'll be fine,' Roy said. 'You were just giving a few language lessons, for Christ's sake. It's hardly fraud on a grand scale.'

Taras agreed but he was being supportive so said nothing. Astrid dragged Roy off to help her cook, and Taras took the opportunity to snuggle up to Katya on the sofa.

'I haven't seen this dress before.' He stroked the red square over her knee. The rich scent of beef frying was seeping through from the kitchen and the answering pang in Taras's

135

stomach sharpened another hunger. He leaned closer to murmur in her ear. 'Maybe you should take it off.'

'My dress?' Katya looked down. 'What is wrong with it?'

'Nothing.' Taras's hand itched to move up to the purple square over her left breast. Would that be seductive, or just crass? 'I'm just saying.'

'You don't like.' She stood up to look at herself in the mirror behind the sofa. 'It is not suitable?'

His hand fell back into the lap of his tracksuit and pressed down, frustrated. He gave up being playful. 'Well, it looks like you're going to a club or a party or something, that's all. A bit dressed up for dinner. But it doesn't matter.'

'Now you are angry with me.' Her fingers dropped away from the sparkly hair-slide she'd been about to adjust, and she turned back to him. 'Why?'

'Katya . . .' He pulled her down on to the sofa again. 'I think we're ready to move our relationship on a step.' His hand stroked her shoulder, edging down towards the boundary of the purple square. 'Stay here tonight.'

'Here?'

'Roy says it's OK.'

'I must go home. I have preparation for class on World Markets.'

'On Saturday?'

'I have to work hard. Scholarship committee will look at grades.'

He sighed. She slipped her hand into his. Her fingers felt small and warm. 'You said you will talk to Carlos,' she reminded him. 'About rent money.'

'Yes, all right.' He was almost glad when Astrid came to call them through to dinner. 'Oh, Taras,' she complained as he picked up his glass.

'What?' He looked down at the dribble of red wine on her book.

'Do you know what these are for?' She held up a coaster.

136

Katya went to the bathroom, and Taras apologised. He hoped Katya wasn't going to be like this when they lived together. How did Roy put up with living with a woman?

'You causing trouble again, Kroheman?' Roy appeared, with a tea towel over one shoulder.

'No, it's me,' Astrid said. 'I'm just a bit tired.'

'You're working too hard,' Roy said. 'We should plan that holiday.'

'We can't afford it. We're saving for a deposit, remember?'

'Doesn't have to cost much. What's that place you were talking about the other day? Skomer?'

'We could all go together,' Taras said eagerly.

Astrid was ladling out meatballs. Her eyes flicked up to Roy's, and she said, 'I'm not really sure it'd be your thing, Taras.'

'I don't know,' Roy said. 'An island full of cute birds? Right up the Kroheman's street.'

Better and better, Taras thought. And Katya in a bikini would top them all. Would it be bikini weather? Well, there'd be a hotel pool or something. Perhaps he could get another credit card, one of those zero per cent balance transfer deals. 'We're all going on holiday,' he told Katya when she emerged from the bathroom. 'How long will it take you to get a visa for Sweden?'

'Sweden?' Katya blinked.

'Or Wales,' Roy said.

'Wales?' Taras didn't get it.

Katya looked between them with a puzzled frown.

'Roy and I are going camping in Skomer,' Astrid said, taking pity on her. 'It's a very small, very rocky island off Pembrokeshire. Puffins nest there, and in the spring you can see hundreds of baby birds popping up from their burrows in the ground.'

'Oh, that is lovely,' Katya exclaimed. 'When can we go?'

'I'm not sure,' Taras said. 'Things are a bit dodgy at work

137

at the moment, I probably need to see what's going to happen there, first.' He glared at Roy, who grinned and raised his glass. That wasn't a holiday, it was a penance. 'And I've got to sort out this crap with our flat. The Bartletts are still insisting that Mami moves out.'

'That's awful,' Astrid said. 'Roy says she doesn't want to move.'

'Well, she's lived there since I was a baby. Before that, even.' Taras said, forking in a mouthful of meatball. It was delicious, mouth-melting, almost as good as his mother's *chiftele*; just the unfamiliar scent of nutmeg let it down. Mami didn't add that. What would she be doing now? Sitting in the parlour, probably, in her stiff-boned chair, with a pile of mending at her feet. When he was little, he used to sit on her footstool and make patterns out of the pins in the fat little felt cushion. He imagined her smoothing her face with her hands: flat, splayed nails and a thin wedding-band on hard-working fingers. He didn't want her to be worried. But she had to learn to trust him, to see that he was a man now, and he'd take care of her.

'Why are they chucking you out?' Roy said. 'Maybe the Mad Monk's holding a grudge from school? Dirty sod.'

'No,' Taras muttered, feeling Katya's eyes on him. 'Anyway, it's his dad, not him. He's a businessman, so maybe he wants to sell it or something.'

'Jesus,' Roy cut in. 'What a bastard thing to do. You should go round there and sort them out.'

That was the answer – of course. Not just a telephone call: anyone could do that. He'd pay the elder Mr Bartlett a visit, and bypass Gideon. Talk man-to-man, and show Mami that he was calling the shots now. 'Yes,' he said, feeling courageous and powerful already. 'That's exactly what I'll do.'

CHAPTER TWENTY-FOUR

Astrid went to bed soon after dinner, pleading tiredness. Roy followed soon after, giving Taras a knowing nudge and wink in Katya's direction. If only, Taras thought grumpily.

'Will you really make this Bartlett man let your mama stay in flat?' Katya kicked off her shoes and snuggled into the sofa.

'Yes, of course.'

Pink-cheeked from excitement, or wine which she didn't usually drink, she patted the cushion beside her. 'And you will make Carlos understand I cannot pay him rent yet. Oh, Taras, you are like knight in twinkling armour.'

Alone in the living room together, with the rest of the flat silent and darkened, it was as if it was theirs. He slid down and began kneading her hip through the patchwork dress. 'Katya, why don't you stay tonight?' He kissed her and she wriggled against him. 'Oh, God,' he murmured. 'I can't wait until we're living together. It's going to be fantastic.' The hem of her skirt had risen, and he moved his hands to her thighs, rolling her underneath him. 'Mmm . . . Katya . . .' he murmured.

'Excuse me.' It was Astrid, dashing past in a vest top and red pyjama bottoms. 'Just getting my book.' Shielding her eyes, she grabbed it and disappeared again. 'Night.'

'Night,' Taras said, mentally cursing her. The mood was broken now. Embarrassed, Katya sat bolt upright and pushed away his hand when he tried to touch her again. 'It is time for me to go home.'

'I'll take you.' He knew she expected him to.

On the way she asked, 'What did Roy mean about Mad Monk and grudge?'

'What?'

'About dirty sod and grudge from school.'

'Nothing,' Taras said, but she wouldn't let it go. Reluctantly he found himself telling her about the paved alley behind the school theatre where the junior school smokers hung out. Taras and Roy generally steered clear but after the summer exams, they'd been swept up in a general mêlée of mischief. Leaning against buckets, and bits of wood, and boxes of props, a group of ten-year-olds clustered around Murdoch, who was holding a bottle of whisky and a duty-free carton of Benson & Hedges.

Someone found a goblet left over from last term's production of *Macbeth*: it was double-handled, with a red glass rim that glittered like rubies. The test was to drain a slug of whisky from it, and smoke a cigarette down to the butt. Then you had to stand on your head while the next boy took his turn. If you did it without collapsing, yakking, or otherwise disgracing yourself, you'd passed. The consequence of passing or failing wasn't spelled out, but everyone felt its significance. Taras was petrified: he'd never tasted alcohol or inhaled a cigarette, and now he was going to be exposed in front of everyone.

The harsh tang of tobacco filled the air, shot through with putrid overtones as the first boy threw up. It came out through his nose, in a yellow-brown stream. The sight and stink nearly made Taras gag too. Whoops of derision rang in his ears and he shrank back against a wooden chest filled with tin swords and shields, wishing he could leave.

A sudden commotion erupted: clattering footsteps, and the curtain being roughly dragged aside. The austere housemaster pushed through. Recriminations followed, then punishments. Boys who had not participated in the drinking or smoking got off with a warning; the ringleaders were suspended for two weeks. Letters went out to parents, some came in for further discussions. Taras succeeded in intercepting his mother's letter before she saw it, but still quaked for days.

A rumour grew. Gideon Bartlett hadn't taken part in the drinking, and he wasn't at the special assembly in which the rest of the class was castigated. He hadn't been punished. Someone said he had been the one who'd called the housemaster. The rumour spread wider. Confronted, Gideon showed no shame. Pushing his pale bowl-fringe out of his eyes, he said, 'Drinking and smoking are against the rules. They're dangerous.'

'So you went and sneaked?' demanded Murdoch, advancing menacingly.

'Of course,' Gideon said. 'You wouldn't have listened to me if I'd told you to stop.'

Baffled by such an inability to perceive the utter wrongness of this action, Murdoch took a step back. Everyone knew telling tales was wrong – it was rumoured that even the housemaster disapproved of what Gideon had done.

'Moron,' muttered one of Murdoch's acolytes.

'Wanker,' added another.

Gideon gazed at them with impervious superiority.

'Mad Monk,' Taras said, infected by the general indignation and forgetting how glad he had been to be rescued before his turn came.

There was a silence, then Murdoch laughed. Immediately, his followers picked it up. 'Mad Monk', 'Mad Monk'. Jeering followed Gideon wherever he went in the school.

Katya was not impressed by the story. 'He would like to throw you out of your flat, because you made up a stupid nickname?'

'No,' said Taras. He knew there was more to it than that. 'Forget it. I shouldn't have told you. Anyway, it's his father, not him.'

'He must be a fool, I think.' Katya's arm threaded tighter through Taras's. 'Why did Roy say "dirty sod"?'

'I don't know.' Taras wanted to get off the subject. 'Here we are. Shall I come in for a bit?'

She looked up at the house. 'Carlos's light is on.'

He saw what was coming. 'I'm not talking to him now, Katya.'

'He wants his money very much. He says I cannot stay in flat if I do not pay rent.'

'I know, I know.' Taras kissed her. 'I'll talk to him soon, I promise. Anyway, it doesn't matter, you're moving in with me, remember?'

'OK.' She kissed him back. 'I hope the father is not fool like son then, and he listens to you.'

'He's not a fool.' Taras remembered those heavy-lidded eyes flickering over him, and shivered. *Sigi's boy.*

CHAPTER TWENTY-FIVE

Taras pushed past a cluster of tourists and looked up at the departure board. Four minutes until the next Southeastern train to Blackheath. Shoving coins into the machine, he grabbed a ticket and rushed through the barrier, leaping on just as the doors beeped and closed. Houses slid by the train window. He'd be able to set things straight with Elliott Bartlett. Once the flat was settled and his mother was safe, he'd find a place for him and Katya. Then he'd tell Carlos to shove it; Katya was moving. All you had to do with a problem was break it down into manageable chunks. Project management. Simple. No wonder Leo had chosen him to organise the morale-booster night. He'd seen Taras was a natural organiser. Shit. The night out. Must do something about that. Hey, hey – no problem. It would get slotted in. He was on top of it.

The train doors rumbled open and with a start, Taras saw the platform sign. Had that been announced? He leapt up and jumped out, just in time. Steel-grey clouds were massing overhead. It was going to rain. Turning up the collar on his suit jacket, he set off towards Shooters Hill. Suppose he couldn't talk Elliott round? Imagining his mother trying to settle in somewhere new made Taras's stomach quail. And could she live on her own? Taras wasn't sure. Well, he'd come home some nights, stay over. Twice a week, say, or maybe even three times. Katya would understand. Wouldn't she?

Sweat was rising under his collar, cooling as it met the air outside. What was Katya like domestically? Roy and Astrid shared the chores, the cooking too. Well, he could get a cleaner, and there were always takeaways. How much would that cost? A bulbous drop of rain struck his forehead. If only he'd been more careful managing his money. He'd always meant to start saving, there'd just never been a good time. He trudged on up the hill.

Rain was splashing down on his shoulders now, soaking through his suit mixing with the perspiration on his skin. Checking the number on the piece of paper again, he stood back. This was it. A four-storey Victorian mansion, glowering westward towards the city. Symmetrical towers of bay windows rose from the hunkered basement to the slate roof, their rolled plate glass set into lime-washed bricks. Two mulberry trees in latticed planters flanked the stone steps that led to the front door; heavy panelled wood, painted the colour of dried blood and topped by a stained-glass frieze.

This house was unassailable. Rooted into the ground; reaching to the sky, it was a citadel: Bartlett history was embedded in the foundations, giving the family their unshakeable stability, their confidence, their sense of belonging. By comparison, Taras and his mother were merely ivy clinging to the surface. If notice were served on the rented flat, it would take no more than a day for all trace of them to be brushed away. A few scratches on the counter-tops and some picture-hooks in the wall would be all they'd leave behind; not much to show for twenty-four years.

But he'd come to scope out the territory, not to be defeated by it. The rainwater had completely seeped through his shirt collar and soaked his chest. At the top of the steps, a bear's head stared down at him, cast in brass and fixed in the centre of the oxblood door with a knocker clasped between its teeth. He took a step closer, brushing against the blunt-toothed mulberry leaves. A shower of water spat into his face. The bear seemed to snarl, warning him off. He stepped back again, nerve failing. He didn't have to knock this time. It was a reconnaissance mission; scouting out the lie of the land. He'd come back tomorrow. Taking a step back, he turned, ready to go, but suddenly the bear was in retreat as the door swung open.

'Very enterprising,' Elliott Bartlett said. 'Did your mother tell you where I live?'

Squirming with embarrassment, Taras muttered something about not intending to disturb anyone.

'I could hardly miss you, dancing about on the doorstep like that. Stop jiggling, boy, you're spraying water everywhere. Worse than a dog.'

Taras retreated a pace or two and blurted an incomplete sentence about wanting to talk, then turned to go.

'Well, you'd better come in.' Those eyes looked him up and down, from his dripping black fringe to the squelching lace-ups, leaving Taras as crestfallen as a misbehaving puppy. 'I suppose I should offer you some dry clothes.'

Taras was handed over to the help; a lump-shaped woman with yellow highlights and smoker's ridges around her mouth. She led the way upstairs and he followed, eyes darting about to take everything in. He hardly dared put his damp hand to the banister, which was elaborately carved, tumbling into a floral cascade, and he was very conscious of the wet trail his squidgy socks left on the painted floor-boards.

'You'll be needing a bath, I'd say.' She gave him a sour look.

Did he smell? Shivering, he nodded. The narrow radiator on the landing wasn't giving out any heat: he needed warmth. She twisted the taps and left him. He'd have preferred a shower, but there wasn't one, just a roll-top tub with claw feet resting on iron balls. Steam rose from the hot

145

water thundering into the bowl, and Taras sank into it gratefully; his pale flesh soon steaming crab-pink. He would have liked to close his eyes and dunk his head beneath the surface, but the door had no lock and though he had wedged his damp clothes against it, he still felt insecure. It seemed inevitable that the handle would turn downwards, and when it did, he grabbed for the towel he'd kept within reach and leapt up with a giant suck and roll of the water.

Elliott Bartlett appeared, long body hunched in the door-frame. 'I've brought you a dressing gown. Mrs E. wants your clothes for the tumble dryer. God knows why she can't come herself. Far too old to be bashful, surely. Appalling woman.'

Taras nodded, knee-deep in water and clutching his towel.

'You're your mother's son,' Elliott said. 'Pale as a clam.' He bent down to pick up Taras's bundle of clothes, holding them in his fingers, as if he found the task distasteful, or was just unused to domestic duties. 'Sigi was the outdoor type.'

He paused by the door. 'Tea will be served in the library when you're ready. First door at the top of the stairs.' And he was gone. Though no need for hurry had been expressed, Taras scrambled to dry himself, and came scuffling down in the dressing gown and slippers a size too large. He entered the library to find Elliott Bartlett in a large wingback armchair with a rug over his knees and a decanter of brandy on a side tray. A brass standard lamp threw light full on his face, making a halo of his silver hair.

'Here.' He poured Taras a glass. 'Mrs E. has brought some sort of tea. Stewed, no doubt. Help yourself.'

Taras took a gulp of brandy for courage and dived in. 'I was hoping you might let us stay in the flat. Well, let my mother stay.'

'Not you?'

'I'm moving out,' Taras said. 'But Mami needs a place to live.'

Elliott contemplated the bottom of his glass before refilling it. 'And why should I help her?'

'Well . . .' Taras was stumped. 'Because your wife did. Because you used to know Mami. And my father. Sigi.'

Saying the name aloud was like breaking a taboo. Exciting. He took another gulp of brandy.

'Has your mother talked to you about him?'

Hardly at all. But Taras didn't want to look ignorant. 'Yes, of course.'

'I see.' Elliott twisted the gold ring on his little finger. 'I suppose you feel I owe you something.'

'No.' Taras said, truthfully.

'No?' Elliott raised an eyebrow. 'You're more forgiving than your mother.' He took a long sip of brandy. 'Sigi might have forgiven me. Had he lived.' He gazed into the fire for some time.

Taras didn't like to interrupt, although he wasn't sure whether Elliott had forgotten he was there. Discreetly, he helped himself to two crumpets from the silver chafing dish, and was just thinking about following up with a slice of Madeira cake, when Elliott broke in, 'Do you know what it's like to betray someone you care about?'

'Mmm,' Taras said non-committally. 'Not exactly.'

'Good. Your mother's kept quiet a long time. Unusual for a woman.'

Taras gave a restrained chuckle, not sure if it was a joke.

'Do you know much about women, Taras?'

What kind of a question was that? He shrugged.

'They want security. An environment in which they can bring up their young. And they'll fight for it. No different to a tigress defending her cubs.'

'Some women don't want children,' Taras said, thinking of Katya.

'Makes no difference. It's an instinct. Coded in. Not their fault, poor creatures. Men don't stand a chance.' Elliott sighed. 'Look at Gideon. Any day now he'll be skewered on a manicured claw.'

Taras remembered the sleek blonde. 'Desirée?'

'Damn depressing.' Elliott filled his own glass again and let the decanter hover over Taras's. The brandy was already going to Taras's head, and he couldn't really handle more, but he nodded anyway.

'Gideon means a great deal to me,' Elliott said. 'I'd like this conversation to remain between us.'

'Of course.' Taras squinted slightly. What had they said?

'Your mother can stay in the flat. I'll tell Banerjee. The same arrangement as before.'

Yes! Taras had to restrain himself from punching the air. He'd done it. No need for aggression or confrontation. He'd done it the clever way: he'd built a rapport. The kind of thing Francis was always banging on about doing with clients. He couldn't wait to tell Mami.

The door clicked downstairs. Someone was home. The rat-a-tat indicated light footsteps running up the stairs. The painted floorboards creaked, then the heavy internal door scraped open.

'Dad, I . . .' Gideon stopped, his mouth caught in a startled curve, and blinked. 'Flounder!'

From the leather sofa, Taras raised his tumbler of brandy in greeting. Wrapped in the crimson brocade dressing gown, with his feet tucked into slippers embroidered in burnished thread, he felt rather magnificent. He certainly blended into the room. Chinese dragons entwined on the thick rug in front of the fire, velvet curtains the colour of claret were tied back with dull gold tassels, and the walls were papered a dark burgundy.

By comparison, Gideon didn't fit in at all. The indigo jeans and a roll-neck sweater which brought out the strange oxidised-copper hue of his eyes, were too urban. Standing outside the flickering circle of firelight, one hand still holding the door, he seemed ill at ease.

'Your father says we can keep the flat,' Taras said. He felt a bit woozy. That wasn't the bit he'd promised not to tell, was it?

In the high-backed library chair, Elliott adjusted the rug over his knees. 'We'll talk about it later, Gideon.'

'I see.' Gideon went over to the fireplace and pushed the poker into the ashes. A tall yellow flame shot up, hard and bright. 'What—'

The door creaked open again. Mrs E. bumped her way in, carrying a large tray. Exhaling noisily as she reached across Taras for the leftover cake, she loaded the tray with their dirty plates. Elliott averted his eyes with a conspicuously pained expression as her large rear swung in front of his face. 'Thank you, Mrs E. We won't need anything else.'

She glanced at the half-empty decanter and sniffed. 'What about dinner then? Is it two or three? Only I've already done the shopping and I can't say it's going to stretch.'

Taras wondered if he was going to be invited, but Gideon said, 'Desirée's coming, Dad. Remember?'

The grooves in his father's face deepened. 'What a treat. I shall take a rest in preparation.' He pushed himself to his feet, letting the rug fall aside. His leg wobbled and he would have fallen if Gideon hadn't caught his arm.

'I'll just clear this away, will I?' Mrs E. grasped the decanter meaningfully and looked to Gideon for confirmation. He nodded, and she tweaked the brandy tumbler out of Elliott's hand, grumbling under her breath as she placed it on the tray.

Elliott's face stiffened. He stood up a little straighter. 'Taras, perhaps you'd like to join us for dinner. Did you have plans?'

'Dad . . .' Gideon said, but Taras was already saying, 'Well, I was meeting someone, but . . .'

'Excellent. Bring him too. That will be five then, Mrs E. For eight o'clock, if you please.' Releasing his grip on Taras's arm, he made his way to the door, and paused. 'You don't have any objection, Gideon, I hope?'

His son shook his head mutely and crouched to push another log into the sputtering embers.

'Good.' Elliott lowered his voice. 'I will not be dictated to in my own home.' Raising it again, he called, 'Mrs E., would you bring Taras his clothes, please. I expect he would prefer to dress for the occasion.'

CHAPTER TWENTY-SIX

Despite Taras's instructions, Katya was late. She phoned from the street corner and he went down to collect her, dressed in his own clothes once more.

'Why didn't you get a taxi? I told you to get a taxi. Everyone's already sitting down for dinner.'

'I called a minicab firm and they said £45. So I got the train.'

'I'd have paid.' Taras had her elbow and was pulling her towards the house, irritated because she still wasn't hurrying.

'Hmm.' She stopped and tugged up a rumpled ankle sock which had slipped down the back of her shoe.

He knew she was remembering the couple of times he'd promised to pay for cabs, and then didn't have enough cash on him. But he'd paid her back later on, hadn't he? Had he? He'd intended to, anyway.

'Come on,' he said, and then took notice of her scuffed trainers and the denim legs protruding from the end of her coat. 'Oh.'

'What?'

'Nothing.'

But she'd caught his look. 'You don't like my shoes?'

'You're not very dressed up, that's all. It doesn't matter. Come on.' He tried to push her along the pavement but she pushed back and held firm.

'You told me I dress up too much.'

'No I didn't. When?'

'At Roy's. You said English people do not find it necessary to come for dinner as for a night club.'

'That's different.' Taras was irritated now; she was deliberately trying to provoke him. 'Look, can we just go in? You're really late.'

It was the wrong tone to take. Her small chin jutted in the air. 'It is not for myself that I have come all this way. You are not even happy to see me.'

'Of course I'm happy,' Taras said, gritting his teeth.

'Oh, nothing changes. This is just like all the times before.' She blinked and jerked her head away, as if about to cry.

'Katya, Katya, Katya.' Taras responded to the danger signs. 'I'm sorry. I didn't mean to be, to be – well, anything. I'm really glad you're here, and I think you look perfect. Now, please, let's just go in.'

She submitted, but there was a frosty slice of air between them as they mounted the stone steps.

'So, this is our mystery guest.' Elliott levered himself to his feet in a courtly manner. 'You surpass Taras's description, my dear.'

That wasn't difficult, since Taras hadn't said anything at all, but Katya brightened. Gideon stood up to shake her hand, his grey-green eyes regarding her without expression. Desirée, sleek in a sleeveless white dress, just inclined her head. Taras had the impression she had taken in at a glance Katya's over-sized orange sweater and stubby ponytail. Her cool gaze rested on him for a moment and his mouth crooked in an apologetic twist before he could stop himself.

Gideon served up the beef casserole that Mrs E. had left in the oven, while Elliott sat still, elbows resting on the carved arms of his chair. The dark green wallpaper cast shadows over the dining table. No one spoke. It made Taras feel awkward, but he was too much in awe to break the silence.

Katya did it. 'I can help.' She was on her feet, reaching for the plate Gideon was filling. Her sleeve brushed against a tall brass candlestick and Taras jumped up to steady it. 'Careful,' he muttered. She rolled her eyes.

'No matter.' Elliott waved a hand. 'Horrible object. Only made bearable by the light it casts, but we seem to have omitted . . . ah, Gideon, thank you.'

With a flick of a match, Gideon applied a flame to the taper. Katya, still trying to be useful, began ladling mashed potatoes on to a plate. She held it out to Desirée who gave a light shudder and waved it away. 'I have a starch intolerance.'

Katya stood blinking, with the plate still extended, and looked back at Taras for interpretation. He flapped his hand at her to sit down. Honestly, of all the times for her to decide not to make an effort, why tonight? She didn't have a scrap of make-up on. Even if she did, it wouldn't give her the satin perfection of Desirée's complexion, or the cloudless blue of her eyes. Imagine the Mad Monk ending up with a girlfriend like this. It was so unfair.

When they were all eating, Taras mustered up the courage to ask Desirée how she and Gideon had met. Unable to meet her eyes, he found himself staring at the tight white outline of her breasts.

'In a club,' she said. 'My friend does the bookings, and she told me about this saxophonist with the cutest British accent.' She flicked a cat-like look at Taras. 'So I thought I'd go see for myself.'

Taras managed to drag his gaze up from her chest, but only as far as those succulent lips. He had the impression she was enjoying his confusion, and he tried to look away, but her slow pink smile was paralysing.

153

'I also met Taras in a club.' Katya's voice was louder than usual, and Taras registered dimly that he should stop staring at Desirée. 'A club for Russian mail–order brides.'

What?! That jerked him out of his hypnosis.

Katya scooped another forkful of mashed potato into her mouth and wrinkled her nose at Taras.

'That's a joke,' Taras told everyone, appalled. Elliott was regarding Katya with interest, Gideon had one patrician eyebrow raised, and Desirée was hiding her pink lips behind frosted fingers.

Katya giggled. 'Yes, I am joking,' she admitted, grinning at Taras.

'It was an ordinary club.' Taras knew he should just shut up, but he wanted to be sure no one was left in doubt. 'A nightclub. The Roadhouse. In Covent Garden. I was on a lads night out. We . . .'

'Taras was too shy to ask me to dance. His friend came and told me.'

'Smooth,' muttered Gideon, making Desirée smirk.

That seemed grossly unfair, considering what a gangling, protruding-Adam's-apple, fervently preachy adolescent Gideon had been. Taras felt furious.

'I think it is attractive.' Katya didn't let anyone but herself criticise Taras. She was like Mami that way. 'I do not like a man to be arrogant. Only a girl with nothing to say needs a man who is always talking.' She looked straight at Desirée.

'I guess the world needs bashful guys like Taras,' said Desirée calmly. 'Just so homely girls can get dates.' She held Katya's gaze.

'Miaow,' murmured Elliott, topping up Taras's wine glass and his own. 'Here come those claws.'

Desirée shot him a sharp glance, Appearing not to notice, he leaned towards her, 'Tell me, my dear – Gideon has been so vague on the subject – what is it that you actually do?'

There was a pause. Desirée flicked her blonde hair over

her shoulder and met his inquiring gaze. 'I was in media relations, but it didn't work out, so I'm taking some time for myself right now.'

'Indeed?' Elliott offered no comment on this. Wanting to show he was listening, not just staring, Taras said, 'Cool,' only afterwards working out that she'd said she was unemployed.

But Desirée seemed pleased. She laid a manicured hand on his arm, giving him goose-pimples. 'It's a great time for me. I'm learning about life.'

'And what about you, young lady?' Elliott turned to Katya. 'Are you also a student of life?'

'No, of economics,' Katya said. 'I have scholarship to study for degree in London.' She laid her knife and fork down on her empty plate, and looked scornfully at Desirée's, which had hardly been touched.

'A brain as well as a pretty face,' Elliott commented to Taras. 'How refreshing.'

Taras glowed. The praise made up for Katya's dishevelled appearance and he felt proud.

Desirée pursed her lips and looked crossly at Gideon, but he was clearing away the plates. As he disappeared to the kitchen, she flung herself to her feet, with a springy bounce that caused Taras some internal anguish, and asked the way to the bathroom.

'The bathroom?' Elliott echoed her words, with an exaggerated frown of apparent puzzlement, then let his brow clear. 'Ah, you mean the lavatory. Of course, my dear. Taras, would you point the way?'

As Taras held the door for Desirée, he made the mistake of briefly catching Katya's eye. She made a little pout, then blew him a kiss. He should have smiled or winked, but he was afraid of looking foolish, so he didn't.

Desirée was too preoccupied to notice. Outside the room, she hissed, 'He's a lush, you know. It'll kill him in the end.'

Who? Did she mean Elliott? Taras decided to pretend he hadn't heard. He took her upstairs, stumbling twice. Too much brandy. Did Elliott always drink that much in the afternoons? And wine at dinner too. Was Desirée right, was he an alcoholic? Taras pushed the thought away; he didn't want to see any flaw in the older man's glamour.

Taking a deep breath, he steadied himself while Desirée paused to examine a large landscape painting on the landing wall. It showed some gloomy-looking horses dotted around a field. He couldn't see anything particular to admire in it.

'Can you read that signature?' she said. 'You think it's someone famous?'

He had no idea, but he said, 'Maybe.'

'Old house like this, anything could be here. Look at that statue on the table.'

It was a marble, delicately made and about six inches tall, of a winged boy kneeling with his fingertips brushing the ground. There was something wistful about the boy's pose, like regret. It was beautiful, Taras thought, surprised at his reaction.

'I bet none of it's insured. Probably not even been valued.' Desirée spotted the toilet door. 'You don't need to wait for me.'

Taras did anyway. He ran his fingers over the feathered marble wings and looked at his own reflection in the darkened window behind. Suddenly a security light flashed on, illuminating the garden beneath and a startled fox dashing away. The light stayed on for another minute, and Taras saw a larger version of the same statue, in stone this time, at the garden's centre. They were turned at the same angle: the larger statue echoing the smaller, like the reflections in a hall of mirrors. The sophistication of the arrangement stunned him. Imagine growing up in a house like a museum, where objects were arranged for a particular view. Did Gideon appreciate his good fortune? The toilet flushed and pipes gurgled. Desirée reappeared, not looking pleased to see Taras. He suspected she'd wanted to snoop around some more.

'Thought we'd lost you,' Gideon said when they reappeared. Dessert was already on the table: a large dish of fruit crumble, and the leftover cherries loose in a bowl. Katya had taken a handful. Taras hoped she hadn't minded him being gone so long.

'We got talking.' Desirée stroked her hand down Taras's arm, making him jump. 'Turns out we have more in common than I thought.' If she was trying to get a rise out of Gideon, it didn't work, but Taras flushed and blurted, 'I only waited in case she didn't know the way back' and then tailed off, aware he was being gauche.

Katya's brown eyes regarded the blonde thoughtfully, ignoring Taras. She flicked out a shred of cherry-skin that had caught between her small, white teeth. 'What, for example?'

'I was only kidding,' Desirée's smile was a touch malicious. 'Don't worry, honey, he's not really my type. Actually . . .' she turned to Elliot, 'Taras stopped to look at that statue on the landing, the one of the kid with wings – is it by anyone famous?'

That made it sound as if *he'd* been the one snooping. Taras was about to deny this, but Elliott just said, 'Ah, the little Eros? A delightful piece. You must take it.'

'Oh . . . I couldn't . . . er . . .' Taras spluttered, taken aback.

'I'd consider it an honour if you would. I'm rather fond of the little chap. It would give me pleasure to think he was with someone who cared.'

'Well, that's very kind of you . . .' Taras didn't want to be rude, but he wasn't sure what to do with a statue of a little naked boy. Where would he put it? His mother wouldn't house anything from the Bartletts, and Roy would take the piss.

Desirée was put out. Casting a meaningful look at Gideon across the table, she waited, and then seeing that he wasn't going to say anything, spoke up herself. 'Elliott, I hate to be rude, but you shouldn't really be giving stuff away. I mean . . . in the circumstances and all?'

'The circumstances?' Elliott looked at her, shadows furrowing the lines on his face. 'Oh, I see.' He glanced at Gideon. 'As you so rightly point out, it's not mine to give. I apologise, Taras. I must withdraw that offer.'

'Dad . . .' Gideon said; a tight, drawn look on his face. 'I didn't—'

'No, no. You're quite right. I have overstepped my bounds.' Elliott tilted his glass and drained the last dregs of red wine. Desirée watched him, lips pinched tight as if preventing herself from saying more.

Transfixed, Katya picked out another cherry and began to gnaw carefully around the stone. Taras, head swimming, felt this was callous, as if she was eating a TV dinner, but he couldn't catch her eye.

'I'm sure your wife was only thinking of what's best.' Desirée couldn't hold back any longer. 'Having money is a whole lot of responsibility.' She eyed Elliott's empty glass. 'She left it all to Gideon so he'd take care of it. And you, of course.'

It slowly dawned on Taras. Mrs Bartlett's fortune had not been willed to her husband, as anyone would expect, but to her son. Gideon was the owner of this house, and everything in it. Not just this house. Taras blenched. Also the flat in which Taras and his mother lived.

'Desirée! This isn't your business.' Gideon's voice was sharp. 'Dad, I'm sorry . . .'

But Elliott was already on his feet. The full length of his stooped height gave him added authority and shadows furrowed the lines on his face. 'I shall go upstairs. If I have your permission to do so, Gideon, of course.'

'Dad!' Gideon jerked his head as if his father had slapped him. 'I didn't ... Oh, for God's sake ...' It was too late, Elliott had stalked out. Gideon glared at Desirée, who shrugged honey-warm shoulders. 'Why the hell ... ?' Remembering they weren't alone, he broke off.

'Listen.' Taras pushed himself to his feet. His brain was too shrivelled by all the brandy and wine to find the right words. 'I'll just ... we should ...' He jerked his head at Katya, meaning it was time to leave, but her bright eyes were flickering between Gideon and Desirée. There were five cherry stones laid out around her plate, and she was nibbling at the sixth.

'Stay out of this, Flounder,' Gideon snapped. 'Why were you poking around Dad's antiques anyway?' He thrust back his chair, rising to his feet, and the crumble jumped in its dish, spattering purple juices on to the white cloth. 'What the hell are you doing here?' Taras felt sick: the dark room was closing in above the dripping candles as Gideon advanced on him, voice battering down. 'Well, forget what Dad told you about the flat. It's my decision, and I say you're out!'

Then Katya was upright too. Spitting the last cherry-stone into her hand, she flung it down on her plate with a chink that turned everyone's head. 'Bully! Stop this now!'

Desirée tittered. 'He doesn't take orders from women, honey. I've tried often enough.'

Katya's ponytail bobbed as she jutted out her small chin, brown eyes fixed on Gideon. 'You are angry with Taras because of stupid nickname at school and now you want to make revenge. *Swinya!* In Russia a man would be ashamed to behave in such a way. I spit on you!'

She grasped Taras's hand, tugging him out of his seat.

Gideon stepped back. 'Nickname?' he said. 'You think I'm angry because of a *nickname*?'

'Yes!' She glared at him. 'Taras has told me.' Tightening her grip on his hand, she dragged him towards the door.

'Did he tell you why I left the school, too?' Gideon called after them. 'Ask him that!'

CHAPTER TWENTY-SEVEN

The autumn term of Taras's second year at St Bartholomew's got off to a dark, gritty start, with a week of rain and mud-swirled winds circling over the top quad. The boys suspended after the summer drinking fiasco were back, rugby season was underway and the school smelled of socks and decomposing leaves. Taras, eleven now, was more confident in his surroundings: another dribble of new boys had arrived, and he no longer stood out. In fact, his spreading of the 'Mad Monk' nickname seemed to have won him kudos. He'd grown two inches over the summer and at breaktime he and Roy got sucked into the stick-fights or mass games of British Bulldog. Then, one afternoon, Murdoch came to him with a plan.

'I don't think I should.' Taras said.

'Why, you scared? Come on, Flounder.' Murdoch threw an arm over his shoulder. 'It'll serve him right.'

It felt good to have Murdoch being so matey. Taras couldn't help but agree to take part. The next day, he cornered Gideon Bartlett in the shadow of the chapel wall. At first, Gideon was suspicious.

'What's brought this on?'

'I don't know.' Taras dropped his eyes. 'I've just been thinking about what you said. God helping the weak, or whatever. I'd like to know more, but if you don't want to help, that's OK.'

'No,' Gideon put out his hand. 'I'm just surprised, that's all. Of course I'll help.'

'I don't want anyone else to know about it, though,' Taras said, as instructed by Murdoch. 'Can you meet me in the AV cupboard after school? Then we can talk properly.'

Murdoch had impressed on Taras the importance of sticking to the planned timings, which made him so nervous that the next day he was uncharacteristically early. The cupboard was actually a small room where the audio-visual equipment was kept. It was unlocked, and Taras, hurrying, flung himself inside. He was plunged into darkness. Unexpectedly, shockingly, he collided with another body, and his blood pressure surged.

'Shit! Who's that?'

'S'all right, it's me, Flounder.'

A light flicked on. Taras was faced with two of Murdoch's acolytes. They seemed irritated. 'Keep your mouth shut,' one said and the light flicked out again. They were setting up the VCR, rewinding a tape, their heads blocking the screen so Taras could only see a lurid glow around them.

Then there were footsteps.

'We've got a treat for you, Monk. Sit down.' Gideon would have refused, but was roughly jerked off his feet, spilling a flurry of papers on to the floor. The screen was unobstructed now, and Taras had a clear view of what was being shown. There was a thick-set man driving a golf-cart. He came to a sudden halt by a sand-bunker and leapt out, striding into the trees to where a blonde woman was searching for her missing ball.

'What's this?' said Gideon.

'Come on,' one of the boys said, but the other muttered, 'Wait a sec, I just want to see this bit.'

Taras's eyes bulged as the woman stripped off her shirt to reveal the largest breasts he had ever seen. They horrified him, but not as much as the woman's next action. She fell to her knees and pulled at the man's shorts to reveal a quivering purple monstrosity. Her mouth split open.

'Oh yeah, baby,' murmured the boy who'd told his friend to wait.

'That's sick!' Gideon snatched at the remote control, and in the scuffle someone hit the wrong button.

In slow motion the mottled foreskin disappeared between the woman's pink lips. Her tongue slithered out to trap the rigid shaft, dragging it down her throat, like a python swallowing a rat, accompanied by a liquid-filled choking sound.

'Urrgh!'

'Shit, what's that?'

'It's Flounder. He's spewing everywhere.'

'Oh shit, it's all over me. Ugh! Open the door.'

Taras was still shaking, with the taste of bile in his mouth, and vomit down the front of his blazer. He'd never seen anything like that before; didn't even know that kind of cannibalism existed. The door opened, and he staggered through it into the corridor.

'Shit, Flounder.' The other two boys were in the corridor with him. 'What do you think you're playing at?'

'Come on, there's no time!' The two of them sprinted off down the corridor.

A knocking on the cupboard door made Taras realise that Gideon was still inside. He turned the handle but it was locked. From the far end of the corner, one of the boys called, 'Leg it, Flounder, you cretin!'

CHAPTER TWENTY-EIGHT

Taras had no intention of telling Katya the full story. She hadn't asked for an explanation, and anyway, he was too upset. They tramped down the hill to the station in the rain, in silence, until he turned to her and demanded, 'What were you thinking? You've ruined everything.'

'I stood up for you! He was shouting at you like big bully.' She put her hand on his elbow and he shook it off. He was sick with disappointment. He'd been so close to reaching a sane, masculine agreement with Elliot, and now it was shattered. He'd failed. He wasn't going to be able to stride triumphantly back to Mami as her victorious hero, after all.

'I won't be able to afford a place for us now,' he told her. 'You know that, don't you?'

'But you promised.' She stopped dead, and when he tried to keep walking, she grabbed his arm and pulled him back. 'You promised!'

'I'm not a magician, Katya. I can't magic up money from nowhere.'

Her small cheeks puffed with air, then flattened with a sharp exhalation. Flinging his arm back at him like a weapon, she stalked ahead. One shoelace was undone: with every step she narrowly missed treading on it. 'Careful,' Taras couldn't help calling but she waved her hand over her head, as if to bat his voice away, without even turning around. They marched down the hill in single file, until Taras began to see the ridiculous side. 'Katya,' he called. 'Katya, I'm sorry.'

'No, you are not.' She didn't stop.

'Yes I am. Wait.' He jogged up to her side. 'It'll be all right. I was just angry. I know you were trying to help.'

'Hmmph.' She butted him with her elbow. 'You will find us a flat?'

'Yes.' He'd make it work somehow. 'Come back to Roy's place. I want you to be there tonight. We don't have to . . . you know. Just stay with me.'

She dug her chin into her scarf and muttered something.

'What?' He couldn't hear her.

'I said, OK.'

On the train, she leaned into him. 'What did he mean?'

'Who?' Though Taras knew.

'Gideon.'

'He got thrown out. For watching a dirty video.'

'Dirty?'

'You know.' Somehow he found the word hard to say. 'Porn.' Shifting in his seat, he added, 'It wasn't really his fault though. He didn't want to watch it. Someone else put it on.'

'You?' Katya asked.

'No!' Taras shook his head vehemently, then admitted, 'But I was there. So I think he kind of blames me.'

'So that is why Roy said "dirty sod"?'

'Yes.'

'Mmm.' She rested her head on Taras's shoulder and looked out of the window.

At London Bridge, they transferred to the tube, rattling and shaking up the Northern Line. Katya remained contemplative until they reached Camden, when she said thoughtfully. 'Are you dirty sod too, Taras? You like these things. Dirty films and strip clubs. Also blonde girls in tight dresses.'

'Sssh,' Taras said, glancing round the carriage, but no one was paying attention: two teenagers had their iPods on, and the elderly couple by the door were reading a guidebook in Italian. 'Katya . . . that stuff, it's just a laugh, it doesn't mean anything.'

'OK.' She nodded. 'As long as you are serious with me.'

'I am!' Did she think he was cheating on her or something? 'Katya, I can't keep trying to prove myself over and over again. I've said we'll get a flat together. That's a big commitment. What more can I do?'

'Do not shout at me.'

'I'm not shouting.' He lowered his voice. 'I'm whispering!'

'It is a whisper that shouts.' She folded her arms and clamped her chin to her chest.

Silence descended for the rest of the journey. At Highgate they disembarked and walked up the road, still without speaking. Katya was yawning uncontrollably, and Taras's head was aching from stress and brandy. He unlocked the front door, and saw the living-room light was on.

'Hey!' he called, 'I've got Katya with me.'

Roy appeared in the hall, curly mop even more dishevelled than usual. His lanky body blocked the door into the living room. 'Kroheman. It's not a great time.'

Over his shoulder, Taras could see Astrid cross-legged on the sofa. Her face was sallow and blotchy: it looked as if she'd been crying.

'Shit.' He lowered his voice. 'You're not breaking up, are you?'

'No. Look, just stay out of the way, okay?' Roy nodded towards the spare room.

Katya sat down on the narrow bed. 'What is wrong?'

'Just a domestic, I suppose.' The allure of cohabitation was rapidly decreasing.

'I need to go to the toilet.'

166

'Wait a bit.'

They sat in silence, Katya squirming. After a while, there were footsteps in the hall, then the whirr of the bathroom extractor fan, and the flush of the toilet. Astrid going to bed, perhaps. Five minutes later, the same sequence of sounds: Roy following her.

'OK, now you can go.'

'Do you have toothbrush for me? And pyjama?'

Of course he didn't keep an extra toothbrush. He told her to look in the cabinet under the sink, reasoning that Astrid might store spares there, and they compromised on an old t-shirt. He waited till she was finished, then went and brushed his own teeth, and checked his breath and armpits. Pretty decent. He sprayed on an extra coat of antiperspirant just in case. When he came back into the bedroom, Katya was rolled on her side under the duvet, facing the wall.

He slid in beside her. She had the t-shirt tucked firmly over her knees and bottom, but the soles of her feet were facing towards him. He gave them an experimental stroke, but she kicked his shins, 'That tickles.'

'Sorry.' He began massaging her waist and hip instead, trying to worm his hand past the barrier of her folded arms.

'Taras, stop it.'

He sighed with frustration and rolled on to his back.

'You said we weren't going to do anything.'

'Well, we're not, are we?' The duvet, only a single, wasn't covering his far leg or shoulder at all. He tried to twitch it away from her, but she had it firmly ratcheted under her hip.

'Taras . . .'

'Go to sleep.' He didn't want to talk.

'Taras.' She lifted up on to her elbow and wriggled over to face him.

Instantly, he got an erection. 'Yes?' He could feel her warmth through the t-shirt.

'I do not wish it to be like this. After argument, when you are angry with me.'

'I'm not angry.' He put out a hand and stroked her hair.

'Good.' She tucked her face into his shoulder and snuggled against him.

His erection rammed against her stomach. 'Oh, God.'

'What is the matter?' She tickled his shins with her toes.

'Nothing.' He tried manfully to stay still, but his hand slid of its own will down on to her shoulder and over her back. At first, she accepted the touch, but when it dipped lower, she wriggled and said, 'Taras.'

'I want to be close to you,' he muttered, hopefully.

'Mmm.' No relenting.

He waited until her body relaxed into sleep, and then got up and went to lie on the sofa, under a throw. It was cold and comfortless, and not at all what he had left home for.

CHAPTER TWENTY-NINE

Sunday, and the tube was up the spout again. Dejectedly, Taras plodded from Roy's place to the bus stop. A constant stream of lorries and cars ground past, heading into London from the north, and a cold wind was spitting in his face. Perhaps he should get a minicab. But he didn't have any spare cash. The thought of being trapped under an enormous rent-bill and condemned to grimy public transport forever made him even more depressed. It would be good just to have things the way they used to be. To patter up to the tiny kitchen and smell lunch cooking on the stove; have his mother fussing round him. Afterwards he could stretch out on his bed and snooze without anyone making demands.

A number 43 bus sailed by with 'NOT IN SERVICE' triumphantly blazoned on its front. If it was going via the stops anyway, why not pick up a few passengers, Taras thought grumpily. It was a good twenty-five minutes before another bus deigned to pass. Taras flagged it down and climbed up to the top deck, leaning his forehead against the damp window and staring out at the grey Archway Road. What if he just told his mother he was sorry? That would put everything right. He'd move somewhere with her, it would all be as it was before. He could even go on seeing Katya, just on a more relaxed basis than they'd been talking about. It was madness to rush things – moving in together was a big step, and he wasn't ready.

The bus rattled and jolted on for nearly an hour before they pulled into the sweep of London Bridge Station. Taras jumped off and sped down the narrow steps that led into the maze of back streets. He was coming home. The sky was brightening; a splash of blue opening behind the chimney stacks. He was panting now but his legs were pumping faster, propelling him into that childhood feeling of accelerating so hard that he might tumble head over heels. Skimming past a couple of surprised old ladies, he was out of control; an almost ecstatic headlong rush as he hurled up the road and flung against the front door.

He pressed the bell, but didn't wait for an answer. Fumbling in his pocket, he pulled out the keys and pushed them into the door. Up a flight of internal stairs, and then he was unlocking the dear old familiar door to home, almost falling inside with a cry of 'Mami!'

Nothing.

'Mami! Mami?' He shouted again.

His voice died away. Stepping into the kitchen, he looked round. No one. The living room was empty, and the door to the bathroom was wide open. His sense of disappointment was disproportionate; he felt bereft. Panic gripped his chest. It wasn't just that his mother wasn't there. Nothing was there. He looked round again, to be sure. The kitchen was empty. No pans, no dishes. He opened all the cupboards to be sure. Bare, scrubbed wood. No ceramic pots. No battered tin of black tea. The chairs had gone from the living room, so had the screen partitioning off his mother's bed. Her mattress on the floor was gone; the wooden sewing box that lived in the corner under the window was no longer there. Just a dimple in the carpet where her trusty leather bag always sat.

He ran down to his bedroom, where nothing of his remained. No clothes, no belongings. All gone. A nail-sized hole on the wall where the tear-shaped icon of the Holy

Virgin had hung. Just the bed, jammed into three walls. For a moment, he felt hurt that she had left it, then suddenly relieved. Feeling around under the mattress, he found the Christmas edition of *Razzle*. That was it. All that was left to show for his life. He sat down on the bed, head in hands, and found himself staring at Russell Crowe's frown. The poster was still on the back of the door; it must have been missed.

A more manly reaction surged in. What had happened? Had the Bartletts sent an overnight eviction crew? His heartbeat raced faster as he pictured a burly set of workmen pushing his mother and her belongings out. No. Reason prevailed. She'd packed up and gone, without telling him. Everything was scrupulously clean, in a way that only his mother could achieve. She must have been in full headscarf-askew, deep-scrubbing mode; he could picture her with the knot tied sharply behind her ears, and the scarf-point rearing out horizontally from the back of her head; elbows flying as she worked furiously into the corners of their stripped home.

Where had she gone? How had she transported all their belongings? It cut him to imagine her organising all this; surely she'd needed his help. Anger flashed up against Katya for coming between them; if it hadn't been for her, he'd have moved back home already. It was just wrong for things to happen this way. He felt he should stay now, though it was pointless. His mother wasn't coming back. There was nothing for him here. He felt stunned; wobbling as if from concussion; not able to walk straight, and had to stop and steady himself against the counter.

A crumpled breast twinkled up at him: the well-worn cover of *Razzle* under his fingers. He couldn't leave that here. Moving stiffly, like a robot, he thrust the magazine into his bag and turned back to the front door. For the first time, he noticed a bulky white envelope on the door-mat: he must have stepped right over it when he arrived. He picked it up. His mother's cramped handwriting, immediately recognisable. 'Mr E. Bartlett', it said. The envelope weighed heavy in his hand. He squeezed it. Keys. His mother's keys. She'd posted her keys back through the letter-box. Without doubt, this was a final departure. His heart flinched.

CHAPTER THIRTY

'But where can she be?' Taras fretted, back in Roy's flat.

'I don't know. You've asked me a dozen times.' Roy pulled on his boots. 'Come on. I'm hungry.'

'She doesn't know anyone, and she hasn't got any money.'

Roy leaned down the corridor and called, 'ASTRID! WE'RE GOING!' There was no reply. Sighing, he followed Taras out of the door. 'Look, I'm not being unsympathetic. But what can I say? She'll be in touch soon.'

Didn't Roy understand? Every moment was an eternity. Taras had called the police, who had listened patiently and said there was nothing they could do. She was an adult, and she'd left voluntarily. He'd swallowed his pride and called Gideon, who'd said shortly that it was nothing to do with them. His only hope now was Mr Banerjee. He'd left four messages, but the office was closed until Monday, and his home number was unlisted. The day was dragging out unbearably.

'Where's Katya?' Roy asked.

'Studying. You know . . . I'm not sure whether she and I are really that well suited after all.'

'Hmm,' was all Roy said.

'What?'

'Nothing.'

'You're thinking something, I can tell.'

'Not going to do any good to say, is it?'

'You don't think we're a good match. You've said it often enough.' Taras scuffed his trainers against the pavement in a dispirited way. It was 3 p.m. and they were walking down the hill to Crouch End, under a bank of grey cloud.

'Look, it's not about what I think, is it?'

'No, but . . .'

Roy looked up at the sky. 'It's starting to rain. Let's go to Banners.'

The café was heaving, as usual, but they squeezed into a small table at the back. Two families with food-spattered toddlers were crammed around the wide wooden table next to them. Even above the general noisy atmosphere, the insistent squeals and clattering of small cutlery-wielding fists was giving Taras a headache. Both the mothers looked like they'd really let themselves go, with hair pulled back into straggly ponytails and saggy, baggy clothes. Mid-thirties, Taras guessed, though they looked older. He jerked his gaze away as one began fiddling with the buttons on her top, about to clamp a red-faced infant to her breast.

'Do they have to do that in public?' he muttered to Roy.

'It's natural, isn't it?' But Roy had shifted his chair so that he didn't have to eyeball her or the banana-smeared toddler snuffling alongside.

Would Katya be the sort to let herself go like that? Taras wondered. Perhaps all women did after they got married. Or even before. When he'd climbed out of bed this morning, Astrid had been huddled on the sofa in an old tracksuit, with unwashed hair and puffy eyes.

'I'm fine,' she'd said when Taras asked. 'Just tired, that's all.' She'd turned down the offer of a fry-up with a graphic finger-down-the-throat mime. 'Ugh. You go. I'm going back to bed, I think.'

'Is she all right?' Taras had asked Roy, who just shrugged and changed the subject. They must be having problems. Roy wasn't as open as Taras; he always needed to stew for a while before admitting anything was wrong. The waitress, a pretty Polish girl, came to take their order. Roy went for the monster fry-up. Taras was going to have the same, but at the last minute changed his mind and ordered the New-Orleans-style French toast with blueberries and wondered if this was what Desirée ate for breakfast. Probably not, with a waist and legs like hers she'd only have the blueberries. Fruit was the key to a balanced diet. On that thought, he decided to just have a smoothie, then at the last minute called the girl back to add the French toast and a caramel latte.

'So,' he prompted, now they were settled. 'You're not sure about me and Katya. That we're an ideal couple, I mean.'

Roy sighed. 'Who's ideal?'

Was that a reference to him and Astrid? Taras decided to come back to it later.

'It's just that – I don't know – she just seems different. More demanding somehow.'

There was some sort of nappy crisis unfolding alongside them. A father was dealing with it there and then, not even taking the baby to the toilet. Taras and Roy's eyes met in incredulous dismay, and both shuffled their seats further away.

'Look,' Roy said impatiently. 'You were desperate to get back with her. Nothing anyone said had any effect on you. Everything was disastrous without her, it was all going to be wonderful with her: you built it up too much.'

The waitress brought their food. Her pin-straight blonde hair fell over one eye as she lowered the dishes and she gave them both a smile. Her white apron was knotted at the back over tight black trousers. Taras watched the white bow wiggle back to the kitchen.

'Well, what can I do now? She thinks we're moving in together.'

'You asked her to move in?!'

'But now I feel pressured.' Taras sucked down a mouthful

175

of caramel foam. 'She owes money to her flatmate, and she wants me to sort him out. I've got too much on my own plate at the moment, I can't cope with Katya's problems as well. It's too much responsibility.'

'You don't know what responsibility is. Jesus.' Roy had cleared his plate so fast that it seemed he must have snorted down the sausage and eggs, and was slumped back, long arms and legs hooked spider-like around his chair. His phone chirruped, and he dug around in his jeans pocket, accidentally elbowing a roaming toddler.

It was a text. He read it, frowning.

'Everything OK?' Taras said indistinctly, through a mouthful of French toast and blueberry.

'Just Astrid. She wants me to pick up a few things on the way back.'

'We could get her a latte.' Taras wanted to do something thoughtful: she was letting him stay, after all. 'Or some dessert? The white-chocolate cheesecake?'

'Nah, she won't eat it. Are you done? All these bloody kids are getting on my nerves. Let's go.'

They stopped at Budgens to pick up Astrid's shopping list of yoghurt and ginger-nut biscuits, then trudged back up the hill.

'Listen,' said Roy. 'What are you planning this evening?'

'Nothing much.' Taras was in the mood for slumping in front of the TV. He had two texts from Katya on his phone but was planning to call later, after it was too late to do anything.

'I think Astrid could do with a bit of space, that's all.'

'You want to stop off for a few bevvies?' If Roy wanted an outlet, Taras could force himself. That's what friendship was all about.

'No, I mean a bit of space for her and me. We just need a bit of time, you know. Maybe you could go and do nothing round at Katya's?'

Had Roy not been listening? Taras felt offended. He'd been pouring out his innermost doubts about the relationship, and now Roy wanted him to go and hang out there for his own convenience? How thoughtless was that?

'Taras!' Katya's face lit up as she opened the door. 'You have come to speak to Carlos? He is not here, but he will be back soon.'

Taras's head hurt. He took her hand and tugged her towards the stairs. 'Let's go and lie down for a bit. I'm exhausted.'

'Poor baby.' Katya allowed herself to be led into the room and pulled the coverlet off her bed. 'Here, I will rub your back.'

'Mami's disappeared,' he said, slumping down on his front. 'She's not in the flat, and it's been completely cleared out. No message, nothing. How could she abandon me like this?'

'She will come back,' Katya murmured in a low, soothing tone and ran her small hands slowly up and down his spine.

'What if she's in trouble? Or hurt?'

'If she was in trouble, she would come to you.' Katya leaned into him, pressing down with more weight.

'Do you think so?'

'Yes.' She pushed her fingers into his vertebrae. 'Taras, tomorrow, I will hear results of scholarship committee meeting.'

'Right.' He couldn't deal with this at the moment.

'I am lucky to have you to help me.'

He rolled on to his back. 'Katya, let's not talk right now. My head's killing me.'

'OK.' She smiled down at him, though her brown eyes were solemn. He nuzzled into her waist, pulling her blue shirt up. Her skin was warm and she smelled like roses. It was a blessed relief from thinking to just feel her skin. His hands pushed up further, and he felt her tense, and then give way. Suddenly alert, he undid a button, then another one, all the

177

way up until her shirt fell apart. She wasn't wearing a bra. The abrupt exposure of naked flesh made him gasp.

'What is wrong?'

'Nothing.' He caught a small pink nipple between his fingers and squeezed it. An image materialised of Desirée's rounded breasts, tightly outlined in the white dress. It merged into a spread from *Razzle*; a well-endowed blonde leaning back on her elbows. 'Ahhhh.' He was breathing faster, burrowing his head against her chest. 'Ah, Katya, I'm so crazy about you.'

'Wait!' She stiffened, listening. 'Is that Carlos?'

Taras didn't care. He flicked at her nipples and tried to ram his tongue into her ear, but she was wriggling away. 'Quick, or he will go out again!' She pulled her shirt together, and called out, 'Carlos!'

'No!'

'Oh.' Her face fell. It was the other flatmate, the Korean girl. She went out for a quick discussion. Taras fell back on the bed and stared at the ceiling. After a while, he got up and went out into the hall.

Katya was in the kitchen. 'Soo saw him at the library. He'll be back soon.' The Korean girl tucked a strand of hair behind her ear and nodded.

'Let's wait for him in your room,' Taras said, but Katya was already filling the kettle and setting out three mugs.

What was he going to say to Carlos anyway? What did Katya expect? A flicker of annoyance lit Taras. It was hardly unreasonable that the guy wanted his money back: he'd done her a favour by lending it. He probably needed it himself. What could Taras do, other than pay him? Was that what Katya was hoping for? He wasn't in a position to do that. It wasn't fair to manoeuvre him this way.

'I've got to go,' he said.

Katya frowned, not understanding. 'But . . .'

'I'll call you.' A quick kiss on the forehead. 'Later.'

CHAPTER THIRTY-ONE

The next morning, Taras arrived at work late, to find the office in uproar. The Chief was back from the States, and enclosed in a meeting room with Francis. Since it was glass-fronted, everyone else was trying to look busy while furiously swapping rumours. No work was being done. That suited Taras just fine. He was in an uproar of his own. Every way he turned, there were problems he needed to resolve, and with every attempt he made, they just got knottier. The one concern filling his head at the moment was his mother, and where she might be. He'd had a restless night, not helped by hearing Astrid get up and go to the bathroom at least three times.

He pushed another empty coffee cup on to Jamal's desk, which was now part rubbish bin, part in-tray. Rummaging for a napkin among the litter of leaflets, unopened payslips and crumpled circulars, he found he was clasping a stiff cream-coloured envelope with thick black print.

'What's this? Where did it come from?' He waved the envelope at Lisa.

Her attention was on the Slim-a-soup she was mixing up. 'You never empty your pigeon-hole, Taras. The receptionist is fed up with trying to cram things in there. You're supposed to check it once a day. She says if it overflows again, she'll dump the whole lot in the bin.'

'Saves me wasting my time doing the same thing,' Taras

grumbled, but this letter looked important. Official. A pulse in his chest was telling him it was bad news. Redundancy. A written warning of some sort. But that was stupid, it was an external letter: the receptionist's mail-received stamp showed it had arrived last week. He should just open it.

'The Chief's been in there with Francis since eight a.m.' Lisa leaned forward with a conspiratorial air. 'Apparently it's about that restructuring memo.'

Taras didn't ask how she knew, Lisa had her sources – she went to Fight-the-Flab with the Chief's secretary. But he wasn't in the mood for gossip and the stink of tomato soup this early was making him feel sick.

'Right,' he said, keeping his voice neutral and his eyes on his screen, and Lisa got the message. Unoffended – she was impossible to offend – she drifted over to another bank of desks, leaving Taras to concentrate on his letter.

He opened the envelope, and slid out the matching sheet of heavy cream paper. It had a large black header, announcing it was from Banerjee & Co, licensed solicitors in Woodstock Road, Croydon. The letter was very short.

Dear Taras,
Your mother has asked me to contact you with respect to her recent move. Please call my office at the above number and I will furnish you with further details.
    Yours etc.
    D. Banerjee LLB

What kind of idiot sent an important message like that by post? Did the man not know about email? Telephones? Taras hurried out to the stairwell, and flicked open his mobile. The number wasn't a direct line. It connected to what sounded like a very elderly secretary. She was unwilling to put him through.

'It's personal,' Taras said at last, plaintively, and somehow this worked where the first two more businesslike approaches failed. Perhaps it was a code: knock three times for entry.

'Banerjee.' Stern, rapped out, no time to waste.

'Where's Mami?'

A pause. 'Is this Taras?'

Well, obviously. What a fool. 'Is she all right? I need her address.'

Another pause. 'Taras, your mother is well. I think you had better come and see me.'

Taras didn't want to see Mr Banerjee, but the Chief's head was bobbing about on the other side of the porthole, and he didn't want to be caught making a personal phone call. 'OK. I'm on my way . . .'

'Let's say at . . .' It seemed Mr Banerjee was consulting a calendar. '5 p.m.'

He was being given an appointment! How derogatory was that? The door of the stairwell pushed open and out came Francis and the Chief, heads together, both frowning.

'I'll make sure to do that,' Taras said into the phone, in as official a tone as he could manage, and hung up.

'I hope we're not interwupting?' Francis laid the sarcasm on, but the Chief seemed unaware. His protuberant, bony face was preoccupied, and he was tapping his nose with his forefingers, which were pressed together, extending from tightly clasped hands like a church steeple.

'Official business. For Leo Harding,' Taras said, hoping he wasn't milking this one too far.

'No one knew where you'd got to,' Francis said. 'Jamal thought you might have *nipped out*.' He enunciated the words with distaste.

'Jamal's back?' Taras's head whipped round to the port-hole. That low-life scum.

'Tao-ahs,' Francis said impatiently.

'Er, yes.' Reluctantly, he looked back. 'You need me for something?'

'Your job, Tao-ahs. If it's not too much twouble.' Francis was in a towering temper. 'The Chief wants sight of that design document we sent over to the States. I believe you've got the most up-to-date version.'

We? That was rich. What exactly had Francis contributed? The heavy cheeks were billowing. He was out of his depth. With confidence, Taras ignored him and spoke directly to the Chief. 'No problem, sir. I can send that across to you now. Leo Harding and I have been working it up.'

Never comfortable talking directly to his employees, the Chief nodded and tapped his nose again, but Taras had the impression he was pleased.

'Wight, send that acwoss to *us* asap.' Francis shouldered in.

'Do you want Version 3 or the 3 star?' Taras enquired politely. He saw the white roll of Francis's bulbous eyes. Ha! That'd teach him.

'The 3 star?' The Chief's voice, almost too soft to be heard, made a rare appearance.

'Oh,' Taras made a show of seeming abashed. 'That's what Leo and I have been calling the design that's more attuned to the American market. It's based on the UK 3 but with some distinctive features.'

'Ah.' The Chief seemed amused, but Francis was furious. Taras fought back a smirk, but he knew its edges were showing. He didn't care. Francis was sinking, and Taras wasn't going with him. The moment was made complete when the Chief scratched the space between his eyebrows thoughtfully, and murmured in his almost inaudible voice, 'Leo Harding arrives tomorrow. I hear he's put you in charge of the morale-boosting team night.'

Taras was delighted. Leo had been talking about him! 'All under control.' He shook his mobile to make the point.

'Good. We must keep him happy. If you need any . . .' the Chief's voice slid away as if hunting for a word and settled on '. . . help, then pop in for a chat.'

'Yes, sir.' Wild success! Taras strutted back into the office, hoping that everyone would somehow know the Chief had invited him to pop in and chat. Not that he would. It'd be painful: the man didn't do small-talk, and he was hardly going to be a good source of entertainment ideas. Who knew what the Chief did in his spare time? Taras supposed he didn't have any.

Back at his desk he found Jamal wearing a Ted Baker sweatshirt and boot-cut jeans, reclining like a sultan in a chair, while Lisa fussed round him, turning Taras's rubbish bin upside down to make a footrest for his cast. She'd shunted all the debris back on to Taras's desk, making it even more of a mess than usual. 'Would you like a coffee, Jamal love? I'll go down and get a proper one.'

'Thanks Lisa.' Jamal gave her his most charming smile, then nodded at Taras. 'All right, mate?'

Taras plumped down in his chair without a word.

'What's up with you?'

'You arsehole. Katya told me what happened.'

'Oh, right.' Jamal reached for the crutches leaning against the join in their desk. 'I hope you told her she owes me one.'

'What?'

'I was gutted, mate. I was really up for this trip, you know? And the travel insurance wouldn't even pay out, 'cause I was on the piss when it happened.'

'When what happened?'

'When she pushed me out of the fucking cab, of course.' He pulled himself up on the crutches and thrust out the cast. 'How do you think I did this?'

'You didn't break it skiing?'

'Didn't even get on the flight. Spent the day in A & E instead.'

'Well . . .' Taras struggled to get back on course. 'Yeah, but she told me *why* she pushed you out of the cab.'

'Gave you a proper earful, I bet. Did she tell you how badly she was coming on to me?'

'She was not!'

'I'm telling you, mate. Sat on my lap, tongue in my ear, everything. I held out for a bit, but I'm only human.'

He was lying. Wasn't he? 'So why'd she push you out then?'

'Who knows? One minute, everything's cool, the next she's gone apeshit. Tears, screaming, the lot.' He shrugged, sounding resigned. 'Women, eh?'

Furious as Taras felt, there was a niggling familiarity about this scenario. Could it have happened like Jamal said? That night they'd all met in the club, Jamal had been the one to get talking to Katya. Taras had only managed to get in there when Jamal went off with a blonde in a mini-skirt. Did Katya fancy him? Had she . . .

'You two back together then?' Jamal winked. 'Better luck this time, eh?'

Taras knew what he meant, and scowled. He should never have admitted that she was holding out on him.

'Anyway,' Jamal shuffled forward a pace. 'Turned out sweet in the end. Might have missed the holiday, but scored an interview instead.'

'An interview? A *job* interview? You haven't . . .'

'Yup.' Jamal adjusted his hands on the crutches smugly. 'Aced it. European team manager. Double the pay, my own office, financial software firm in South Ken.'

Even allowing for the inevitable exaggeration, it must be pretty good, or Jamal wouldn't be smirking like that. 'Have you told Francis?'

'Doesn't even want me to work out my notice. I'm a free man as of Friday. Poor old Fucknugget. He'll probably be out before me. I hear you've told the Americans what a dozy twat he is.' Jamal tucked Taras's *Metro* under his arm and hobbled off towards the toilets.

CHAPTER THIRTY-TWO

'Off somewhere?' Francis stood in the doorway, thick eye-brows drawn together at the sight of Taras in his duffel coat with his bag over his shoulder at only 4 p.m.

'Yup.' It was liberating to no longer be afraid of Francis's heavy-set opinions. Taras chose not to offer an explanation, silently daring him to ask for one.

The eyebrows bristled but Francis just muttered some-thing and stooped back over his desk. Victory! This was power indeed.

He'd printed off a streetmap of Mr Banerjee's office address and was surprised to find it was a residential street. Only ten minutes walk from Croydon station, in a row of suburban 1930s houses, there was a brass plate fixed to the doorbell. 'Mr D. Banerjee, LLB', it read. Taras pressed the bell and was greeted by a steel-haired lady in her sixties: the secretary he'd had such difficulty getting past on the phone.

'He's on a call at the moment,' she said. 'I'll let him know you're here.'

Taras couldn't see any evidence of her actually doing this. It was ten to five and she seemed more concerned with gathering her belongings into her large carpet bag. The reception area was effectively an alcove off the hallway: to the left was a firmly closed wooden door with another brass panel declaring 'D. Banerjee'. Despite the businesslike labelling, it was clearly the ground floor to a house.

By the time the minute hand hit the hour, the secretary had buttoned up a fawn mackintosh and was buckling herself into outdoor shoes. Finally she picked up her phone and pressed a button. A metallic squawk issued, presumably Mr Banerjee.

'A Mr Krohe to see you,' she said, and another staccato squawk came out.

'You're to go through now.' She nodded at the door, and picked up her bag.

Wondering how she could tell, Taras went through, and saw with surprise how small Mr Banerjee's office was. Used to working in open-plan spaces, he found the idea of having an enclosed room odd. This was so cramped. Nevertheless, it was obsessively neat, with the maximum amount of storage: bookcases, shelves, filing cabinets; and squashed into the centre, a wide wooden desk with right-angled folders and a fountain pen. Behind this sat Mr Banerjee.

'Thank you for coming, Taras.' As usual, he pronounced it correctly, Tuh-rash, emphasising the final syllable, but doing so with a quick, clipped precision that cut off the sound as quickly as possible, as if the very name irritated him. 'There are some matters we must discuss.'

Taras sat down in the visitor's chair, which appeared to be both harder and lower than Mr Banerjee's own, setting him at a disadvantage. He had taken off his duffel coat in the hallway, but there was nowhere to put it, so he draped it over his knees.

'Your mother has been very upset by your behaviour. She expected you to respond to my communication immediately. This has been a difficult time for her.'

Taras had not come here to be brow-beaten. He'd explain himself to his mother, not to freckleface. He opened his mouth to demand to know where she was.

'However.' Mr Banerjee forestalled him. 'The regrettable situation with Gideon has no doubt distressed you also. He has been most headstrong. He did not listen to my advice, and insisted you and your mother must leave the flat. Of course, he has suffered a bereavement, and that is never easy.'

Taras remembered being nine, and his mother telling him he must be especially polite to Mr Banerjee when he came that month. 'Wife dying, pourchi. Cancer eating away bones. Nasty nasty.' She'd shivered and crossed herself. 'Poor man, may God have pity.' Taras had prepared himself for red eyes and sniffling, but was surprised to find no visible change. Mr Banerjee had been as severe and disapproving as ever.

'This is contrary to his mother's wishes,' Mr Banerjee continued. 'But since she did not make it a legal require-ment, he has that right.'

Taras didn't have time for this. 'Where's Mami?'

'I am coming to that.' Mr Banerjee concentrated on align-ing his fountain pen with the papers on his desk. He cleared his throat twice. 'My association with you and your mother has been a long one. Over time—'

'Where is she?'

Mr Banerjee attempted to continue as if Taras had not spoken. 'Over time, I have developed a considerable respect—'

'Is she all right?'

'. . . and under mature consideration—'

'She's not in hospital is she? Did she have an accident? Traffic?' Taras was panicking. 'Do you even know where she is?'

There was a long pause. They looked at one another. Then Mr Banerjee stood up, square and solid in his snug-fit-ting shirt and suit trousers. Unhooking his jacket from a hanger on the back of the door, he compressed himself into it, and a soapy smell of aftershave squeezed out. 'I shall take you to her.'

Taras followed Mr Banerjee through the hall to the living room. It was square and boxy with lilac floral curtains and a creased but extremely clean white leather suite. There were ornaments on the mantelpiece: a china figurine and a brass incense holder in the shape of an elephant. The artificial smells of furniture-polish and air-freshener wrestled in the air. None of this made more than the faintest impression on Taras. His attention was fixed on the woman seated ramrod-straight in the armchair; dressed in an unfamiliar skirt and jacket of navy piped with red beading, her dark head bolt upright and not touching the tartan rug draped over the chair-back.

'Mami!' He rushed forward, but she stayed still. Nevertheless, he could detect the familiar lighting up of her eyes at his presence, even if her face was stern.

'I have not discussed everything with Taras,' Mr Banerjee said, placing a stress on the word 'everything'.

'Absolutely, Deepak,' Mami said. 'I am explaining.'

Deepak? Taras thought, disliking the familiarity but relieved to see that Mr Banerjee was withdrawing, leaving Taras and his mother alone together.

'Mami, everything will be all right.' Taras rushed to her chair, too excited to sit down. 'I'm not going to leave you.'

His mother frowned at his shirt collar.

'Very crumpled, Taras,' she said. 'You are not doing iron-ing of proper kind.'

He tried to explain again but his words got tangled up, and he broke off in the middle with a huge sigh. 'Oh, Mami. I made a big mistake.'

At this, his mother's black brows broke apart, and her face softened. 'Very foolish boy. Taraşhu.' She opened up her arms and he knelt down beside her chair and put his head in her lap with a child-like feeling of utter relief. His mother's hand came up and stroked his hair, and tension drained from his body.

Something was different though. Her hand felt different. He shifted, and cricked his neck. On her fourth finger, where the thin slice of her wedding band had always been, was another, different ring: he had never seen it before. Raising his head, he drew her hand closer to see it better. Fretworked silver with a ruby.

Almost coyly, his mother said, 'Taraşhu, there is some news for telling.' A sick feeling galvanised his insides: somehow he heard her words before they actually appeared, so that her voice became a mocking echo of his thoughts. 'I am to be marrying with Deepak.'

Still kneeling in front of her, Taras felt himself in a horrible parody of a proposal. Mr Banerjee's square, ungainly body might have been squatting in this very position as his ring slid on to Mami's finger. With incredulous dismay, Taras scrambled to his feet. 'But Mami . . .'

'Very good man, pourchi. Will be taking care for me. Not true Orthodox Faith, but Blessed Virgin is woman and she will forgive.'

'No!' Taras howled, clutching her ankles. 'I'll take care of you! You don't need him, you've got me!'

With a cough, Mr Banerjee was in the room. He came up behind her, laying a square hand on her shoulder. 'I hope you will be happy for us, Taras.'

It couldn't be true. He found himself climbing to his feet and drooping into Mr Banerjee's hard handshake. He didn't think the solicitor was any more delighted than he was at their new relationship, but Mami's face was lit by a wide beam, and they were both trapped within it, unable to break the spell.

'When is it going to happen?' Taras said, feeling as if he was asking about an execution.

'No date yet, pourchi. But engagement party on fourth.' She patted his shoulder and kissed his cheek. 'I am making new shirt for you. Blue and yellow over red, like flag of Bukovina.'

CHAPTER THIRTY-THREE

It was a long journey from Croydon back to Roy's place. Slumped over the escalator at Highgate tube, Taras listened despondently to his messages.

'I need you.' Katya's voice, sounding weepy. 'I have problem . . .' Her voice dropped to a mumble and he could just make out the word 'Carlos', and then 'call me'.

He was too tired even to replay it. Delete.

Dragging up the hill had never felt so slow. Hopefully Roy would be back by now: Taras needed a beer and some sympathy. 'Anyone home?' he called as he came in.

'In here!' Astrid was lying face-forward on the beanbag, scribbling notes on a computer print-out. On the floor beside her, a long spoon stuck out of an empty jar of roll-mop herrings.

Taras scrunched up his face against the vinegary smell and dropped his bag by the sofa with a dramatic thump. 'I've had a really shitty day.'

'Me too.' She rolled off the beanbag. 'I'm going to take a nap. If you're watching TV, keep the sound down.'

Left alone, Taras screwed the lid back on the herrings and consigned them to the bin, then opened a window pane to get rid of the stink. Eating stuff like that was really inconsiderate. And she hadn't taken a moment to ask him what was wrong.

The doorbell sounded. Expecting it was Roy being too lazy to fumble for his keys, Taras scudded down the hall and flung open the door. 'Thank God . . . Oh!'

It was Gideon Bartlett. Shrugging off a sheepskin jacket, he stepped over the threshold. 'All right if I come in? Banerjee gave me the address.'

Taras stepped back, startled, and Gideon stalked through into the living room, stopping by the long ceiling-to-floor window and stared down at the patchwork of gardens below.

'So what does "*Swinya*" mean?'

'What?'

'Your girlfriend appeared to have a rather low opinion of me. What's the translation?'

'Er . . . "pig", I think. She might have got the wrong end of the stick from something I said.' Taras scratched his neck. Why was Gideon here? 'Sorry about that.'

'Hmm.' Gideon looked down at the garden again. 'If the situation was reversed, I can't imagine Desirée throwing cherry stones and calling you a pig.'

Taras couldn't either. Was it his fault Katya was over-emotional? 'We've moved out of the flat, if that's why you're here.'

'I know. Did you find your mother?'

'Yes.' Taras didn't want to discuss that. 'Just crossed wires. She wasn't really missing.'

'Good.' Gideon ran a hand over his chin. His cream jeans and taupe jersey fitted perfectly, and they'd been ironed. Taras felt at a disadvantage in his crumpled work suit. 'Listen, Flounder. What Katya said, about me taking some sort of revenge on you.'

'Forget it.'

'No. It's been bugging me. She has a point. I do bear a grudge. You were part of it, weren't you? The set-up.'

'Set-up?' Taras said, but he could see it was no good. 'I didn't know what was going to happen,' he said. 'And

191

Murdoch was setting me up as well. He meant me to get caught in there with you.'

'That wasn't the issue. The head knew I hadn't locked myself in to wank over a video: he just didn't want to investigate any further. It was the leaflets that did it.'

'Leaflets?'

'I brought them for you. "Words of Life". A Bible-reading plan. Stuff about the Salvation Army, that sort of thing. Proselytising on school premises, he called it. I accused him of suppressing religion, then he said there was evidence that I was forcing my brand of it on others. Ma got on her high horse, and the end result was that I was out. So, not really your fault, after all.'

Taras bit his lip.

'Ma and Dad were both bitter people. I grew up in an atmosphere of resentment. But I don't want to be like that.' Gideon's eyes were tired: as if he hadn't slept. 'So . . . you and your mother can have the flat back. For the time being, at least.'

'That's nice of you . . .' Taras said.

'Thank Katya, not me.'

'. . . But it's too late. We don't need it any more.'

'Oh?' Gideon uncrossed his arms. He looked taken aback. 'You don't?'

The sound of a door opening interrupted them, then the clatter of voices in the hall. Roy's tangled head appeared. 'Kroheman. Code black situation here.' He saw Gideon and broke off. 'Sorry, didn't realise . . . Fuck me! It's the Monk!'

'Hello, Lewin,' Gideon said, unmoved. He might have added more, but from behind Roy, a dishevelled Katya burst in. She was wearing her padded parka over a short woollen dress in jagged shades of red and orange, with silvered tights and her purple ankle boots. It looked as if she'd thrown on clothes at random. Across her shoulders and in both hands were an assortment of bags, stuffed so full that most of them wouldn't close.

'I have no home,' she declared, throwing the bags down in front of Taras. 'Now you will have to take care of me. Oh!' She noticed Gideon. 'You. Rude man. Why are you here?'

'Katya, what's going on?' Taras picked up a bag and dropped it again. 'What's all this?'

'I have lost scholarship. And I am homeless. Carlos said if I cannot pay, I must leave.' She pushed back her dark fringe, dislodging a sparkly hair-grip. 'You have been asking me to live with you. You want to take care of me. Well, it is time to begin.'

'Er . . . look, Katya. It's a bit difficult right now.' Taras glanced to Roy for help.

Misunderstanding, Roy shook his head. 'Not here, mate. Frankly, one extra guest is already one too many.'

'You see? I haven't got a place to live myself. It's not great timing.'

'You think I choose this timing?' A red and orange arm gesticulated, narrowly missing Gideon. 'Well? Where can I go?'

'Katya . . . I don't know.' I'm not your father, Taras thought crossly, I can't do everything for you. 'There must be someone you can stay with temporarily. What about Margarita or Anya?' He wasn't sure if he'd got the names right, but she had a whole group of Russian friends: angular, bold-eyed girls who talked in loud, unintelligible voices and made him uncomfortable with their mocking laughter.

'Of course.' Katya threw herself on to the sofa, buckles on ankle-boots flashing as she crossed her legs. 'They have Russian hearts, of course I can go. But Margarita has baby and husband out of work and not enough space for themselves, and the flatmates of Anya will not accept extra person without extra payment. It is not possible.'

'Well, what about university accommodation,' Taras said, flapping his hands to indicate she should calm down. 'Or maybe a B & B? Just temporarily, until things get sorted. There's lots of options . . .'

'There are no options!' Katya's voice rose. 'No options with no money. I cannot pay. Do you not understand? You want me to humiliate further by saying over and again?'

'OK, OK,' Taras took hold of her hands and squeezed them. 'Just calm down.'

'And without scholarship, I must pay university fees myself. These are already overdue, if I do not pay then I must leave course.' The sparkly hair-grip was dangling over her face: angrily, she dashed it aside. 'Never mind. I do not want help. I go!' She grabbed for her over-stuffed bags and one tipped over, spilling a brightly coloured flourish of clothes and books on to the floor.

'Katya, calm down.' Taras grabbed her and tried to push her back on to the sofa. 'You're over-reacting.'

'Leave me alone!' She scooped up an armful of clothes and a spray of underwear, white and pink and pale blue, sprang out like a magician's bouquet. Taras seized at it and they tussled for a moment. He let go, and she staggered back. 'You want? Very well!' She upturned each of the other bags one after another, tipping out their contents over Taras. 'There! Are you satisfied?'

'Katya . . .' Taras shielded himself from the flood of possessions: tangled t-shirts, lever-arch files, a glint of hooped earrings. 'Don't!'

Her silvered tights glittered as she kicked the pile. 'There! Oh!' She pounced on the last bag and pulled the zip open. A pair of large, man-size trainers fell to the carpet, followed by a sweat-stained t-shirt and tracksuit bottoms. A striped towel caught in the zip and flapped loose as a stale smell of perspiration evaporated into the air.

'That's not your bag!' Taras wrestled it from her. 'Stop it!' But the shiny cover of a magazine was already emerging, brightly coloured pages flipping as it landed with a soft slap on the carpet.

'Whoops,' said Roy, as Katya took a step forward and

demanded, 'What is that?' Gideon looked down at pome-granate-pink splayed flesh glistening up from the shiny pages and raised a sardonic eyebrow.

Briefly, Taras considered denying all knowledge, but the sports kit was too obviously his.

'What's all the commotion?' A voice cut through from the corridor and Astrid appeared. Short hair flattened, in a t-shirt and pyjama bottoms, she stared at the chaos and demanded, 'Roy, what's going on? Then she saw the magazine. 'What the hell is this?' Pincering the corner between her fingers, she dangled it aloft like it was a dead mouse. 'Taras?' she said, accusingly. The page ripped with a rough sound, and the rest of the magazine fell to the floor, leaving Astrid with a slice of hip, breast, and Santa hat. Her face tightened and she flapped the fragment in his face, as though he was responsible for its mutilation.

'You know how I feel about this stuff. How can you bring it in here?' She crumpled the paper up with a vicious twist, right in front of his nose. 'Do you know how I spent today? I went to a nasty little pub in Vauxhall, where vulnerable women get exploited by disgusting men like you.'

'Astrid, it's just a magazine. It was a mistake bringing it here, but—'

She ignored his interruption. 'Leering, beer-soaked idiots who're too cheap to pay the prices the bigger clubs charge. These girls are foreign, poor, they don't have the right per-mits, so they strip in places like that.' Stalking over to the coffee table, she picked up a sheaf of papers and shook them. 'All I can do is make a report, try and shake up people's opinions. And what good is that? It's all pointless.' She dropped the papers so they floated down around Taras's feet.

'Astrid, come on,' he said, trying to defend himself, 'Half the girls in this magazine are in *Big Brother*, or putting out a pop song. No one's getting exploited.'

'Oh, for God's sake, Taras,' Astrid sat down on the sofa

with a thump. Her eyes were watering, or was she, heaven forbid – she was, she was crying. Taras spun around for Roy, who rolled his eyes but went over to rub her shoulder. She shrugged him off, and marched out of the room with him in pursuit.

'Jesus, Astrid,' Taras heard, and then the click of the bed-room door.

Keeping her back to Taras, Katya picked up the pages of Astrid's report, one by one, looking through them as she sorted them into order. Gideon stroked his chin, then turned to her and said. 'Taras's old flat's empty. You can stay there for the time being.'

'Didn't you hear before?' Katya thrust Astrid's report back on the coffee table. 'I cannot pay you any rent.'

'That's all right. Neither did they.'

What did Gideon mean, 'neither did they'? They'd paid rent, £500 a month, Taras had shouldered the responsibility himself since starting work. Now Katya was looking at the man with shiny eyes, as if he was St George with a sword steeped in fresh dragon-blood. 'Thank you,' she murmured in that quiet, breathless voice that set Taras's skin tingling.

'Come on,' Gideon said. 'Get your things together. The car's outside. I'll drop you there.'

With a shake of her dark hair, she jumped up and began shoving fistfuls of belongings into bags.

'Wait,' Taras said. He wanted to thrust Gideon aside. But what was he going to do? Insist on accompanying her him-self, by tube? 'I'll come with you.'

'It's a two-seater, Flounder.' Gideon passed Katya a hand-ful of underwear and a *Little Mermaid* notebook.

She didn't even look at Taras as they left. The door banged shut, leaving him alone. He stuck his head out of the open window, hoping the cold air would clear it. What did Gideon mean about the rent? Taking his mobile out of his pocket, he dialled Mr Banerjee's home number.

'Household of Banerjee.'

'Mami?'

'Taraşhu!' She sounded delighted. 'Deepak and I are just talking about you.'

'Oh. Is he there?'

'Yes, of course. You wish to be speaking?'

'No! No, no. I just wanted to ask you . . . Mami, the rent on our flat. It was five hundred pounds, wasn't it?'

There was a pause. 'You know this, Taraşhu. Why asking?'

'Mami, why would Gideon Bartlett say we were living there rent-free?'

More silence. Taras thought he could hear Mr Banerjee's voice in the background. The cold air was making his ears ache. He closed the window and noticed something glitter on the carpet. As he bent down to pick it up, his mother came back on the line. 'No need for speaking with Bartletts,' she hissed.

'Mami . . .'

'Rent money in past now.' Still in a low voice, as if she didn't want to be overheard.

'Mami . . .'

'Come for dinner tomorrow, pourchi.' Back to normal volume. 'Bring shirts for ironing. And blue sock for darning. Big hole in heel.'

She hung up, leaving him none the wiser about the rent. It didn't make any sense. A suspicion arose. Could Mr Banerjee . . . no, it was ridiculous. He wouldn't . . . but what if . . . what if? His fist tightened around the object he'd picked up from the carpet. He would confront Mami tomorrow and make her tell him the truth. Unclenching his fingers, he found Katya's butterfly hair-grip twinkling back at him. Why had he let Gideon take her away? What if he pounced on her, like Jamal had? He'd admitted he held a grudge against Taras, maybe that was his real plan for revenge. Taras knew he hadn't reacted well to Katya's

197

bombshell, but it was just that she'd sprung it on him. If only he'd had more warning, he could have dealt with it better. He took out his phone and dialled her number. It rang out without reply. Shit. Shit, shit, shit. He'd messed up again.

CHAPTER THIRTY-FOUR

Taras overslept the next morning and was relieved to find Astrid had already left for work. He cornered Roy in the kitchen and complained, 'It was just a magazine. I haven't committed a crime or anything.'

'Yeah,' Roy's eyes were bleary, as though he hadn't slept. 'She's a bit emotional at the moment. Working too hard. Just let it go.'

'Mmm.' Taras reached for the Weetabix. It wasn't the same as having Mami's *mamaliga*; he was putting on weight because he couldn't make it through to lunch without a mid-morning Tracker or Bounty. 'I texted Katya twice, but she hasn't replied. Do you think she's ignoring me?'

'I heard a joke on the radio this morning. Want to hear it?' Roy didn't wait for Taras's shrug. 'If a man is alone in the forest, with no woman to hear him, is he still wrong?'

'Ha.' They'd run out of milk again. He'd have to make the Weetabix with water.

'Listen, Kroheman, don't take this the wrong way, but you're going to have to find somewhere else to crash.'

'What?' Taras dropped the cereal packet. 'Because of a stupid magazine?'

Roy made a sketchy gesture in the air. 'Just . . . this isn't a good time. Look, you don't have to go right now. We're going to go away next week. Take that holiday early. Just find somewhere else by the time we're back, OK?'

Taras was devastated. He brooded about it all the way to

Bank, where he changed tube and spent the rest of the journey thinking up convincing excuses for being late.

Sneaking into the office via the back entrance, he found the first person he met was Colin. Great, no need to be cool. 'Is he here yet?'

'Who?'

'Leo Harding!' Who else? How could Colin be so dense?

'Yep. The Chief took him round and introduced him to everyone.'

Oh shit. 'Do you think he noticed I wasn't there?'

Colin ran a hand through cobwebbed remnants of hair. 'Yep.'

'What did he say?'

A shrug as one hand rested on a skeletal hip. 'The Chief pointed out your desk, and Leo said, "So where's Tear-ass?" Then Jamal said . . .'

Shit, shit. 'What?'

'. . . He said you might have nipped out to have a fag. And Leo looked surprised, and the Chief said "That doesn't have quite the same connotation here, you know."'

'What the hell did Jamal say that for?' Taras was incensed. 'I don't even smoke.'

He rushed through to his desk, and found Lisa filling in a testing schedule sheet. Her hair looked frizzier and the broken veins on her cheeks redder than usual, or perhaps Taras was just seeing things from a more objective perspective, imagining what Leo would make of all this. He wished she didn't have that photo-frame of her kids: two gawping, funnel-faced adolescents. It looked so middle-aged.

'Oh, there you are, Taras love.' She looked up. 'Leo Harding's just been round.'

'I know,' Taras said grimly. 'I've already heard what Jamal said.'

Lisa giggled, with a snorting sound. 'Apparently beaver is quite rude in America, did you know that?'

Beaver?! 'What are you talking about?'

'Jamal said it was funny you weren't here, you're usually such an eager beaver. And . . .'

Oh God. Taras looked round the office and found Jamal by the coffee machine, looking sleek in his jeans. He directed an evil glare that way until Jamal felt the force of it and turned. A broad grin split his face and he lifted a crutch to execute a cock–aim–and–fire gesture at Taras, who hurried over.

'What the hell are you playing at?'

Jamal didn't bother denying it. 'Just having a bit of fun, mate.'

'You might have another job to go to, but I haven't! It's not a joke.'

'Chill, my man, chill. No harm done. The stupid Merkin doesn't get anything I say anyway.'

'Shush.' Over his shoulder, Taras saw a large ruddy-faced stranger approaching. He wore a suit, but no tie, and his open shirt–collar revealed a neck as thick as a tree-trunk.

'Hey, Tear-ass. Good to meet'cha at last.'

'Leo! Mr Harding! Sir!' Taras narrowly avoided saluting.

'We need you over here, Tear-ass. This Francis guy's just talkin' out of his ass. I'm runnin' out of patience.'

This was it. His big chance. Every other part of his life might be crashing around him, but his career was poised for take-off. Full of purposeful determination, Taras strode after Leo and wondered how best to avoid talking out of his ass.

Leo breezed through everything like a whirlwind. In ten minutes, he had the entire office assembled for a team update. The Chief gave a long, digressive and unconvincing introduction about the aims and ideals with which he'd founded IBS, and how well they sat with a big, hungry American take-over. Blah, blah, blah. Taras's fingers tight-ened over the sparkly hair-grip in his pocket. What business did Gideon have muscling in like that? Taras was Katya's boyfriend, it was his job to sort her out. Was he still Katya's boyfriend? He'd sent three more texts, and still no response.

Now Leo was rising to his feet, grabbing Taras's attention. Heavy-set and ruddy-faced, he dominated the room with a physical energy that the Chief completely lacked. 'No point beating yourselves up over what's gone by,' he drawled.

Jamal elbowed Taras and muttered, 'Can we beat up Francis, though?' but Taras ignored him.

'But now things are gonna be different round here.' Leo hammered the point home with a shake of his fist. 'We're gonna be go-getters! We're gonna make shit happen!'

Yes! Taras thought. Yes! Yes! He was going to be different too. Go-getting, dynamic, making shit happen.

Next Francis was huffing and puffing at the front. 'I won't beat about the bush,' he said. 'Costs will have to be cut . . .'

What was it with beating today, Taras wondered. Francis should trim his nose-hair. Did no one ever tell him that? Mr Banerjee trimmed his. Taras had seen an electric prong device in his bathroom. How could his mother marry a man who needed to trim his nose hair?

Leo was on his feet again. '. . . night out to get to know all you guys.'

There hadn't been time to organise anything yet. Hopefully Leo wouldn't . . .

'So, Tear-ass, let's hear the plans.'

. . . he would. Shit. Taras pushed himself up and glanced round for inspiration. He saw Jamal fold his arms and smirk. 'Well. The plan is . . . er . . . the arrangements are . . .' It wasn't his fault, he hadn't had time. '. . . Not to beat around your bush, er . . .'

There was a stir. What? He glanced round, surprised. Jamal was shaking silently, hand gripping his mouth. What had he said? Oh shit. He'd just made a tit of himself in front of Leo. '. . . I mean, not to beat up a bush . . .'

202

Now Colin was chirruping with laughter, Lisa too. It was spreading. Only the Chief and Francis were po-faced. Taras couldn't look at Leo.

'You're giving us the comedy act here, Tear-ass?' A massive paw slapped his shoulder. 'Hey, Francis, you gotta be careful what you say in front of this guy.'

Leo thought he'd done it deliberately. Taras exhaled with relief. Francis was glaring at him, but it didn't matter. Leo thought he was being funny. He *was* funny. Now he felt calm and confident. 'There'll be dinner and drinks,' he told everyone. 'Details to follow by email.'

'Yee-ha!' Leo crowed. 'It's gonna be a great night, guys. All on my dollar. Any questions, see Tear-ass here. He's the man with the plan.'

'So, man, what's the plan?' Jamal mocked, when they were back at their desks. 'Or isn't there one?'

'What's it to you? You resigned, so you're not coming.' Taras said. 'And it's all in hand.' Only it wasn't. Two days to go, and he'd done sod-all. Stabbing the internet icon on his screen, he then spent twenty minutes surfing Toptable. It didn't help: he couldn't tell which places were naff and which were cool. Maybe they were all naff. The best person to talk to, clearly, was Jamal. But Taras wasn't going to lower himself to beg for help from a girlfriend-molesting scumbag.

'You'll arse it up.' Jamal had flicked his chair into recline mode, and was buried behind the *Metro*.

Taras thought so too. What if it was a crap night? All the good work with Leo would be wasted. The Chief would be disappointed. Francis would be cock-a-hoop. Oh shit, he hadn't sent that document they wanted yesterday. Asap, Francis had said. To annoy him, Taras put only the Chief's name in the 'To' field and relegated Francis to 'Cc' status, making it clear he was a mere bystander in the conversation.

The *Metro* rustled. 'Want some help?'

'No.' Taras went back to the internet and tried googling 'cool bar London'. A load of tourist sites. Anyway, a place that really was cool wouldn't list itself as 'cool bar', would it?

'Tell you what. Make sure I'm on the list, and I'll sort it for you. Bookings, guest list, all that.'

'You've quit,' Taras pointed out. 'Francis isn't going to let you come.'

'Not up to Fucknugget, is it? You're in with Leo, you can swing it.'

Taras made a show of thinking it over, resenting the fact he had no choice. Was he compromising his principles? But Jamal did say that Katya had made a move on him. He was lying, obviously. She wouldn't have done that. But maybe there had been some sort of misunderstanding. 'OK. But you'd better make sure it's a top night. I've got a lot riding on it.'

CHAPTER THIRTY-FIVE

At dinner with his mother and Mr Banerjee, Taras felt like a gooseberry. Not because there was any canoodling taking place – heaven forbid – but because of something unseen, unspoken, that just hung in the air, telling him he was no longer the centre of his mother's world. In a new two-piece outfit of duck-egg blue with cream trimming, she was bustling in and out of the dining area.

'Take more *tokanitza*, Deepak. Sauce is containing Indian spice for extra taste.'

The stew tasted wrong to Taras. Any idea of adapting traditional recipes for non-Bukovinian palates should have been anathema to his mother.

'Thank you, Maria.' Mr Banerjee inclined his head in a way which Taras found unbearably slow and irritating. 'By the way, I have bought a new bulb for the bedside lamp in your room, to replace the one you have said is flickering. I will fit it for you.'

Was this being said for Taras's benefit, to underline the fact that no sin was being lived in? It was hard to tell. He scrutinised Mr Banerjee's chunky jaw chewing on a spicy chunk of cabbage, and the only conclusion he drew was that Mr Banerjee did not like the taste either. He was eating it out of what? Politeness? Love? Taras looked back at his mother. She was beaming across the table at them both. And she was wearing eyeshadow. He searched for something nice to tell her. 'I think I've got a good chance of being promoted at work,' he said finally. 'This American takeover could work out very well for me.'

In the afternoon, Leo had brought him into a top-level meeting with Francis and the Chief and two important-looking faces on video-conference from the States. Though the on-screen gestures of the Americans were jerky and their voices had lagged behind the mouth-movements, Taras had been impressed by their sheer decisiveness. A dozen issues seemed to be pummelled into submission in as many minutes. It was nothing like the weekly team meeting run by Francis. At one point, a mouthing American face asked Francis what he'd done about the increase in client complaints after the last release.

'Well . . .' Francis uncrossed his disproportionately puny legs, then crossed them again. 'Obviously I flagged it on the weekly status weport.'

'Yeah,' mouthed the American face, followed a second later by the voice. 'And . . . ?'

'And . . . I passed it upwards.' Francis glanced at the Chief, who looked away, distancing himself.

'Passed it upwards,' said the American face, then the voice. 'Ri-ight.'

Leo caught Taras's eye and gave him a meaningful look, which Taras returned. The moment of camaraderie was no less sweet for its acid undertone of uncertainty: Taras didn't know what else he would have done in Francis's situation. The IBS process was to pass things on. But if the Chief wasn't stepping in to explain this, then neither was Taras.

'We could set up client-resolution teams,' Taras said instead. 'With the responsibility to follow through a complaint until the client's satisfied.'

'Every darn employee should be a client-resolution team,'

said the American face. Taras saw the word 'darn' before he heard it, and froze. Had he made a mistake?

But it seemed to be OK. 'Good job, Tear-ass,' Leo said at the end of the meeting. 'You got the idea. Go balls-out to keep the customer happy. Thay-att's whut it's about.'

It wasn't an image Taras relished, but he lapped up the praise.

'I'm organising an office night out on Thursday,' he told his mother. 'My chance to really impress Leo Harding.'

'Thursday?' The tell-tale line appeared between his mother's eyes.

'Sure,' Taras said. He'd picked this up from Leo, it sounded much cooler than a plain 'Yes'.

His mother looked at Mr Banerjee. A silent communication passed between them.

'What?' Taras didn't like being left out. 'What's the matter?'

There was a pause, while Mr Banerjee finished his mouthful. 'Taras, perhaps your mother forgot to mention to you the date of our engagement dinner.'

'Oh, sh-shish.' Taras managed to convert his original choice of word to something more harmless. Of course his mother hadn't forgotten. And of course Mr Banerjee knew she hadn't. She'd said the fourth. And Thursday was . . . he counted on his fingers. Yes. The fourth.

'Taraşhu, it is very important occasion. Many relatives of Deepak making journey to come. Uncle, sister, nephews, all.'

And the only relative his mother could call on to support her was himself. Taras knew that. But the date for this office night out was set: it was the last night before Leo flew back. It couldn't be changed. 'Mami, you don't understand, this is work.'

Usually there was no stronger call he could make. His

mother venerated his career above all things. But for once, her frown did not ease. He could see this really mattered to her. It was a shock. Their interests had never diverged before.

'Maybe I can change the night,' he said, without much hope. 'I'll see what I can do.'

She took this as confirmation he would be there. Her smile returned.

After dinner, Mr Banerjee disappeared into the kitchen. Taras saw his chance to talk to his mother, but she said briskly, 'Come now, pourchi. Time to be helping. Dishes for drying.'

Taras was stunned. He had never been asked to do this before. A stiff, new tea-towel, embossed with views of Buckingham Palace, was pushed into his hand and he took his place next to Mr Banerjee, who was immersed up to the elbows in soapy water, meticulously rinsing each item. He'd taken off his cardigan, and underneath the apron he was wearing to protect his clothes, was a tailored shirt with lurid green and yellow spiral swirls.

'Is something the matter, Taras?' Mr Banerjee had noticed him staring.

'Mami made that shirt, didn't she?' Taras hated these violently coloured creations and tried to avoid wearing them, but seeing one on Mr Banerjee's rotund frame felt like a betrayal.

Mr Banerjee smiled fondly and passed him a wet plate. 'Your mother is very talented. I am thinking of giving her a new sewing machine. As a wedding present.'

A wedding present! Taras couldn't get his mind off the words. They made all this sound real and permanent.

'Of course she will not need to sew for other people any more. But I think she has too much talent to wish to stop altogether. There is a model I have looked at in John Lewis. It is electric and comes in different colours. I thought perhaps sunshine yellow. What is your view?'

Taras had grown up seeing his mother's head bent over the battered khaki beast, one stockinged foot pushing rhythmically against its metal claw. 'I don't think she wants a new machine,' he said.

Mr Banerjee looked disappointed. 'Well, perhaps you are right.' He held a patterned side plate under the tap to rinse, then passed it to Taras, who rubbed it against the face of a Coldstream Guard.

Who did Mr Know-it-all Banerjee think he was? Pushing his way between Taras and his mother. As if anyone wanted him here with his stupid big belly and his round balding head. He could just . . .

'Careful, pourchi.' His mother bustled back. 'Not to be banging dishes like such. Expensive china and also matching set.'

And how exactly had he paid for it? Taras followed her out of the room and cornered her behind the dining table. 'Mami, I need to talk to you.'

His loud whisper made her stare. 'What is matter, pourchi? Trouble with throat? Wait, I am making salt water gargle.'

'No, no!' He clutched at the cream trim on her jacket, and raised his voice slightly. 'It's about the rent on our flat.'

Her black eyebrows scissored together. Taras saw her glance at Mr Banerjee's shadowy outline through the rippled glass in the kitchen door.

'I think Mr Banerjee kept the money. Gideon said there wasn't any rent. But we paid Mr Banerjee.' It was obvious. Imagine the things they could have done with an extra five hundred pounds a month.

'What is this foolishness?'

'I'll talk to Gideon. The Bartletts have been defrauded too, he took the money in their name.'

'No, no and no.' She wheeled round, a deep groove in her forehead. 'I forbid for talking to Bartletts. Not father

Bartlett, not son Bartlett. No trouble-causing Bartletts. Are you understanding me?'

'Maria?' Mr Banerjee put his head through the door. 'Is everything all right?'

'I'm just saying goodbye,' Taras said. He wasn't going to dry any more expensive plates for this thief and fraudster.

They both came to the door with him. Taras looked back from the street and saw them framed in the white hall light: Mami leaning into Mr Banerjee's portly frame.

But he stole money from us! Taras wanted to shout. All the way back to East Croydon station, his feet tapped out the rhythm: 'stole money from us, stole money from us'. How could Mami marry this man? He must save her.

On the train he made his decision. He had to override Mami's command, for her own good. This was how he could show her he was a man. And Gideon would give them back the flat. It was all coming together. He'd save Mami from the predator's claws and bring her home again. She'd be grateful. Pulling out his phone, he tapped in a new message:

Need talk urgently your mother and mr b fraud

Sent. He felt the clarity that comes with taking action. He was dynamic. A go-getter. A Leo Harding kind of guy.

A moment later, it occurred to him that for Mami to move back into the flat, Katya would now have to move out. Who would Taras go with? Mami, or Katya? Was the choice even his any more?

Further down the carriage, two drunken teenagers were snogging: all burger breath and groping hands. Taras averted his head and stared out at the yellow lights beyond the blackness of the train window. Reflected in the glass, the flickering shapes of the young couple had a passionate intensity that their real bodies lacked. He didn't know why seeing this gave him such a pang.

CHAPTER THIRTY-SIX

At London Bridge, Taras made a second decision. Exiting the concourse, he stopped to buy flowers. Ideally he wanted a single rose, but they were only selling them by the half-dozen, and he didn't want to seem cheap, so he got two bunches. Down past the hospital stairs, and up the street towards home. Towards the flat anyway. It wasn't home now. He saw his mother again, in that rectangle of light, with Mr Banerjee's hand on her shoulder, turning away.

The dark street felt cold, lonely. He took out his key and unlocked the door.

'Katya!' he called. He didn't want to scare her. But the flat was unlit and silent. For a moment, he panicked. Had she disappeared, like his mother? He checked the bedroom and breathed out in relief: her bags were there, spilling clothes and books over the floor.

That was strange. Katya's belongings in his bedroom. He felt like a ghost watching someone else live his life. The Russell Crowe poster was still curling on the back of the door: he felt pleased that Katya hadn't removed it and then a touch jealous in case she was enjoying looking at it too much.

Where was she? He sat on the bed, clasping the flowers, and checked the time on his phone. Nine thirty. When would she be back? He needed to unburden himself about this situation with Mr Banerjee. If Roy hadn't been so insensitive about asking Taras to move out, he'd have called him.

When Katya came home, they could cuddle up. And then . . . but it might be an hour or two before she came back. And she wouldn't want to cuddle up. They'd have to talk; he'd have to apologise for not being quicker off the mark at Roy's place. A yawn stretched through him.

An idea struck. Brilliant! The situation called for a grand romantic gesture. He turned out the light and stripped off his clothes, deciding at the last minute to keep his briefs on. He didn't want to unnerve her. Her heart would be warmed by the sight of him curled up and waiting. Carefully, he arranged the roses on the pillow beside him. First he fanned them out, then he laid them in a heart shape. Even better. He was glad he'd got twelve now. The bed was wonderfully soft after sleeping on a futon for so many nights. How did Japanese people manage? They must have spines of steel. Katya's sheets were pretty: embroidered daisies. Though she hadn't starched them, like Mami always did. He closed his eyes. How many times since hitting puberty had he dreamed of a woman here, in his bed? Not long to wait.

A dim thudding penetrated the fog of Taras's sleep. He rolled over and yelped as rose thorns ripped his neck. Aaagh! He was bleeding. Jerking up, he shivered as bed-warm flesh met frigid air. The thudding had been Katya's footsteps. Now she was opening the front door. Did she know he was here? Why hadn't she come to bed? It was daylight. He pressed a pillow to his injured cheek and checked his phone. Nearly 9 a.m. He'd slept for more than twelve hours.

Who was at the door? He could hear a voice. Male. His mind jumped to the geriatric ponytail: was he on the scene again? Or Jamal? Had he been telling the truth about Katya's behaviour in the cab? Maybe she'd called him, and . . . The voice was getting closer, mixed with Katya's own. Were they coming into the bedroom? Not wanting to be caught in just his underpants, Taras leapt up and clutched the first thing that came to hand. Katya's dressing gown. He scrambled it on, wincing at the frills. But they passed the door, and went on up the stairs to the kitchen.

Easing open the door, he crept after them, still clutching his phone. He needed to know what was going on. Music clicked on: a clunking great radio-cassette player that Katya had bought from a market stall for three quid. It masked any sounds as Taras hovered by the doorway. Katya was boiling water in a saucepan and the intruder was reaching a box of teabags down from a cupboard.

Thick blond hair. It wasn't geriatric ponytail. Or Jamal. The face turned into profile and Taras stepped back behind the door.

'It is very kind of you to bring me the television.'

'It's an old set. Ma had it in her room while she was ill. You might as well get some use out of it.'

'You must miss your mother very much, I am sorry.' Her voice was warm and quiet: hardly audible above the radio. Had she moved closer to Gideon? Perhaps touched him? Taras felt a stab of jealousy.

'I hadn't seen her for a long time,' Gideon said, sounding non-committal.

'I did not talk to my father before he died. He drank too much, always, and I did not forgive him.'

Whenever she was annoyed with Taras, Katya would accuse him of being worse than her father. He'd never taken it seriously. After all, if she nagged him, he might tell her she was just like Mami. But that was affection, not hostility. He didn't know she didn't like her father.

'Your mother loved you though,' Katya said. 'She made a will to leave you all her belongings.'

'Mmm. Maybe she was just angry with Dad.'

'Why?'

'Nothing. It doesn't matter.'

'Are you angry with *her*?'

213

'Why would you say that?'

'Your face, it is all . . .' She struggled for a word. 'Locked. Like a door. Shut very tight.'

'She used her money to manipulate people. And she's still doing it, from the grave.'

'I do not understand.'

'Her will. It left everything to me, but under one condition. That I go back to the church. Train to be a Salvation Army officer.'

'Officer?'

'Like a minister. It was always her ambition for me.'

'Ohhh.' Katya considered. 'I do not know very much about religion.'

'I know more than enough.'

'Then you do not believe in it?'

A pause. The radio announcer introduced the next song. Gideon must have shaken his head.

'That is easy then.'

'Let the money go? I've been living off Ma all my life. Even when I disappeared off to America, she still gave me an allowance. A pretty generous one. I don't know the first thing about supporting myself.' There was another pause, and he said, 'What?'

Katya hadn't spoken. She must have made a face. Taras could picture it: the expressive little pucker of the lips. 'This is not very manly.'

'Ha!' Gideon sounded as if he'd been punched. After a while he said, 'The first time we met, you called me a pig. Now I'm less than a man. I suppose that's progress of a sort.'

Was he about to make a move on her? Taras wanted to swoop in to interrupt them, but he couldn't let Gideon see him in a dressing gown for the second time. Especially this one. It was embroidered with humming birds. He'd go downstairs and put his clothes on first.

'Progress?'

'Never mind. Have you spoken to Taras? I got a weird text from him last night.'

No way was Taras leaving the doorway now. He tightened the scalloped belt on the dressing gown and leaned closer.

'He is here.'

'Here!' Gideon sounded startled. Taras was delighted.

'I come back and I find Taras snoring drunk in my bed. So I have to sleep on floor in living room.'

He hadn't been drunk! That was his big romantic gesture! Why did she have to jump to the worst conclusion?

'Do you want me to get rid of him?'

What!

'No-oo.' Katya sounded half-hearted. 'He is big stupid, but he loves me, I think. Was it about me that he sent you text?'

A long musical interlude. Taras wondered why Gideon was keeping quiet and then realised that he must be showing her the message. They must be standing very close together to do that. Clamping his hands to the wall for balance, he tried to crane his head round to see.

'That is very strange,' Katya said. Taras jerked his head back. 'What does it mean?'

'No idea.'

'It does not make any sense. What is em-ar-bee fraud?'

'Still no idea,' Gideon said.

'And I do not understand this about "our mother".'

Thank God this new phone saved sent messages. Taras pulled his phone out and scrolled down. There it was, blinking back at him:

Need talk urgently our mother and mrb fraud

What? That wasn't what he'd written! Well, not what he'd meant to write, anyway. Still, it was just a slip of the finger. Two slips. But surely that should be easy enough to work out, for anyone with half a brain.

Apparently not. 'Whose mother does it mean?' Katya

sounded baffled. 'You and Taras do not have the same mother.'

'No,' Gideon said, a sardonic edge back in his voice. 'Though certain other combinations had occurred to me.'

'What?' said Katya.

What? thought Taras.

'Nothing,' Gideon said. 'I'd better go. Tell Taras to ring me when he sobers up.'

What did he mean? Taras's mind raced as the radio chattered on.

'Wait. I have something for you. On top of fridge.'

'What are you doing?' Gideon's voice. 'Careful!'

The radio cut out, leaving a resounding silence.

'You knocked out the lead.' Gideon again. 'Let me get that . . .'

Scraping, clambering sounds. Then a sudden 'oops' from Katya, then a thump and a half-grunt as if Gideon had just been winded. Taras couldn't bear it any longer: he rushed into the doorway – Gideon was on the floor, head against a cupboard and Katya was spread-eagled across him, denim skirt riding high over red tights. The fridge door flapped open above the counter. She must have climbed up and slipped.

'Get off her!' Taras roared, swooping down on them like an avenging angel, frilly dressing gown flapping round his thighs. 'Get off her now!'

'Oh, Taras!' Katya began to giggle. 'You look very sweet.'

'Technically, Flounder,' Gideon pointed out, dropping his head back to the floor, 'she's going to have to get off me.'

'So, what's on top of the fridge anyway?' Ten minutes later, Taras was still sulking. They had both treated his intervention as a joke.

'Oh . . . chocolate,' Katya said.

'Chocolate?'

'Russian hospitality. I cannot just offer tea. Chocolate is all I have.'

'Why is it on top of the fridge?' Gideon was leaning against the counter, green eyes glinting against lightly tanned skin. This new, relaxed mood suited him; he looked younger.

'To hide from Taras, of course. He is here, with hangover, he will eat all my chocolate.'

Gideon's loud whoop of laughter added to Taras's aggrievance, but Katya was already asking, 'What does your message mean? What is "mrb fraud"?'

'Not mrb,' he said impatiently. 'Mr B. Mr Banerjee.'

The smile died from Gideon's face as Taras explained. 'Fraud? Ma's solicitor has been stealing money?' His voice was tight with anger. 'Are you sure about this?'

'I can't prove it.' Taras backpedalled in the face of Gideon's fury. He hadn't expected to be taken seriously with such speed. 'But I think so.'

'My God. No wonder he's keeping so tight-lipped about her affairs. All that guff about her wishes for privacy.' Thrusting his hands in his pockets, Gideon paced the kitchen. 'Wait till Dad hears this!'

'Oh, your poor mama,' Katya exclaimed. 'She is marrying a thief.'

'Marrying?' Gideon looked up in disbelief. 'Your mother's marrying Banerjee?' His eyes were cold with suspicion. 'What are they up to?'

Taras was slow to cotton on. 'Up to?'

'Are they working together on Dad? What . . . ? Wait a minute.' He rubbed his jaw. 'Let me think.'

'Mami?' Taras's voice rose. He was outraged. 'Of course she's not up to anything. We're the victims here. What are you suggesting?'

'I've got to go.' Gideon's face was hard again. 'Don't say anything to your mother, Flounder. Or to Banerjee. I'll be in touch.' He strode out of the kitchen, and they heard the internal door slam, then a moment later, the communal front door.

'How dare he?' Taras turned to Katya. 'What does he mean about Mami?'

'I do not know.' She was puzzled. 'He has a lot of anger inside, I think. Building up pressure. Boom!'

'And what were you doing on top of him?'

'Oh, Taras. Are you jealous?' Katya giggled again. 'You look so funny. Big hairy legs.' She patted one.

He brushed her off. 'I'm going to get dressed.'

'Oh, do not be cross.' She followed him out of the room. 'It was very sweet, how you rushed to defend me.'

Taras stomped down the stairs to the bedroom and pulled on his trousers. Katya held out his shirt and he whipped it from her hand without a word. It was quite nice having her run after him, for a change.

'What is this on my pillow?' she wanted to know. 'It is blood!'

He showed her the thorn scratch on his neck. She looked at the roses and counted them. 'Who is dead?'

'What?'

'Taras, in Russia an even number of flowers means a funeral. It is very unlucky. Did your mother never tell you that?'

Mami was full of superstitions, but he didn't know that one. With a hint of shame, he realised that he'd never seen her receive flowers. Certainly not from him. 'I was just trying to be romantic,' he said. Nothing turned out the way he meant it. 'And I wasn't drunk, I just wanted to be with you.'

'Ahh. That is very sweet.'

He wished she'd stop using that word. Dynamic go-getters weren't sweet. 'I'm moving back here with you, Katya. It's not safe for you on your own.'

'You are coming to protect me?'

'Don't you want me here?' He kissed her.

'It is very lonely by myself,' she admitted. 'But Taras, I cannot be going backwards and forwards like this all the time. I need someone that I can depend on.'

'You can depend on me.' Saying it made him feel strong. 'How much money do you owe Carlos?'

'Two thousand pounds.'

Taras whistled.

'But that is not all. I have to pay for loss of scholarship also, and money to bank.'

'How much?' He felt manly. 'I'll sort it out.'

'Twelve thousand pounds. It is a lot, I know.'

More than eight months of his salary, after tax. He had no idea she owed so much. He gaped at her. 'Katya!'

'I need help, very much.'

'What's that smell?' He sniffed. 'Something's burning.'

'Oh!' She leapt up. 'The water is still on the stove!'

They ran into the kitchen and found the saucepan had boiled dry: it was blackened and bent.

'Never mind.' Taras switched off the gas. 'Let's have some of that chocolate.'

'Chocolate?' She stared at him as if he was mad.

'On top of the fridge. I'll get it.' He reached up on tiptoe.

'Taras, there is not any chocolate. I made it up.'

His hand felt something. An envelope. He reached it down. His mother's handwriting: 'Mr E. Bartlett.' He'd seen it before. The one with the keys.

'We found it when Gideon brought me here last night. He pulled out the keys and gave them to me. But later, when throwing away, I saw there was something else in the envelope.'

Taras was already feeling inside. A square of newspaper rolled inside a ring. His mother's wedding ring. The one that had been removed to make room for Mr Banerjee's ruby.

'Your mother meant it for Mr Bartlett. So I thought I should give it to Gideon. But then you came running in to rescue me. So I waited, to show you.'

The paper was old and soft, wedged tight inside the ring: an edge ripped as Taras tugged it free. 'Have you looked at this?'

She shook her head. It was a page from the *South London Press*. September 15, 1981. Taras's eye scanned across, stopping at a paragraph near the bottom edge, by the tear.

Tower Bridge Suicide

A body found last week floating in the Thames has been formally identified as East German immigrant, Sigismund Krohe. Krohe, 24, of Southwark, had been married just ten months and was last seen by his wife, Maria, 23, last Monday afternoon. Eyewitnesses saw a young man of his description behaving 'wildly' on Tower Bridge shortly after midnight. It is thought that Krohe jumped from the bridge and drowned. No other parties are being sought in connection with the incident.

1981. Taras hadn't been born until January of 1982. Taking his wallet out of his trousers, Taras fumbled for the newsprint picture of his father. He laid it down beside the paragraph he had just read. The torn edges matched exactly. Mami had torn out the picture from Sigi's death notice, and given it to him as a keepsake. He shivered.

'What is this?' Katya looked over his shoulder. 'Is this your father? Why is your mother sending this to Elliott Bartlett?'

Taras didn't answer. In his head, he heard Gideon's sardonic voice again: '*Certain other combinations had occurred to me.*'

CHAPTER THIRTY-SEVEN

Taras was late into work again, but it didn't matter because Leo and the Chief were out all day in meetings with IBS clients. He sauntered in, giving Francis a nod. The corpulent cheeks were sagging today: perhaps the strain of being on the way out was getting to him. Taras almost pitied him, but there were more important things to be done. His mind was on power-drive: he needed chocolate to fuel it. Scoring a Dairy Milk and a Kit Kat from the machine, he slid into his desk just as Lisa came back from a system test meeting.

'Nearly two hours long,' she said brightly. 'That really was a *testing* meeting, ha ha.'

Taras ignored her. She'd come out with that so many times it didn't count as a joke any more. He saw Jamal hobbling over from the programmers' compound. He'd managed to get a suit over his cast today. It looked like a new one: a pearlescent grey that shone against his dark skin, with a pale yellow tie and a high collar.

'Jammy git,' Taras said. 'Why should he be the one to get a new job?'

'Well, he had the get-up-and-go to apply for it, for a start.' Lisa peeled cling-film off a Hob-Nob. 'And he probably interviews ever so well. He's very charming. And so well-dressed. Plus he's quite good at his job, when he takes the trouble. And . . .'

'Yes, all right.' Taras bit down hard on his Dairy Milk and tried to apply his mind to the bigger issue. What could make a newly married twenty-four-year-old with a baby on the way so desperate that he leapt off a bridge?

'Hey, Cow-arse.' Jamal reached them and paused to rest on his crutches for a moment before lowering himself into the chair. 'Fancy getting us a brew?'

Taras had no intention of being Jamal's tea-mule. 'Have you sorted Thursday yet?'

'In the bag, my man, in the bag.'

'You'd better not let me down.'

Jamal gave him a wink, and tapped the unopened Kit Kat. 'Broken through the wrapper yet, mate?' He was insinuating that Taras hadn't got anywhere with Katya. It was doing Taras's head in. If it wasn't for needing Jamal's help with this fucking night out . . .

The desk phone rang. 'Kroheman?'

'Roy! Thank God.'

'Want to watch me buy a fuck-off plasma screen? I'm just in Selfridges.'

'I'll be there.' Taras slammed down the phone and grabbed his coat.

'Where're you off to?' Jamal wanted to know.

'Out.'

Twenty minutes later, he sailed off the bottom of the escalator to find Roy scratching his chin in front of a 60-inch Pioneer.

'That'd look good on the living-room wall,' Taras said, examining the price-tag, and taking a step back when he saw it was over £7,000.

'It would, wouldn't it?' Roy didn't turn around. 'They don't have it in stock, but they're checking the order time.'

'Woah!' Was he serious? 'Aren't you supposed to be saving to buy a house?'

'Jesus Christ.' Roy raked a hand through wiry black curls. 'I mean, how old are we, Kroheman? Haven't we got better things to do than worry about interest rates?'

'Like watching TV?' Taras didn't know why Roy was so keen to throw away money he didn't have. Astrid would kill him. And then she'd probably blame Taras. More importantly, this was a useless place for proper conversation. Sunshine was flooding through the glass doors downstairs. 'Come on. We'll go to Green Park.'

They pushed through the crowds on Oxford Street. A dog seemed to be snarling after them. Taras looked down at Roy's groin. 'Is that you?'

'New ringtone. Cool, huh?'

Was Roy having some sort of mid-life crisis? Quarter-life crisis? Couldn't he see Taras needed to talk? The snarling erupted into furious barks. 'Well, answer it, then.'

Roy dug out the phone. 'Yeah, hi . . . Fine.' Energy drained from his voice. 'Just out . . . With Taras . . . Yeah . . . I don't know. Later . . . Yeah, all right . . . Yeah . . . Bye.' His manner was sullen as he pushed the phone back into his trousers.

'Everything all right?' Taras asked, glad it had been so quick.

'Fan-fuckin-tastic.' Hands stuffed into pockets, Roy shouldered through a bevy of tourists.

Taras had to scuttle to keep up with him. 'Listen. Something weird's happened . . .' But Roy didn't seem to be paying attention. Eyes to the pavement, hand rummaging through black curls, he was sunk in contemplation.

'Are you all right?' There was an edge to Taras's voice. It wasn't pleasant to have your problems ignored.

Roy shrugged. 'I suppose.'

'Good.' They were at the crossing, waiting for a pause in the shuffle of red buses and black cabs. Taras tried to marshal his thoughts. How to explain the grinding suspicion that

Gideon's overheard comment had left? It seemed crazy to put it into words. 'Listen. I'm beginning to wonder . . . It might sound mad, but . . .'

The lights changed and they had to weave around a red-faced woman with twins pummelling each other in a buggy.

'It might sound mad . . .' Taras said again, but Roy was looking back at the red-faced woman. It was hard to see why. Her jeans were slipping down her hips, but not in an attractive way. Kinder to ignore it, really. 'Elliott Bartlett,' Taras said, louder, nudging Roy. 'I think maybe . . .'

He paused as they turned out of the frenzied bargain-basement melée into the more rarified air of New Bond Street. The crowd thinned and it was easier to talk. Roy was already rubbing his chin thoughtfully and looking across at him.

'. . . maybe he might – I know, I know, this sounds crazy—'

'Who wants to buy a place anyway?' Roy interrupted.

'What?'

'It ties you down. I mean, what if I want to move to Australia or something?'

'You're not moving to Australia, are you?' Taras couldn't deal with another shock.

'You're being as literal as Astrid. Christ!' Roy's voice rose. 'I'm just saying, *if* I did. If I wanted to move to Australia, then this would be the age to do it. Live a bit.'

'I suppose.' Taras waited a moment for the air to clear, then went on, 'So Gideon said something, and then I found this newspaper cutting—'

A pulsating tone from his own pocket interrupted him. 'Oh, for God's sake.' He looked at the screen. Jamal.

'Cow-arse, you slacker. We're sorted.'

'What?'

'The plan. For tomorrow night. Come on man, get with it. Gaucho Grill for dinner, then guest list at Light Bar.'

'Isn't Light Bar a bit pretentious?' Taras said impatiently. 'Look, can we talk about this later—'

'Course it is. That's the clever bit. This lot won't like it. They'll all make excuses and drift off to get their trains to Farnham and watch *Inspector Morse*. Then the real fun starts . . .'

Taras's eyes drifted back to Roy, who had slowed down and was frowning at a windowful of snakeskin shoes. Why was everyone being so difficult today? He had this one important thing to discuss, and Roy wouldn't pay attention, while Jamal was butting in at just the wrong moment. Couldn't they be more considerate? Now Roy was nudging him. For God's sake, he'd only been on the phone a moment.

'Look, Jamal. I'll be back in the office soon. Talk then.'

'Wait, I haven't told you—'

'Yeah, bye.' Taras stuffed the phone in his pocket. 'What the fuck's the matter with you?' he demanded as Roy nudged him again. 'Can't you even . . . oh.'

Following the direction of Roy's thumb, he saw that on the other side of the window was a blonde. A sleek, corn-fed blonde with breasts jutting from a slash-fronted dress and one hand raised to tap on the window. Tapping at them. Taras goggled, only just tearing his gaze up towards her face. She flapped her hand, inviting them inwards.

'Anything you want to tell me?' said Roy.

'Don't be stupid. That's Desirée. The Monk's girlfriend. Come on.' Taras was already hurrying up the steps.

The interior of the shop was spacious and wooden, with large mirrors and androgenous staff. It wasn't the kind of place in which Taras felt welcome, but Desirée was perfectly at ease.

'What do you think?' She turned her back to Taras and admired herself side-on in the mirror.

He wasn't sure whether he was being asked to comment on the dress, which was some sort of electric-blue silky flounce, or the expanse of luscious sun-warmed flesh exposed from neck to hip.

'Great,' he said, hedging his bets. In the mirror, he saw her raise an eyebrow. 'I mean . . . Cool . . . er . . . Sexy.'

Oh God, what did he say that for? Still, Desirée gave him a half-smile, though it could have been a mocking one, and turned round.

'I'll take it, I guess,' she said to the assistant, then to Taras, 'What trouble have you been causing?'

'Um, I don't know.' Taras's current trouble was placing his eyes. The dress was so low-cut he could see the swelling undersides of her breasts. How did the material stay put, was there some sort of sticky tape?

'There's a big old argument going on right now, all 'cause of you.' Desirée moved a shoulder strap to flick away some invisible speck and slid into a slatted changing cubicle. There was a gap of a few inches at the bottom. Taras tried not to watch her ankles. 'Hi,' he said to the lurking assistant, who stared impassively past him. Outside the window, Roy was tapping his watch and gesturing impatiently. Taras mouthed 'WAIT!' and turned back.

'Gideon and his daddy just set to like no one ever saw.' Desirée's voice floated through the wooden slats. 'Gideon went right ahead and called that lawyer, Mr Banjo.'

'Banerjee,' Taras said.

'Whatever.' The ankles were stepping into dark trousers. 'He came straight on over, mad as all get-out.'

Oh, God. What had he started?

'So your mom's getting it on with this Banjo guy?' Desirée pushed open the changing-room door. 'Elliott got pretty fired up over that.'

It was easier to look at Desirée now she was wearing trousers and a silk shirt, even though the shirt was skin-tight. She moved to the mirror to examine herself, front and back. Taras and the skinny assistant watched. Desirée undid a button on the shirt. Taras winced. The assistant managed to shoot a sneer at him before gushing at Desirée. 'So stylish. Not many people can carry off animal print, but with your figure . . .'

'Yeah.' Desirée smoothed a complacent hand over her hip and looked at Taras. 'Gideon gave me his credit card, sent me out shopping. Wanted to finish that fight in peace, I guess.'

'Shall I put it to one side with the rest?' Skinny wasn't giving up.

'Oh, I don't know.' Desirée pouted. 'Where am I going to wear any of this stuff anyway? Gideon never takes me anywhere. For a guy who's just inherited seven million bucks, he's pretty miserable.'

'Maybe because his mother just died?' Roy, tired of waiting, had stomped into the shop.

Taras frowned at him, but Desirée was unperturbed. 'They weren't close.'

'Hmm.' Roy was about to speak again but Taras elbowed him aside. 'Uh, Desirée, I know somewhere you could wear this stuff. Light Bar. Tomorrow. My boss is financing a night out. You and Gideon could come.'

'For real?' Desirée's face broke into the first genuine smile he'd seen. It was overpowering. All those sparkling, perfectly even, white teeth, only just held in by the stretch of immaculate pink-lined lips. Taras blinked at the onslaught, but managed to stammer out, 'Yes, absolutely. It's on the firm.' He'd swing it with Leo.

'Guess I'll take it all then,' Desirée said, and the skinny assistant jumped into action.

Taras turned back to Roy. 'You could come too. And Astrid.'

'Hey, thanks,' Roy said sourly. 'Don't want to interrupt your fun with your new friends.'

227

'No, you don't understand.' Taras looked round to make sure Desirée wasn't listening. Drawing Roy into a corner behind a rack of sequinned halter-tops, he hissed, 'I think Elliott Bartlett is my real father!'

Roy's face didn't change. 'Right.'

'Didn't you hear me? I said, I think—'

'Yeah, yeah.'

Taras couldn't believe it. How significant did something have to be before Roy got excited? 'Don't you get it? His wife found out. That's why she made the will leaving everything to Gideon. And no wonder Elliott went mad when he found out my mother's living with Mr Banerjee. He's probably still in love with her himself! And—'

'Kroheman, last week you thought Mr Banerjee might be your real father.'

'No I didn't! Well, only for a minute. That wasn't serious.'

'And this is?' Roy scratched the back of his head and took a few steps away, then turned. 'I think you're going off your rocker. You don't have a father. He died when you were a kid and you can't remember him. Tough. Get over it.' And with that, he walked out of the door.

CHAPTER THIRTY-EIGHT

Taras didn't go back to the office. Instead, he headed to London Bridge. He wanted to see Katya, but yet again, she wasn't home. And, what was more, she'd dragged the mattress off her bed and dumped it in the parlour. His bag was on top. Did she mean he should sleep there? Didn't she understand what cohabitation was all about? His mobile chirruped and he grabbed it, thinking it might be her, but it wasn't.

'Taraşhu, what am I telling you? Am I not making clear that you must be staying away from Bartletts? Why must you be nose-poking and trouble-causing? I tell you not to bother with foolishness about rent-paying. I forbid you to be talking to Bartletts. This is words coming from my heart. Are you remembering?'

'Mami . . .'

'Deepak very upset. Accused of many bad things. This is no good. No good at all.'

'I was just thinking of you, Mami. I was worried. He's been stealing from us. I don't want you to be hurt, that's all.'

There was a long pause. Then his mother sighed: a deep, heavy sigh that took him back to childhood. He could see her, in this very room, headscarf over furrowed brow, hands resting in her lap as she faced up to whatever new expense was confronting them. How could Elliott Bartlett have left her to struggle like that all those years? It was cruel.

Luxuriating in that large house with his wealthy, ageing wife, knowing he'd abandoned his young mistress and illegitimate son. Worse than cruel. Vicious. Mami was only twenty-three when Taras was born. Elliott must have been well over forty. He'd taken advantage of her. Overwhelming feelings of loss and betrayal flooded him. Not for himself but for her. It was a new, frightening sensation.

'Deepak very angry. He says that without apology you are not welcome at engagement party. I say I will not have party without Son. So this is finish. No party. Maybe no engagement. He says then Son must apologise and set right.'

'Mami, I'm sorry . . .' Wasn't this what he wanted? But he felt no triumph, only sourness. 'Mami, I can't.' He'd refused to apologise before, and this time was, if anything, even more unpalatable. He wouldn't do it. 'You don't need him. You've got me.'

'Oh pourchi . . .' Her voice choked for a moment. It seemed like forever since she'd called him by that name. 'You are not little child any more. It is time for Mami to letting go.'

A fat tear welled up in the corner of Taras's eye and slithered down the side of his nose. Tightness in his throat made it hard to breathe. He wanted to be little again; to bury his face in her skirt and have her stroke the back of his head, crooning to him till he felt safe and warm. The phone clicked and she was gone. He pressed the hard shell against his ear, wanting it to hurt, biting back the surge of unhappiness he felt.

Then the door creaked, and Katya's face appeared, pale and pixie-like, with untidy hair. She took it all in: the phone, Taras's hunched posture, his wet cheeks. Without saying anything, she slid down on the mattress and clasped her arms around him, laying her head on his shoulder and hugging him from behind. Immediately, the feeling of warmth for which he'd been longing suffused him. He leaned back, letting her enclose him, and shut his eyes. They slipped lower, until they were lying together on the mattress, and he rolled to face her, pressing his mouth over hers, pushing his tongue through her small lips. The familiar smell of her hair; honey and oranges, was all around him.

'Oh God, Katya,' he murmured, reaching his hands under her t-shirt, lifting it up. 'I want you so much.'

She wriggled, letting him drag it over her head. He dug his hands into her waistband, tugging the jeans off. 'I need you,' he muttered, pulling on his own zipper, cramming his suit trousers down, licking the pinkness of her nipples. She squirmed, then twisted; resisting, and he reached both arms around her, putting his lips to her ear. 'I love you,' he whispered, and then her body gave way, opening under him. 'Oh, Katya, Katya, Katya.' The climax was quick and immediate. Afterwards, he held her tight and murmured, 'Thank you.'

'Is OK. You needed, I give.' Her bright brown eyes looked into his.

He felt exhausted, as if all the energy had been bled out of him. With a little sigh, he let go and sank into sleep.

When he woke, hours later, it was dark. Katya was still there, the warmth of her body radiating through his shirt. He could hear the gentle rhythm of her breathing, soft against his shoulder, as his body released back into a dream.

The next time he awakened, the sky was lightening beyond the glow of the street-lamp. He tried to hold still as long as possible, to hold on to the feeling of her snuggled against him, but his shoulder was stiff and his legs were cramping and when he shifted, her eyes blinked open. He twisted his head and saw the momentary blankness before she remembered where she was.

231

'Katya.' His fingers played over her pale wrist. 'I'll help you with the money you owe. I can't give you twelve thousand pounds, but . . .'

'It is more money now.' She sat up, bare arms wrapped round bare knees. 'It is sixteen thousand pounds.'

'What?! How could that happen?'

'I borrow from Russian. Friend of friend. He give me twelve thousand pounds. Cash. I must pay him thirteen hundred pounds every month for one year.'

'But that's outrageous! It's . . .' Taras tried to do the maths in his head and failed. '. . . ridiculously high interest. You could get a bank loan for a fraction of that.'

'You, maybe. Bank will not lend money to me.'

'But this guy, he's robbing you.'

'He is helping me, Taras. I have no options.'

Her passivity frightened him. It was a monstrous amount of money. It loomed over his head: a terrifying burden. Was it really up to him to shoulder it? Her naked skin was a reproach now. He pushed her t-shirt into her lap and turned his head away as she shrugged it on. She wasn't wearing a bra: last night he'd found that erotic; now he wondered if it was because her breasts were small. Her toes brushed against his leg as she wriggled into her knickers, then her hand touched his neck as she got up. Last night hadn't been a trap, had it? Did she think he'd be bound to help her now?

'I can't give you £1,300 a month, Katya. For God's sake. It's more than I earn.'

Padding over to the window, she pulled at the blanket tucked over the empty curtain rod. 'I have an idea.'

He didn't want to hear it. Resentment rushed in. He was entangled in something beyond his control. There was too much going on; it was hard for him to breathe. 'I want things to work out between us, I really do. Why does everything have to be so difficult?' He jumped to his feet, heading to the bathroom. 'I can't talk about this now. I've got a big day today.'

'Taras.' The blanket fell to the ground, and pale light filled the room. Silhouetted against the glass, the slight bow in her bare legs was more obvious than usual. Her hair was kinked on the side where she'd been lying and rumpled on the other: together with her small nose and clean skin, it gave her a boyish, unprepared look.

He sighed, like a balloon deflating, and turned back. 'It'll be OK, Katya. One way or another.' But right now, he didn't see how.

CHAPTER THIRTY-NINE

Taras was in work before eight, a bacon sandwich oozing ketchup in his hand. As he emerged from the lift doors, he came face to face with Leo and hastily stuffed the sandwich in his coat pocket.

'Hey, Tear-ass! Just the man. I need an honest opinion here.'

'Sure, Leo.'

'We'll take Francis's cube.' Leo shouldered in and fixed Taras with a stern look. 'How'd'ya think IBS is doing right now? From a market perspective.'

From a what? Taras scanned Leo's face, looking for the answer. Now they were standing head-to-head, eyeballing each other. What should he do? Dropping his gaze would be weak, but he couldn't keep staring like this. Leo's irises were china blue; they'd be pretty on a girl, obviously without that glaze of red veins. What was he thinking? He was still staring into Leo's eyes. Stop it. Look away. Say something! But nothing was coming to mind.

'You don't need to pussyfoot around with me, Tear-ass.'

'Well . . .' Time to take a risk. He looked away, then met Leo's eyes in a frank, manly way, not that rabbit-in-headlights stare, and said straight out. 'It's, um, not what it could be.'

'That's for damn sure.' Hurrah! He'd got it right. 'Customers are not happy. The story I've been hearing out

234

there is way worse than your Chief guy made out. Slipshod analysis. Buggy code. We've gone into half-time trailing big.'

Taras nodded, not sure where this was leading.

Leo lowered himself into the visitor's chair. 'So, whad'ya think, Tear-ass? My guys buy this thing, can yours buckle down, grind out a victory?'

'Yes.' Taras hesitated. Would Leo hold him personally responsible for that? 'Well, probably. It depends who you mean.'

'Ha! That dog'll hunt.' A big hand slapped the table. 'C'mon, Tear-ass. Siddown and gimme the lowdown.'

What did he mean? Obediently, Taras wedged himself into Francis's chair, tensing his stomach against a rumble. A waft of bacon tickled his nostrils. The room felt airless. Perhaps that was why Francis left the door open so often, not just to spy on the rest of them. A hot prickle started at the back of his neck.

The door rattled and burst open, with Colin gripping the handle. He stuttered something, his eyes widening as he saw Taras ensconced in Francis's seat.

'Whad'ya want?' Leo said impatiently.

'Er . . . umm. It was just . . . I mean . . . the Chief wants Francis.' Even first thing in the morning Colin was rumpled. Where did he buy those shirts? They were made of some special ultra-thin nylon that couldn't be ironed, like a cheap school uniform. 'I'll, er, look somewhere else.'

'Right. And I wanna see the both of 'em. You tell them that. In here, ten minutes. OK?'

Colin nodded, eyes bug-wide and scuttled out.

Leo waited until the door was closed again, then leaned forward, till Taras could see the wide pores around his nose. 'You're sweating, Tear-ass. Don't blame you. No fricking air-con. Feels like being stuck down a fricking hole.' He looked round. 'That's working life, Tear-ass. Trapped in a cube with a pedantic old fool. Till one day the air clears and you find the old fool's gone. Now you're stuck with an impatient young whippersnapper. For a moment, you think that's good, then you realise that no, it's not good. It just means you've become the old fool. Huh?'

'Huh?' repeated Taras.

Leo sprawled back, elbows spread. 'You're an impatient young whippersnapper, hey, Tear-ass?'

Taras nodded and then froze. So who was the old fool? Surely Francis? It would be a dreadful mistake to imply Leo. Aargh! Leo's fist was swiping forward in a hefty punch!

'Ha!' Leo's hand clamped on Taras's shoulder. It wasn't a punch, more of a clap. A good-humoured, cheery sort of clap, though with plenty of weight behind it. Taras had to resist the urge to rub his arm.

'Winning teams execute offense, hey Tear-ass?'

'Yes, sir.' Taras had lost all hope of following the conversation. Leo was grinning, so things must be going well.

'Yup. Wey-ell, thanks for this little talk.' Leo nodded as if they were finished. Taras got up and almost collided with a jittery-looking Chief hovering at the entrance.

'We gotta talk,' he heard Leo saying, as he made his exit.

Outside, Jamal was hobbling back from the stationery cupboard with a printer cartridge under each arm. 'Hear you're taking Fucknugget's spot?'

'What? No!' Taras glanced around and saw Colin, hand on hip, reporting to a growing bank of faces.

'Serves him right, the titface.' Jamal shifted his crutches and dropped the printer cartridges in a box on the floor, already overflowing with fresh notebooks, pens, CDs, Post-its, even a stapler. 'Lisa said he only put a quid in my leaving collection.'

'Really?' Taras hoped Lisa hadn't reported his own contribution: 20p and an old franc someone had slipped him in a pile of change. 'What are you doing?'

'Clearing my desk.' Jamal winked. 'Why? You going to report me for it, now you're management?'

Wispy hair crackling with excitement, Colin was scuttling back. 'Francis is here! He's going in to see them now.'

All over the floor, heads whipped round to watch Francis, heavy eyebrows beetling with disapproval, as he stumped past. As he pulled open the door, they all got a glimpse of the Chief with his head in his hands, and Leo, standing up with a phone to his ear, and then the door banged shut.

'Salad dodger's getting his marching orders,' Jamal said.

A squeeze of excitement tightened in Taras's chest as he squinted at the tinted glass. 'Do you think?'

Fifteen minutes later, Francis emerged, head down, heading for the coffee machine, and pressed the top button, for double espresso.

'Yup.' Jamal made a throat-slashing gesture. 'Total de-installation.'

Francis swallowed the espresso shot in one gulp, then turned and stalked across the floor to the main doors. A tranche of silence opened up in front of him, like the parting of the Red Sea.

The Chief came out a few moments later. Another wave of silence spread over the room as he headed at high speed into his office and called his secretary in for a conferral.

'Can you believe it, my train was late again.' Lisa arrived, shaking raindrops off her patch-pocket coat. 'When you think how much I pay for a season ticket . . .' She looked round. 'Is something happening?'

'Taras talked to Leo and got Francis sacked,' Colin blurted.

'Oh, dear.' Lisa plumped down in her chair and looked at Taras reprovingly. 'That can't be very nice for the Chief. Imagine having to sack your own brother-in-law.'

'Brother-in-law?'

'The Chief's married to Francis's sister.' She thought for a moment. 'Or is it the other way round?'

'I didn't know that!' Taras stared at Jamal, who shrugged.

'They keep it quiet.' Lisa waved at the Chief's secretary

and gestured towards the Ladies, for a debrief. 'I expect he'll be very cross.'

Minutes later, an email pinged round the office. Tonight's morale-boosting team event was cancelled.

'Oh, shit.' Taras slumped at his desk. 'What have I done?'

'Hey, Tear-ass.' Leo breezed past. 'I'm outta here. We all set for tonight?' He winked heavily. 'The unofficial version. Be a pity to waste all that planning. Whad'ya say?'

'Yes, sir!' Taras sprang to attention and executed a salute.

Leo laughed; a big, shaggy, bear-laugh, and the warmth of it spread through Taras's veins. 'Gimme the details. I'll meet'cha there.'

Jamal leaned forward once Leo was gone. 'You're well in with Merkin.' There was an unfamiliar tone in his voice. Could it be respect? 'Maybe he really has got you down for Francis's spot.'

Taras shook his head, but a bud of hope was flowering in his chest. As long as tonight went well, everything might just work out.

'We should stay in touch.' Jamal fished a pack of Post-its out of his box and scribbled down his personal email address. 'Contacts. The secret of success. Come on. I'll buy you a pint.'

'It's not even midday.' Taras looked round the office.

'So? Half this lot are going to be out on their ear tomorrow. What do you care?'

Jamal might be an arsehole, but he was right. Taras took a deep breath. 'Let's go.'

CHAPTER FORTY

It was well before the lunch-time rush at the Cittie of York, and their footsteps echoed on the flagstoned floor. The baronial hall was almost empty, with only a few solitary drinkers dotted along the long bar.

'You all right to get this one?' Jamal patted his trouser pocket as the bartender came over. 'Forgot to stop by the cash machine this morning.'

Typical, Taras thought, but paid up without complaint. If Jamal delivered on a cracking night for Leo, then it'd be worth it.

'Hey,' Jamal nudged him. 'Isn't that your mate? Curlyboy?'

Further down the bar, wiry black curls wild and unbrushed, was Roy, chin in hand and slumped over a half-empty tumbler.

'Hey, Doc!' Jamal yelled. 'Bit early for the hard stuff, isn't it?'

Roy swivelled, lanky legs shooting off the bar stool. 'Kroheman! I was just waiting till lunch-time to call you.' He got up and nodded towards the small wooden booths near the fire. 'Let's go over there.'

'Righty-oh.' Jamal wasn't offended. 'I'll have a go on the fruity then. Got any shrapnel, Cow-arse?'

Taras fished some pound coins out of his pocket, and Jamal headed for the twinkling slot machines. Following Roy over to the end booth, Taras said, 'What's up?'

Roy stared at the huge wall-mounted vats. 'Nothing.'

Something in Taras snapped. He banged down his pint. 'Right. I'll just go then.'

'Come on, Kroheman.' Roy looked at him, startled. 'I'm sorry about yesterday. I've had a lot on my mind.'

'*You* have? What about me? I told you about Elliott Bartlett, and you just walked off.'

'Christ.' Roy rolled his eyes. 'You really believe he's your old man?'

'It all fits.' Taras leaned forward. 'The tension between him and Mami at the funeral: it was obvious there was history there. I should have realised straight away. That's why his wife paid for my school fees and everything. Mami must have told her, and she felt they owed it to us. She was very religious.'

'Makes him a bit of a shitty bastard. The Monk's only a few months older than you.'

Taras had been so taken up with the possibility of finding a father that he hadn't even considered the fact that that would make Gideon his half-brother. A brother! If only it could have been Roy.

'You know, Kroheman, you shouldn't build this up too much. Even if it's true, so what?'

'So what?' Taras stared at him. 'That's easy for you to say. Your family's like something out of a kids' story. Do you know how much I used to envy you? With your dad coming to every prize-giving, every concert.'

'Yeah, I know, my old man's great. He's a saint.' Roy sighed. 'I'm just saying, a lot of blokes aren't like that. They don't stick around. And yeah, maybe it's not ideal, but if the mother decides to go ahead, then that's how it is. Old man Bartlett obviously didn't want to be your dad, so why rub it in his face now?'

'You don't get it.' How could his best friend fail to appreciate something so fundamental? 'Not having a father is . . .

well, it's a hole. A big fucking hole in your life. A black shadow where something should be. You don't know who you are or where you come from. Elliott Bartlett doesn't have the right to turn his back on me. Yeah, he doesn't measure up to a dad like yours, but even if he's the shittiest loser, that would be better than nothing.'

'You really think that?' Roy's forehead creased, and he drummed his fingers on the table. 'Jesus.'

'Yes, really,' Taras said. 'And anyway, Elliott Bartlett might be a shit, but he's not a loser. You should see the house he lives in.'

'So what are you going to do?'

Talking helped make everything clear. 'I'm going over there to have it out with him.'

'What? Now?'

Taras looked at his watch. Francis was out of the picture. Leo wasn't around. Jamal was right: no one else mattered. There'd be time to go out to Shooter's Hill, confront Elliott once and for all, and still be back in time to meet Leo. He downed the rest of his pint, feeling brave, inspired, like Maximus stepping out to meet Commodus in the arena. 'Yes, now.' Standing up, he felt his nerve falter. 'Want to come with me?'

Roy shook his head. 'Sounds like something you need to do on your own. Listen, Kroheman, Astrid and I are going away tomorrow. I wanted to talk to you about something.'

'I know, I've got to move my stuff out of your flat. I'll do it this weekend, OK?'

'Not that.' Roy tugged on his hair, straightening out the curls till they pulled at his scalp. 'Kroheman, listen. It's important.'

Taras was itching to be off. If he lost momentum, he'd run shy. 'Come to Light Bar tonight. We can talk then.'

Roy sat back. 'I don't know.'

'Come on,' Taras urged. 'I want you there, anyway. This is

my big night. If it works out, then it could make all the difference to my career. Come on, man, I need you.'

He knew Roy would give in, but something about his posture, hunched against the wooden bench, made Taras feel bad about rushing off. Pushing the feeling to one side, he told himself that he'd sort it out this evening.

CHAPTER FORTY-ONE

One hand on the bear-head knocker, facing the dark red door, Taras felt his throat spasm tight. Then, as the tall, stooped figure of Elliott Bartlett appeared, calmness enveloped him. He was here. He'd done it. Now the truth was going to unfold.

'Well, my boy, what do you want?'

My boy! Taras tingled with delight. Opening his wallet, he took out the envelope Katya had given him. Elliott looked inside and frowned. Taras had replaced the newspaper cutting, just as he'd found it, inside the wedding ring. Elliott unfolded the paper and looked at it, then closed his eyes for a moment, kneading his forehead with age-spotted fingers. 'Your mother sent this?'

Taras nodded. 'It's time we all faced up to the truth.'

'I see.' Elliot took a deep breath. 'You'd better come in.'

They didn't go into the library this time. Elliott ushered him down a plain passage with whitewashed walls and cracked tiles on the floor. 'This is the back part of the house. No one to bother us here.' Pushing open a door, he waved Taras in.

'Eurgh,' Taras clamped a hand over his nose. Redolent of old smoke fumes, the room had small leaded windows and little natural light. In contrast to the rest of the house it was dingy and uncared for. The stiff maroon wallpaper was peeling in the corners and above it the intricate ceiling coving was discoloured by decades of nicotine. Two winged leather armchairs flanked a small carved table topped with a brimming ashtray.

'My wife never came in here,' Elliott said. 'The dismal Mrs E. poked her nose in, but soon thought better of it. You'll have a drink.' It was a directive, not a request. He poured a generous measure of peaty amber liquid into two tumblers. 'Talisker,' he said, setting them down. Then he removed his woollen cardigan, hung it outside the door, and pulled on a heavy silk smoking jacket. 'Absorbs the odour. The unamiable Desirée seems to find it even more repulsive than did my late wife. Will you join me in a San Cristóbal?'

The down-at-heel look of the room faded, replaced by a feeling of sophistication as Elliott unlocked a dark wood cabinet inlaid with crinkled leather. 'How many cigars is that?' Taras exclaimed.

'Oh, about seven hundred.' Elliott seemed pleased with the question. 'Dreadful creation, this.' He stroked the door. 'My great-grandfather shot the beast and added insult to injury by transforming him into a humidor.'

'It's real crocodile?'

'Lined with Spanish cedar, of course.' Elliott saw Taras's blank expression. 'Repels the fearsome tobacco beetle.'

'Oh.' This was what Taras had always wanted. A father who could introduce him into the realm of masculine secrets. It was almost too much. 'I know I don't have any claim on you—' he began.

'Good.' Elliot took a silver cutter and clipped the cigars. 'In any case, I have very little to give.' He laid both on a white plate and offered it to Taras. 'Perhaps you know this house was built by my great-grandfather?'

Taras shook his head, then, copying Elliott, passed the cigar meditatively under his nose. Woody, leafy. Tobacco, basically. He hoped he wasn't going to be asked for an opinion.

'Five generations, unbroken. Hardly the stuff of antiquity, but meaningful nevertheless. I always felt it important to continue that tradition, to have a son and pass it on.'

His son? But hadn't it gone to Gideon already? Or, could he mean . . . ?

'My firm too.' Elliott struck a match with a quick, inwards, flick of the wrist and turned the foot of the cigar just above the flame. 'Bartlett and Sons. Handed down from one generation to the next. Until I broke the link.' He frowned as Taras fumbled with the Swan Vestas. 'Not like that. You're warming the tobacco, not setting fire to it. Yes. Better.' He rolled his cigar between his fingers, gesturing at Taras to do the same.

For a moment, Taras wandered into a reverie about Cuban girls doing this with their bare thighs. Shaking it free, he said quickly, 'Gideon said your company made shoes.'

'How prosaic of him. It was a very old company. Our roots can be traced back to the Great Fire. And it made very fine shoes. Nowadays people would rather marinade their feet in plastic monstrosities churned out by Chinese sweat-shops.' Elliott angled his cigar in his mouth and as if by magic, a flame seemed to leap from his hand to the foot of the cigar. Slowly, he turned the barrel and then drew deep so the end glowed warm. The lined face filled out, blurring the wrinkles and making him seem briefly younger. Then the lips puckered, expelling a ring of smoke, and his heavy eyelids snapped open again. 'I went bankrupt, near as dammit. Three hundred and fifty years of history destroyed.'

Taras didn't know what to say. 'I'm sorry.'

'Indeed.' Folding one leg over the other, Elliott picked up his tumbler of whisky. 'My dear wife bailed me out, just enough to allow me to wind up the business in a decent way, without the stain of insolvency touching either of our reputations. After that, I took over the rather less taxing occupation of managing her portfolio of investment properties. Which allowed me to hone my destructive talents further.' Elliott raised his cigar and took another slow puff. 'I met most of her tenants at one time or another, but one couple made an immediate impression. Sigi and Maria were very young, and very beautiful. Newly married. Full of the excitement and promise that I lacked.' A contemplative smoke ring drifted towards the ceiling. 'Well, you know the rest. No need to dwell on past sins. My wife found out, naturally. She chose to forgive me. In her way. And in return, I signed over this house and everything in it to her. Stock, lock and barrel.' Elliott raised his cigar and took another slow puff. 'So you see, I have nothing left to give.'

'But that's not why I'm here,' Taras said. 'I'm not asking for money. Nothing like that.'

The lizard eyes flicked over him in wary contemplation. 'No? Then what do you want?'

'You.' said Taras simply.

A smoke ring quivered and broke. 'Indeed?'

Taras fumbled with his cigar. One edge was briskly burning but the rest remained resolutely unlit. Could one smoke half a cigar? He turned it, like Elliott had, and with relief saw the rest ignite. But the cigar was already short on one side, lopsided. Ridiculous. 'I'm making a mess of everything.'

'Blow on it, dear boy. It'll even itself out.'

'Not the cigar.' But he did, and found Elliott was right. 'My life. It's all going wrong. I need to change, but I don't know how.'

Elliott reached for the decanter. His tumbler was already empty: Taras hadn't noticed that happen. Hurriedly, he took another sip from his own. The peaty taste mingled with the aromatic cigar smoke: a heady, masculine fragrance. Like Lynx deodorant. Taras resolved to buy some tomorrow.

Elliott took a long slug, then sat back, looking into the distance. 'My behaviour must seem inexcusable with hindsight,

I know. All I can say is that I was in love, which is a strong force, but I was also a coward. It seemed easier to turn away, and I couldn't foresee the consequences.' He turned his silver head, and looked Taras in the eye. 'So, if it is not an impertinence, let me offer you a piece of advice. Do not make the mistake I did. Look into your heart, accept what you find, and then act without fear. It may be difficult, but believe me, to look back upon a wasted life is infinitely harder.'

The two armchairs were angled towards each other, only a foot or two apart. Elliott was leaning forwards slightly, tense with the force of what he was saying, while Taras was bolt upright, hands clenched between his knees. He wanted to say something, to tell Elliott that he understood, but the ensuing silence between them was too powerful. Eyes locked together, they both leapt as if an electric current had jolted through them as a fist pounded on the door, and a voice called out.

'Dad? Are you in there?'

Elliott flung up a hand, warning Taras to stay still. 'Yes, Gideon.' His voice wobbled a little. 'What is it?'

'Mr Banerjee telephoned. He's on his way here. He wants to see you.'

A frown crossed Elliott's face. He went to the door and opened it slightly, but not enough to allow Gideon to see inside. 'It's not a convenient time.'

'He didn't ask if it was convenient. He's going to be here any minute. I think he's got something to tell you.'

'Put him in the library. I'll be there in a few moments.' Elliott waited, watching Gideon disappear through the hallway, and then brought Taras out to a plain side-door.

'You can get out this way, through the garden.' He sounded withdrawn. 'I would prefer that Gideon knows as little as possible about what we've discussed. I'm sure you understand.'

Taras understood that he was being dismissed. A feeling of

betrayal pierced him. There was going to be no public admission of their relationship: he was being smuggled out of a clandestine back entrance. He wanted to drop to his knees and wrap his arms around the old man's legs. Elliott's hand touched his shoulder lightly: a gesture of affection, perhaps, or apology. The intimacy between them felt rekindled. Taras opened his mouth, wanting to say something.

'Dad?'

For a second Taras felt as if the word had come from his own mouth. He held still, transfixed, but Elliott was already turning.

Gideon was at the other end of the corridor. He saw Taras and his face tightened. 'Mr Banerjee's here. He's not alone. I thought I'd better warn you. But perhaps you already know.'

'Know what?' Elliott sounded impatient.

'He's brought Taras's mother with him.'

Back straight, arms folded, jaw firmly set, Mr Banerjee was standing in the library. His round, bald, head was thrust forward and his tight-fitting suit, straining at the side-seams, was barely holding in his determination to be heard. Although he was short, his presence was commanding. He looked like a challenger ready to fight.

Taras and Gideon entered on either side of Elliott's tall, frail frame; rival princes flanking an ageing king. When Mr Banerjee saw Taras, a twitch went through his body and he clamped his elbows tighter into his chest. Guilt, Taras decided, although it might also have been anger.

Behind him, Mami was seated in a high-backed library chair in front of the curtains with their dull gold tassels. She was wearing a dark green dress that Taras hadn't seen before. With her hair in a looser style than usual, and Mr Banerjee's ruby flashing from her left hand, she was a noblewoman, waiting to reward the victor. Her black eyes widened as they met Taras, and her frown deepened as she looked from him to Elliott. Did she see a family likeness? The thought exhilarated Taras and at the same time loaded him with guilt.

'Accusations have been made.' Mr Banerjee's barrel chest projected. 'I have been placed under suspicion. I am here to clear my name.'

Looking tired, Elliott waved his hand, signalling him to continue.

'It has been said that I fraudulently collected rents from Mrs Krohe, when the London Bridge property was leased to her free of charge by your wife.' Mr Banerjee was using his most stiff, correct manner. He turned to Taras's mother for affirmation, 'Maria?'

Her black eyes were still on Taras. They flickered and hesitated.

'Maria?'

Looking down, she said in a small, even voice, 'No rent was being charged. I was not paying, and Mr Banerjee was not collecting.'

'But Mami!' Taras said, astonished. 'That can't be true. I gave you the money.' Twenty-five crisp twenty-pound notes, every month since he'd begun working.

She looked at him again, a quelling stare that silenced him.

'You saw the money handed over?' Elliott asked.

'Well . . .' Taras blinked. 'No, but Mami gives it to him on his quarterly visits, when I'm at work.'

'This is all damned lies!' Mr Banerjee roared, his chest swelling. 'Maria, tell them!'

For the first time, Taras saw a hint of uncertainty in her gaze, and that scared him. 'Mami?'

'Money was not for rents, Taraşhu.'

'But . . .' Taras didn't know what to say. He would have given her money if she'd asked for it, any amount of money. Why lie? Something inside him crumpled. His eyes fell to the gold dragon on the rug in front of the fire.

249

'You extorted money from the boy?' Elliott exclaimed. 'My God. If Sigi were here now!'

Her black eyes ignited. 'You are daring to talk of Sigi to me?'

Elliott turned away from her. 'Well, Banerjee. I suppose I owe you an apology. But I think you can see that your personal involvement,' he said these words so coldly that they sounded shameful, 'with Maria muddied the waters.'

Mr Banerjee's freckled skin darkened. His lips clamped together.

Taras's mother leapt to her feet, hands chopping through the air. 'Because you are man without moral, you think I am also like this? *Mitokan!* You are worth less than nothing.' Taras jumped forward to catch her arm, but she shook him off. 'Taraşhu, you are very foolish boy. This is bad-feeling man. Family-breaking man with cold heart and liar face.'

'Gideon, would you go and call a taxi for our visitors?' Elliott said, staring him down with an autocratic frown until he obeyed. 'I believe they are ready to leave.'

'You are afraid for son to hear what I have to say? You wish to be protecting him? Ha! What for *my* Son? Who is protecting? I find him here, in your house?' Running forward, she struck Elliott on the chest. 'No! He is not for you!' Her white hands flew up towards his face.

'Maria!' Mr Banerjee was pulling her away, and Taras caught Elliott as he stumbled back. 'Maria, what are you doing?'

There were scratches on Elliott's face, blood welling up on his lined cheeks. Steadying himself, he kept hold of Taras's shoulder. 'You talk of robbing? You, with your rapacious demands, your constant threats? If there is a robber here, I think it must be you, Maria.'

In a fury, she would have wrenched free and thrown herself at him again, but Mr Banerjee was holding her tight. His round, freckled head was bent towards her. 'Maria, please.' Then to Elliott, 'What do you mean by talking like this?'

'You pretend you don't know?' Elliott's lip was curling. 'You were my wife's lawyer for thirty years. You dealt with . . . with this creature, on her behalf.'

Mr Banerjee was bewildered. Still holding on to Taras's mother, he said, 'Mrs Bartlett made certain financial provisions for Mrs Krohe and Taras. I ensured they were carried out.'

'And why do you think she made such "provisions"?' Elliott mimicked Mr Banerjee's careful manner. 'Out of sheer charitable goodwill?'

'Mrs Bartlett was involved with many worthy causes. I did form the impression there was a, ah, more personal flavour to this particular concern.'

'Ha!' Elliott's long body was trembling now, whether with emotion, or the effort of remaining standing, and Taras was forced to grip his arm tighter. 'Threats of public exposure, of shame and scandal. Is that what you mean by motives?'

'You are wrong, sir.' Mr Banerjee was curt.

'My God.' Elliott stared at him. 'You're marrying the woman and you have no idea what she is. She's devious, calculating . . .'

'Stop it, stop it,' Taras cried. He dropped Elliott's arm and then caught it again as the old man collapsed forward, coughing. 'Brandy . . .' Elliott muttered between racking coughs, and Taras hurried to pour some from the decanter on the side-table. He felt his mother's eyes following him accusingly as he returned and held out the glass. Mr Banerjee had let go of her, and was now on the other side of the room, his head bowed and one hand covering his face.

Alone by the fire, Taras's mother looked around at the three of them. She was standing very still, her dark eyes intense in her white face, but otherwise calm. 'Man can be having principles, maybe. Woman have not time for such. I am alone with baby coming. No money. Dead husband. Yes, I go to Mrs Bartlett. She want no fuss. I want no fuss.

We understand each other. Man makes mess, woman must be practical.'

'Maria, is this really true?' Mr Banerjee's face was grey. The distress on his plump features was plain, and a twinge of pity rose above Taras's long-held resentment. Tonight should have been their engagement party, but Taras's interference had already put paid to that. Now he was beginning to be afraid of what further destruction his meddling might have caused.

'The taxi's here.' Gideon came back into the room, hurrying to his father's side at the sight of his strained face. 'Dad? What's the matter?'

Taras felt his mother's black eyes turn upon him. He seemed to be in the centre of the room now, with Elliott and Gideon behind him, and his mother and Mr Banerjee on either side. How could she have taken money from him under false pretences? Why? She saw his hesitation and hurt rushed into her face. 'Not needing taxi,' she said, picking up her worn leather bag and clutching it to her chest in the posture that she always believed warded off muggers. Dark head held high, she marched across the room, without a glance towards any of them. Her green skirt swished through the door, her heels clicked against the hallway parquet, and the heavy front door creaked open, then slowly swung shut.

'Wait!' Taras's heart thundered in his ears. 'Mami! I'm coming with you!'

'No.' Mr Banerjee put out a hand. 'Whatever she has done, your mother is my responsibility now, Taras. Please allow me. I will go.'

CHAPTER FORTY-TWO

Taras got the cab, alone. Mr Banerjee had gone after Mami, and Gideon was helping Elliott upstairs. There was nothing else for Taras to do. The driver was tetchy at being kept waiting, and turned the radio up full blast in protest. Fifty yards down the hill, Taras saw his mother and Mr Banerjee.

'Pull over! I'm getting out,' he called, but it took a minute or two for the message to get across, and then the driver protested that he'd been told a fare to Croydon. Taras ended up agreeing to give him twenty quid, and by the time they came to a stop, he was much further down the road.

Plodding back, he watched them. Mami was tugging the ruby off her finger while Mr Banerjee leaned forward, lecturing her. She stopped, waved her hand at him, then pulled open her satchel and rummaged inside. Something emerged: Taras couldn't see what. Mr Banerjee took out his glasses and frowned at it, then put his head on one side and asked her a question. She nodded. He gestured emphatically. She shook her head. He turned away. She tugged at the ring again, but he turned back and caught her hand in his. She whipped it away and said something: he replied. Then she gave him her hand back again. He took it, gently, and held it for some time. He was pushing the ring back on, Taras realised. They stood like that for a moment, and then Mami stepped into Mr Banerjee's arms. Her head went on to his plump shoulder.

His arms tightened around her. Despite the wind and the spitting rain, they looked peaceful.

Taras came to a stop. Mr Banerjee didn't approve of what Mami had done, but his commitment was unshaken. *My responsibility now*, he'd said. All the years of Taras's childhood, the short, plump solicitor had been a constant in their lives, stepping forward in times of trouble. However much Taras resented his ideas of discipline, he could no longer deny that the man deserved respect. He'd stood by Mami, when Taras himself had flinched. It was an uncomfortable realisation. To shake it off, Taras opened up his phone, and a flurry of messages bounced off his voicemail.

'Cow-arse, where the fuck are you? Get down to the Gaucho, now.'

'Hey, Tear-ass, I'm havin' a senior moment here. Whut-all's that fricking Grill place called?'

'Cow-arse, this had better not be a wind-up. We've got a tab of three hundred quid here, who's going to pay it?'

'C'mon, Tear-ass, switch on the cell for frick's sake! Forget the goddam restaurant. I just got a burger. I'll see'ya at the bar.'

'Cow-arse!' The message descended into obscenities. Taras pressed delete.

So he was late, but could no one handle the simplest task without his personal supervision? Taras left a message for Leo, then dialled Jamal's number and tried to convince him to get everyone in a cab and over to Light Bar. But Jamal refused to move until someone sorted the bill, and since he was essential for the VIP entry at Light Bar, it had to be done. It took Taras more than an hour to negotiate trains and tubes, and he ended up sprinting into the Gaucho Grill to load a five hundred pound charge on to his Mastercard. There'd been three rounds of Jagermeister shots since he'd made the phone call, and someone, almost certainly Jamal, had ordered a £40 lobster main.

He was just tucking the limp card back into his wallet, when he was hailed with a loud, 'Hey, Tear-ass!' Leo was striding in. He'd stripped off his jacket and rolled up his shirt-sleeves to reveal brawny forearms and a big titanium wristwatch. 'Remembered the name. Pretty fancy place, huh? Y'all had yourselves a good time?'

'Er, yup,' said Taras, wondering if Leo was going to offer to reimburse him.

It seemed not. 'OK, wait up while I hit the can, and I'll be with you momentarily.'

'Shame you can't stay longer,' Jamal muttered.

'Do whut?' Leo caught that.

Jamal wasn't fazed. 'We'll be out all evening. It's a shame you can only stay for a moment.'

Raising his eyebrows and tapping his head meaningfully at Taras, Leo headed for the toilets.

'Are you trying to wind him up?' Taras demanded. 'Stop it.'

'Doesn't matter.' Jamal grinned. 'As of now, I'm a free man. Never gonna see any of these losers again.'

'Well, it matters to me.' Taras wondered if he was included among the losers. 'So shut up, all right?' Perhaps he could just drop a hint to Leo about the bill, somehow?

'Let's go!' Leo was back, and in high spirits. Taras didn't want to spoil things by carping about money. He'd do it later. As predicted, most people wanted to get off home, but Taras managed to round up two taxi-loads to move on. He and Jamal were in the first cab, with Leo and the red-haired receptionist.

'Hi, gorgeous,' Leo said, manoeuvring himself into the back seat so he could throw an arm behind her shoulders.

Jamal rolled his eyes at Taras and swiftly transferred to a tip-up seat.

'Hey, baby,' Leo murmured, flicking away a strand of auburn hair so his lips brushed her ear. 'Gonna miss me when I'm gone?'

On the other tip-up seat, Taras braced his feet against the stop-start jerks of the traffic and hoped he wasn't going to spend the night watching Leo seduce a receptionist. Especially one he secretly fancied, and who always ignored him.

As it happened, Leo's interest in the red-head proved short lived. 'Hoo!' He exhaled heavily as they entered the bar.

Taras followed his gaze to a mass of thick, blonde hair plunging over bare skin. And down to the firm round bottom and long legs sheathed in electric-blue silk.

'Now that is one sweet patootie.'

'I'll introduce you,' Taras said, feeling suave, and touched a bare shoulder. 'Desirée? This is Leo Harding. Leo, Desirée.'

The look of approbation from Leo almost made up for Desirée's cringe as Leo squeezed closer and said with a wink, 'Desirée, huh? That name's worth a drink.'

'I've got one already.' She raised her Martini glass and turned her back on him. 'Taras, I'm waiting for Gideon. He's supposed to meet me here.'

'Tear-ass, whut'll you have?'

'Oh, erm, what she's got,' Taras said, flustered. 'Are you sure he's coming? Maybe you should give him a call.'

'The lady's got good taste, huh?' Leo gave her a broad smile.

She ignored him. 'On what? My cell doesn't work in this stupid country.'

'Use mine.' Leo pulled out his Blackberry. 'Good anywhere on the globe. C'mon, let me refresh that glass for you.'

'If it'll get rid of you.' She held out the glass.

Taras joined Leo at the bar, afraid he might be offended by Desirée's rudeness, but he seemed delighted. 'Good play, Tear-ass. The more you pass, the easier it is to score.'

'Umm, she has actually got a boyfriend, I'm afraid.' Taras felt obliged to break the news.

'Hey, I'm just playing tag 'n' release.' Leo held up both hands. 'I'm a married man myself. Not aiming to plug anyone.' He turned and called, 'C'mon, little lady, come and tell the bartender what goes in this glass here.'

It was clear she only complied because she didn't want to stand on her own. Then, with a flick of blonde hair, she leaned over Leo's shoulder. 'Is that a platinum Amex?'

'Working on the black, honey.' He winked at Taras, who discreetly slipped away.

Jamal had been watching. 'You are in with the big man, aren't you? Reckon he's going to give you Fucknugget's job?'

'Don't know.' But the hope was growing. 'It could happen.'

'Where's my guy? Tear-ass! Here ya go.' Leo was passing something over people's heads. A Martini glass. Cold. Cloudy. Taras waved thanks and took a gulp, relieved to find that the bite of the vodka was drowned in sweet pineapple.

'Hmm.' Jamal chewed the inside of his cheek. 'I mean it about staying in touch. We should sink a few pints sometime. I'll give you a bell when I'm settled into the new place.'

'Sure.' Taras knew what was happening, but it had a certain appeal. So this was what it was like to be a player. He could get used to it.

'Flounder!' Gideon was shouldering through the crowd, still in the jeans and crew-neck jumper he'd been wearing this afternoon. How had he got past the bouncer? 'Where's Desirée?' Following the line of Taras's gaze to the bar, he paused, brows drawing together. 'Right. I needn't have been in quite so much of a hurry. Should have guessed she wouldn't be alone for long.' Drawing Taras to one side, he handed him a dark blue plastic wallet. 'Banerjee brought your mother back to the house. He wanted Dad and me to see this.'

Easing out a matching navy booklet, Taras opened it and exclaimed. 'My Squirrelsaver passbook!' Opening the account had been a big event on his ninth birthday. He'd deposited the pound that the Lithuanian man downstairs had given him, and the 57p he'd made from returning bottles to the newsagent. For a while, the cardboard cut-out of a squirrel holding a calculator had taken pride of place beside his bed, until he spilled a mug of hot milk and the squirrel's face had gone soggy and peeled off. There had been a few more deposits over the next couple of years, but not many, and the account had been long forgotten.

There was his name. Taras Sigismund Krohe, and that first deposit, on his ninth birthday: £1.57. The next deposit was three months later, £2.50. Over the next four years, the total had grown to a massive £7.32. And then, jumping suddenly to the summer he'd left university and started work, there were a whole series of deposits. September 30: £500.00, October 31: £500.00, November 30: £500.00. And so on: each month without fail, right up to last month. A total of £18,360.45. He stared at the figure. Eighteen thousand, three hundred and sixty pounds. And forty-five pence. In an account belonging to Taras Sigismund Krohe.

'Banerjee wanted Dad to know that your mother wasn't stealing money from you.'

'Of course she wasn't.' Taras had known that; he just hadn't understood. He stared at the book again. He was a rich man! The deception was all for his own good. He was under no illusions about what would have happened to the money if she hadn't taken it. It would have been drunk, or frittered on gadgets or wasted in one way or another. He was wiser now. 'I can bail Katya out!'

'Out of what?' Gideon frowned.

'Nothing.' Should he do it? That would be all his money gone: before he even knew he had it. In his mind's eye, he saw Mami leaning her head on Mr Banerjee's shoulder. Commitment. Principle. *Look into your heart and act without fear,* Elliott had said. A man should make his decisions and stand by them. But was it the right decision?

'Katya's in trouble?'

'It's nothing. I'm dealing with it.' Taras slipped the pass-book into his pocket. He'd give her the money. Gideon could butt out. 'They're OK now, aren't they? Mami and Mr Banerjee.'

'Banerjee obviously doesn't approve of what she did. Holding threats over Dad's head. But he told us she'd been in very difficult circumstances, and it was now up to him to make sure she was never in such a situation again. I was impressed by him, frankly. I think Dad was as well, though he's very bitter about your mother.'

'Here, Tear-ass!' Leo was passing over another pineapple Martini. Taras waved thanks. 'It's not her fault,' he said loyally. 'She wanted it for me, not for herself. He shouldn't have tried to abandon us.' He broke off, wondering if he'd said too much.

'Mmm.' Gideon rubbed his chin. 'Dad said a few things when I was taking him upstairs. I think I've got a pretty good inkling about what happened. You know, don't you?'

Taras nodded. His breath caught in his throat. Was Gideon about to acknowledge him as a brother?

'Hey, Tear-ass!' Leo was yelling above the hubbub, tilting his hand towards his mouth. 'How's about another?' Giving him a thumbs-up, Taras turned eagerly back to hear Gideon say. 'Perhaps we should just leave it there, then. Dad's an old man. His health's bad. It won't help anyone to drag up old grievances, and it doesn't make any difference now.'

Crestfallen, Taras nodded. So what if Gideon was under-whelmed at having a brother? It didn't matter. Elliott valued him. He'd called him *my boy*.

'Gideon, sweetie,' Desirée had seen him at last. She broke away from the bar, with Leo in tow, and leaned into Gideon, resting her chin on his shoulder so that the bright wheat of her hair merged into the dark gold of his.

'Hey, Tear-ass. You enjoying thay-att drink? Know whut it's called?' Leo demanded, with a wink at Desirée.

Disengaging from Gideon, she clinked her Martini glass against Taras's and said something Taras didn't hear. The music in the bar was cranking louder. She mouthed again, but he still didn't get it. 'What?'

'BIKINI MARTINI,' bellowed Leo. 'Kinda faggy, huh? Oh,' turning to Jamal. 'No offence.'

'You what? Why would I be offended?'

'You're a member of the team, right?'

'I'm what?' It dawned upon Jamal. He scowled. 'You think I'm gay?'

'Aint'cha? Don't bother me none.' Leo waved a hand at Jamal's narrow-legged Paul Smith suit. 'You got the whole look going on, thay-att's all.'

Taras sniggered, delighted at Jamal's discomfiture. Colin, who'd been hovering on the fringe of the group, joined in with a high-pitched snort.

'What's so funny?' Gideon asked coolly.

'Leo thinks Jamal's a bender!' Colin said, socially embold-ened by a few drinks.

'You're the bender. Shut up,' Jamal snarled, and Taras snickered again.

'Witty stuff.' Gideon's face was icy. 'Desirée, it's time to go. Do you have a coat?'

'But you only just got here.' She pouted. 'We never have fun any more.'

'C'mon, stick around,' Leo said. 'You and your pretty lady

here. Don't worry, I'm not trying to steal her. Wouldn't mind borrowing her awhile though. Just kidding.' He elbowed Gideon in the ribs. 'Whad'ya drinking?'

'All he ever has is sparkling water,' Desirée said with a note of complaint, then seeing Gideon's stony face. '*All right*. I'm coming.'

'Listen, thanks for bringing this.' Taras tapped the Squirrelsaver book in his pocket, not sure why Gideon's mood had changed so abruptly. 'I'll give you a call.'

'I wouldn't bother. Dad and I could do with some space. I think it would be best if you and your mother steered clear. Do you understand me, Flounder?'

Taras didn't, but neither did he want to get into family discussions now, in front of Leo. Trying to mould an expression which would strike Leo as breezy, while communicating hurt and disturbance to Gideon, he nodded. It made his face ache.

'Just as well,' Leo said, watching them leave. 'She's a hottie, but she'd have got in the way of the entertainment, hey Tear-ass?'

What did he mean? Taras didn't have a chance to ask, because his phone was buzzing. He held it to his ear. 'Roy! What? I can't hear you.'

'There's your mate. Curlyboy,' Jamal said, pointing through the crowd. 'Just in time. We should move on before we're totally fubared, or we won't get in.'

'Get in where?' Taras asked, waving at Roy.

Leo winked. 'I hear you boys have got a slice of real London planned.'

Had they? Taras blinked as Colin gave his sparse hair a twitchy tug and declared, 'Jamal says we're going to a nudie bar.'

'Jesus Christ,' Roy heard him as he joined the group.

'Hey!' Leo didn't like that. 'No fricking blasphemy.'

The red-headed receptionist bobbed up behind Colin. 'Did I hear right? You're going where?'

Leo held up both hands. 'Not my call, honey. Tear-ass here's showing me London. What can ya do?'

'We don't have to go,' Taras began. He didn't remember this being part of the plan. Was this what Jamal meant by *the real fun starts*? Oh, God. He panicked for a moment in case he'd said that aloud. Was God more blasphemous than Jesus Christ? Shit, shit, shit. He should never have delegated the organisation to Jamal. Maybe Leo was deeply offended. Maybe . . . His thoughts trailed to a halt as he saw that Leo's red face was beginning to glower, like a sulky child being denied a treat.

'C'mon, Tear-ass. No bailing now. You got a plan, let's stick to it.'

'Right,' Taras said, taking control of the situation and projecting leadership. 'Everyone into a cab. We're on our way . . .' He hissed into Jamal's ear, 'To where, exactly?'

CHAPTER FORTY-THREE

'Hey Tear-ass, aint'cha got better'n this?' Leo kicked back his heels and gazed indifferently at the girl on the dais with the slash-fronted evening dress.

Better than this? Taras didn't know what to say. The girl looked good to him: tall and blonde with hair that swung out as she glided round the metal pole. The dress was silver, glittery under the spotlight, with splits that ran up each long thigh to her hip-bones. Perhaps it was the music? Leo probably wasn't an R 'n' B man, what would he like? Country and Western? Did they do requests here? Taras twisted his neck round, as if hoping to see a DJ with giant headphones in a corner cubicle.

Everyone else here seemed to be enjoying themselves. The knot of striped-shirts on the sofas had a champagne bucket with two blondes in strapless metallic dresses laughing loudly and showing a lot of throat. Further back, in the screened off cage area, a fat suited man lolled on a throne, broad thighs spread around two writhing girls in g-strings.

'Would any of you gentleman like a dance?' Another blonde was leaning over them, with a pretty young face and sparkling eyes. All the girls were so friendly. In a normal bar, girls this good-looking would be frosty and unavailable to a group like them, but here they were not just wreathed in approachable smiles, but actually making all the moves.

'Not right now, honey,' Leo said, and the girl moved

acquiescently away, still smiling. No fuss, no awkwardness. Even through his drunken haze, Taras thought this revealed an important point about modern society, and decided to share it. 'Y'know, ordinary girls all ought to be like this. More . . . more . . .'

'More naked?' said Jamal and guffawed, annoying Taras, who had been trying for something more philosophical. He turned to Roy, ready to express himself more fully, but Roy's arms were folded and his eyes were locked on to the girl on the stage.

She had lost her evening dress now. Her breasts were high and pointed. Definitely real, they sank down a touch as she gripped her knees around the pole and tipped her head back, dusting the stage with a long sweep of blonde hair.

'Tear-ass?' Leo was leaning forward now. 'C'mon, now. I can go to a joint like this any night, anyplace. I wanna see the real scene. The London that Londoners know.'

Taras's head spun wildly as he considered the options. What was identifiably London? The Trocadero? It had a bowling alley and video games. Leicester Square? Fine if Leo wanted an over-priced Coke and a blockbuster film. *The Mousetrap*? Taras didn't think Leo was really a culture vulture, and besides the theatres would all be empty by now. What did he want? As far as Taras was concerned, Jamal had hit the jackpot with tonight's entertainment: it was way slicker than anything Taras could come up with. Not that he'd ever admit that to Jamal, of course.

'Would you like a dance, sir?' A different blonde this time, in a green fish-tail dress. They all went straight for Leo, as if they could pick out the size of his wallet through his trousers.

'Whut's your name, honey?'

She gave him a coquettish smile. 'I'm Chantelle.'

'And whut's the name of the girl up there on thay-att stage?'

'That's Angelique. We can give you a special show, together.' She smiled again, not pushing, just offering.

'Maybe later, honey.' Leo looked her over frankly and gave her a nod of dismissal. As soon as her tightly packed bottom had wiggled out of sight, he said, 'Chantelle? Angelique? What the hell?'

'They're stage names,' said Taras helpfully.

'Yeah, you think?' The heavy dose of sarcasm in Leo's voice was a surprise – weren't Americans famous for their lack of irony? He jabbed the air with a finger. 'See, that's what I'm talking about. There's nothin' real here. I coulda asked the concierge at my hotel and he'd send me here or someplace identical. C'mon you guys. Show me what real Londoners do.'

What did real Londoners do? Taras thought frantically. The ones he knew just went to the pub. He was about to make a joke about it, when he was struck with a brilliant idea.

'No problem, Leo. I know just the place.'

It took a while to extricate Colin from the toilet, where he'd fled within minutes of their arrival. They filed out of the club and into the street where the doorman hailed them a cab. Taras pulled Roy to one side.

'What's the name of that pub? The one in Vauxhall?'

'What?' Roy stared. 'The one Astrid did her report on? No way!'

'I need it,' Taras hissed, clasping Roy's shirt desperately. 'Help me!' Roy was still hesitating. 'Come on.' Taras made clucking sounds, flapped imaginary wings and pretended to peck at Roy's face, then held a thumb upside down over Roy's head. 'What are you, a doormat?'

'Get off! Oh, for Christ's sake. It's the Princess Victoria.'

CHAPTER FORTY-FOUR

The pub was large, but not crowded. A traditional wooden bar ran the length of the room, opposite shabby banquettes curved around low tables. It had a rough-edged, working-man feel. Taras's group stood out in their suits: everyone else wore jeans and sheepskin or leather jackets. A few of them sat at the tables, but most were leaning against the bar, pint-glasses in hand, watching the raised plinth that took up half the space.

'Good job, Tear-ass.' Leo took in the blacked-out windows and old beer-mat smell.

The girl on the plinth had peroxide hair with a half-inch of dark roots. She was wearing a fake-fur bolero, cowboy boots, a suede fringed thong and nothing else. Two men were pumping their arms in the air, yelling encouragement as she teased them, half-opening the bolero and closing it again. Thrashy and loud, the music followed her thumping hips as she swivelled and slapped one buttock to cheers, then stripped off the bolero and brandished it above her head, turning all the way to reveal heavy breasts, larger than any Taras had seen outside a magazine. She was grinning, laughing back at the whooping lads in front of her. It was all very good-humoured, but he wasn't sure if it was sexy.

Leo seemed to like it. Brimming with renewed energy, he slid into the banquette next to the stage and clicked his fingers in the air. 'OK, let's get some drinks here.'

'Uh, I think we have to go up to the bar,' Taras said.

'For real?' Leo seemed surprised, then pleased. 'That's London, huh? OK, Tear-ass, go get 'em.' Thrusting a fifty into Taras's limp palm, he added, 'A typical Brit drink for everyone. Y'know, Old Fusty-whatever. Go, go.' He shooed him away.

Taras stumbled off to the bar. The bolero girl was off the stage now, standing next to him, chatting animatedly with one of the lads who'd been cheering her on. She'd pulled on a pair of boy-shorts, cut high to expose two firm ridges of buttock. Not sure if it was bad form to leer when a girl wasn't actually on the stage, Taras looked away, and saw a dark-haired girl approaching Leo's table. She had smooth light-brown skin and a belly-button ring that winked between her short red skirt and matching halter-top. There was an old-fashioned pint glass in her hand, half-full of coins and crumpled notes.

Leaning over Leo – why did they all flock to Leo? – she said something and held out her glass. It didn't seem appropriate to be begging in here. Taras wondered why no one was stopping her. He said so a few minutes later when Roy came over to help him with the drinks.

'She's not begging, you prat,' Roy said. 'She's collecting. When her cup's full she'll get on the stage and do her strip.'

'Oh right.' Taras felt a fool.

'They don't get paid here like the other place. In fact, they pay the landlord to get a slot. But they keep their earnings.'

'How d'you know all that?' Taras wondered if he was the only naïve one in the room.

'Leo asked her,' Roy admitted. 'Look, Taras, I think I'm going to head off, all right?'

'Noooo!' Taras's wail came out louder than he'd expected. It made the bolero girl jump and glance over her shoulder. 'You can't. I mean . . . I need you here.'

'You're fine. The big boss is happy enough. He just gave the Brazilian girl a twenty.'

Taras hadn't known she was Brazilian. She was climbing on to the stage now: he glanced at the red skirt and wondered if that meant she would be . . . hmm. A movement from Roy recalled his attention. 'No, man, you can't go. I need moral support. Come on, you're supposed to be my best mate. I'd do it for you.' He couldn't think of a more poignant plea. How could Roy even think of deserting him now?

The music changed to a slower, more insistent beat. The Brazilian girl stamped her red platforms, tossed her hair and unclasped her halter-top. Instinctively, both Taras and Roy shifted slightly to get a better view.

'Look, just stay for one more drink,' Taras said. 'Leo's paid for them already.' He passed over a pint, and made a snooker-rack out of his hands to carry the other three over to the table.

'Helluva place, Tear-ass,' Leo said, not taking his eyes off the stage. A pale girl with too little bikini and too much lipstick had inserted herself next to Colin, who was sitting bolt upright and goggling down at the table with a rosy flush rolling up his neck.

Taras went back up to the bar, where Roy had half-drained his pint, still watching the Brazilian girl. She was very sexy, Taras thought; much more so than the bolero girl. There was a knowing smile on her lips, but she wasn't laughing at her audience, it was more as if she was inviting them to share a secret. Her breasts were tight and firm, like the toned muscles of her warm, glistening arms and that undulating stomach with the twinkling silver ring. He felt a pleasurable twitch in his groin, and let himself give in to it as she tugged her skirt away, revealing red fringed pants. Sexy, he thought, watching her hook her thumbs into the pants, very, very sexy. Oh, not shaved, interestingly enough, just trimmed. Winding herself round the pole and catching his eye with just the suspicion of a wink. Wow.

'You see that?' Roy said.

'Mmm.' Taras wasn't ready for conversation just yet.

'You know what it is?'

'What?'

'That scar.'

Taras had no idea what Roy was talking about; then he saw it, a raised furl of flesh, hardly visible beneath the neat hairline.

'That's a C-section. A couple of years old.'

Taras wasn't quite sure what a see-sex-yun was. 'Mmm,' he said. His eyes slid back up to her breasts.

'So she's making her money from guys like us, then going home to her toddler. Makes you feel sleazy, doesn't it?' Roy put down his pint-glass, unfinished. 'Does me, anyway. I've had enough, Taras. I'll see you later.'

He stalked out, not glancing at the stage where the Brazilian girl was sitting on a chair now, refastening her halter top and skirt as the pale girl mounted the steps for her turn. Taras wondered whether he should go after him, but Leo was signalling for another round of drinks, and there was no time. This was the thing about starting to take work more seriously, Taras thought, waving at the barman, it required integrity, he couldn't just do what he liked all the time. He was a man with responsibilities now. Placing the order, he turned to watch the pale girl shake off her bikini top.

When he got back to the table, Leo had disappeared.

'He's getting a private dance from the Brazilian bint,' Jamal said. 'In the back room.'

'Oh.' Taras felt odd. Almost jealous. He took a mouthful of lager and watched the next dancer climb the stage.

When Leo came back, he was full of praise for a hot little number he'd seen giving another customer a lap-dance.

'Real cute. Great ass. I'm goin' back for that one.' He stuck a bunch of notes under an empty glass. 'Don't be left out. You have yourselves a good time.' He was watching the door to the back room over Taras's shoulder, and a few minutes later he was off again.

'Would he mind if I used mine for a cab home?' Colin said, still avoiding looking at the stage.

The bolero girl had spotted the money being exchanged and was leaning over the table. Taras didn't fancy her at all and looked away, not wanting to be impolite, but Jamal was already on his feet, reaching for his crutches.

Taras nipped off to the loo, and when he came back, Colin had also gone, whether to the back room or home wasn't clear. Taras sat down and picked up his drink, avoiding looking at the stage. It was one thing to be here with a rowdy group of mates, but now he felt like a sad old raincoat.

'May I dance for you?'

He looked up. It was the Brazilian girl; long dark hair falling over pale brown shoulders. Her eyes were friendly but mysterious too, green with long lashes. That hint of a wink again, and desire came flooding back. He didn't have to say anything; she scissored the note from his hand and tucked it away.

'Wait.' She checked the curtain shielding the door to the back room. 'Full. One or two moments, that's all.'

Taras felt stupid queuing, as if they were in a post office. Another girl came out, following a burly man in jeans, and murmured to the Brazilian girl who gave her a wink. Now Taras was ready to walk away, but the Brazilian girl was leading him through the curtain into a dark cave-like space. A circular bench ran round the rim, and the Brazilian girl pushed him into a gap. There were other men positioned at more or less equal intervals around the irregular circle, each with a girl gyrating in front of him. It made him self-conscious, although no one was looking at him.

The Brazilian girl straddled him, blocking his view, and

began to sway. Her movements were mesmeric, especially this close. She ducked down to rub her cheek against his, and he felt her rub against his chest. Perhaps he should sit on his hands, to avoid mistakes – he knew that all the touching had to come from her. She unhooked the halter-top and pressed her breasts forward, like a gift, in front of his eyes, then ran her hand down over the belly-button ring and tugged off the skirt. Starkers. He had a naked woman wriggling over his thighs. She straddled him backwards and bent down, spreading her buttocks. Ugh! He didn't want to see that. His eyes jumped away, and he caught sight of Jamal, almost opposite, watching fixedly as the naked bolero girl thrust her pelvis forward.

There were six naked women in this room. Taras really should keep his eyes on his own, but the touch of forbiddenness about gawping at the other flesh was distracting. Where was Leo's hot little number? The Brazilian girl was facing forward now, he couldn't look away, she was spreading her fingers down between her legs, pushing the lips apart. Did she have to be so graphic? He wasn't her gynaecologist. Shit. Now he'd thought about that scar again.

She must have seen the recoil in his eyes because she stopped doing that and began fondling her breasts instead. That was better. They were beautiful. She teased them forward, almost into his face, if he put out his tongue it would catch her nipple, no, mustn't do that, though it seemed like she wouldn't mind. The guy next to him was standing up, his dance over, leaving, and beyond him Taras caught a glimpse of Leo; rubicund face slack with satisfaction as a naked brunette undulated over him, arms raised above her head.

The hot number had a very sexy bottom, pert and round. Even with two Brazilian breasts pushed up against his face, Taras couldn't help watching it swivel. It turned, hinging forward at the hips as the girl's hands went down to clasp her ankles, then slid back up her thighs. Leo leaned forward, seemingly eager to get that buttock-spread view which Taras found so repellent, and the girl's head came up, dark fringe opening like curtains to reveal a small, oval face. Two upside-down brown eyes met his, widened, and then Taras jumped up with a cry. The leer froze on Leo's fleshy red face. On the other side of the room, Jamal's teeth flashed as his mouth dropped open. 'Fucking hell!' The Brazilian girl had jumped away, startled; now the bolero girl had stopped her dance as well and everyone was turning, looking as Taras stared at the doubled-up brunette and whispered, disbelievingly, 'Katya?'

CHAPTER FORTY-FIVE

He turned and ran, pushing past the bolero girl and the trimmed Brazilian, through the heavy emergency exit and out into a narrow back alley. Panting as if he'd just run up a flight of stairs, he bent forwards, arms braced on knees, facing the smooth brick wall. His head was spinning and he thought he might throw up, but the cool darkness was a relief, and his breathing began to slow.

'Taras?'

He turned. Silhouetted in the glow from the emergency exit door, smooth and pale, was Katya.

'Go away.' He averted his head.

'Taras, we must speak.'

He would have walked away himself, but his legs felt wobbly. It was all he could do just to straighten up.

'I cannot come outside, Taras. I have no clothes.'

With a half-sigh, half-yelp of frustration, he stripped off his suit jacket and flung it at her, still looking away.

Wrapping it around her, she padded out barefoot and put one hand on his arm. He shook her off and covered his face with his arm.

'I am sorry, Taras. I know this is big shock.'

'Uhh!' Speechless, he lashed out and struck the brick wall, scraping the skin off his knuckles. The sharp rasp of pain brought relief. She tried to take his arm again, but he fended her off. 'For God's sake, Katya, get away from me.' Against his will, he glanced at her; hunched inside his jacket, which could have lapped her small body twice, one foot standing on the other and toes scrunched against the cobbles. Her knees and pale legs looked cold; despite everything, he had the impulse to scoop her up to his chest. 'How could you do it?'

If she'd dropped her eyes then, or they had filled with tears, he might have wrapped his arms around her, but instead she hugged herself and fixed him with squirrel-brown eyes. 'Is it worse for me to dance than for you to watch?'

Was she making fun of him? 'Yes, of course!' he roared. 'Katya, you kept this a secret from me. You lied to me!'

Her head tilted to one side. 'You said that strip club is not for talking about. Just somewhere for laugh and does not mean anything.'

'Oh, for God's sake, Katya—'

'You know I owe money! I told you I have idea to pay off debt. You don't ask any questions. You do not want to help, so you choose not to know.'

'I was going to help!' He reached towards her and plucked the Squirrelsaver passbook out of his jacket. 'Look. I was going to give it to you.'

'Too late!'

'That's not fair. I didn't have it before.'

'The money is not the point. You did not help. Help is . . .' She cast about for a word, 'Understanding. Coming together to think of plan. You did none of this.' Small, determined, with her mouth set, she faced him, and Taras felt a quiver of uncertainty. Could he have done more?

'Taras.' She said it softly, sounding very Russian; Tuh-rass, and the low drawn-out voice tugged at his chest. Her eyes, normally so twinkly and bright, had a sorrowful look that reached inside him and unleashed a familiar sense of guilt. He'd let her down. He was a stupid, insensitive fool. It wasn't

274

her fault, it was his. She should be wrapped in his arms, not his jacket. He . . .

'Taras!' A male voice, jaunty. It was Jamal. He pushed through the emergency exit, wedging it open with a crutch. With a wink, he added, 'Hey, Kit Kat.'

She tightened her grip on the jacket and didn't respond.

'Didn't know you had such talent. Waste of time studying economics with moves like that. I'm well impressed.'

She glared at him. Taras's mind leapt immediately to that night Jamal had taken her home, and his own lingering suspicions. Unconsciously, he took a step away from her.

'Here.' Jamal handed her something. It looked like banknotes.

'What is this?'

'From Leo.' Jamal turned to Taras. 'He says he's fricking sorry. Didn't know, etcetera, etcetera. Wanted me to tell you that you did a great job tonight, put on a real London show, thumbs up all round.'

'He's gone?'

'Back to his hotel.'

'There is two hundred pounds here,' Katya said.

'What can I say? He's a big-hearted guy.' Jamal winked at her. 'Beats giving Russian lessons, eh?'

'It was you.' Katya's head jerked up.

'What?'

'You told the scholarship committee. They said they received information. I could not understand who would do this. But it was you.'

Jamal began to shake his head, but then his mouth relaxed in a contrite fold. 'Sorry, Kit Kat. I was angry, you know. Did they give you grief?'

'If you are asking, did they take away my scholarship, the answer is yes.' She gestured down at her bare legs, as if to point out that this was why she was here. 'I am made example of, as warning to other students.'

'Shit.' Jamal's eyes widened, then his gaze flicked to Taras, as if registering that he'd just admitted the story he'd told before about Katya coming on to him wasn't true. He gave a rueful half-smile and shrugged, then turned back to Katya. 'I was just arsing about. I didn't think they'd actually, you know. What a bunch of merchants.' He rummaged through his pocket and pulled out his wallet. 'Here, let me . . .'

Taras stared at his girlfriend, wearing nothing but his suit jacket, clutching a fistful of banknotes while his beer-sodden colleague thrust more at her. Unwanted images flooded him: her pale legs spread in front of Leo's bloodshot leer, pointed nipples pushing forward, dark hair falling back as her brown eyes met his own. A shudder ran through him, disgust crumpled his face. He took another unthinking step back, and then realised Katya was looking right at him, a stricken expression in her brown eyes. Shoving Jamal's money aside, she ducked under his outstretched arm; back inside the pub. Still trying to press the notes on her, Jamal turned too, the door swinging behind him.

'Katya!' Taras yelled, running towards them, but too late. The emergency exit slammed shut with a resounding thud. He banged against it, leaving a smear of blood from the hand he'd scraped. What now? He couldn't face going round to the main entrance, walking through the sniggering whispers. The story must be round the whole pub by now: some stupid punter found his girlfriend working inside.

Slowly, he trudged up the alley to the main road at the top. The yellow light of an empty taxi beckoned. He broke into a run, flagging it down. He needed to be with someone he could trust now; the one person who wouldn't let him down. 'Thanks,' he said breathlessly, grasping the door. 'Highgate, please.'

CHAPTER FORTY-SIX

'Is that blood?' The driver was craning his head over his shoulders. 'Get it on my seats and it'll be fifty quid for cleaning.'

Taras waved a weary hand. It was only a scrape. He considered stuffing the money through the opening in the safety partition, just to avoid any further discussion, and even got as far as reaching for his wallet when realisation struck. All he had was his Squirrelsaver passbook. His wallet was still in his jacket, along with his keys, mobile phone, everything. And the jacket was wrapped around Katya. His first instinct was to tell the driver to turn around and go back, but he'd have to walk through that pub again. And what if Katya refused to give him the jacket? What if she'd left? No, better to carry on. Roy would sub him.

By the time they were speeding up the Archway Road, that plan seemed less appealing. Last time he'd suggested to a cabbie that he pop indoors to get the money, the man had insisted on accompanying him. And now it was two in the morning. What if Astrid answered the door? He'd have to cadge money off her with the taxi driver breathing over his shoulder. It would be awkward. Without his phone, he couldn't even ring and set things up in advance. A better idea came.

'Drop me anywhere here,' he called, and the cab slowed and pulled in. Taras reached into his pocket and at the same time said, 'I don't think I've got anything on the seats. Take a look if you like, and if I have, I'll pay up.'

'Nah, you're all right, mate,' the driver said, flicking the doors unlocked. Taras got out and came around to the passenger door, feeling for an imaginary wallet. 'Can I get a receipt?'

The driver sighed but reached down for his pad, and Taras swivelled and sprinted off in the opposite direction, down an alleyway. 'Hey!'

Heart banging, Taras heard the slam of a car door, and more shouts. The driver was chasing him! He dodged down another sidestreet, doubling back the way he had come, back on to the Archway Road. Risking life and limb, he darted out into a gap in the traffic, raising a blood-stained fist at a driver who beeped him, and was rewarded by the sight of the cab driver panting to a stop on the far side of the street. Exhilaration pumped through him. Was this how fugitives felt? Taras began to see the appeal. At a more moderate jog, he sloped down Shepherd's Hill to Roy's block of flats. He wished he and Roy had had the foresight to set up a code for just this type of occasion. Two short rings on the doorbell and one long one, say, so Roy would know to come to the door. Perhaps he would anyway. What kind of man sent his girlfriend to answer a mystery ring in the middle of the night?

One like Roy, it turned out. Taras's heart sank as he saw Astrid's distorted outline in the ridged glass.

'Sorry, Astrid, sorry, sorry,' he said. 'I didn't mean to wake you.'

'You didn't,' she said. 'Roy's in the shower. What do you want?'

'Can I come in? Wow, you're looking fantastic,' he said, meaning it. The hollow, exhausted look she'd had for the previous couple of months was gone. Her skin was brighter and the blonde spikes of her hair were sharp again. In jeans and a bright red t-shirt, she seemed full of energy. Not positive energy as far as Taras was concerned, unfortunately. She sidestepped, blocking his attempt to enter.

'I don't want you here, Taras. I don't even want Roy here. How dare the two of you use my report for your sordid little night out?'

How had she found out? Total abasement was the safest response. 'I'm really sorry. It was all my fault. Roy didn't want to go. He complained the whole time and barely even looked at the girls.'

Astrid's face didn't soften. 'I should have known something was up when I found there was a page missing. You took it, for the address, didn't you?'

That wasn't fair, he hadn't done anything of the sort. It must have been Katya, he realised belatedly, but Astrid didn't look ready to listen. She folded her arms and the red t-shirt rode up to reveal a wide elasticated waistband on her jeans. Not very cool, unless this was a new trend Taras hadn't caught yet. Best to stick to defending Roy.

'It's true, really. And he left early too.'

'So that makes it all right, does it?'

'Well . . .' He wished Roy would get out of the bathroom. 'I'm just saying you don't have anything to worry about. There wasn't any touching, nothing like that. Roy would never cheat on you.'

She stared at him. 'You just have no idea, Taras, do you? I'm not jealous, you moron. I'm ashamed of him.'

The words hung in the air as Roy emerged in a cloud of steam from the bathroom, with a towel around his waist.

'Get rid of him,' Astrid said. 'I don't want to look at either of you.' She disappeared into the bedroom, slamming the door behind her.

'Shit.' Taras stepped over the threshold. 'How did she find out?'

'I told her,' Roy said flatly.

What?! How stupid was that? 'You must be more pissed than you look.' Taras sniffed the air: was that coffee? Exactly what he needed. 'Listen, I've got something to tell you. The most unbelievable thing happened tonight.'

'Kroheman.' Roy nodded him back towards the door. 'Some other time, right?'

'No, you don't understand. This is major. It's Katya. She was . . .'

'Some other time.'

Taras gaped. 'But . . .'

'Listen, Taras, I've been a bit of a fool.'

Too right. It would take ages for Taras to get back in Astrid's good books now. But that wasn't the important thing. He opened his mouth again.

'Astrid's pregnant.'

It was a kick in the solar plexus. Taras couldn't breathe. When had this happened? How come Roy hadn't told him before? He thought he might faint.

'Yeah, I know. Big news.' Roy dug his thumbs into the fold at the front of his towel. 'I've been a complete twat. But I'm getting it together. No more arsing about. I'm not going to be the kind of selfish prick to this kid that old man Bartlett's been to you.'

'But . . .' Taras sucked in a gasp of air. He didn't know what to do or say.

'I'm sorry, Kroheman.' Roy held the door open. 'Things have got to change.'

He was actually . . . Roy was sending him away? Stunned, Taras stepped back outside. 'But . . . I need your help!'

'I'll call you in a day or two.' Roy patted his shoulder, then gave it a little push.

How was that going to help, when he was here now, with no wallet, no cash, no phone? Taras opened his mouth, but the door was already closing. Through the glass, Roy raised a hand in a silent salute, and then padded away.

Taras stood outside, gripping the useless Squirrelsaver passbook. What good was being rich, in a situation like this? Without someone to depend on, he was stuffed. What was he going to do? He didn't dare hail a cab: he wouldn't get away with that trick twice in one night, and besides, what if he got the same driver? The guy might be trawling the area, looking for him. Everything was falling apart. Everyone had let him down.

CHAPTER FORTY-SEVEN

Taras was hunched in the darkness, shivering. His jacket and tie were missing, and his shirt was damp from sweat and dew. He'd lain down on the grass by the winged statue for a while, but it was cold and uncomfortable and now he was sheltering under a latticework of vines. He was exhausted, a bone-deep exhaustion, and he couldn't stop his eyelids from flickering shut. He slumped, passing in and out of sleep, and wasn't sure if he'd been here for minutes or hours when the clatter of footsteps jerked him awake.

'Up! Now! Or I'll shoot!'

Taras started up into a half-crouch, whirling round to find where the voice was coming from.

'Out of the pergola, where I can see you.'

Stumbling away from the post he'd been leaning against, Taras raised his hands.

'Out of the pergola, damn you!' A heavy metal object struck his back and prodded up against his neck. It felt like the barrel of a gun.

'Aaargh!' he screamed, closing his eyes. 'Help! I don't know what a pergola is! Help!'

The barrel dropped. 'Taras?'

'Oh, God. Oh, God.' Taras was panting. Staring through the darkness, he made out a figure, hidden amongst the vines. 'Elliott?'

'Good God, boy, what are you doing? You've trampled my clematis.'

Taras's legs wobbled beneath him, and he collapsed on to the tiled ground. 'I'm sorry. I didn't mean to disturb you.'

Metal scraped along the tiles as Elliott pulled a bench closer and sat down, swinging the gun across his dressing-gowned knees. 'I saw someone skulking round the garden. What the devil do you think you're doing?'

'You could have shot me.' Taras was still shaking.

'It's an antique. Hasn't been fired for a century, I shouldn't think. Rather a fine piece. Austrian.'

Taras didn't find this reassuring. 'I meant to wait until morning, I thought you'd be asleep.'

'Insomnia. Curse of the elderly.'

'I didn't know where to go. Roy threw me out. There's no one left, but you.'

As he spoke, the moon emerged from a bank of cloud, silvering a large crack in the sky.

'Good grief, boy, you're filthy, and soaking wet. Is that blood on your hand? You'd better come inside.'

'No, no.' Taras didn't want Gideon to see him and think he'd come to pester for attention. 'I'm all right. I've been walking. I lost my wallet, phone, everything.'

He was grateful that Elliott didn't ask how. The last thing he wanted was to talk about it. That moment would be with him for the rest of his life: Katya's face through a curtain of hair, eyes widening, and above, Leo's fleshy red leer. Dropping his head on to his knees, he groaned. 'I can't bear it.'

A hand came down and rested on his head. The weight and warmth of it was enormously comforting, like a security blanket.

'It's all been a mistake,' Taras mumbled. It was easier to talk like this, with his eyes shut and under the steady pressure of Elliott's hand. 'Katya . . . an awful, horrible mistake . . .'

'Sssh. It's all right.' The hand stroked his hair, then his shoulder. 'Who's this Roy character?'

'His girlfriend's pregnant, and he doesn't want me around. He told me to leave.'

Elliott's hand held still for a moment. 'Yes. I understand. You know, Taras, I gave you some advice . . .'

'I know! You told me to look into my heart and I did. I was ready to act. But it all went wrong.' Taras sat up and put his hand on Elliott's, keeping it pinned on his shoulder. 'What can I do?'

Above them, the silver crack in the clouds was widening, casting a glow over the grass. On the raised veranda, under the twisted creepers, it was still dim, but the greyness was draining from the world, and now the big double-headed petals on the flowers were mauve-blue, contrasting against bright yellow stamens. After the misery of the night, hope began to glimmer in Taras's heart.

'Oh shit, I promised I wouldn't, but I can't help it.' He clutched Elliott's papery hand tighter and twisted to look up at the hooded eyes. 'Gideon warned me to stay away, but it's no good. I need you.'

'Taras . . .' Elliott tried to pull his hand back.

'No . . . please.' All the longing for a father which had been banking up since the earliest days of childhood came bursting out, washing away the horror and hurt of the night. He clutched tighter. 'I need you.'

'Taras . . .' Elliott leaned forward, his hooded blue eyes scrutinising Taras's brown ones. The smoky reek of whisky filled the air as his hand tightened on Taras's shoulder and then his lips were rasping over Taras's mouth in a pungent, sandpaper kiss. Abhorrence swelled to fill Taras's skin but like a nightmare he was transfixed, and then Elliott was easing his hand away and saying, 'I'm far too old for you, my boy. You should think of me as a father.'

'I do!' Taras's strung-out senses splintered and his voice

shot up into a squeal. 'I mean . . . you are my father! Ugh! Ugh!' Rubbing at his mouth, he leapt up. 'Get away!'

'Taras, careful . . .' The shotgun clattered to the floor, exploding with a bang. A burning sensation tore through Taras's shirt and he fell writhing to the ground. 'Argh, I've been shot!' The pain was indescribable and then everything seemed to crumple inwards into a black nothing.

Surfacing was limpid, like slipping through water. Taras opened his eyes. Daylight welcomed him. He was on velvet, in a red haze.

'Are you all right?'

He raised his head. Gideon was looking at him.

'Where am I?'

'We carried you into the library.'

Slowly, Taras recognised the tall bookcases and the gold tassels tying back the dark red curtains. 'I got shot.' He felt the bandage on his side. 'Oh my God. Am I dying?'

'It's just a powder burn.' Gideon sounded brisk. He nodded towards the garden. 'Eros took the brunt.'

Taras looked out through the open doors. The statue was still kneeling on his marble plinth, but his wings were blasted off, lying in broken pieces around the glass. 'My side hurts.'

'There's paracetamol here.' A small packet lay on a side-table. Gideon squirted soda from a canister into a crystal glass. He was barefoot, in pyjama trousers and a white t-shirt. 'You should probably see a doctor, but it'll be fine.'

From the doorway, Elliott spoke. 'I'm sorry you misunderstood, Taras.'

Taras twisted to look over the back of the couch. Still in dressing gown and slippers, Elliott looked back at him.

'We seem to have been at cross-purposes. Of course I'm not your father. You look a little like him, you know. Something about the profile.'

'But, I thought you and my mother . . .'

'No, Taras. Not your mother.'

Taras's head hurt. He wanted to slide back into uncon-sciousness. 'What then?'

Elliott rubbed his lined forehead. Taras gazed at him in bemusement.

'Oh, for God's sake, Flounder.' Gideon cut in. 'It was your father. Sigi.'

Taras still didn't understand. He looked from the blond head to the white one, his face creasing with the difficulty of it, and then realisation began to seep in. 'Oh my God.' He jerked upright. 'Not . . . you mean, you and Sigi?'

Elliott nodded. His lined face looked very tired as he lowered himself into a high-backed chair. Gideon moved to stand behind his father, one hand resting on his shoulder. Their long, aquiline noses and deep-set eyes were so alike that Taras felt even more of an outsider. His thoughts scrambled into panicky clots. Sigi was his father. His father was gay. What did that make him? Was Katya dancing at that club because he wasn't enough of a man? Could people tell? Leo? Jamal? Were they sniggering behind his back?

'Flounder.'

He looked up. 'Sorry. I . . . er . . .' He shook his head to clear it. 'I still don't understand. How . . . ? What happened?'

Gideon looked impatient, but Elliott's tapered fingers closed on his elbow, telling him to wait. 'I went to the London Bridge flat,' he said. 'A trivial matter – some paper-work that hadn't been signed. Maria opened the door. Long, dark hair and big black eyes regarding me with great suspi-cion. She didn't speak much English and she didn't want to let me in. She called for her husband, and Sigi appeared behind her. He was wearing jeans and his hair was wet. It was one of those once-in-a-lifetime events. An electric jolt that sets one's life on fire. We both knew, instantly.'

'You had an . . . an affair?' It was difficult to get the words out.

'More than that. It was all-consuming. But we were both married. No good could come of it. Sigi was young, impetuous. He wanted us to run off together. I was tempted. My marriage was not fulfilling. But then Ursula became pregnant. After more than a decade of trying, when we'd all but given up. She told me it was a sign from God, and I half-believed her. I told Sigi we should wait, to see if the baby was a boy.' Elliott glanced upwards at Gideon. 'I wanted a son so desperately. Sigi didn't understand. He came here, railed at me in this room. Cursing, shouting. I was afraid Ursula would wake up. I ordered him out, told him I never wanted to see him again.'

'Is that why he killed himself?'

Elliott closed his eyes. 'We'd both been drinking. He wasn't in his right mind. And he didn't know about you, Taras.' The hooded eyes opened again and Taras felt the force of their blue stare. 'No one knew. Your mother could only just have conceived. I resented you when I found out. I didn't want to think that Sigi slept with his wife too, but of course he did. Maria was a beautiful girl. He'd told me that he was mad about her when they met. Perhaps he would have been again.'

'But he didn't get the chance.'

'No.' Elliott got to his feet: his long frame unfolding. 'Ironic, isn't it? He would have forgotten me. He was a boy. No older than you are now. But I . . .' He waved away Gideon's proffered hand. '. . . I was never able to forget him.'

A cool breeze was blowing in from the garden. The sun was brightening.

'I'll get you a cab, Flounder.' Gideon said as his father left the room.

Taras started to say he didn't have his wallet and then stopped. Who cared? His life was in tatters. He had no father: Sigi had died without knowing he existed. He'd made a catastrophic fool of himself with the Bartletts. Katya had betrayed him; he never wanted to see Leo again; Roy had shut him out. And his mother, the rock he'd taken for granted, was starting a new life without him. While Gideon went to phone, Taras got up and slipped out through the garden to the street. There were only a few people about: a knot of workmen in orange vests; one Saturday commuter in a suit; a mother pushing a hooded pram. None of them took any notice of Taras. He walked on, down the hill, torn shirt flapping over the bandage on his chest, not knowing where he was headed. There was nothing left for him, no one waiting.

CHAPTER FORTY-EIGHT

Taras woke up earlier than usual and whiled away an hour surfing his new ultra-light MacBook, then ambled out on to the balcony of his river-view studio, dressed only in Calvin Klein boxers. Below him, a tourist boat was chugging past and the distorted amplification of the guide's voice drifted up through the late summer air. Two kitchen workers in white jackets dragged rubbish sacks out of the restaurant opposite and then leaned on the railings to have a cigarette. Taras watched, letting the morning sunlight stripe his skin until the warmth prickled into discomfort and he retreated back indoors.

Ten minutes under the power shower revived him. Its shiny chrome and deep pulse jets were a prime reason he'd taken this flat – that and the view, which he rarely noticed any more. Pulling on his tracksuit bottoms and a hoodie, he saw that the projection clock said it was a quarter to nine. Usually he slept till after midday, watched cartoons on the plasma screen and found the afternoons trickled effortlessly past. But this was a special day: a day marked out for contemplation. It was the anniversary of his father's death.

Down in the cobbled street, he stopped at the kiosk with the yellow awning for a frappachino and then strolled along the river bank with the pleasing chill of the iced cup in his hand. An endless tide of commuters was washing past him and he wondered what they all did. It was only six months since he'd been one of their number, but now the rush and flurry seemed mystifying. Getting back into it was going to be tough. He didn't want to think about it. Ahead, the turrets of HMS *Belfast* blended into battleship-grey sky. Two small children were running at the ramp, tugging their father by the hand. As a boy, Taras had been desperate to go aboard but it hadn't occurred to him that it was even possible. It wasn't the sort of thing he and Mami did.

He mounted the steps to the bridge. This would make a good running route. Free, too. For the last few months, he'd invested all his exercise time in the gym below his apartment block. It had air-conditioned rooms, with mineral water and fluffy towels. He endured a gruelling session with his personal trainer most evenings, then took a sauna to detox his liver before another onslaught of clubbing. This was the life he'd dreamed of, so why did it feel so joyless?

Waves of commuters pulsed from the rail station over the bridge, and Taras allowed himself to be swept along in their grey midst. The bus he used to take to work, a number 521, was stranded in the traffic; glazed faces framed in its windows. There was a good smoothie shop somewhere round here which would make a healthy breakfast. All this time in the gym had drained his flab reserves, uncovering a body which was sturdy if not yet sculpted. An olive-skinned brunette flashed him a smile, and he'd flexed his shoulders and nodded back before she held up a collection tin, and he realised she was asking for contributions. Plus, her eyes were too wide apart and she wasn't really his type. He sidestepped, and luckily a guy in a suit had already stopped.

'What's the charity?' he heard the man ask.

'Samaritans.' She rattled the tin. 'Emotional support for people in despair. Twenty-four hours a day, three hundred and sixty-five days a year.'

Taras walked on, feeling bad. He should have given something. Especially today of all days. Should he go back? He'd look a bit of a fool. Still deliberating, he turned down a side street and found a tall stone tower rearing above him. The Monument. He recognised it: they'd had a school outing here once; his whole history class, with him panting and sweating up the spiral stairs, lagging far behind everyone else. A short, squat man in a blue uniform was unlocking the turnstile. On impulse, Taras went in. Three hundred and eleven stone steps. He counted them as he jogged up. His breathing quickened and the back of his neck dampened but it felt good. He'd come a long way.

Bursting out into daylight, he found the whole city laid out for inspection. Amazing. He didn't remember being so impressed the first time, perhaps because his heart had been hammering through his chest and the ascent had taken so long that he'd only had moments to look before they set off back down again. There was the ball and cross on the dome of St Paul's, to the west. Funny to think that another class of boys would be sitting in the form room a few feet from there; maybe even another plump, hopeful body in the desk Taras had occupied.

His gaze flicked fractionally north, straining to find Holborn, but there were too many buildings in the way. Was a team meeting in progress right now? Lisa laboriously taking minutes while Francis strutted and Colin spluttered? No Jamal to snooze through it any more. Taras had been profoundly grateful that Black Thursday, as he thought of it, was Jamal's last day at IBS. Taras wouldn't have been able to deal with everyone at work knowing about his humiliation. As it was, coming in that Friday afternoon had been hard enough. Every glance, every smile seemed directed at him. And when Francis beckoned him into his office, Taras had been paranoid, certain that it was somehow connected to Katya.

'What's Leo said?' he'd demanded, not even sitting down. 'Did he call from the plane?'

'I think Leo said all that was necessawy yesterday.'

Francis sounded cold, and Taras belatedly remembered that he had good cause. 'Oh yes, I'm sorry about that.' He glanced around the tiny cubicle, noting that there was no sign of packing up yet. 'I really didn't mean to cause trouble for you.'

'Your behaviour was unpwofessional.' Francis leaned back, crossing his undersized legs. 'The Chief was shocked. You told Leo that IBS was incapable of impwoving its performance.'

'No, I didn't!' Taras was incensed. He'd been talking about Francis, not the entire staff. Although he could hardly explain that now.

'It was undoubtedly a contwibutory factor in Leo's decision to—'

'I didn't tell him to—' Taras began.

'—pull out of the deal.'

'—sack you.'

Francis's piggy stare drilled into Taras. 'What did you say?'

'Nothing.' Taras backtracked. 'Pull out of what deal?'

'You suggested Leo should . . . *sack* me?'

'No!' Taras waved his arms to show how completely he hadn't suggested that. 'Pull out of the deal? The Americans aren't buying IBS?'

'It leaves us in an extwemely awkward position vis-à-vis our clients and the, um, genewal marketplace.' Francis was clearly still mulling over Taras's revelation. His eyebrows beetled together in a frown.

Taras began calculating his position. Perhaps it was for the best. It would have been impossible working for Leo after what had happened. This way, even if the rest of his life was a cataclysmic disaster, at least work was untouched.

'In addition, the Chief asked me to stwess the absolute inappwopwiateness of your behaviour yesterday. Organising a twip to the type of entertainment venue you chose. It's highly offensive not only to our female staff, but to the Chief personally.'

This was so unfair. Circumstances were conspiring against him. Taras opened his mouth to say that he hadn't organised it, Jamal had, but Francis frowned him down and Taras slumped back.

'The Chief also suggested that in view of your disloyalty and lack of judgement, you were no longer an asset to IBS. I could hardly disagwee, but I did advise further considewation. One should never inflict unemployment lightly.' Francis's beetle-brows bunched more tightly. 'However, it appears you think otherwise.'

'No, no,' Taras sat to attention but it was too late.

'You will weceive a month's pay in lieu of notice. Have your desk cleared by 5 p.m. and make sure HR has up-to-date details for mailing your P45.'

At the top of the stone column, Taras tugged up his hood against the breeze. His eyes shifted north, to the rise of Highgate Hill. Roy and Astrid didn't live there any more; they'd just bought a place in Barnet with a deposit from Astrid's father. Three bedrooms, a garden, right on the end of the Northern Line: it was practically in the countryside. Two weeks ago, their baby had been born; a boy with translucent skin and a dusting of black hair. Taras had visited and fallen in love with the frail little limbs that jerked in panic when unswaddled and the tiny mouth always working, trying to suck even in sleep. If Sigi had known he was months from fatherhood, he surely couldn't have abandoned a vulnerable scrap of humanity like this? Taras had found his eyes filling with tears as he eased the baby back into Astrid's arms, and seeing this, she had relented towards him. Yesterday, he'd received a card in the post with a pen and ink drawing of a hungover-looking Taras in church with an expression of consternation as a shrieking bundle wriggled out of his arms and plummeted into the font. 'Godfather Taras', it said underneath. Looking down now from this great height, Taras clutched the envelope in his pocket and resolved to be a constant presence in his godson's life.

His gaze swept eastwards, towards the big blinking tower at Canary Wharf. It had taken two months to persuade Katya to see him. He'd phoned, emailed, then posted notes through the door of the flat, and in her pigeon-hole at college without success, until finally he demanded the return of his possessions, and she called him back. Her voice was small and distant.

'Taras?'

'Katya! Thank God. I've been thinking about you all the time.'

'Give me address and I will send courier with your belongings.'

'I don't care about that.' He'd replaced his credit cards and his phone, and what use did he have for a suit jacket now? I know I behaved badly, Katya. Let me see you. Just to talk. Please? Tomorrow? I'll come and meet you from lectures.'

'I do not have class tomorrow.' She paused, then said, reluctantly, 'You can meet me at work.'

A long silence followed. He didn't know what to say.

'Not that kind of work, Taras. Come at 1 p.m. to Canary Wharf.'

He'd waited in the reception while one of a bank of receptionists filled out a form with his details and contacted Katya. It was a huge vestibule, with sleek black leather furniture and electronic gates guarding the lifts. Taras was the only person not wearing a suit, or a security uniform. He'd come in his tracksuit, to give the impression he wasn't trying too hard, while simultaneously showing off his sleeker physique, but as soon as he saw Katya crossing the floor, he wished he'd dressed up. Her heels clicked against the floor, and her hips swung under the pale-blue knee-length skirt. He couldn't help thinking about the last time he'd seen her; naked but for his jacket, and it seemed not to make any sense.

'Thanks for seeing me.' He almost added, 'finally', but restrained himself.

'I have brought your things.' She handed him a carrier bag. Inside was the jacket, folded neatly, with his wallet and mobile nesting on top. She hadn't given him the London Bridge keys.

'Thanks.' He glanced around. 'Looks impressive here. What's your job?'

'I find data for presentations, that is all. Two days a week only. But it pays something, and it is good opportunity. Maybe I will win summer internship.'

Her hair was different: brushed back and parted at the side. It looked business-like.

'That's great.' It felt like talking to a new acquaintance. 'How did you get it?'

'You don't think I can do this by myself?' She cocked her head and then relented. 'Gideon helped me. The head of European Operations knows his father. He arranged interview, but rest is up to me.'

'I didn't mean to imply you couldn't do the job. I know you're talented, I'm sure you're great. It's just, this is all so different. Look, can we go somewhere and talk? I'll buy you lunch.'

'I have lunch date already. I will walk you out.' She unhooked the security pass round her neck and slipped it into her bag. They walked out into the shopping centre, through a fluorescent glare of clothes and snack outlets. 'Goodbye, Taras.' Briskly, she marched off, and he trotted after her, dodging office workers. 'Wait! Katya!'

'Go away, Taras.' Tipping her head back, she waved upwards. Taras craned to look, and saw a hand rising in response as a tall figure with a dark blond streak of hair stepped on to the escalator.

'Gideon?!' Taras's brain fired into gear. 'You . . . you're going out with him?'

She inclined her head slightly.

'Why? Because he's rich?' Taras watched Gideon's long body being drawn inexorably closer until he stepped off the escalator, casual in cream jeans and a t-shirt. Blond hairs glinted on the fading tan over his arms as he held out his hand. 'No hard feelings, I hope, Flounder.'

'He thinks that I am selling myself to you for money,' Katya said.

'That's not what I said!' Taras exclaimed. 'I just . . .'

'It'd be a pretty poor bargain.' Gideon rested an arm over Katya's shoulders. 'I don't have any. I'm not going back to the church, so everything Ma left goes to them. They've agreed to let Dad stay in the house, but they'll have it after he's gone. I'm starting afresh.' He squeezed Katya closer, smiling fondly at her. 'Someone gave me the courage to do it.'

Katya was reflecting the same absorbed smile. They seemed lost in each other.

Taras stared in horror. 'But . . .'

'Taras.' She broke her gaze away from Gideon and took Taras's hand. His body jolted with electricity, but it was just a momentary touch, for emphasis. 'I have scholarship again. Gideon helped me present case to committee, to show that more money is necessary to live, and a job can be complementary to my studies. He found me interview. And he persuaded Russian money-lender to take back my loan.' Her eyes snapped back to Gideon again. The two of them seemed to be caught in a magnetic pull.

'Right!' Taras was desperate to break the spell. 'And why do you think he did all this, Katya? To get into your pants!'

With a thump, he skidded back and hit floor-tiles. People spilling off the escalator divided around his sprawled body as if he wasn't there. Gideon leaned down. 'Sorry, Flounder. But you can't say stuff like that.'

Katya bent over him. 'You wanted also, Taras.' A few strands of brown hair had slipped into her eyes, and she brushed them away. 'But you did not do so much.'

She stepped on to the upward escalator. Gideon followed, bracing his arm over her shoulder. Slumped on the ground, Taras watched them glide slowly into the skylight. His own jacket, spilling out of the carrier Katya had given him, smelled faintly of lilies: her perfume. He lifted himself up on one elbow, still staring, and at that moment, Katya looked down. Her gaze met his, and his truculence evaporated. The sadness in her face reminded him of the Blessed Virgin icon that Mami had hung opposite his bed all those years ago, and he shivered.

Up on the Monument, Taras shivered again, although the breeze was warm. He pressed his face against the metal bars enclosing the viewing platform. On the school trip, they'd been told that this cage was erected in the mid-nineteenth century to discourage suicides. His eyes followed the line of the Thames, wiggling inland to the monolithic castellation of Tower Bridge. He imagined his father; drunk, distraught, climbing up on to the iron railings in the darkness. Had Sigi hesitated there, hanging above the inky river, or did he let himself drop without fear? If he'd known about Maria's pregnancy, would that have checked him, or was the pull of unrequited love too strong? He'd been so young, only the age Taras was now, and barely a year out of East Germany: there was so much he hadn't known. The pointlessness of it made Taras feel weary. Moving round to the southern edge of the viewing cage, he looked out towards Blackheath, thinking of Elliott, alone and growing older. Millions of bodies living all around him, and yet he'd never found another one to love. Perhaps Taras would be the same.

Away to the south stretched bunched rooftops. Somewhere beyond that massive conurbation was the registry office in Croydon, where Taras had stood and watched Mami become

297

Mrs Banerjee. In a cream hand-stitched suit, with Mr Banerjee resplendent beside her in a matching *sherwani* with gold trim; she'd made her vows in a clear, firm voice. Taras, entrusted with holding the rings, had managed not to let them down, and afterwards made polite conversation with the bevy of relatives welcoming his mother into the Banerjee fold.

'Good pourchi.' Mami kissed him and cut him a slice of braided wedding cake. She'd decorated it with traditional Bukovinian bird figures, and a small elephant-trunked ganesh.

'This is for you, Mami. A wedding gift.' He tried to stuff the building society book into her leather bag. 'Just in case you need it one day.'

Tugging his arm away, she snatched the bag under her feet where he couldn't get at it. 'No, no, Taraşhu. This is money for you.' She sighed and rubbed his hair, then kissed him again on the nose. 'For future. Only sense-talking.'

Reluctantly, Taras had taken the book back. Watching the presents from other guests pile up on the white linen cloth covering Mr Banerjee's glass table, he felt he should have tried harder.

A week later, he showed up at Mr Banerjee's house. 'I know you weren't planning on taking a . . . er . . . wedding trip,' he told his mother – somehow he couldn't quite articulate the word 'honeymoon' – 'But, this is something special. From me.'

Forehead creasing, his mother opened the envelope. 'What is this?'

Mr Banerjee leaned over her shoulder. 'Aeroplane tickets, Maria.' He took his gold-rimmed glasses out of his inside pocket, and looked closer. 'To Bucharest?'

'And then a car, to take you to Bukovina,' Taras interrupted.

'To Bukovina?' His mother seemed stupefied.

'I've arranged everything,' Taras was bubbling over with

excitement. 'Top-notch hotels, a car and a private tour guide, excursions, everything. Though it's flexible too, you can change the details if you want. I don't know exactly which places you might want to go . . .' He tailed off. Mami's eyes had welled up, and she was blinking hard. Was this a terrible idea? After all, the memories the past held must be bitter ones. He'd screwed up again.

Mami had one hand over her mouth, pressing hard. 'Taraşhu,' she managed to say, 'Taraşhu.'

He crouched down beside her chair. 'Mami, I'm sorry, I didn't mean to upset you. I should have thought more . . .'

Her hand slid over his head. He could feel the ridge of her new wedding ring, and Mr Banerjee's ruby rubbing against his scalp. 'Not upset, pourchi. Only . . . only . . .' A sob sputtered out and she snatched her hand back to her face, then shot out of the room.

'It is a very thoughtful gift, Taras.' Mr Banerjee was still looking through the pages of the itinerary. There was a note of surprise in his voice. 'You must have gone to a great deal of trouble.'

'It was a mistake, though, wasn't it?' Taras leaned his head against the chair arm. When the idea came to him, he'd been so excited, he hadn't stopped to think.

'No.' Mr Banerjee put his glasses down. 'No, Taras. It was not a mistake. Your mother is overcome for a moment, that is all. This means a great deal to her. More than she can possibly say.' He hesitated, then placed the envelope on the chair seat between them. 'I wonder . . . Taras, this will be a very important journey for your mother. Perhaps you would rather be the one to accompany her?'

Taras looked up at the bald, freckled head bent towards him with the slight, perplexed frown he'd seen so often during his childhood and had always registered as disapproval. Now, for the first time, it struck him that Mr Banerjee's expression wasn't disapproving, but concerned.

'No,' he said slowly, feeling that he was treading new ground. 'No, Deepak. I meant this as a gift for both of you.'

And as his mother came back into the room, face composed again, Mr Banerjee held out his hand and Taras took it, in a firm, square handshake.

'Very naughty, pourchi.' His mother's eyes were still damp, but a smile was undercutting her words. 'Not to be spending such money on old baba.'

'It's done now, Mami.' Still gripping Mr Banerjee's hand, he put his other arm around her shoulder.

She rapped his knuckles, but not hard, and her smile stretched. 'No more, then, pourchi. This is not for why Mami is saving. Big handsome Son must have nest-egg, to make home, find good wife.'

As proud as he had felt that day, now the memory of her beam made him feel sick. There was less than seven thousand pounds of the nest-egg left. He'd spent the rest. On what? A flash apartment, pointless gadgets. Looking westwards, he winced at the thought of all those boozy nights with Jamal and his mates, when he'd bought popularity along with another round of tequila shots or the door fees at one club or another. He'd been lonely. Roy, preoccupied with impending fatherhood, hadn't been around. After a couple of months, Taras had given Jamal a call, just to see how the new job was going. Apart from one awkward conversation, when Jamal said, 'So, are you still seeing the Kit Kat?' and Taras shook his head, keeping his face turned away, and said, 'All over,' they hadn't discussed Katya. Taras had the impression that Jamal felt ashamed, though he'd never say so. Instead of talking, they concentrated on drinking and clubbing, and even a week's skiing with Jamal's new work buddies, who were all young and up for it. Living the dream. For what that was worth, which felt like very little right now. He should cut down on Jamal. In fact, he should cut Jamal out altogether. To make life feel more worth-while, he needed to be worthwhile himself. He needed to change.

Nudging against his stomach was the hard edge of his cheque book, still in his hoodie pocket from paying the trainer last week. Taras fingered it thoughtfully, then pulled it out. There was a broken biro under a couple of dead leaves in the corner of the platform. He bent down and retrieved it, hoping the person who'd dropped it didn't have any communicable diseases. Leaning against the metal bars, he wrote in scratchy but legible letters: 'The Samaritans', and 'Six thousand pounds'. It meant he'd have to move out of the riverside apartment, but what the hell. There was something pleasingly formal about such an old-fashioned method of payment: it was more meaningful than swiping a piece of plastic, or clicking on a computer screen. There. Carefully, he tore it out. More money than he'd ever spent in one go before. He wouldn't benefit from a penny of it and yet this felt better than all the larging it up of the past months. Sigi wasn't coming back, but with this money, the Samaritans could prevent the waste of other lives, and maybe some kid somewhere would grow up with a father because of it.

Slipping back to the galleried dome of St Paul's, his eyes dropped to the buildings and quadrangles of his old school. The day after the porn film incident, he had been called in to the headmaster's office.

'I expect you know why you're here, Krohe.'

It was all round the school that the Mad Monk had been caught wanking to hardcore filth, but Taras shook his head.

'Bartlett says that you were with him in the audio-visual cupboard, when a certain unpleasant incident took place.'

Another shake of the head. Could he get away with deny-ing it?

But that didn't seem to be the issue at stake. 'Have you

seen this before?' The headmaster held up a dog-eared copy of 'Words of Life'.

Taras shook his head.

The headmaster frowned. 'Are you sure? Did Bartlett show you this, or other papers like it?'

His heavy grey head was thrust forward over the desk, eyes locked on Taras. The answer he wanted was clear, and a powerful compulsion was moving Taras to give it. He fought, briefly, and then nodded.

'Yes? Bartlett pushed evangelical ideas on you?'

Was evangelical the same as religious? Gideon mentioned God a lot, definitely. Taras nodded again.

'You're Eastern Orthodox, aren't you, Krohe?' The head-master leafed through a file on his desk. 'The School takes religious freedom seriously. The governors are very exercised about the issue. Several feel that certain influences on the board are leaning too far. Financial support is one thing, but it cannot be allowed to alter the School's character.' He tapped the file. Taras stared at him blankly. 'What I'm trying to say, Krohe, is that if you sign a letter to the effect of what you have just told me, then such influences can be restricted. And there would be no reason to pursue the matter of your involvement in yesterday's incident.'

'A letter?'

'A confidential letter. The ensuing discussions won't men-tion you by name.'

He'd obeyed, though somewhere inside he'd known it wasn't right. During afternoon break, Roy had nudged him and pointed towards the quadrangle. Gideon, blond bowl of hair round a pale, set face, was striding away behind a plain, stout woman in a buttoned-up coat. The similarity of their gait: stiff and heavy on the heels, with smartly swinging arms, rammed home the realisation that this must be Gideon's mother. Her lips were pulled thin; bloodless, beneath a tight grey twist of hair, and at the ends of her dark

302

sleeves, her hands were clenched tight. Taras had shrunk back, as if seeing him might alert them to what he'd done. The guilt festered all afternoon, coming to a head in the last period. It was Latin: they'd been studying the Punic Wars, and Taras had faltered in the translation they were all supposed to have prepared.

'Buck up, lad,' the master had barked. 'This should interest you, of all people.'

Taras had looked blank.

'That's where your name comes from. Taras, founder of Taranto, a Greek colony in southern Italy. Later known by the Romans as Tarentum.'

Stumbling through the translation, Taras had to read it again by himself to make sense of it. That evening, lying on his bed, with the four walls of his small bedroom leaning in around him, he'd pieced it together. In 212 BC, the Tarantines had betrayed the Roman garrison in their midst to the Carthaginians, allowing Hannibal to march in and lay waste to it. Three years later, they double-crossed their new masters and betrayed them to the Romans. *Tarentum*, said the text book, *a city repeatedly betrayed from within*.

That's me, Taras had thought, crossing his arms behind his head, and staring up at the blank wall where later the icon of the Blessed Virgin would hang. Something inside made me do it. I couldn't help it. He was ashamed of the whole thing: trying to suck up to Murdoch by getting Gideon in trouble, then weaselling out in the housemaster's office and letting himself become a pawn in a bigger political game. He'd never told anyone about that last event, not even Roy, and with Gideon's disappearance from school, the guilt had faded until it seemed not to exist any longer. Now, holding on to the cold bars of the iron cage, with the sun prickling at the back of his neck, he shivered. *Betrayed from within*. A sense of shame flickered inside him, growing, overtaking the sun as a source of heat. He'd been selfish, thoughtless, stupid, letting down everyone that mattered in his life. And the end result was that he'd destroyed his own chance of happiness. Taking what he'd wanted in the short term had lost him what he truly needed.

Above him, topping the Monument, a flaming copper urn symbolised the Great Fire that had rampaged through the streets of the city three and a half centuries ago, burning up the rat-ridden slums, boiling off the disease-ridden sewers running into the river. The fire had purified the streets, burning away the plague that had decimated London. And now the heat of this shame was purifying Taras too.

Slowly, he descended the winding stone stairs, holding the cheque tightly in his hand, feeling more sober and determined with each step. He wanted to be principled. He wanted to be the kind of person that others turn to in trouble. He wanted his little godson to grow up respecting and admiring him. It was scary, but also exciting; a real intention to change was coursing through his body. He broke into a jog, knuckles trailing along the dark stone wall, knees pumping, breathing under control. This was it: a watershed in his life, a turning point. His head was full with the glory of it, singing like a choir of angels, as he burst out into the open air.

'Oi, mate.'

That wasn't an angel. Taras looked round to find the stout official in the navy uniform brandishing a piece of paper.

'D'ya want your certificate?'

'Sorry?'

'You made it to the top, dincha? So you get a certificate. Commemorate your achievement. D'ya want it or not?'

Taras accepted the stiff piece of paper. At the far end of the street, he saw the olive-skinned brunette, still shaking her tin. Wadding the cheque between his fingers, he strode towards her.

'Excuse me.' He pushed the cheque through the slot, ignoring her questioning look. The old Taras would have made sure she saw the amount, but the new Taras wasn't trying to impress. 'Thanks.' His head felt clear, and his feet were buoyant as he set off eastwards, towards Tower Bridge. Tourists were clogging the pavement: a young couple strolling entwined, an older pair snuggling up for photographs. Leaning over the railings, blocking out the chatter, Taras stared down at the steely grey water. It was thick and viscous: he seemed to see Sigi plummeting into its depths with hardly a shiver of the surface as it closed up over his head. Disrupting this image, a girl with windblown hair shrieked excitedly into her phone, ignoring the friend standing beside her. Taras grimaced. That could have been him, frittering away his energy instead of spending it on the people who mattered.

Today, he needed to sacrifice more than money. He needed to wave a symbolic goodbye to his old life. He'd throw his phone in the river. Bending over the side, he dangled the silver handset between his fingers, wanting to see it hit the water: one small splash and it would be gone.

As if fighting for its life, the phone suddenly vibrated. Taras's fingers jerked and the handset shot up. Instinctively, he leaned further over, trying to catch it, as it leapt like a slippery fish from one hand to the other. There! He had it. Panting, he dropped back to safety, clasping the phone, and put it to his ear.

'Yes?'

'Hey Tear-ass! Thay-att you?'

'Er . . . Leo?'

'You betcha. How's it hanging, Tear-ass?'

'Er, all right, I suppose.' Taras had never known how to answer that one. Presumably saying his life was a disaster and he was reinventing himself as a better person didn't fit the bill.

'Uh-huh. Well, I'm gonna get right down to business. We're cutting a major deal here, Tear-ass. New venture. A

lotta similarities to your IBS outfit, in fact. And I need someone like you to be point man. Whad'ya say?'

'Er . . .' Taras shook his head, bemused. 'I . . . er . . . don't
know.'

'Playing hardball, huh? Well, I respect that. Listen, Tear-
ass, I worked my ass off for this. We're talking top dollar,
relocation package, all that crap.'

'Relocation?'

'Sure. The job's in Southern California. You got a problem with sunshine?'

'Well no, but . . .'

'I figured. Young single guy like you, mobile as shit. He-
eyy, guess who I hooked up with, a month or two back?
That blonde cutie, Miss Desirée. I slipped her my number
that night in the bar, and whad'ya know? She's back
Stateside. Took her on a little trip to Vegas. Woah, Mama!
So, Tear-ass, whad'ya say?'

'Desirée? But I thought you played, what's it called? Tag
and release.'

'Well, some you hold awhile before you throw back,
right?' Leo snickered. 'Quit bouncing off the rim, Tear-ass.
What's your fricking answer? You want in?'

'No.' Taras took a deep breath. 'No, Leo, I don't.'

The words were out. It was terrifying but also liberating.
He'd made his decision about the future, and he was going
to stick with it.

There was a long sigh. 'You're not still sore at me for that
night in the club, Tear-ass? How's a guy supposed to know
she was your girl, for frick's sake?'

'No,' Taras said quickly. Even the mention rubbed him
raw again. 'No, it's not that.'

'OK then. We'll throw a car lease in too. C'mon, I need
a guy with prior experience on this thing. Take down this
number and call me back in a few hours OK? I gotta board
a plane.'

306

Taras had no intention of calling him back, but he scribbled the number down on the edge of his Monument certificate anyway, and then stared at it. What had he done? He might just as well have scrawled a huge 666 over his promise to change. The devil was defacing his moment of enlightenment. He was being tested. Well, that wasn't a problem: his strength was great enough. Wasn't it? Banging down the stone steps into Shad Thames, he ducked into Starbucks to shake off the momentary temptation.

Moseying up the cobbled street, in the shadow of converted warehouses, he munched away on a chocolate muffin, deep in thought. Overhead, the autumn clouds were darkening, and a faint drizzle sprang out of the air. Shitty English climate. In Southern California, it'd be different. Not that he was going. He pulled his hood over his face and mooched on, fingers clenched around his phone. No point throwing it away now. He wasn't on the bridge any more, it wouldn't be symbolic. His trigger finger was itching. He'd just decided that he needed to distance himself from Jamal, but . . . one call couldn't hurt, surely? Besides, Jamal had been around for him all these months while Roy was distracted: how lonely would Taras have been otherwise? Quickly, before he could think about it too hard, Taras dialled.

'Cow-arse. Wossup?'

'Nothing much. Well, actually, Leo Harding just offered me a job in Southern California.'

There was a pause while Jamal took this in. 'No way.'

'Yup.' Taras felt a little flush of triumph.

Jamal whistled. 'Sweet. What kind of job?'

Taras realised he wasn't quite sure. 'Uh . . . heading up a new venture. A bit hush-hush at the moment, can't say more.'

'Fucknugget would flip his lid. You need to find a way of letting him know.'

That was a warming thought. Taras savoured it.

'I'm being called into a meeting. See you later, Cow-arse? Drinks on you tonight.'

Taras sauntered on, smirking. After a few steps it occurred to him that he hadn't told Jamal he wasn't taking the job. The rain thickened, soaking through his sweatshirt. He chucked away the empty muffin wrapper and brushed off his hands, stepping round the claw-toed pigeon that darted in to peck up the crumbs. An unprompted image of sandy beaches came to mind, festooned with corn-fed blondes, all in red bikinis. You could be a good person in California as well as anywhere else, couldn't you? Taras tilted his face upwards, letting the rain course over him, and grinned. Sure you could.

ACKNOWLEDGEMENTS

I owe many thanks and much appreciation to:

Oxana and Andra for their careful reading and helpful suggestions.

Emily and Alison at City University, and Andrew, Jo and Susanna at Royal Holloway, University of London, all of whom were inspirational tutors.

Ant, Caroline, Eleonore, Gerard, Helen, Justine, Lawrence, Matthew, Natasha, Remy, Rebecca, Richard, Ryan and Sue: brilliant writers and perceptive critics.

Caroline and Jenny, my agent and editor, who have made the path to publication a pleasure.

My parents and brother, for their inexhaustible support and superb childcare.

And most of all, to my husband, Nathan, for giving me the freedom to write, and to our children, for putting firm boundaries on that freedom.

THE WEDDING WALLAH

Farahad Zama

Mr Ali's marriage bureau remains busy helping clients
find perfect partners, while Mrs Ali tackles pesky crows and
greedy neighbours. Pari receives a proposal from a handsome
aristocrat, and her prospective mother-in-law will stop at
nothing to convince her to marry – will Pari remember that
if something seems too good to be true, generally it is?
Mr Ali's son Rehman, meanwhile, is still mourning a broken
engagement, unaware that someone else now loves *him*
but she's afraid to make the first move.

As communist insurgents go on the warpath in rural Indian
hinterland, so do India's gays in the cities, and soon Mr Ali's
able assistant Aruna will discover her own world threatened
by these unpredictable forces in Southern India . . .

ABACUS
978-0-349-12268-7

A RELIABLE WIFE

Robert Goolrich

COUNTRY BUSINESSMAN SEEKS RELIABLE WIFE.
COMPELLED BY PRACTICAL REASONS.
REPLY BY LETTER

Rural Wisconsin, 1907. In the bitter cold Ralph Truitt stands alone on a train platform waiting for the woman who answered his newspaper advertisement. But when Catherine steps off the train she's not the woman that that Ralph is expecting. For she is motivated by greed. But what Catherine has not counted on however is that Ralph might have plans of his own for his new wife . . .

'High drama evolving out of avarice and lust' *Guardian*

ABACUS
978-0-349-12236-6

Now you can order superb titles directly from Abacus

☐ The Wedding Wallah   Farahad Zama   £8.99
☐ A Reliable Wife   Robert Goolrick   £7.99

The prices shown above are correct at time of going to press. However, the publishers reserve the right to increase prices on covers from those previously advertised, without further notice.

───────────────── ⟨ABACUS⟩ ─────────────────

Please allow for postage and packing: **Free UK delivery.**
Europe: add 25% of retail price; Rest of World: 45% of retail price.

To order any of the above or any other Abacus titles, please call our credit card orderline or fill in this coupon and send/fax it to:

Abacus, PO Box 121, Kettering, Northants NN14 4ZQ
Fax: 01832 733076   Tel: 01832 737526
Email: aspenhouse@FSBDial.co.uk

☐ I enclose a UK bank cheque made payable to Abacus for £
☐ Please charge £   to my Visa/Delta/Maestro

Expiry Date ☐☐☐☐   Maestro Issue No. ☐☐

NAME (BLOCK LETTERS please) ....

ADDRESS ....

....

....

Postcode .... Telephone ....

Signature ....

Please allow 28 days for delivery within the UK. Offer subject to price and availability.